Life as Carola

''Here is an unusual book that shines with fire...that is packed with incident, that is vivid, dramatic and skillfully put together—and yet one that this reviewer finds harder to value correctly than any that has ever fallen into his hands.''
—The New York Times

''In many ways, *Life as Carola* is a fascinating glimpse into life in Italy just before the advent of the Renaissance. Through Carola's eyes, we see the beginnings of modern theater, the tremendous extremes between the life of nobility and the common man, and even the awakening of Europe to the existence of the Americas. Yet the real power of this book is its personal account of a very intimate story—the growth and development of the inner character of a young woman, and her capacity to triumph in even the most adverse situations. This is a book filled with all the best qualities of human nature.''　　　—Books of Light

BOOKS BY JOAN GRANT

Far Memory Books:
Winged Pharaoh
Eyes of Horus
Lord of the Horizon
So Moses Was Born
Life as Carola
Return to Elysium
Scarlet Feather

———

Far Memory

———

The Scarlet Fish and Other Stories
Redskin Morning

———

The Laird and the Lady
Vague Vacation
A Lot To Remember
Many Lifetimes *(with Denys Kelsey)*

LIFE AS CAROLA

by Joan Grant

ARIEL PRESS
Columbus, Ohio

First published in Great Britain in 1939
First Ariel Press edition 1986

This book is made possible by a gift
to the Publications Fund of Light
by Judith Renaud Ross

LIFE AS CAROLA

ISBN 0-89804-144-9

table of contents

1	Daughter of the Griffin	3
2	Return of Orlanzo	13
3	The Spanish Bride	28
4	Donnelli	42
5	The Strong-Man	50
6	Revolt in Padua	64
7	The Farm	78
8	The Jester	86
9	Companions on a Journey	94
10	Love and Lucia	103
11	The Drab	119
12	The Alchemist's Daughter	130
13	The Lotus	141
14	Fugitive	149
15	The 'Santa Maria'	157
16	House of the White Sisters	173
17	Anthony the Glass Maker	182
18	Green Blood	196
19	Snow in Heaven	212
20	The Lame Nun	223
21	Return from a Dark Journey	240
22	The Ark	251
23	Blind Alley	263
24	Lalage	274
25	Godson of Carlos	285
26	The 'Crimson Rose'	300
27	Torch Light	311

JOAN GRANT

Joan Grant was born in England in 1907. Her father was a man of such intellectual brilliance in the fields of mathematics and engineering that he was appointed a fellow of Kings College while still in his twenties. Joan's formal education was limited to what she absorbed from a series of governesses, although she feels she learned far more from the after-dinner conversations between her father and his fellow scientists.

When Joan was twenty, she married Leslie Grant, with whom she had a daughter. This marriage ended soon after *Winged Pharaoh* was published in 1937—a book which became an instant best-seller. Until 1957 she was married to the philosopher and visionary Charles Beatty, who is the author of several books, including *The Garden of the Golden Flower*, a treatise on psychiatrist Carl Jung. In 1960, Joan married psychiatrist Denys Kelsey.

Throughout her life, Joan has been preoccupied with the subject of ethics. To her, the word "ethics" represents the fundamental and timeless code of attitudes and behavior toward one another on which the health of the individual and society depends. Each of her books and stories explores a facet of this code. As Denys Kelsey has written, "The First Dynasty of Egypt once knew the code well, but lost it and foundered. Eleven dynasties were to pass before it was recovered, but those were more leisurely times when the most lethal weapon was an arrow, a javelin and a club. We feel that in the present troubled days of this planet, these books must be presented."

To Charles Beatty
from
The I That Was Carola

author's note

Although the author could have availed herself of the 20th century facilities for historical research, she has preferred to seek no documentary confirmation and to leave this story bound by the limitations of Carola's own experience.

Carola judged people and institutions only as she saw them—through the eyes of a bastard of the Lord of the Griffin in 16th century Italy. This is perhaps particularly noticeable in those chapters which describe her days as a novice in the House of the White Sisters. At first she was under the rule of a wise and benevolent Abbess, and it was only when the new Abbess, a woman unworthy of her office, assumed authority, that Carola came to hate the Church—not, until several years later, being sufficiently experienced to realize that a religious system cannot be condemned because certain of its adherents misuse their power.

That the fanatical Abbess subjected Carola to torture in an attempt to make her recant of her heresies, does not mean that this was a usual practice in convents, but only that a woman driven by hatred took the law into her own hands. The reader may find it strange that Carola submitted to torture without demanding a trial for witchcraft; but a strolling player has little knowledge of the temporal laws under which she lives.

life as carola

CHAPTER ONE

Daughter of the Griffin

I was born early in the morning of the fourth of May, in the year of our Lord fifteen hundred and ten.

Though I was conceived in the great bed, I opened my new eyes for the first time in the north-west turret of a castle of the House of the Griffin, which lay two days' journey from Perugia in the country of Italy.

My cradle was of dark, carved wood, very old, and my mother used to rock it with her foot while she laid her long thread into smooth stitches. All through my first summer I never saw the sun except when it shone through the high window in a clear-cut shaft of light and lit a blue sheen in her black hair; but when the cold weather came she used to take me out under the sky, where I could watch the clouds and see the winter trees flaring in the wind.

Sometimes she carried me through vast, shuttered rooms, where the storm cried in the wide chimneys and the furniture was blind and shrouded in the dusty gloom, into a long gallery where there were many pictures. She would hold me up to them and talk to the portraits as if they were living people. Often she would begin to cry, and I would feel her tears falling warm and wet on my face.

Even when I could run very fast my mother still had to carry me up the stairs of the turret because they were so very steep and there was nothing to hold onto. There were two rooms in our turret, one above the other, and we lived in the top one. The walls were so thick that the embrasures of the three high windows were almost like passages leading to the light. I often used to curl up in them, for the windows were too narrow for me to fall out of, and look down at the country far below me. At the bottom of the castle hill there were vineyards and ploughland, and on days of clear air I could hear the voices of the drivers as they shouted to their oxen. The sound was very small and thin, because of the distance, and the oxen looked like toys I could pick up in my hand; as if I should have to be small as a grasshopper to ride on them.

The privy was in the corner of the room, up three little steps. The hole was very big and I was always afraid of falling down it, like an unwelcome guest down an oubliette, until Mother got the carpenter to make a little wooden seat for me so that I should feel safe. I did not play there in summer, because it was very smelly, and in winter there was a cold draught. But in spring and autumn I used to collect pebbles or horse chestnuts and pretend they were my enemies whom I had at last brought to justice; then I dropped them into the privy and heard them go clattering down till they fell into my dungeon.

Because my mother was the daughter of Donna Isabella's steward, who had died the year before I was born, she looked after the rich materials that were stored in four great chests in the room below ours: rolls of cut-velvet, damask and brocade; stamped cloth-of-gold, satins and lawn for ruffs; and bundles of black horsehair to stiffen sleeves. She used to embroider with the gold and silver threads and precious stones that were kept in a little cabinet, its drawers inlaid with mother-of-pearl, whose key she always wore on a chain around her neck.

Sometimes, though not often, she took me down there and let me play with the jewels. I loved the blue ones, and the green, but the red ones made me think of the dove that had fallen on the parapet after a hawk had plucked out both its eyes: I think I comforted it a little before it died between my hands, but the blood that dripped from its beak onto its breast reminded me of white velvet sewn with rubies.

Mother often sat all day at her embroidery frame and I had

4

to play alone, but on other days she would be gay, play hide-and-seek, or, in the spring take me out to the hillside to gather wild iris. From autumn to early summer we were alone in the castle, except for a few servants in the kitchen quarters, and I was free to wander wherever I liked. I used to help in the herb garden and when they were gathering the herbs to make cordials and simples, and run races with the kitchen children on the stone terraces where I fed the birds in winter.

The great empty castle was a very good place to play in. One room was floored like the Long Gallery, with alternate squares of black and white marble, and when I crossed it I was always very careful never to step on the black squares; I don't know how this game started, but it always seemed very important. I could even go into Donna Isabella's own apartments, where the furniture was crouched in the shadows like wolves waiting to spring on an unwary traveler, and the mice had grown so bold that if I stood quite still they would creep out of their holes and watch me with their little bright eyes.

I had three dolls, and my favorite one was a blackamoor that Mother had made for me out of a scrap of velvet. He was dressed as a negro page, with a yellow turban, and pantaloons of silk striped in green and mulberry, and he even had shoes with curling points. His eyes were very real, for the craftsman who came to mend one of the inlaid cabinets had made them from a broken piece of mother-of-pearl. He was called Salim, after the famous negro page, because I had always loved the story of Salim and made her tell it to me very often.

On Sundays, when Mother took me down to the village to hear Mass, I wore a green velvet dress and a skull cap embroidered with wild flowers in brilliant colored threads. My hair was a bright sienna red, and Mother rolled it in rags so that it would curl up round my cap. The little damp knobs were very uncomfortable to sleep on, and I often wished I were like the kitchen children whose heads had never felt a comb.

5

When Donna Isabella left her palazzo in Sienna and came to the castle for the hot weather, everything was different. I could not understand why she must never see me, and why Mother was so frightened of her, but I knew I had to stay in our turret whose stairs she was too crippled to climb. I was kept almost like a prisoner and was not allowed to go out of doors except very early in the morning when all the grand people were still sleeping. It was only after I overheard Maria talking to my mother that I realized Donna Isabella was my grandmother.

Maria was the head cook, and I was very fond of her; she was fat and friendly and always gave me nice things to eat when I went into the kitchen. Three days after her eldest daughter's baby was born, she took me down to the village to see it. The baby was very small and red and it cried a lot, but Maria seemed to love it already though she had only known it such a short time.

While we were walking back to the castle I asked her, "Why doesn't my grandmother love me as you love your grandchild?"

At first she pretended not to hear me, but I went on asking her until she said, "It is because Donna Isabella is not your real grandmother—at least your mother is not her daughter-in-law, and a tie of blood is often a tie of hatred when it has not been knotted by a priest."

I said, "I know I am a bastard..." I didn't know what a bastard was, but I had heard people say I was one and I knew it was caused by having a mother who wasn't married. "...but I can't see what difference it makes. As far as I can see I am just the same as your children, and I know they aren't bastards because I asked them." Maria didn't say anything; I thought she was offended, so I added, "In the Long Gallery there are two portraits of men of the House of Griffin who were bastards, and no one seems to be ashamed of *them*."

"That is quite different. You see, their mothers were

married and the father of one of them became a cardinal, and, anyway, it all happened a long time ago.''

''I think it is very silly and unfair. Next time Donna Isabella comes to the castle I shall go and ask her why she hates me, and when she sees I'm only an ordinary little girl she may like me after all.''

''If you do that, you and your mother will be turned out of the castle! She will send you far away from here to some horrible place where you will never have enough to eat and not even a roof to shelter you. There is no place in Donna Isabella's heart where kindliness can hope to find a lodging!''

''Why is she so cruel?''

''She is of the true line of the Griffin, not only by marriage, but by blood, for she married her first cousin. I have often wondered by what strange chance your father, Orlanzo, was born into this eagle's nest. Have you never heard the stories that the servants whisper below the creaking of the turning spits? How Guido, whose portrait hangs at the end of the Long Gallery, drank of viper's broth when he was young to make him wily as a serpent? He snatched a bride from the Duchy of Milan; he poisoned her brother while he was his guest and then took her as though he picked up a gage that challenged him to show his power. Some say he died a traitor's death, but I have heard that it was his wife, a girl turned to a bitter woman, who gave him the toast to drink that he heard answered by the keeper of the gates of hell!''

''Does my mother hate Donna Isabella as you do?''

''I have heard her say, 'The day she dies the summer trees will all put forth their buds, though it be winter, to show how they rejoice that she will never walk the paths they shade again!' ''

After this, in my imagination Donna Isabella became as fabulous as a dragon. I felt that she might fly past my window with the beating of heavy leathern wings, as though the griffin on the banner had flown down from the roof.

I had always made up stories to myself while I was in bed

7

at night, but they had been happy stories about the knights and princesses in the tapestries on the walls of the banqueting hall. I had joined with them in their remote green world; ridden pillion behind the man in armor while his white horse galloped through flowery thickets to the castle in the distance, where Mother and I lived with a joyous company and being a bastard didn't matter at all. I also made up stories with dragons in them; very large, fierce dragons who ate all the wood-cutters in the forest until I, as a young knight in golden armor, slew them in single combat.

Now I began to weave stories in which my mother and I were imprisoned in a castle by an ogre. The ogre was very tall, but I made him too tall to get up the stairs to my room so that I was safe from him when I was in bed. He used to stride across the countryside plucking up cottages as if they were mushrooms, and he never ate anything but human flesh. He was so huge that he could eat a company of soldiers at one bite, and while he was munching them their arms and legs stuck out between his pointed teeth, like wisps of hay stick out of the mouth of a browsing donkey.

Then I decided that Donna Isabella was more frightening than any ogre I could imagine, so I changed him into a female ogre and gave him a face like I thought hers must be. Mother said all ogres were men, but I told her that even ogres must have mothers or they would die when they were baby ogres.

Mother always said that when Orlanzo came back everything would be different. When Donna Isabella was away she used to take me to see the picture of him that hung in the apartments on the east side of the castle. It had been painted before I was born, when he was only fifteen, and it showed him standing against a dark and windy sky, with his hand on the collar of a great boarhound. Sometimes I used to go there alone and ask him, so hard that it was like praying, to come home to us very quickly.

fiesta

At the end of the summer there was always a fiesta in the village for the vintage. I had never been to the fiesta, but when I was five Maria persuaded my mother to let me go to it, as Donna Isabella had been ill and was still confined to her room.

I was so excited the night before that I hardly slept at all. I woke while it was still dark, but had to wait until the sun got up before I was allowed to. I joined Maria's children in the kitchen, and after we had had some bread and goat's cheese we started off along the ridge of the hill towards the terraced vineyards, stopping on the way at the house of Maria's sister to join her nephew, the village cooper, who had promised to look after us.

Although the sun was quite strong when we reached the highest terrace, it was still cool between the vines. The bloom was cloudy on the grapes, but when I touched them it vanished like mist on a mirror, and they looked hard and shiny. Each time I ran backwards and forwards along the rows I carried two great bunches to put into the pannier-baskets, which were loaded on to the waiting pack-donkeys as soon as they were filled. My hands were soon stained with juice and my bare feet red with dust, so I was glad that Maria had taken off my dress and let me wear only a cotton shift like the other children.

As it grew hotter, little green lizards came out to sun themselves on the narrow walls. They pretended to be asleep, but when I tried to pick one of them up it flashed into a crack between the stones. An old woman was looking after the babies whose mothers were helping in the picking. Beside her there was a pile of water-skins which had been brought up to refresh the vintagers, and when I was thirsty she gave me a drink from an earthen-ware cup.

After the last of the vines on the terraces had been stripped, we went down the hill to where the grapes that grew in the vineyards on the level ground were being collected into ox-carts. The oxen had been groomed, and some of them had bunches of flowers or corn tied to their horns. Several of the carts had been newly painted; one had pink wheels picked out in green, another was orange, and a third was blue. One of the drovers put me up on the back of his ox. It was very uncomfortable, but I was proud to be there.

It was quite a long way to the pressing tubs; and when I reached them, women with their skirts tucked high up round their thighs were already beginning to tread out the grapes. There were to be six children in our tub, and we had to take off our shifts before we climbed up the ladder to get into it. I was very hot, and before the fruit began to pulp it felt beautifully cool and smooth. We jumped up and down, clapping our hands and shouting. At first we tried to keep in rhythm with the treading-song that the grown-up people were singing; but soon we were playing together as happily as piglets in a swill trough.

In the evening an enormous meal was spread for the vintagers on long tables made of planks laid across empty barrels. There were huge bowls of meat stew, into which we all dipped our bread; or picked up the hot savory mess in our fingers, until, as I heard one man say to another, there was not a beard or a chin there that had not enough gravy on it to feed a poor family for a week.

I thought my mother might be cross if she saw me naked and dirty, so I wandered off by myself across the fields to the stream. I climbed down the bank by a willow root and found a patch of sand which I used to rub off the sticky juice; then I lay in the running water until I felt cool and clean again. It was so nice being there that I thought I would collect my clothes from the house of Maria's sister and go home by myself without waiting for the others.

I walked upstream until I came to the ford, splashing through the shallow water and sometimes seeing a fish flash away in the shadows. Growing out of the damp earth in the shelter of a boulder, I found a clump of late forget-me-nots; I picked some, and on the way home I plaited them into a garland, because I wanted to take back something for my mother from my strange and happy day.

Ðonna IsaBella

One day Mother went down to the village to see a woman who was sick, so I was alone all day. Although she had left enough food to last me until evening, black bread, marchpane, a square of cheese, and goat's milk in an earthenware pitcher, I had finished it all before midday. There was sunshine in the far distance, but it was raining near the castle; I could see the rain slanting across the windows like silver harpstrings. I was tired of telling stories to Salim and I had no chestnuts to play the privy game, so, although I knew that I ought to stay in my room because Donna Isabella was in the house, I decided to go and play 'squares' in the Long Gallery.

I had nearly crossed it, hopping on one leg and never once jumping on a black square, when I heard the tapping of Donna Isabella's stick. I had no time to reach the far door before she would see me, but there was a chest of gilded leather, standing between two of the windows, in which I could hide. I knew there was nothing in it except some spare hangings, for I had crept into it before, when I was playing hide-and-seek in the winter with my mother.

It was very dusty in the darkness and I began to be frightened that I should sneeze. The chest was old and the lid did not fit very well, so I could see out of it through a long narrow slit. Donna Isabella was alone. She was dressed in black, with a widow's cap hiding her white hair. She was very small and withered—very small to be the familiar of giants and monsters! She was a little lame, and leaned heavily on her stick. It was made of ebony with an ivory ball

11

for a handle. Her hands were narrow and shriveled, with long nails. Suddenly I knew what it was they reminded me of: the griffin's claws holding the ball, the gilt griffins that upheld the table in the banqueting hall. Her lips were very thin and bloodless, as if she had never kissed anyone or laughed or sung. Her eyes were black and glittering and very alive; yet terribly tired, like the eyes of the old jackdaw in the wicker cage that hung in the doorway of the shoemaker in the village.

I wondered whether her hair had ever been red like mine, or whether when she had been young it had been black and shining like her eyes.

She coughed, a dry harsh sound like the branches of an old tree complaining in the wind. There was a pomander in a silver case hanging from her girdle. She stood by the window sniffing it. I wondered why. Surely she was not afraid of plague in her own house? I knew what a pomander was, for my mother had shown me one, telling me that people carried them when they went to cities where there was a pestilence because the strong aromatic smell kept off the evil vapors.

I wondered whether it was true that this small old woman was the most wicked of all her line, for it was difficult to believe some of the stories that were told about her. It was said that her husband had had ten men murdered because he had suspected them of loving her. I heard Maria tell this to another servant, but I could not understand why any man should have loved Donna Isabella, even fifty years ago when she was young.

Now I had seen her close to, all alone, and lame, and sniffing at her pomander because her cough hurt her, I knew that I shouldn't be frightened of her any more. My favorite ogre that I had made up to frighten myself with, the one that was so big it couldn't get upstairs to my room, would have to have a new face, *much* more frightening than Donna Isabella's.

CHAPTER TWO

Return of Orlanzo

I did not see my father until the summer after I was six. He had been on a long journey to the Island of King Harry to visit a kinswoman of his uncle who had married an English wife. This had kept him from Italy for two summers, and before that he had been fighting under his cousin the great condottiere, so though my mother told me that when I was a baby he had often come secretly to our turret room to see us, I could not remember him.

His friends and kinsmen were coming many leagues for the great banquet by which his return was to be celebrated. Even before the arrival of the steward, who came a month sooner than Donna Isabella to see that all was ready for her arrival, the sleeping house was startled into life by the scurrying of women-servants and the clatter of provision carts on the cobbles of the kitchen courtyard. The tapestries were uncovered, and hangings, smelling of the rosemary and sprigs of box in which they were packed to keep away the moth, were taken from the presses. The clumsy goose-feather mattresses were carried down to sweeten in the sun, and the lawns whitened, as though there had been snow at mid-summer, with bed-linen and napkins set out to bleach. Hinges of creaking shutters were oiled; floors were waxed until they were honey-smooth; and the chimney-boy brought down tangles of rotten feathers and jackdaws' nests on to the hearths of long disused rooms.

Mother worked all day long on the doublet that my father would wear at the banquet. It was of white satin, slashed with orange and embroidered with seed pearls and silver thread. While she sewed she told me how she used to hang a bright scarf from our turret window to show Orlanzo that she would be watching him as he returned from the hunt. When they rode up the hill he would gallop a little ahead of his retinue, which was a message to her that he loved her, just as the scarf was a message to tell him that he had all her heart.

"You will see, Carola, it will be the same as it was five years ago, only now that he has come to man's estate he won't be frightened of his mother and there will be no need for secrecy. He has been without news of us for so long. Perhaps even now he is praying to the saints that my scarf will be hanging from the window to show him I have not changed. He will be so impatient that he will gallop far ahead of the others. The servants will be lined up in the great courtyard; he will have to greet them first and hear the speech of welcome from the steward; but soon, so very soon, we shall hear him running up the turret stairs. He will scratch on the door and we won't answer for a minute, just to tease him a little— but it will be a very short minute! Then I shall call to him to open and he will see me, and his daughter grown so tall and beautiful, and we shall be together again."

They were to arrive at the castle on the twenty-fourth of June, and for five weeks I had counted off the days, with lines scratched on the stone window-sill. When I could say, "To-morrow he is coming!" I was so excited that I couldn't just sit still and wait for him. I wanted to help get everything ready, so I went down and asked Maria to give me something to do.

Every one in the kitchen was very busy, and I noticed that the great spits had been cleaned of the grease in which they had been wrapped for the winter. Maria was pouring melted lard over pates of goose liver and wild boar, all strongly spiced. She was in a very good temper, and when she finished she gave me a bit of sugar loaf to suck; it was dark, and so strongly sweet that it was almost bitter. She told me not to bother her, so I watched one of the other cooks making sweetmeats, of egg-yolk and sugar flavored with rose-water, coriander or cinnamon. They were not to be baked, so when she had set them out on trays she told one of the scullions to take them outside to dry in the sun. Then she began shaping marchpane into little pleasure boats, each with almond oars and a cargo of sugar plums.

A cart came up the hill from the village with barrels of wine for the guests' servants. While it was being unloaded the two white oxen stood patiently in the heat and let me stroke their noses. Children were plucking ducks and goslings in the courtyard, and I helped them gather up the breast feathers, which were collected in sacks to be put away until they were needed to stuff pillows or mattresses. An old greyhound bitch was digging in a pile of garbage by the door; rotten fruit and pig's entrails, bleached soup bones and the head of a white goat, eggshells and the bloated carcase of a carp; all decaying under a widow's veil of flies.

The next morning Mother and I got up very early. We swept out our two rooms and then I scattered the herbs I had been collecting on the hillsides, sage and wild lavender and camomile, among the fresh rushes on the floors.

I hoped that my father would say he preferred a brown skin, because for twenty days I had had to go to bed with my hands smeared with an ointment, which Mother made out of honey and crushed almonds and lemon juice, to whiten them. At first I had quite enjoyed this, because when I was left alone to go to sleep it was fun licking it off; but when she found out what I was doing she tied up my hands in little bags. I told her I thought it was a silly idea and that if ever I became the chatelaine of a castle I should get brown all over and make a special law that all the people on my estates could walk about in the sun without any clothes on as much as they liked.

At last she had finished combing my hair and washing me, and I put on the beautiful green dress, embroidered with flowers, that she had made for me. The morning seemed very long, for I had to sit quite still on a high wooden stool and wasn't allowed to run about or play in case I got dirty.

It was after midday when the fore-rider arrived to say that the retinue was drawing near. When it came in sight Mother let me stand with her at the window from which she had hung her scarf. I could see the great lumbering coach, drawn by six mules with red harness, in which Donna Isabella traveled; and behind it came a long train of pack animals, with traveling boxes slung across their backs instead of panniers. There was a man riding on a black horse beside the coach, and, although he was still too far away for us to recognize, Mother was sure it was Orlanzo. Then they disappeared round the curve of the hill, but I knew when they were approaching the great gate for I heard the trumpeters in the south-west tower sounding their fanfare.

My father had ridden ahead of the retinue, and when he came in sight again he was so near that I could see the muscles in the shoulders of his horse rippling under the shining coat like sunlit lake-water moving in the wind. He was dressed very richly in white with a scarlet cloak, and the plume in his hat was scarlet too. Mother, forgetting her fear of Donna Isabella, leaned out of the window to look at him—she was so sure he would look up at our turret and had ridden ahead only because he longed to see her.

But he never looked up at us. I knew that her happiness died like a guttered rush-light, and, though I did not know this until much later, it was then she realized that Orlanzo had forgotten the sewing-woman whom he had loved for a little while when he was sixteen.

the tear in the tapestry

Orlanzo never came to our turret, and I only saw him in the distance, walking on the smooth lawns or on the terraces where white statues gleamed in the formal arbors of glossy shrubs. Sometimes when I looked from our high window I saw him riding out to the hunt, his greyhounds running beside him and his falcon, in its little scarlet hood, on his wrist. It was so difficult to realize that he was my father, for he seemed as remote as the strange gods on the painted ceilings, as remote from other men as was the scarlet griffin from the white pigeons that strutted on the parapets.

I thought that if only I could see him close, not just a glimpse of him in the distance, and hear him talking, it might be that I should find out how I could approach him in some way that would make him understand he must not make my mother so unhappy. I would tell him he must come to see her, for I was sure that when he saw how beautiful she was he would forget all the grand ladies with their brilliant clothes, to whom he seemed so gallant, and remember only that he had loved my mother when he was young and that they must still love each other when they were old.

One day Mother put me to bed very early and told me that it would be a long time before she came up to me because she must finish the doublet for Orlanzo to wear at the banquet in honor of the Spanish envoy to Tuscany, who would break his journey to Perugia here on the following night. It was of orange velvet, quilted with gold thread and studded with pearls, and with it he would wear trunk hose with knots of violet ribbon at the knee. I had heard Maria say that Donna Isabella was dining with the women in her own apartments and that with my father would be only the men he had gone hawking with that morning.

Suddenly I remembered that behind the tapestry in the banqueting hall there was a niche, which must have been made to hold a statue. It was a deep niche; sometimes I had hidden there when I had been playing at being a beautiful princess hiding from robbers in the forest; and it was not too dark, because there was a little tear in the fabric which let in a ray of light.

I was glad it was a hot night, for my clothes were in the lower room and I only had on a bedshift of white cambric. The door creaked as I opened it and I expected to hear Mother call out to me. I listened, and heard her walk across the room to the cabinet where the jewels were kept, and then the scrape of a stool on the stone floor as she went and sat down again by the window.

I hid in the little-used ante-room until the banqueting hall was empty of servants, and then I managed to climb up into the niche without anyone seeing me. The tapestry hung away from the wall, and I had to balance myself very carefully on the edge of the niche because there was nothing to hold on to when I leaned forward to look through the tear.

It seemed a very long time before the servants took up their places behind each chair. Even Gervase, in spite of his pock-marks, looked quite handsome in the household livery of white and scarlet. I could see the chair where my father would sit; a high-backed chair, more like a throne, the arms richly gilded and the scarlet griffin blazoned on the Spanish leather.

I heard voices, and my father came in with his hand on the shoulder of one of his companions. There was a heavy seal ring on his little finger; I had seen the same ring in the paintings in the Long Gallery, the griffin not cut into the stone but in high relief. He was dressed in white and yellow and wore a gold chain set with emeralds and a single pear-shaped pearl in his left ear. His little greyhound sat beside him in the great chair and shared the food from his plate. It was an arrogant little dog and snarled at the two boar-hounds, which I think belonged to the man on my father's left, as they prowled around the table or quarreled over the food which their master flung to them.

The wine-flagons and goblets were of gold or silver, some richly enameled. The crystal bowl of rose-water, which the steward carried round between each course for the company to rinse their fingers, was edged with a wreath of jeweled leaves, and the napkin on which they wiped their hands was of white satin with a silver fringe.

I could understand very little of what Orlanzo said, for most of the time he spoke in a foreign language to the man who had come with him from England—which is a land of barbarians that cannot speak our tongue. I began to get very sleepy, but at last the peacock and boar's head, stuffed pike and cockscomb, lark pasties and syllabubs, were finished and the servants were dismissed. The wine flagons had been left on the table, and I heard a goblet clatter to the floor, echoed by laughter which did not stop the snores of the man who had drunk himself to sleep.

I suppose I was tired, or careless, for leaning too far forward I lost my balance and had to clutch at the tapestry to stop myself falling. The boar-hounds must have seen it move, and they leaped at it, trying to tear it down, their hackles rigid and growls rumbling up from their throats. I was very frightened, and cowered back as far as I could. I heard cries of ''An assassin!'' Then the weight of the dogs pulled the tapestry down from its hooks, and as it fell it enveloped them so they could not get at me.

The men had sprung up from the table and two of the chairs had been overturned. They had drawn their daggers and stood ready to face an attack. For a moment we looked at each other as if I were a statue and they a fresco. There was no sound except the wine from an overturned flagon dripping on to the floor.

Then my father began to laugh. ''Be seated, my friends! There are seven of us and I think we can defend ourselves against one so small.'' He turned to the Englishman, ''James, get hold of your dogs.''

The foreigner was smiling at me as if he were vastly amused. He shouted at his dogs, who had at last managed to free themselves from their sudden burial, and they crept shamefacedly to his feet.

My father came and picked me up and stood me on the table. I realized that I was very cold and I shivered. He looked kindly at me and said, ''There is no need to be frightened.''

I was angry with him for thinking that I shivered because I was afraid, when it was only because I was cold, so I said,

"Why should I be frightened of a lot of men who are frightened of a little girl behind a tapestry, and two stupid dogs who don't know the difference between me and a wild boar?"

My father frowned, for all the men laughed; then he began to laugh too. He looked puzzled and asked me, "How did you get here? I have never seen you before."

"I came through that door, and that you have never seen me before is no fault of mine!"

Two of the men beside me were talking, and one said to the other, "Look at the line of the jaw and the ear—Orlanzo's are exactly the same. Look at those straight eyebrows and the way she carries her head."

My father still looked puzzled and said, "I must have seen you before—you look so familiar."

Another of the men laughed, a drunken, stupid sort of laugh: "Look in your own picture gallery, Orlanzo, then you will see why she looks familiar."

My father said to me, "Who are you? What is your name?"

And I answered, "Your daughter, and my name is Carola. I am six and a half years old—in case you have forgotten!"

He seemed to forget there was anyone else in the room as he said, "You are Olivia's child. I didn't know that she was here any more. I had forgotten...."

"Didn't you know that she sewed the doublet you are wearing?"

"No, I never thought about it."

Then one of them cried out, "A toast to the daughter of the Griffin!" and a man who was curled and ribboned like a pet spaniel put the hilt of his dagger into my hand saying, "Signora, you are indeed an assassin! Your beauty has wounded me in the heart even as your mother wounded Orlanzo—but not perhaps in his heart."

He giggled like a silly kitchen wench, and my father said angrily, "Quiet, Deccio!" as though he were speaking to one of his dogs.

But the man called Deccio went on giggling, "You are a belated champion, Orlanzo! Was I not respectful enough to your bastard? Or perhaps you deny her—though her face gives you the lie."

Then my father suddenly got very angry and shouted, "Deny her? No! She shall wear the great seal of the Griffin that only my line can wear."

He took off his ring and held it in the candle flame, but I don't think any one realized what he was going to do. He put his arm round my shoulders—he was so tall that although I was standing on the table we were of the same height—and said, "Carola, I claim you for the Griffin! We of the Griffin are brave."

He pulled down the bedshift from my shoulder and pressed the red-hot seal against my flesh. It hurt a lot but I managed not to flinch.

After it was finished I found myself crying, and shaking as if I had a fever. I said, "I am very sorry. I am not really a coward. It's only because I am six, and I am very tired."

Nobody was laughing any more, and they looked as if they wished they were somewhere a long way away. My father picked up his short cloak, which was lying on a chair, and wrapping me in it he carried me out of the room.

It was very dark on the turret stairs, for the moon had not risen. There was a crack of light under the door of our room, so I knew that Mother was still working. She must have been startled at the sound of any one coming up the stairs so late, because when my father opened the door she was standing with pearls and a tangle of embroidery threads spilt on the orange velvet at her feet, where they had fallen when she sprang up.

Perhaps it is in the nature of all children to think that their parents are old; for it was only when I saw her standing there, with her loosely braided hair hanging to her waist and her eyes heavy with sleep like a tired child, that I realized how young she was.

They stood looking at each other, then he said, ''Olivia,'' and she held out her hands uncertainly towards him, as if he were a vision that might vanish, or she were in a dream from which she was afraid of waking. And then he said, very gently, ''Come up and help me to put our daughter to bed.''

He tucked the covers round me, just as if he were an ordinary father who lives with his family and puts his children to bed every night. He asked me whether my mother sang to me as she had sung to him when they were young, and whether she still played on her lute.

I was very tired, but before I went to sleep I remember seeing her sitting on the window-sill—it must have been much later for the moon was very bright—and my father on a cushion at her feet, looking up at her as she had hoped to see him when he rode past our turret on his return from England.

I remember her face, very pale against the dark sky, and how I thought that the nightingales must have flown away, because there was no sound until she sang an old love song to him, in a high clear voice like a bird singing in a tall tree.

Serene Interlude

While Donna Isabella was still in the castle, although my father came very often to our turret there was still an urgent need for secrecy. He was always afraid she might discover that he was keeping his bastard under her roof, and so, instead of coming himself, sometimes he sent his body-servant with a precious gift for my mother; a crystal cup to hold the flowers I gathered for her; a box of sugar-plums, its lid painted with garlands; or silver candlesticks to hold the long tapers of scented wax we burned instead of the rush-lights that used to gutter in the draught.

After Donna Isabella went back to Sienna, he was with us

nearly all the time and he even took me with him when he went hawking, his arm holding me before him on the saddle-cloth. He loved his falcons, and I don't think he ever knew I was frightened of them. They would rise up in heavy spirals, like smoke on a still day, and when they returned to his wrist his glove would be stained with the blood of their prey.

He used to tell me stories of his journey to England and of the strange people who lived there; or of how, when he was only seventeen, he had fought against the Milanese. I told him about the games I had played and the adventures I had imagined; but when I told him my ogre story, and how I had had to change the face of the fiercest one after I had seen that Donna Isabella was only a little old woman whose cough hurt her, he didn't smile but told me quite angrily that it was churlish to laugh at one's elders or superiors. I said, "If people were really one's superiors I don't suppose one would ever want to laugh at them." This only made him look angrier still, so I didn't say any more, although I wondered how my grandmother had the power of making people so afraid of her that even her son dared not cross her will.

Except sometimes when he was in a bad temper, my father was very nice to me, and when his favorite greyhound bitch whelped he gave me one of the puppies. I called her Mimetta, and as soon as she was old enough to leave her mother she followed me wherever I went. She was nearly as small as a rat, a smoky grey color with a coat so smooth that it felt more like newly-ironed linen than fur, and she had a collar of soft red leather with a gold buckle. She hated the cold, and when there was a patch of sunlight on the floor she followed it across the room, and, although she had a beautiful cushion, with a gilt tassle at each corner, to lie on, she used to creep into my bed at night and huddle up beside me for warmth.

Now they knew I was the daughter of the Griffin, the kitchen children were shy of me when I went to play with them. It made me feel rather lonely, and instead of going about barefooted with the others I had to wear a long dress that I tripped over if I tried to run, and when Mother took me to the village I had to hold her hand, as if I were a little princess going out for a walk with her nurse.

We still lived in our tower, but now the lower room was furnished with chairs and stools covered in green brocade, and there were tapestries hanging on the stone walls. When the days grew colder there was always a fire on the wide hearth. We burnt olive wood, which had been dried for a long time in the sun and needed little kindling to leap into weird blue flames and aromatic smoke, for since my father had found us we no longer had to go into the woods to collect the sticks and fir-cones with which we used to try to light the green logs that were all that we had been allowed to take from the wood-store.

One night, when we were all having supper there together, he gave me a pendant that he said was made by the greatest goldsmith in Italy. It was a mermaid, a kind of sea fairy, and her body was made from a pearl which nature had shaped to the curve of a woman's belly. Her fish tail was set with little emeralds—or scales of green enamel, and it seemed that she rested on it, leaning back to look up at one she loved who smiled down at her.

When his servant had taken the food away, I sat on his knee, with his arm round me and my head resting against his shoulder, while he told me this story about the mermaid.

Long ago, when the hill on which our city is built was the home of many eagles who were the only guardians of an empty plain, this mermaid was born in a palace built of honey-colored marble by the Sea of a Thousand Islands. Though she was the only daughter of a king, the sea was her foster-mother; the little waves sighing among the rocks were her lullaby, and the sad crying of gulls was sweeter to her than nightingales. She would not play in the gardens, but ran down the steps between the cypresses and along the steep path to the beach. She found branching coral more beautiful than hyacinths, and scarlet seaweed in the clear water of the rock pools more splendid than a peacock when he spreads his tail.

She was as fearless of the water as larks are fearless of the air; and as she grew older she became even more beautiful, and her beauty was equaled only by her wisdom and her kindliness.

Princes voyaged far to woo her, and the fame of her traveled even beyond the mountains until other princes journeyed across deserts where men die of the hot wind, and passes where the snow lies even in summer. Some of them were strong, and some were wise, and some were even handsome as well. In a thousand ways they tried to win the heart of Iccari; but, however tender their wooing, they could not enchant her, and however angry her father became, because he thought her capricious, she only smiled.

The suitors declared that until Iccari had made her choice none of them would leave the island, for they all hoped that it would be he upon whom she smiled. They had come richly attended, and even though the palace was a great place, it was difficult to house them, for there were eighty-seven, each with his retinue. The king grew weary of this bounteous hospitality, and the king's vizier sighed as he saw the gold dwindling in the treasure chests. So the vizier went to the princess and told her that because she would not choose a husband her people would go hungry, and the ships of her father's fleet be without new sails.

The princess asked him, ''Which prince shall I choose to save my people?''

And the vizier answered, ''For that you must listen to your own heart.''

''I cannot hear what my heart tells me. Perhaps it does not speak to me, because it knows I listen only to the voice of the sea.''

Then the vizier said, ''If all the princes are the same to you, and your heart cannot decide among them, it would be

wise if we thought of some challenge to their skill by which
your husband might be chosen. Then no man can say that we
have favored one for his riches, or that we fear another for his
strength.''

''I will marry no man who comes from beyond the mountains, for I should die if I had not the sea to comfort my loneliness.''

The vizier was a wise man, and so he said, ''All in our
country know that none can swim as fast or as far as the
Princess Iccari. If you proclaim that the first man who can
show himself a swifter swimmer than yourself shall be your
husband there will be no danger that the victor—if there be a
victor—will be a man from beyond the mountains.''

So the heralds proclaimed the challenge. It was decreed
that on the seventh day all who accepted it were to assemble
on a ledge of rock whose sheer edge rose high out of the deep
water. Then the king's trumpeter would blow three blasts; at
the second Iccari would dive into the sea, and at the third the
others would follow her; and he who overtook her could
claim her for his bride.

Of the eighty-seven princes only sixty assembled, for the
others could not swim. When Iccari dived it seemed that the
sea opened to receive her. On and on she swam, smoothly
and tirelessly, and one by one the princes had to signal to the
boats, which the king had thoughtfully sent after them, to
save themselves from drowning. At last Iccari saw that none
followed her, and she was content, for she knew herself free
of their importunities.

Then she heard someone swimming beside her, and she
saw that it was a young man, strange and beautiful. His
eyes were blue as a calm sea at midsummer, his skin was
green as deep waters, yet he seemed familiar to her as her
own reflection. And though the voice of the sea was loud in
her ears her heart cried out to her that she loved him. They
talked together and he told her that she was his beloved;
and she knew that it was his voice she had heard when she

26

listened to the sea.

She said to him, ''Why have you made me wait so long for you—did you not know how lonely I have been?''

''I have watched you swim out towards me, yet I could not come for you for I do not belong to the country of the sun.''

Then for the first time Iccari noticed that he had no legs, for at the waist his body tapered into the tail of a fish. She asked him, ''Are you the son of the god of the sea?''

He shook his head. ''The children of Neptune, and all his people, have bodies fashioned like human beings; though their skins are green and they are more beautiful than mortals.''

''Then why are you half man, half fish?''

''When I was a baby, my mother, who was a king's daughter, took me on a sea journey. A storm arose and drove our ship on a reef. All were drowned save me, whom the waves carried to a ledge of rock that was uncovered at low tide. I cried, for I was small and lonely and frightened. Then I saw a woman leaning over me, a woman whose flesh was green as seaweed and whose eyes were lucent. I held out my arms to her, and she picked me up and comforted me, singing the song the conch shells still echo. But as the tide began to rise she wept, knowing that as I was a mortal baby the sea would destroy me. Neptune heard her weeping and, as she was his favorite daughter, he came to see what made her sorrowful. She told him that if he could not save me she would walk out of the sea to shrivel up and die on the dry land. Neptune said to her, 'I cannot make this child a god, because he is born of a mortal woman whom no god has favored, but I could turn him into a fish. I think he would be quite happy as a fish.' But his daughter went on weeping, saying, 'The sea is full of fishes! I want this little boy, with the golden hair and the strange blue eyes, to love.' So Neptune promised that he would do half a magic, so that I should be half of the sea and half mortal; and with that his daughter

27

had to be content...."

As he finished speaking, Iccari knew that it would be better to drown in his arms than to live without him under the sun. And she said to him, "I will never return to the land but together we will swim towards the horizon until I am too weary to swim any farther. Then you must carry me down into the quiet green depths; so that my heart will be too rejoiced in love to know of fear; and the memory of you shall guard me in eternity, where I shall wait for you."

So they swam out together along the silver wake of the moon.

But Neptune, who was very fond of his foster-son, had been listening to them talking; so he changed Iccari into a mermaid, and for a bridal gift he gave them immortality....

It was a very long story but I remembered all of it; and while he was telling it to me Mother watched him, and by her eyes I knew she held that all the happiness of the world was compassed by the curve of our turret wall.

That is how I always try to think of her; smiling quietly at us in the firelight, serene as the madonna lilies in the walled garden.

CHAPTER THREE

the Spanish Bride

My father stayed with us until the last leaves had fallen from the vines, the last embers of the summer heat had cooled to a quiet umber on the hillside. Before he rode off he promised that he would take us away from the castle and that we should live in a little house of our own in the hill city where he would come often to see us so that we should never be lonely any more.

My mother no longer wore a plain dress of woolen stuff, but laid her stitches into dresses she would wear herself. Though it was the fashion to wear brilliant colors, she chose satins the soft grey of a wood pigeon or colored like far hills at twilight, moss-green velvet, or proud brocade that matched the dried rose-petals which kept their scent through the long winter. She no longer had to cut up discarded gowns to make my clothes, but let me choose which length should be cut from the great bales and rolls, kept in their pungent wrapping and leaved in rosemary, lavender, and bergamot.

When they were finished she laid them away in a dower chest which my father had given her. It had belonged to my great-grandmother, and at each corner there was a gilded griffin, supporting the lid on their outspread wings. In the center panel there was a painting of the young Virgin kneeling before the archangel who told her she would bear the Holy Child. She wore a white coif, fine as mist, through which you could see the curve of her smooth head. Her hands were long and tapering, like magnolia buds reaching towards heaven, and the grass on which she knelt was tall with lilies.

While my mother sewed, she used to tell me how we should live when we went to Perugia.

"It is a very splendid city, far away across the plain—so far that we could not see it even if the shoulder of the mountains did not hide it from us. I was only a little older than you are, Carola, when I went there. There is a great wall round it, with many towers, and the steep streets climb up between the merchants' houses and the palaces. There are five churches, and the bells sing together to call their people to God. We are going to have servants, as if I were a great lady, but I think that sometimes I shall pretend that we are poor again so that we can go down to the market and buy our own food. I used to do that when I was there with my mother. The people were very friendly and kind; sometimes when they had finished bargaining they would give me a flower or a bunch of grapes because they were feeling happy."

I said, "It is two months since he went away. Won't he be sending for us soon?"

"You mustn't be impatient. The house may not be ready yet. Perhaps he is having a fresco painted by the young artist he told us of—you remember, Carola, the one who is working in the cathedral, I forget his name. He knows he must give me time to have everything prepared, so that my new servants will see that I am worthy to be the mother of his daughter."

"I have been telling Mimetta that she will really have to learn to lie on a silk cushion and allow herself to be combed and scented—instead of always running away when I let her off the lead and trying to chase rats or burrow in the kitchen midden."

"He is going to send a coach for us. I have never ridden in a coach—I wonder if it will have two mules or four?"

"Perhaps it will have *six* like Donna Isabella's!"

My mother was so happy she used to sing like a brook or a bird, as if joy were her melody.

Then the messenger came from my father. It wasn't to tell us to make ready to join him; but to say that he had been sent by his uncle on a perilous journey to Spain.

Though I often told my mother he would soon return, it was as though the chill of the future were already upon her, and I could not make her laugh any more. I used to ask her why she was so afraid, but she would not tell me. Perhaps she thought that to put the dangers she envisaged into words would give them a stronger reality.

Maria and the other servants never spoke of my father when I was there, but sometimes when I went into the kitchen I heard them talking about him, and although they stopped as soon as they saw me, from broken phrases an image grew in my mind. I knew they thought my great-uncle had sent his nephew to Spain because it was a land of bandits and assassins, where death is a frequent guest at banquets and may be hiding behind the bedcurtains when a man thinks he is sleeping in security; and that the head of our house was jealous of my father, jealous of his brilliant youth and of the wide lands he would inherit from his mother.

That year Donna Isabella did not come to the castle, so there was no bustle of preparation, no shouting of orders or scurrying of servants, to disturb the drowsy summer months. As day after day passed with no sable messenger to warn the castle of Orlanzo's death, Mother was reassured; she used to play with me again and sometimes I even heard her singing.

The garden and the hills were quiet with the first snow when we heard that my father was bringing a bride out of Spain. I could not understand how he could want a foreign woman when he had us; but Mother told me that though a man can have only one wife, he may love many women, though in the eyes of the Church their children are born not of love but of sin. I had been at the wedding of Celia to the falconer's son, and I could not understand how the slow Latin phrases could change the quality of their love for each other. If it was right that they should live together in the same house because they loved each other, why did they live apart until they were married? Surely God judges His children Himself, and does not leave it to a priest to decree whether they must flock with His holy lambs or herd with the black goats of Satan. I tried to speak these thoughts, but even Mother would not listen to them, and Maria crossed herself and said I was bewitched.

The Spanish bride was the daughter of a prince and had a great dowry. I always thought of her as being old and wizened like Donna Isabella until I heard that she was only fourteen. I asked Mother what she would be like, and she said that I should never see her, because before she arrived we should have gone to Perugia. I was told that in our time men seldom loved their wives, for it was the custom to marry a woman for the size of her dowry or for some family alliance, and I began to be sorry for the little foreigner. Perhaps far away across the sea she was crying, because she didn't want to leave her family and go into a strange country where everyone spoke a language she could not understand. I hoped my father would be kind to her so that she wouldn't be lonely; for I knew that being lonely is so much worse than being cold or hungry, and that although she would have rich apartments and eat off gold and silver dishes, she might envy the hogkeeper's daughter, who lived in a hut with her parents and her brothers and sisters.

My father must have realized his bride would feel strange in Italy, for with his messenger he had sent plans and foreign workmen so that the rooms she would occupy could be altered to the Spanish fashion, in which she would feel familiar. Plasterers and gilders, wood-carvers and painters, came to rebuild the apartments that overlooked the eastern terrace. The great bare rooms were made smaller, with partitions pierced by archways framed in twisted pillars with foliated capitals. The high stone groins were hidden by false ceilings of elaborate plaster or canopies of painted canvas stretched on wooden battens. Three span of oxen were yoked to each cart that brought the ocher-colored marble from Sienna. Bales of gilded leather from Cordoba came to hang in the new anterooms, and the deerskin rugs were stored away; for when the Spaniard came, tapestries were to be spread on the marquetry floors for her to tread on.

The foreign workmen were lodged in the granaries opening off the kitchen courtyard, where, in times of danger when the castle might have to stand another siege, grain and fodder for cattle were stored. The other craftsmen, who had come from Perugia and Sienna, hated the Spaniards, but I thought some of them were very friendly. I used to like watching a carver changing the plain wood into flowers and leaves, as if by the magic of his knife he made the dead tree blossom again. The man I liked best was Carlos the gilder. He used to let me watch him laying on the gold leaf; it was fine as cobweb, yet docile in his large hands, and he showed me how the edge of each little square must be smoothed and burnished until the cherubim and twisting vines seemed carved of pure gold.

It was April before we heard that Orlanzo and his bride were nearing Italy, and every day we thought the coach would come to take us to Perugia.

Banishment

I was talking to one of the Spanish workmen, who was nailing canvas to a wooden stretcher, when I heard Maria calling for me. She was in great distress, invoking the saints and weeping noisily. She wouldn't tell me what was the matter, but took me into the kitchen and sat me on a table while she filled a pannier-basket with food. Some of the kitchen girls and the other cooks stood round looking at me pityingly. I couldn't understand why they were sorry for me; but as they kept on telling me not to be afraid I began to be frightened.

Then my mother came into the kitchen. She wore a traveling cloak of grey cloth and carried over her arm the red cloak, lined with squirrel fur, that my father had given me. Behind her were two men, in Donna Isabella's livery, carrying between them a small trunk made of cow-hide with a rounded lid. They looked very stern and unfriendly, and I could see that the kitchen servants were hostile towards them.

I shall always remember that scene, as though it were a fresco on the wall of a room in which I have lived for a long time; the glare of the fire below the two kids glowing orange in the heat, and the turn-spit boy standing quite still, gaping in amazement with his greasy black hair falling over his eyes; the brilliant colors of fruit and birds' feathers on the long table and the sharp light of the meat-chopper in Piero's hand; the white and orange liveries of Donna Isabella's servants, who held the little old trunk which showed the leather where the hide had been rubbed bare; and my mother standing there in her long grey cloak with the hood framing her still face.

She looked as though she were on the other side of a dream, as though she could not see the people around her but was walking all alone through the land of the sorrowful mist. I did not know what had happened, but I knew that she was very far away and that somehow I must get through into the country she was in—and stay with her always.

I jumped down from the table and ran to her. She didn't say anything, but she held my hand very tightly. The others must have thought she was bewitched, for they shrank away from her as she walked very slowly and quietly towards the door to the courtyard.

An ox-cart was standing in the spring sunlight. I thought of the coach that my father had promised to send for us—I had been so sure that it would have six mules. There was a group of workmen by the door of the granary, and Carlos ran forward to help her step from the hub of the wheel into the cart. She smiled at him, very gently, but as if she were acknowledging the courtesy of a stranger.

The taller of Donna Isabella's servants lifted me up beside my mother and threw the trunk after us. Maria was the only one who had followed us out of the kitchen. She was carrying the basket of food I had seen her making ready, but as she tried to give it to me he held her back saying:

"It is Her orders that they take nothing but one trunk, and no valuables save three pieces of gold. They are to be three leagues beyond Her lands before to-morrow, or it will be—unfortunate!"

Maria screamed at him, "When Orlanzo comes back he will have you tortured for driving out the daughter of the Griffin and her mother! Tortured in a manner worthy of Donna Isabella's household!"

The man answered, "Orlanzo himself has sent a messenger to Donna Isabella—commanding her to make every preparation for the happiness of his bride!''

The oxen moved slowly forward. We passed under the archway of the courtyard, down the steep hill to the village, and took the road to the west.

The castle where I had lived all my life grew smaller and smaller in the distance—until we couldn't see it any more.

I was asleep when we reached the first village beyond the lands of the Griffin. It was dark, and the narrow cobbled street was deserted. The man who had driven the cart was banging on a door and shouting to the landlord to open to him. The inn-sign, three arrows piercing a red shield, creaked in the rising wind, and it seemed a long time before we heard the bolts being drawn back.

The landlord was very fat; not with the kindly fatness of Maria's husband, but as if he had a monstrous cruelty like the great black sow that always ate her young. I suppose he thought we were prosperous travelers, for he told us that he would hasten to prepare his best room; protesting that although his was a small inn we should find none other so clean or well-served in the whole of Umbria or Tuscany. He said that he would show our coachman where to stable the horses. But while he was talking we heard the ox-cart turn and go back down the street.

When the inn-keeper found that we had no coach, no grooms or servants, no traveling boxes of gilded leather, his manner changed and he became surly, as if we had tried to dupe him. He accused us of having wakened him from his bed on a false errand, but when Mother showed him a gold piece he said that we could sleep on the settles by the fire. When she said that we were hungry he grumbled, but went off to the back room, which must have been the kitchen, and brought us some stew in a wooden bowl.

The settle was very hard and I was bruised by the jolting of the ox-cart. I tried to make myself believe that I was excited at this adventure; that I was a knight in a song of the troubadours, riding out to find a beautiful princess who needed saving from a dragon. I told myself this very firmly but I couldn't help knowing that it wasn't true. I pulled my cloak over my head, as if I were cold, so that Mother shouldn't hear me crying.

Olivia the Embroidress

For many days we traveled: sometimes in ox-carts, sometimes walking behind a mule-train when a friendly drover tied our trunk on one of his pack animals.

I knew that soon we should have no money, for already our last gold piece had been broken into bronze. I tried to persuade Mother to stay in some town where she could earn our lodging by doing embroidery, and I told her that I should go from house to house until I found friendly women who would pay well for her work. But when I tried to make her talk of what we should do in the future, she wouldn't listen to me.

She used to ask me, over and over again, ''Don't you remember, Carola, how he told us we should never be lonely any more? Why did he play this jest upon us? Was the Spanish woman an enchantress who poisoned him with love potions and put the waters of forgetfulness into his wine? Perhaps she is very beautiful and has so filled his heart that there is no corner of it that we can claim. She is there now, Carola, sleeping in the great bed of the Griffin in which you were conceived.''

Though I tried to comfort her, I couldn't call her back into the sun. I never believed that it was my father who drove us away, I felt sure it was Donna Isabella, who had twisted his message.

Sometimes I saw a solitary horseman galloping after us down the long white road, and I thought that it was a messenger sent to summon us back to the castle, or even that it was my father himself who had come to find us. But the horseman never drew rein, and we went on our journey alone.

I think Mother was ill though she had no fever, for quite often she talked about the house in Perugia as if we had really lived there.

"Orlanzo was waiting for us when we reached Perugia. The rooms were sweet with plum blossom and flowering almond because he knew I loved them; and through the windows I could see a smooth lawn sprigged with flowers, such as our great painters spread beneath the feet of their goddesses.

"He had thought of everything for our happiness. In the courtyard there was a white mare, caparisoned in scarlet, and he was going to teach you to ride on her so that he could take you hawking with him in the autumn. He had brought you a husband for Mimetta so that there would be puppies for you to play with, and he said that even if they tore the tapestries he would not be angry—for it was all ours.

"There were scented tapers in high silver sconces to light me to bed. My skin looked very white against the red coverlet—the red he loves, the red that is vivid as sunlight shining through wine. As I lay listening for my ardent lover, I used to hear the fountain, whose living water echoed the nightingales. There was a magnolia tree under my window, and its buds, smooth as closed eyelids, bemused us on summer nights...."

I used to hear her crying in her sleep. Then she would wake and lie staring up at the ceiling, her eyes wide open but with no outward vision. She would describe her own life as if she were telling me a story....

"I thought him more than mortal, Carola. I was fifteen, Olivia the embroidress. I had been late in finishing a doublet, and when his body-servant came to fetch it there was a little square of embroidery on the left sleeve still unfinished. I dared not say that it was not ready for I might have been punished, and I hoped it would pass unnoticed in the candlelight.

"I waited till the household was asleep, and then I crept down to the little room, next to his own, where his clothes were kept. The doublet was not there, so I realized he must have dismissed his servant before going to bed and that it would be in his room. I knew his dogs would be with him and that they guarded him well; but they both knew me, for I had helped the groom to look after them when Herta, the bitch, had been ripped in the shoulder by a boar's tusk.

"The door opened quietly. The dogs were lying by the fire; Herta woke up and began to growl, but when she recognized me she stretched out and went to sleep again. The flames were licking up from the logs and the room was warm with their light. The doublet was lying on the floor under the center window, and I had to go round the bed to reach it.

"Orlanzo was breathing smoothly as though he were in a deep sleep. I had never seen him so close before; to me he had always been the young Griffin, riding out with his falcons or jousting in the tilt-yard; a legendary figure of power and splendor like the knights that my stitches had made to live on tapestries. He looked very young, though already his beard was trimmed into a point. His skin was pale and had the sheen of polished olive wood. I picked up the doublet, and had nearly reached the door when I felt myself checked. At first I thought my dress had caught on the carving of the bed, and then I knew it was his hand that held me back."

Then my mother's voice would change and she would smile. It seemed that she had slipped from the sorrow of the present into a happier past.

"I shall always remember the gentle mockery in his voice as he said, 'I was dreaming that I sat alone in the banqueting hall. Drowsy with wine I stared up at the ceiling, which was painted in my grandfather's time, and thought how melancholy was my fate, which decreed I must sit alone under the fond eyes of goddesses and the amorous glances of delectable cherubs. Then I noticed that a little Pan, who piped the melody to which they danced, was beckoning me; and I found myself one with the painted company. The breasts of the goddesses were warm under my hands and I found that under their smiling mouths their teeth were eager.

" 'The most fair among them—I think she was Athene—was about to surrender to me the most secret, and yet the most obvious, of her delights, when you must come into my room and wake me up—make me discover myself to be couched, not in the arms of a goddess but upon a mattress stuffed with goose feathers! A melancholy ending to a muse which was fathered by the mind of a poet and suckled by two flagons of my best Falernian!

" 'Come closer, so that I can see you.... Perhaps the goddesses have pitied me—for it seems that for sweet fancies they have sent me sweet flesh!

" 'Such modesty would be overplayed if you were a marchesa! Are you a marchesa? Or the shepherdess that comforted Endymion when the moon-goddess left him desolate? Be tender to me and let me quench my thirst upon your mouth. Take off your shift and let me see the moon unveiled by clouds.

" 'Forget who we are, forget to be afraid, forget that I am lord of this dismal house. Join in my dream and let us forget the dawn. We mortals act our melancholy parts, and strut, and smile, and lust, and fight, and die, thinking ourselves the last reality.

" 'Let me play Adam to your willing Eve and forget the serpent of the commonplace that poisons all our days....

" 'Listen! The songs that men think nightingales are cherubs singing, amorous and glad to watch ourselves as their apt pupils. Your hair is like a veil that shields me from the harsh light of my thoughts, which walk with me through leaden-footed years. Your thighs are lilies and your breasts are doves. I am the wine and you the crystal cup, and so, together, we shall drink of love!' ' "

39

Sometimes this memory would warm her heart as if once more she lived in its reality. At last her voice would fall away into silence and she would sleep, folded in peace.

the Shining One

Since I was very little, my dreams had been like the memory of yesterday, but even my mother had not believed me when I told her of them. Now that I knew she was so unhappy, I used to pray, not to Our Lord or His majestic saints, but to some little archangel who would not think my prayers too foolish for his compassion. I used to pretend that I could see him standing at the foot of my bed: he had no wings, for I knew that even mortals could fly when their bodies were asleep; his robe was blue as the morning, and his hair, luminous as the petals of a celandine, was bound to his smooth brow by a silver fillet. I told him that my mother sorrowed even while she slept, for the tears slid from under her dark lashes and no smile curved her mouth. I asked him to help me to take her to the house in Perugia, so that she could hear the fountain of which she had dreamed and walk in the early dew when the scent of herbs is strong in the air.

For many nights I talked to him, and still my mother slept with sorrow for her companion. Then I saw my archangel stretch out his arms to me; and the palms of his hands were kindliness and his fingers were strength. I got up from my bed and I felt his hands on mine, warm and living as though we were of the same flesh. He pointed to the bed on which I had lain down to sleep and I saw a child lying there, and it was my reflection.

I think this was the first time Carola knew that the body of Carola moved only because my spirit had put on this flesh: just as the leaves of a tree are still until the wind beckons them to dance.

He led me to where my mother was sleeping, and I saw

that although her body lay there she did not stand beside it free and radiant, as I did, but crouched by the dead ashes of the fire in a grey shroud of grief. My companion called her by name, and at first she would not listen. Then she raised her head, and I saw that her eyes were blind.

The Shining One turned to me and said, ''For you to sleep is to be born into the light, and to wake is to return into the darkness. On Earth you may walk in shadow, for there are clouds over the sun, but you will tell men that above the clouds there is warmth and beyond the darkness there is light. It may be that some will listen to you and be comforted; but there are many who will hate you and try to afflict you with their own blindness.

''Long have we known each other, upon Earth and away from Earth, under many names and in manifold disguises in the flesh and in the spirit. As Carola you have a solitary journey. But I shall be with you, until the past and the future are one.''

When I awoke, the sound of his voice was strong in my ears. And I went out into the young morning, for I wished to be alone under the sky with the memory of my vision. I felt far wiser than Carola, with a wider understanding than my child mind could compass, because I knew that sometimes in my dreams I had seen truth, and that what other people thought were fancies were the only realities.

The mist was lying on the water-meadows, shining like clouds under the sun. I stood watching a broken ant-hill, and I thought that the ants were like little priests in black cassocks scurrying about their business without knowledge of the immensity of the wide heavens. I realized why I was so unwilling to go to Mass: it was because while I was there the longing to be spoken to with divine authority was more intense than at any other time. Now I should not sorrow that this longing was not fulfilled on earth, for I could escape from the little prison of Carola's body into the presence of the Shining One.

CHAPTER FOUR

Ɖonnelli

At last Mother began to realize that unless we earned some money we should starve, so she agreed to stay for a time in the next town that we reached.

We had been following a mule train for two days and were very tired. When we were in sight of the town walls the muleteer picketed his animals in a little wood, for if he had taken them through the city gates he would have had to pay a tax on his merchandise. He left the mules in the care of the boy who helped him look after them, saying to us that, as he was not going to drive them across country to rejoin the high road on the far side of the town until the following morning, he would carry our trunk as far as the first inn. He shouldered it and strode off down the road, whistling a marching song that I had heard some of the troops of foreign mercenaries singing as we passed them. The ruts were deep in white dust, and in the strong sunlight the shadows of the plane trees were clear-cut as an inlay of ivory and Macassar ebony.

We did not stop at a proper inn, but at a little wineshop just inside the town gate. The muleteer was a kind man; he bought us a large bowl of onion broth and as much bread as we could eat and would not let us pay him anything. I kicked off my shoes under the table thinking no one would notice, but the innkeeper's wife saw my feet. She made a great fuss of me and called me ''poor poppet.'' Then she took me into the kitchen to bathe my raw heels with sour wine and wrap them up with rags dipped in oil. I was very grateful to her, but I said that I shouldn't be able to keep the rags on very long, as I couldn't get my shoes over them. She said that I was in no fit state to walk and that my mother and I must stay with her until I was better. It was not really an inn, but she had an extra room, where her two sons used to sleep before they went off to the wars, and she said it was kept ready because she was always expecting them back.

It was a very nice room. The bed had a goose-feather mattress, and a white woolen cover carefully, but not skilfully, embroidered with flowers and fruit in dark blues and greens. There was a clothes chest and two benches, and even a few sprigs of willow-herb in a crock on the window-sill. She said I looked so tired that I must go to bed, even though it was only two hours after midday. I didn't want to, but I thought it would be rude to argue when she had been so kind. I must have fallen asleep almost at once, for it seemed only a few minutes before I woke, to see the moonlight shining through the windows and Mother asleep beside me.

The innkeeper's wife was called Donnelli. We told her that as we had hardly any money left, we couldn't stay with her more than a few days. But she said she wouldn't let us go until we were tired of her company, and she ought to pay us for keeping her sons' bed aired, because the amount we ate wouldn't keep a sparrow alive. She got the cobbler to mend my shoes, and he put little pads of soft leather into them so that they shouldn't rub my heels.

house of the magnolias

Mother now began to worry because she wasn't earning any money. I told her that soon she would have more embroidery to do than she could manage, for I thought that once they heard about her, lots of the rich people in the town would want her to embroider their doublets or quilt their satins, and I should be kept busy collecting orders and taking back the work when it was finished.

I decided to go from house to house until I found the sort of people we needed. I washed my hair and curled it with rags as Mother had done for me when we lived in the castle. I still had one good dress, and I brushed it very carefully before I put it on.

The knocker of the first house was too high for me to reach, and though I banged on the door with my fist nobody came. The servant at the next one said, ''We want no beggars here!'' and when I tried to explain to him that I was not a beggar he shouted at me and pushed me off the steps. I fell, and grazed my hand quite badly; but it didn't matter, because my dress wasn't torn. At house after house no one would listen to me; they all thought I was trying to beg, or that I summoned the doorkeeper just to annoy him.

When I reached the top of the hill I came to a large villa set back from the road in its own garden. The wrought-iron gates were locked, but through them I could see four magnolia trees shading the path to the front door. They were in full leaf, though the flowers had not yet opened. A branch spread over the wall and I reached up and broke off a leaf: one side of it was hard, smooth as polished agate, and the other was a glowing brown, soft as Genoese velvet. I was standing playing with the leaf when I heard the gates being opened. A young woman, very richly dressed, came out of them in a carrying-litter. She looked kind and was quite young, and I thought this might be the only chance I should get of speaking to the sort of woman who could afford embroideries, so I made a very low curtsey, as if she were a princess, and called out, ''Beautiful lady, may I crave your favor?'' She laughed and told her litter-bearers to stop. A man dressed in black with a gold chain round his neck, whom I took to be her steward, commanded me to go away. He wanted to appear generous and threw me a little bronze coin, but I took no notice of it. She said, ''You are a fool, Fernandi. Can you not see that this is no beggar but a child of quality? Perhaps she has run away from her nurse, or climbed the wall of her father's garden in search of adventure!''

Then she turned to me, ''Am I not right, little girl? Are you not playing a prank on some attendant by hiding? I used to do that when I was your age—I can still remember the excitement of it, but I have forgotten the scoldings of my nurse, and the stern upbraidings of my father. Have you got a stern father, little girl? Come, do not be shy! Tell me your name!''

''My name is Carola. I have no father.''

''An orphan as I am! My poor sweet, surely we must be friends!'' Then, to her servants, ''Set down my litter, I am going into the garden to talk with this enchanting child. Fernandi, go to the Contessa's house and tell her that I am desolate I cannot join her to gossip about her husband's mistresses over her sugar cakes and the too sweet wine with which she embalms herself in fat. Tell her—you know what to tell her, Fernandi—'My humble duties,' 'I am desolate, but a sudden malaise has afflicted me...' ''

She stepped out of her litter, and when I curtsied she offered me her cheek to kiss. Taking me by the hand she led me through the gates. It was very cool and green under the great trees, and at the back of the house there was a kitchen garden. She found some early strawberries in a sunny corner and said I could eat all the ripe ones I could find. She told me about the greyhound that had belonged to her when she was a little girl, so I told her about Mimetta; but I didn't say that I no longer had her. She chattered on, telling me she was having a new coach and it was to be grey with the wheels picked out in yellow, and inside it was to be lined with quilted satin.

She said I must ask my mother to be so gracious as to permit me to visit her again. She was very gay and laughed as easily as her lap dog barked. She was very proud of her little dog. I don't know what breed he was; he was very small, with a pointed nose and white silky hair that would have fallen over his eyes if it had not been tied up with a blue ribbon, and his feet were as cold and scratchy as a bird's claws. She said she played hide and seek with him, and I was to hold him and cover his eyes with a silk scarf while she hid, so that I should see how clever he was at finding her.

We played this game for a time, and then she hid behind a thorny shrub which tore a long rent across her overdress. When she saw it was spoiled she began to cry. As she dabbed her eyes with a lace handkerchief, I wondered if she had ever cried real tears; if she had ever been really unhappy she wouldn't have been moved by such a little thing as a torn dress when she must have had so many dresses. She seemed so distressed, that I told her my mother was even more skilled at embroidery than whoever had made her dress had been, and I was sure she could mend it so it was even better than it was before. She said, "I could not ask your mother to mend my dress—as if she were a serving woman!"

"But she *is* a serving woman—at least a sewing woman. We have very little money, so won't you let me bring her to see you or let me take this dress to her? When you see how beautifully she has mended it there may be other things you want her to do for you, and then perhaps you will tell your friends about her."

The lady gathered her skirts away from me and looked at me as if I had turned into a frog.

"Fernandi was right. You are a beggar after all! What a fool I have been to spend my morning playing with a scullion's child!"

"I am *not* a scullion's child! My mother and I are poor. She has to embroider clothes like you wear for a living!"

She slapped my face, which I suppose I deserved, and said, "If ever you come near my house again I shall tell them to set my dogs on you!"

I looked very hard at the little ball of yapping fluff she called a dog and said, "You need have no fear that I shall try to see you again! Among all your possessions you prattled about you forgot to mention your boarhounds—which is a pity as I like large dogs!"

So the only time I might have been able to get somebody to help my mother I was a fool and lost my temper.

Prelude for Strings

I decided not to tell Mother what had happened until I had talked it over with Donnelli. She was in the cellar, pounding butter in a wooden churn, and when I had told her everything, even about losing my temper and being so rude, she said, ''I know the woman who lives in the House of the Magnolias. An ill-bred, pretentious strumpet who is not fit to mend your mother's shoes! Even the old man who keeps her for his amusement doesn't trust her—that's why he sends his steward on the pretext of looking after her servants. He is really a spy to see that none of the money is being spent on the favors of young gallants. ''

''Can you think of any way I could persuade people to let Mother work for them?''

''If I could, my little one, I'd have done it already. My husband used to keep a stall in the market, where he sold the produce of his farmer brother, before we saved enough to buy this wineshop. I used to take the fruit and vegetables round to many of the big houses and I became quite friendly with some of the kitchen servants—though some of the others thought that just because they wore livery they were blood brothers to dukes! I have been round to see all of them who I thought might remember me, but it didn't matter what story I told I couldn't get any work for her. It was always the same answer, 'What has she got to show us? Perhaps if she could bring her work here one of the upper servants might deign to bring it to the notice of the mistress of the house.' When I told them she had no embroiders to show, they just laughed at me and said that they wouldn't even buy a cabbage before they had seen it, or a basket of berries until they had tipped them out to see that the fruit under the top layer wasn't rotten. ''

''Isn't there any one,'' I said, ''who would give her a bit of velvet—even the skirt of an old dress—and some silks that have got into a tangle which most people are too impatient to

47

unravel? I could smooth them out; I'm very good at knots—even little ones that have been there a long time.''

"If I were a rich woman—or could find where my husband keeps his savings—she should never lack materials. Griggori is a good man in many ways; as mild as an ox and nearly as stupid, but the goddess of generosity never stood by his cradle. If he had not got drunk one night, and so forgotten to take the money from me after a fiesta, I shouldn't even have been able to buy new kneeboots for my sons to wear to the wars. Sometimes, when a few people want food with their wine, I can sell a cheese of my own making without his noticing. But he is a difficult man to live with! Perhaps men are only born into the world to teach women patience—who teaches *them* I have never discovered!''

This gave me an idea, and I said, "Sometimes after a market-day the men who stop here to play dice have a purse full of money. They don't seem to mind losing it to each other, so it can't have been hard to earn. Do you think it would matter if I took just a little of it? I'd only take from people I didn't like—the cross-eyed carter who goads his oxen, or the tanner who is always shouting at his wife.''

"Your mother would rather starve in the gutter! Yes, even *this* gutter, dirty as it is, than have you turn thief to help her. Thieving is a sure way to the gallows. Do you want to lose a hand or have an ear lopped off? Anyway I couldn't allow it! If you did it anywhere else you might get caught and break your mother's heart—and mine into the bargain—and if you did it in my house it would give it a bad name. I may be only the wife of the keeper of a wineshop—as my cousin who married the landlord of the Golden Bantam never tires of telling me—but at least a man can drink himself insensible on my wine and not wake up to find his throat cut or his pockets any emptier than before he spewed. Which is more than she can say, even if she *has* sometimes got four traveling coaches standing in her stable-yard at the same time, and every one of them with a coat-of-arms on the panel!''

"Are the things Mother would need to work with very costly?"

"I have heard that velvet out of Genoa is sometimes two gold pieces the span, and they give silver for a hank of embroidery silk so small that you could hide it in your fist."

"And the gold thread and the jewels?"

"It would need a scholar to count their cost, and Casparri the silversmith to know their value."

As I went up the cellar steps I heard the sound of a lute, very soft and far away as if it were only memory brushing the strings. It came from our room, and while I stood listening outside the door the music grew louder as if the strings had persuaded my mother's fingers to pluck them more strongly. The harmonies lamented as if the lute were tuned to sorrow, and then she began to sing the same song that I had heard on the night that my father returned to her.

"A nightingale is singing in the wood where nymphs are
    dancing in a silver glade.
A white hind watches them, startled yet not afraid to see
    them weave enchantments.
At dawn they vanish, yet their spells remain. And when
    two mortal lovers
Tread the grass their feet have trod, their hearts shall be
    enthralled
Each unto each, so that they beat as one until they die
    and join the happy ghosts."

The song broke off, and I opened the door so that she shouldn't have time to cry to herself. She smiled, and asked me if I had had a happy day.

I said that I had been outside the town, playing with some children, and had forgotten how far the sun had traveled. I picked up the lute and said how I had missed hearing her play it. I asked her to play the songs that were my favorites; gay songs that the vine-pickers sing, and songs that would make even a one-legged man begin to dance.

Suddenly the door was flung open and there was Donnelli, her arms covered in flour, holding a twist of baking dough in her hand. ''Here have I been calling on the saints to give you work as an embroidress and you can sing to a lute sweeter than I have ever heard! You have only to sing songs like that in the front room and all the customers will be pouring out of the grandest inns in the town to come and listen to you. Why, even the coaches will stop here! I must tell Griggori to order ten more barrels of wine before next market-day, or there will be gold thrown on the tables and no wine to sink it in.''

And that was how my years as a strolling player began.

CHAPTER FIVE

The Strong-Man

It was on the evening of a market-day that my mother first sang for Donnelli's patrons. The room was very noisy, two carters were wrangling in a corner and one of the dice players must have stopped at another inn before he reached ours. When she came in carrying her lute no one took any notice of her. At first her quiet, falling melody was lost among the raucous sounds of the wineshop, as the sound of a rivulet is lost when thunder challenges a storm; but I think the very fact that they took no notice of her made her forget her nervousness.

In a few minutes her voice soared out pure and clear above the tumult; and gradually, one by one, the men grew silent until her song was ended. Then they shouted their acclaim of her, and when she would have run from the room in confusion they made her sing again, and again. They laughed with her when her songs were gay, and when she played ''The

Lament for a Dead Mistress'', they were as quiet as mourners round a bier. It was as though she had recaptured some forgotten power that gave her strength; her eyes were brilliant with renewed courage, and I saw the mother I had known before we left the castle, coming back to me.

After this, she played the lute every day, and the wineshop became more and more crowded. Sometimes she went up to the market place and sat by the booth of Donnelli's brother-in-law. At first she fingered the lute strings as if she were only testing the truth of their note, and the passers-by stared curiously at her but walked on; then she began to sing very softly, as if to herself, and they would pause; soon a crowd had collected, and only after she had finished singing did she pretend to discover that they were there. We never asked for money in the market, but the booth-woman got all the people who had been listening to the song to buy vegetables from her stall, and at the end of the day she used to give us a quarter of the day's takings. Some of the keepers of the other booths began to realize that their patrons were being enticed away from them, and they even told Mother that if she did it again they would break her lute over her head. But she only smiled at them, saying, ''When the town herald announces that a new order has been passed which forbids a woman to play a lute in the principal square for her own amusement, I hope I shall be fortunate enough to hear him. For surely it will be an order unique in any duchy!''

At the end of July, a fair was held in honor, I think, of the birth of a child to the House of Este. Oxen were roasted over open fires, and all the people in the town could eat until they had forgotten even the name of hunger. The fountain in the square ran with wine; it looked very pretty, though it ran dry long before noon. I heard a man grumbling that the wine was only from the dregs of the casks and even those did little more than color the water, but as I didn't taste any of it I don't know if he was right. As well as all the food that could be had for the asking, there was a booth where a man was selling

51

slices of roast sucking-pig, and another one where they sold fruit syrups and brightly colored sweetmeats.

A ragged jester went amongst the crowd banging people over the head with an inflated pig's bladder on a long stick. I saw him knock off an old woman's cap and then, pretending he had done it by accident, he handed it back to her with a stately bow and turned her anger into laughter with a quip.

There was a dancing bear being made to do its tricks by having a wooden spoon, dipped in honey, held just out of its reach. It had a collar round its neck, which must have been too tight, for it had worn the fur away. The man who owned it made it the foil for his humor: he would ask it a question and then pretend to repeat the bear's answer.

I heard him say, pointing to a market woman, ''What do you think of that fine lady in the red cloak?''

Then he put his ear to the bear's mouth, as if it were whispering to him, and said in a voice of mock horror, ''Oh, you rude animal, how dare you say such monstrous things about a human being! Even if what you say *is* true, she is still superior to you.''

He often cuffed the bear over the head, not very hard but enough to make it look even more bewildered. It used to rub its face with its forepaws, as if it were trying to hide itself away, and when it got tired of standing up on its hind legs and tried to go down on all fours to rest it was jerked upright again.

After a time the crowd became bored and wandered away, and the man tied the bear's chain to the ring in a hitching-stone. Mother had given me two small coins, telling me I could spend them as I liked, so I thought I would buy something for the bear to make it feel a bit happier. I wondered what bears liked to eat, but before I could ask the owner, he left it and went off to one of the booths. I stroked the bear and scratched its ears, until it went to sleep just as Mimetta used to do. Its coat was harsh and full of dust, and on its right side the hair was clotted round what looked like a knife thrust.

When the bear-leader came back he was very drunk, and he went up to the bear and kicked it in the side. I pulled out the long silver pin that Donnelli had given me and drove it as hard as I could into his leg. He bellowed, and swung round. Then he made a grab for me and I just had time to say, "I *hate* you!" before I started to run.

I had thought he was much too drunk to chase after me, but I found he wasn't. Cobble stones are very difficult to run on and I was afraid of slipping, but I went much faster than I had ever gone before. I could hear the bear-leader thundering after me and shouting out all the horrible things he would do when he caught me. With every step he got bigger and bigger, and I got smaller and smaller, until I felt as if I were being chased by an ogre. Just as I thought he was going to catch me, I saw a crowd and dived through it amongst their legs. I found myself in a little open space ringed round with people, who were watching an enormous man bending an iron bar as though it were made of plaited leather.

I heard the bear-leader shouting, "Let me get at her! She's half-killed me, and I'll flay her for it!"

I saw him fighting his way through the press of people and I couldn't see any way to escape. Then I saw that the strong-man was smiling at me, and he said, "What's the matter little girl?"

"There's an ogre—I mean a bear-leader, after me. He's going to kill me. Please stop him!"

As the man broke through the crowd and rushed at me, the strong-man caught him by the shoulder; then—I don't know how it happened it was so quick, the bear-leader's arms were twisted up behind him so that he couldn't move. His captor said, "Not so fast, my friend! You should not waste your strength on a child. If there is a fight in you that must be let out, I, Bernard, will do you the great honor of joining with you in a wrestling bout!"

He turned to the crowd, ''Will you be our patrons and provide us with a stake to fight for?''

They shouted their approval, for they had taken this yellow-haired giant into their favor. Now that I had stopped being frightened I could enter into the jest; and, at a word from Bernard, I snatched off my cap and carried it from hand to hand until it was full—there were even silver pieces amongst the bronze!

The bear-leader had forgotten me in his anger at being mocked. He drew a knife out of his belt, but Bernard caught his wrist and the knife spun through the air. Always the bear-leader's mad rushes were turned against himself: Bernard side-stepped, tripped him, threw him a half-score of times, and at last picked him up bodily and, after whirling him round his head as if he were a sack of flour, he flung him into the crowd like a stone from a siege engine.

I thought Bernard was the nicest man I had ever met. He said I must help him spend the money we had collected; he took me from booth to booth to buy syrup and sugar-plums, and he gave me a little donkey, carved out of wood with real panniers, and a silk scarf to wear over my head.

I asked him where he was lodging, and he told me he had only reached the town that morning and had left his pack-donkey in the stable yard of the Grey Eagle.

I said, ''The landlord of the Grey Eagle is a robber, and it is even whispered that some of his patrons have their throats cut if their money bags are too heavy!''

I had really never heard of the Grey Eagle, but I wanted Bernard to come with me to Donnelli's. I went on, ''If you come with me I will show you the best wineshop in the town, where I am sure you will be happy. You must come, please, because my mother will want to thank you for saving me.''

''What will your mother say when she finds you have made friends with a strong-man? Women of quality look on people of my trade, jesters and tumblers and mummers, as being fit companions only for rogues and vagabonds.''

"But we belong to the same trade as you do! Mother earns our lodging by singing to her lute, and I collect the money and make people laugh so that they will feel generous. People flock to listen to her, and they call her Olivia the Beautiful."

"That is the best news I have heard since the Jew my brother owed money to died of the palsy! You, and a sweet singer, and a strong-man—already we have the beginning of our own troupe of strolling players!"

Then he swung me up and set me on his shoulders. "We must hurry for I am impatient to see her—to see Olivia whose name shall be joined with Carola and Bernard for the fame of Italy!"

When we reached the Grey Eagle we only saw a loutish stable boy and I was very glad to find that the landlord was at the fair. Bernard looked into the panniers to see that nothing had been stolen, and then he let me ride on his pack-donkey all the way home.

fRESCO

Bernard stayed at Donnelli's wineshop for two months, and when the autumn came, Mother and I went northwards with him. He had never been to the Republic of Venice, but had heard from other strolling players that there the songs of a troubadour reaped a plentiful harvest. He was sure we should soon grow rich on his feats of strength and my mother's singing—not forgetting how I was to smile at our patrons and collect their money.

He said, "The Venetian ladies are renowned for their chastity and the gallants for the strength of their ardor. Impatient lovers do not turn easily to weaving songs, and if men must tarry to serenade under the window they long to enter, it will not be with their own verses; for it is easier to make love songs by candlelight than at high noon, and gallants do not waste their nights on driving quills! Olivia will compose their serenades, and I shall teach them how to grow strong so that they can twist the iron grille from their lady's window or throw her jealous husband into the canal."

Although he could not pay for us to travel in a coach, Bernard said that he could at least save us from having to walk, and so he bought us a little donkey. She was only two years old and very gay, with a shaggy grey coat and long velvety ears. She had only been trained to carry panniers, but in three or four days we taught her to carry a riding saddle without lying down when it was put on her back. When the kind cobbler heard that we were leaving, he made Celestina, for that was the donkey's name, a beautiful bridle of red leather; and Casparri trimmed it with two little silver bells.

The old pack-donkey was much bigger than Celestina, and as its panniers were shabby Bernard had new ones woven to carry all our possessions. Although it was Donnelli who had persuaded my mother to go north for the winter, telling her that the wineshop had so few patrons in the cold weather that sometimes they never even bothered to take down the shutters, she wept bitterly when we went away.

When Mother, wearing the hooded traveling cloak of azure cloth that Donnelli had given her and carrying her lute, rode on our little donkey, she looked like a picture that I had seen in some town we had passed through, of the Holy Mother fleeing into Egypt with her child in her arms.

She often took me with her when she went to Mass. I loved the singing shape of the candle flames and the memorable smell of incense, but I preferred being in a church when the priests were not there to break in on my thoughts with their mumbled Latin. When there was no service going on it was much easier to pray, because I could pretend to be looking up at the windows when I was asking God about something. I had often been told that it was rude not to look at the person to whom one was talking; so I could never understand why, in churches, the harder people pray the more they seem to address their appeal to Satan, cringing as if they were ready to receive a scourge on their backs for their impertinence in addressing their Creator, instead of standing upright, looking towards heaven where they hope their words will be heard.

On our journey I saw a picture, which I kept on remembering however much I tried to forget. It was frescoed on the wall of a cloister: at the top there was Heaven; where God, surrounded by His holy saints and a company of musical angels blowing horns, was enthroned in the sky. Below them, on Earth, there were many scenes: a noble and his lady, in old-fashioned clothes, riding out to the hunt followed by their courtiers; a man, with goats' feet, holding a naked woman in his arms; another man, of great fatness, with wine flagons and boars' heads and sucking-pigs heaped beside him; a young woman admiring herself in a mirror, while in her other hand she clutched a casket overflowing with jeweled brooches and heavy necklaces; and there were lots of other people I can't remember. Here and there, skeleton arms were sticking out from the ground, and what at first looked like boulders were skulls or thighbones; the path that the falconer was riding along led through a flowery meadow, but ended in steps that led down into a black pit. Hell was underneath the Earth, and from each of the people in the Earth part of the picture there was a little ladder leading down into it. In Hell you saw what the people above were going to suffer: there were men on racks, stretched out so far that they were twice their own length; women having their feet branded with irons; a boy being flayed—you could see all the muscles and veins where his skin had been rolled back. There was one scene I minded much more than all the rest: a ladder led down from five gallants who were lying on the grass watching a naked girl dancing, to where the same five men were lying with empty eyesockets and the blood running down their cheeks; the devil, who had just done the gouging, mocked at them as he threaded their eyes on a string to make himself a necklace.

I think I must have been blinded myself once, because although I could stop myself thinking of the rest of the fresco, this part of it kept on coming back very strongly when I was alone. I used to wonder if the artist who had painted it really knew about these things. I almost began to believe in Hell, and I thought the earth was so thin that it was only a crust over Hell, like a crust of pastry over a meat pie. I prayed very hard to my Shining One to let me know the truth; so that if Hell were really true I could start learning to be brave about it, but if it were not I could stop thinking that at any moment my foot may go through the ground, and that up from the hole would come terrible cries and the groans of souls in torment mingled with smoke and flames.

After I prayed I found that even if I tried to think of the fresco I saw another picture instead. At the top, there was the same Heaven as before, but the Earth part had been changed. Now there were no ladders leading downwards, and each group of figures was shown twice: in one group there were two men fighting, and then there were the same two men with the victor binding up the wounds of the vanquished. There were lots of people being wicked or foolish, but beside them were the same people after they had gained wisdom, undoing the results of their own actions. Hell had vanished, and in its place the same Heaven that was at the top of the fresco had been repeated.

After I had seen this I wasn't frightened of Hell any more; because I knew that there is sky on the other side of the Earth, as well as on this side that every one knows about, and that beyond both skies there is Heaven. No one need be afraid of falling into a bottomless pit, because you can't fall into the sky—you have to learn how to fly up through it into Heaven.

Village to Village

I had thought that Mother and I were going to be so happy with Bernard, and that soon we should be able to have a little house of our own instead of always having to wander from place to place. But before long I began to wish that we had never left Donnelli's. When we had lived there, we had had a clean room and were never afraid of being hungry; I had known a lot of friendly people, there were children to play with, and when I was tired I could go to sleep. Now, as soon as the people of a village had begun to cease being strangers we moved on somewhere else. Bernard was always telling us that in a little while everything would be better, for we should have become rich and famous and could have whatever we wanted. But soon even I began to realize that his confident speeches held no real promise.

Mother was often ill, and sometimes she coughed so badly she couldn't sing. The rooms we slept in were cold and dirty, and usually we had to share them with other women whom Mother would not let me speak to. When I asked her why we stayed with Bernard although neither of us was happy, she told me it was because she had no money. I said, ''What happened to all the silver pieces that you saved while we were with Donnelli?''

''Bernard took them from me. He said it was dangerous for a woman to carry money, because she might be robbed, and that in his possession it would be safer than a cardinal's coffin in a cathedral vault.''

''And he has lost it? Who took it from him?''

''The dice lost it for him. Or perhaps I lost it, by being so simple-minded that I never realized he would use it to gamble with. A hundred silver pieces—enough to have kept us in safety for six months, all lost by a bragging giant who swills his wine and cannot hold it!''

I was surprised at the bitterness in her voice, for I had thought she was as fond of Bernard as I was. I asked her,

"Then you will never marry Bernard?"

"What should I marry him for? A home, when he is a vagabond? Security, when he cannot be trusted to look after a single coin?"

"I thought perhaps you loved him."

"Loved Bernard! No, to love once is enough for any woman. She must be a fool who loves a second time, for even a fish does not catch itself twice on the same hook."

"Bernard is very kind to me. Is it wrong to love him, even a little?"

"If you see Bernard as he really is, he will never hurt you; his body is as strong as the iron bars of a prison window, but he is unstable as water. If he looked after you, he would give you such a rich supper one night that you would be sick for two days, and then he would lose the rest of his money at dice and the innkeeper would throw you both into the street. He might carry you on his shoulders for five leagues and then leave you in a strange village and stay drunk in a wineshop while you searched for him. He has asked me, many times, to marry him; but I have told him to seek some barren woman who needs a grown-up child to look after, or a kitchen-girl who will love him for his strength."

I still went on thinking that when we got to Venice things would be happier for us. But some weeks later, when I tried to find out how long it would be before we got there, Mother said, "The plan to go there was only more of Bernard's windy talk. In a town it is only in the poorest inns they let us play—for shelter in the stable and a meal of old crusts with thin broth to moisten them! How should we get a hearing in a great city?"

"Won't things *ever* get any better?"

"Some people say that next year the whole country will be more settled. But everywhere we go there is fighting—our own people fighting against themselves, and foreign mercenaries being paid to cut Italian throats."

"What are they fighting about?"

"How should I know the secrets behind the plots of princes and the intrigues of cardinals? Perhaps your father and his brothers-in-arms know what they fight for, but I no longer hear even what is whispered in the kitchens of castles. We belong to the poor, the poor who plant vines that fill other men's wine flagons and grow corn to make pasties for a fine lady to feed to her lap-dog; who entertain the dregs of the people in taverns, so that they laugh and forget their wrongs—and march to the tune their master's trumpeter sounds!''

It was a long time before Bernard gave up boasting of what we should do in Venice, though he seemed quite content to drift from village to village. It was always the same story: the first two or three days the patrons of some little inn would applaud us, and the landlord might be willing to give us a few small coins or a bowlful of meat stew; but within a week we had to move on. Then we would saddle Celestina and the pack-donkey and set off aimlessly along another road.

Sometimes Bernard made a little money by wrestling. Once he fought the village bully in an inn-yard; two travelers who were watching from the balcony wagered on the fight as if the men were two gamecocks. The man who had wagered on Bernard was so excited when he won that he gave him five gold pieces. Mother managed to get hold of two of these and sew them into her dress, but the rest of it Bernard spent on a feast for all the patrons of the tavern—which delighted the inn-keeper and didn't prevent us going hungry again three days later. When Mother tried to reason with Bernard he said, ''It is better to play the duke for an hour than to live like a prosperous shop-keeper for three days!''

I think it was very unfortunate that Bernard had not been born the eldest son of a duke; for while he was emptying the ducal coffers of their hoarded treasure, his people would have been happy and contented; and his justice would always have been very merciful.

Sorrowful Woman

I am not sure why we never went back to Donnelli's, but I think it was because Mother was too proud to let her see that none of our fine hopes had been realized, that we were still living from day to day, still beggars instead of the bringers of gifts that we had thought we should be when we returned.

The hardships she had experienced during the two years since we had left there had changed my mother; she no longer seemed the same woman who had so often told me stories and legends to teach me that love, even unhappy love, is the essence of the teaching of Christ. Even her voice had been different: gentle, calm as muted strings: ''There are three goddesses, three sisters: they are Love, and Sorrow, and the third is Hatred. He that knows Love only is blessed. He who knows Sorrow may know Love also and be comforted. He who has taken Hatred for a companion to shield him from Sorrow, so that he cannot see the face of Love, dies like a scorpion—of his own poison.''

It seemed to distress her that I had not grown bitter as she had. I remember her saying to me, ''You are a strange child, Carola. Once I hoped to keep you safe against the world, with peace and beauty as your counselors. But in the last two years you have seen much of poverty and hate; of hunger, avarice, and dumb despair; yet you have seemed content. Has all this taught you nothing? Remember, to love another is to invite an unknown guest to dwell with you, a guest whom you can never bid depart. And this, so welcome, guest comes through the door with her face veiled. You are so sure that when she shows her face it will be joy that shines upon you, but when she lifts her veil it is often grey sorrow that has come to keep with you eternal company.''

''How can I stop loving? I don't want ever to love anyone as you loved my father.''

''It is hard to know Love so that one may bolt one's door against her; for she is a master of disguise, a mummer of a

62

thousand parts. She will shower many gifts upon you to gain your confidence. She has given us each other; flowers, clouds, the young green of willow leaves in spring and the quiet benediction of snowflakes. The stars are her comfits; and she will give you warm apricots, and melons for your thirst. She will beguile you with ice-flowers on a winter thorn tree and water-weeds flowing in a stream. The gentle breezes are her messengers and singing-birds her lute-players. Yet how can I teach you to defend yourself against her, when all that has brought you joy since you were born has been her gift?''

I found it difficult to understand why love always seemed to bring sorrow also. Sometimes even Bernard was sad because he loved Mother and she could not love him. I said, ''I wish that loving people was like loving things. I loved my little mermaid, I knew that even though she was a sea-fairy she couldn't love me, and it didn't matter. But when we knew my father didn't love us any more we were so unhappy. Could a woman learn to love a man as she loves a tree, learn to take pleasure in her own love and yet be indifferent to what she receives from him in return?''

''I think to do that she would have to be more than mortal. Only the love of God and the Blessed Virgin, perhaps of the Saints, has that serene quality; their love is like the sun, which sends down its rays with a sublime indifference whether they call the leaves from reluctant boughs or parch the water from a thirsty plain.''

''Why did Christ tell His people to love each other, if it makes them more sorrowful?''

''Perhaps the true meaning of His words has been forgotten. He told us to seek humility. It is easy to give alms to a beggar and not be thanked; it is easy to play the lute and hear no praise; but it is bitter sorrow to give love and not receive it.''

I thought men were fortunate to have so many other things than love to fill their lives. I said, ''I wish I were a boy, then

63

I would apprentice myself to a craftsman. I should like to be a goldsmith, or perhaps a wood-carver. Why can't women be apprenticed?''

''Men are jealous of women, because a woman can make a child out of flesh and a man can only make a statue out of marble. They are proud and arrogant, they hate to remember that the greatest of them once screamed for a woman's breast, and if she had denied him the charity of her milk, he would have died. Even the Pope once wet his swaddling clothes and had to be cossetted to break his wind! God Himself allowed His only son to spend long months within a woman's womb, but He could find no man worthy of divine fatherhood.''

''Then why was Jesus born a man and not a woman?''

''Because He took upon Himself the form of the lowest of God's creatures—as the symbol of His supreme humility!''

''Are all the legends that the troubadours sing nothing but lies, the songs of knights and princesses who have loved each other in joy until they died?''

''I have seen very little of the world, even of Italy. It may be that somewhere there is happiness; there may be men who do not tire of women when they have possessed their hearts. Perhaps it is women's dreams of heaven that have made these songs. It may be that you will find them true, Carola—in some strange land where mermaids and dragons dwell, where gazelles talk and flowers sing madrigals.''

CHAPTER SIX

Revolt in Padua

We seldom went into a big town, but when we were in sight of the walls of Padua the pack-donkey put its foot into a hole and broke its leg. The panniers were put on to Celes-

64

tina, and as Mother could not walk very far we decided to stay in Padua until we had collected enough money to buy another animal.

It was a market day, and carts were streaming into the city from the surrounding farms. Bernard persuaded a carter to let Mother and me sit up amongst the grain sacks whilst Celestina trotted along behind us. There were soldiers at the gate who questioned nearly everyone before letting them through, but they must have known the carter, and perhaps thought we were part of his family, for they did not make us halt.

When the carter set us down in the market square, he told us the way to a little wine shop, the house of his sister's husband, where he said we should be well looked after. It was in a narrow alley that ran along inside the town wall, and although it was small there was good stabling, for people who came in from the countryside to attend the market often left their animals there for the day. The owner and his wife were friendly people, and they said we could have the empty room next to the winestore without payment until Bernard had found work for us. The only furnishings were some wooden pegs driven into the wall and a plank bench under the window, but the man spread some clean straw to make a pallet, and his wife lent us two woolen covers of her own weaving.

Bernard took me with him while he went from tavern to tavern trying to find an inn-keeper who would let us entertain his patrons. Everywhere we went the people seemed nervous and furtive; there was a feeling of unrest hanging over the town, palpable as the mist over a swamp. I didn't want to stay there, and I begged Bernard to take us away even if we had to sleep on the bare hillside; but he was in one of his moods when he thought to-morrow would see a change in our fortunes, and he laughed at me for being frightened.

Perhaps I had disturbed him more than he would admit, for after a few days he decided that we had better move on to a smaller town, and it was arranged we should leave on the following morning. He came to wake us while it was still dark; not to tell us to get up, but to say that Mother was to keep me with her in our room all day and that on no account were we to go into the street. I asked what had happened, and was told that during the night there had been some disturbance among the townspeople but I was not to be afraid for it would soon pass. I felt something terrible was going to happen, and however often I told myself not to be silly it did no good.

Although Bernard knew there had been fighting between the foreign soldiers and the townsmen, he insisted on going out to see what was happening. A wounded man had been brought to the inn while I was still asleep. He was hidden in the wine-store, and through the thin partition I could hear him groaning and muttering to himself. I wanted to go and see if I could help him, but I was not allowed to. Soon after dawn he grew quiet—I didn't know whether he had died or fallen asleep.

Our only window was boarded up. I pulled out some of the straw that we had stuffed into the chinks between the boards to stop the draught, and tried to see into the street. For a time it was deserted; and then we would hear the galloping of horses or the angry muttering of a crowd.

I knew Mother was frightened although she kept on telling me we were quite safe and that Bernard would soon come back. When I was tired of staring out through the narrow chinks of the window, she made me a manikin with some of the straw from her pallet.

No one came near us and I began to be very hungry. We had a loaf of black bread and some mutton slices, which Mother had prepared to take with us when Bernard had said we were to make ready to leave the town. The meat was almost raw and the fat grey and sticky, but we had nothing else.

Towards evening we could smell smoke, strong and acrid on the wind, and see the red glare of a distant fire. Mother

told me she thought it was in the direction of the merchants'
quarters. She said, ''Perhaps the mob have set light to some
of the houses, so that their oppressors will have to fling open
the iron-barred doors that guard their treasures. When they
try to escape they will find the poor, who for so long have
plotted against their masters, waiting for them—as dogs wait
for the rats to bolt from a burning hay-rick.''

''What will they do to the merchants?''

''Their bodies will be stripped and thrown into the river.
In a few days a corpse may glide past a village further downstream; and if a fisherman wonders who once wore that
swollen flesh, his passing thought will be its only requiem.''

''Are you sure it will be only the merchants who are
killed?''

''No, child. This riot, an angry crowd sullen with hunger
who at last turn to fight, is like all wars. It is the same when
men pick a quarrel in a tavern brawl, the sack of a city, or
when kings ride out to battle and the people of two lands are
joined in conflict. Where men sow hatred, Death is their
harvester.''

Dark Harvest

It soon grew quite dark, and as we had neither candle nor
rushlight, we lay down on the same pallet and tried to sleep.
I was very thirsty because I had had nothing to drink since
early in the morning. I tried to forget about it but it grew
worse and worse, and I kept thinking of the spring trickling
into the stone trough where the mules were watered.

I was lying between Mother and the wall but I managed to
creep out without waking her. I slid back the heavy wooden
bar that secured the door and slipped quietly past the store-
room towards the stable-yard. The house was very quiet;
usually at this time there would have been several people
drinking in the front room. I pushed open the door and

peered in. It could not long have been deserted, for logs were still smoldering on the open hearth. The shutters were bolted across the windows and the two heavy settles had been barricaded against the door leading into the street.

I ran down the passage to the room where the innkeeper and his wife slept with their two children. Both the chests were open; one was empty, but the other still held some winter covers that must have been too heavy to carry away. On the bed, some clothes and a wooden horse that I had seen the baby playing with were tied up in a cotton quilt. I realized that they had forgotten all about us—perhaps their panic had driven everything from their minds, or else they thought we had gone with Bernard.

I went back along the passage into the yard. The glare of the distant fire was so bright that I could see enough to find a crock and fill it at the spring. After I had drunk I splashed my face with the cold water, because I had always found this was a way of making myself feel brave.

I filled the crock and carried it back to my mother because I thought she must be very thirsty too. She didn't wake until I touched her; she must have been exhausted, for usually she slept so lightly. When I told her that the inn was deserted, she said she was sure the innkeeper would not have left his house, which was by far his most valuable possession, unless he knew it would be very dangerous to stay there. She told me to get a candle out of the front room and light it from the fire, which I had said was still burning, and then go to the kitchen to look for some food. I was to tie in a cloth as much as I could carry, for she was going to take me out of the town where we could hide in some patch of woodland until it was safe to return to look for Bernard. I asked her whether, instead of going into the hills at the back of the town, it would not be better to go down the river valley where there were farms and people who might help us. But she said that her plan was the safest, for when the foreign soldiers, who had been brought in to quell the rebellion, had restored order, revenge would be taken on guilty and innocent alike.

I took three smoked sausages which were hanging from the rafters; there were some hams hanging there also but they were too heavy to carry; some cold stew I found in a basin, a piece of salt pork, the heel of a loaf of bread, and a few raw onions. When I went back with them I saw Mother coming out of the wine-store next to our room. She told me the wounded man had gone, but I knew she wasn't telling me the truth. I said, ''Are you *sure* he's dead?'' And she answered, ''Yes, quite sure.'' So I knew that we needn't worry about him, because he was much safer than we were.

Celestina was in the corner of the stable where I had left her; there was still some hay in the rack and water in the bucket. She didn't like being taken out of her stable at night, but after I had stroked her ears she let me put on her bridle and strap the panniers on her back. Celestina was small enough to get through the wicket of the big stable-yard gate; we couldn't close it behind us but we wedged it to with a piece of wood.

The inn was built against the town wall, and we followed the narrow street that led down towards the East Gate. At one place there were steps, but we managed to make Celestina go down them. When we neared the East Gate, Mother told me to stay with Celestina while she went forward to see if it were open.

When she came back I could see she was frightened. She told me the gate was heavily guarded by the Duke's men and that she had seen two people who were trying to leave the town seized by the soldiers and dragged into the guard-room.

She decided that our only chance of escape was to go back the way we had come, in the hope that the gate near the merchants' quarter would be unguarded. She said, ''Neither mob nor mercenaries will trouble to attack a woman and a child. Even if there is danger there, it is better than to risk being taken by the Duke's men. If you were stripped and searched they would see your brand; and no one with the blood of the Griffin can hope for clemency in Padua.''

From the way the fire was spreading and the shouts of the distant crowds, it was clear that on the far side of the town the mercenaries had not vanquished the rebels. We left the main street and went by dark alleyways; sometimes dragging, sometimes cajoling Celestina. She found some cabbage leaves in the gutter and insisted on stopping to eat them. Although the way we followed turned and twisted between the houses, it was easy to keep our direction because of the fire.

As we approached the market square we met people fleeing in terror from the advancing flames. Some had their faces blackened with smoke and their clothes charred, and many of them were carrying bundles, perhaps their own possessions or else things they had stolen from the burning houses. I saw a woman stumbling along, her eyes blank and staring as though she were bewitched, carrying a dead child under one arm and a great silver candelabra under the other.

Celestina grew more and more stubborn and I had to drag her along by the bridle to keep her moving. It must have been market day, for there were broken booths lying about, and cheeses and fruit were crushed into the mud. By an overturned stall there were some live chickens tied together by their legs; and an unmilked goat, tethered to a post, was bleating incessantly from the pain of her swollen udder.

The fire must have just reached the back of the buildings on the far side of the square. The houses were silhouetted against the flames, as if they were not real houses but a painted backcloth to marionettes.

From the corner of the square opposite to where we had come into it, a wide street led down to the Market Gate. The houses that lined it were not yet alight, though if the wind veered nothing could save them. The street was very crowded; by each doorway there were several men armed with cudgels, and I thought of what mother had said about the dogs waiting round the hay-rick. Nobody hindered us, though some of them looked curiously at us or laughed at my efforts to urge Celestina forward. As we drew near the Market Gate we saw that it was open and unguarded. In a few minutes we should be safely outside the walls, climbing slowly up the mule track into the hills where we could sleep in safety under the stars.

Suddenly I heard a trumpet call. It came from beyond the gate, and there were cries of, ''The Duke's men! The Duke's men!'' from the crowd. We tried to run back up the street, but the crowd closed in behind us. I think they all realized that in a moment they would be fighting for their lives, and that if they could not seize the city and hold it against the Duke, soon they would plead before his torturers for death.

There was no alleyway up which we could run, so we crouched in a shallow doorway. On one side of us there seemed to be a wall of faces, of the type I knew so well from watching them in the taverns. Many had lost an ear; many were marked by the pox, or scabbed with the green sickness. They were armed with the tools of their trade; meat-choppers and fleshers' knives, blacksmiths' hammers and sickles.

As the soldiers came through the gate we could see that they were not the Duke's men but mercenaries. They wore helmets, and ''back and breasts'' of blued steel over brown leather tunics and were armed with halberds and long daggers. They were well-trained troops and advanced in steady file, ten abreast, spanning the street from wall to wall.

The crowd did not retreat. When the soldiers were within twenty paces of it, they halted while their captain commanded the mob, in the name of the Republic, to throw down their arms.

A man, nearly as big as Bernard, who shouldered a blacksmith's hammer, shouted, ''If you want our knives come and get them! You'll get them in your backs!'' The crowd roared its approval. The captain shouted to his soldiers to advance, and at the same moment the crowd surged down towards them.

Soon the street was a turmoil of fighting. A man's arm was cut off by a halberd and the blood spurted over Celestina's forelegs. I had covered her head with my cloak to try to stop her from bolting, but when she smelled the blood she broke away from me and plunged into the crowd. I ran out in an attempt to catch her, and Mother followed me.

We were caught in the press, like straws caught up by a gust of wind at a street corner. Mother had her arm round me and was trying to protect me. We were carried up the street into the market-place. At last we found ourselves on the edge of the crowd, opposite a narrow alley which led steeply up between the high garden walls of two merchants' houses.

Mother told me to run up it until I found somewhere where we could hide. She walked very slowly and I was frightened someone would come after us, so I urged her to hurry. She stumbled, and nearly fell. Even then I didn't realize she was hurt; I thought she was only dazed by all the noise of the fighting and that she couldn't see her way in the dark passage.

There was a buttress jutting out from the wall with a small level place behind it where there was enough room for us to rest. I told Mother we could hide there till the fighting was over. She nodded, and then stumbled again and fell forward on her hands and knees. I put my arm around her to help her up. Her cloak was hot and wet, and then I knew that she had been stabbed.

She was panting as if she had been running a long way. She said, ''Don't be frightened.... It's only a little wound and will soon heal.... Let me rest a little....''

I sat down with my back against the wall, and supporting her across my lap I took her head in my arms. The moon shone through the clouds and I could see her face. She was so pale, and there was a heavy dew of sweat on her forehead. I asked her if she were in pain. She said, no, but she must rest a little and then she would be strong enough to go on.

I knew that she was very ill. I tried not to cry, but I could feel the tears running down my face. I wondered how I was going to be able to look after her while she was ill. Celestina was lost, and with her had gone everything we possessed, our food, and our clothes, even my mother's lute.

I stroked her forehead and told her that now she must be my little girl and I would look after her and be her mother. She tried to smile and said, "Don't be frightened...I'll soon be..."

Then she tried to sit up. Her face was working as though she couldn't breathe, and suddenly blood drenched out of her mouth and poured over my hand in a hot stream. Her head fell back against my shoulder and two great scarlet bubbles formed on her mouth.

Then I knew that it was no good my calling to her. But I couldn't help calling to her, because I was so frightened without her, and I thought that somehow she might manage not to die.

I held her in my arms and comforted her, as she had comforted me when I was little and had a sorrowful dream.

the Cold Stranger

I knew that she was dead, but I tried to make myself believe that she was only asleep. The sorrow lines had gone from her face; she looked young and happy as she had been when my father was with us.

I wondered when Bernard would find us. I listened for his voice but no one came up the alley. I found myself smoothing my mother's hair and telling her not to wake into the dream that I was seeing. Her face was cold under my hand and I tried to tuck her bare arm under the cloak, but I couldn't move it. For a moment I thought she was trying to resist me and that she wasn't dead. Then I found her body had gone hard, like a statue; and suddenly she wasn't my mother any more, she was something I was afraid of.

I tried to get up, but I had been sitting such a long time with her weight across my knees that my legs wouldn't obey me, and I couldn't move. Blood from the wound in her back had soaked through her clothes on to my dress; it had dried, hard as wood; it was as if she and I were frozen together. I could feel my mouth trying to scream but I couldn't hear any noise.

I suddenly thought that she was turning into a statue...the figures on the tombs in the cathedral must have been dead people who had turned into stone. They looked so peaceful with their hands folded over their breasts—if only I had known that this was going to happen to her I shouldn't have let her die in such an uncomfortable position. Why had her clothes not turned to stone also?...I remembered my terror of the ilex avenue at the castle, where the white statues gleamed in the dusk against the dark trees. Were they all women to whom my father's kinsmen had denied Christian burial so that their beauty changed to marble as their only immortality?

I tried frantically to break the draw-string of my skirt so that I could get away from this cold stranger. At last it gave and I could draw my legs from under her. I stood up, shaking with cold and fear. There was a patch of blood on the front of my cotton shift; I wanted to tear it off but I had nothing else to cover me.

I started to run down the hill towards the noise of the crowd—they might be enemies; but they would be warm, and alive. Then I thought that I was being a coward to leave my mother, and I went back up the hill, between the high walls of the narrow passage, and crouched beside her until daybreak.

The grey morning light was getting stronger when I saw an old priest pass the dark corner where we were hidden. I ran out and caught him by his robe and implored him to come to my mother. He hesitated for a moment and then followed me. When he saw the silver cross that she wore, he said a short prayer over her which I could not understand. He

74

promised me that he would bury her in consecrated ground and do all that was possible to save her soul, even though she had died by violence and so had not received the sacrament of extreme unction.

He told me to wait beside her until he sent someone to take her body to the burial place; then he would take me before the Civil Authority where I must try to describe my mother's assassin. I told him I knew nothing of what had happened, except that we had been caught up by the crowd and carried along until we had been flung out of the press of people; that I hadn't known my mother was hurt until she had stumbled and fallen and told me to drag her into this dark corner where we should be hidden from the passers-by; and how the blood gushed from her mouth while she was telling me not to be frightened, because she would soon be well again.

But the priest still said that I must go before the Civil Authority when he returned. Bernard had told me always to avoid the law; for laws were made to harrass strolling players, to put the hungry into prison, and to protect the rich. I didn't want to go to prison. I had heard stories of what prisons were like; how the mad people were chained to the walls, and the prisoners wore irons that chafed the flesh until the bones showed as white as a skeleton's.

So when I saw the priest coming back and knew that which had been my mother would be safe in his care, I ran away to search for Bernard.

I ran as fast as I could until I got to the bottom of the passage. I couldn't hear any sound of fighting and I crouched in the deep shadow beside a buttress, watching to see who would pass along the street.

The front of the house opposite had fallen to the fire, it looked like the setting of a giant's puppet show. A dead man lay across a charred beam of the upper floor; he must have been killed whilst searching for the merchant's riches, for the clothes were not blacked; he looked like a marionette of whom his satanic master had grown weary.... Perhaps only

75

those people who go to heaven are turned into stone; people whose body God wishes to preserve, so that they may be remembered upon earth while their spirit is joined in His celestial company.

I was so tired that I couldn't be frightened any more. I kept thinking that I should see Bernard coming to look for me: he would pick me up and take me somewhere where I could sleep, so that I could find my mother and tell her I had looked after her body, and that it was safely laid in consecrated ground beyond the reach of demons and warlocks.

A troop of soldiers marched up the street towards the market-place. I realized the townsmen had been overcome and the wineshops would be closed. Until then I had thought I had only to go from tavern to tavern until I found Bernard; but now I didn't know where to go.

There were more dead men lying in the market-square. I saw a mongrel boar-hound carrying a man's arm in its mouth; the hand was still clenched into a fist. I went back by the same alleys through which I had come with my mother. All the hovels were shut and their doors barred. I heard a child wailing and a woman's voice trying to comfort it. I knocked on the door, for I thought she might help me as she had a child of her own. The crying was stifled, as if a hand had been put over the child's mouth. I implored the woman, in the name of St. Catherine, to let me in—but she would not answer.

Further on some mercenaries were battering down the doors with the hafts of their halberds, searching the houses and dragging the people into the street. I saw one of them tear open the bodice of an old woman and find a gold crucifix on a faded purple ribbon. He told her that the Duke had proclaimed all houses were to be searched and anyone having on his person or property any object of value that could not be in his possession by lawful means was to be summarily put to death. She fell on her knees and swore by the saints that it had been in her possession since she was a little girl, and that it had belonged to her mother and her grandmother; but he threw the crucifix to another soldier who put it into a leather sack. When the old woman tried to stop him, he kicked her in the belly. She lay on the ground moaning, until he drove the haft of his halberd down on her temple. Then he said, ''One less for the dungeons! The executioner should be grateful to me for saving him this extra burden—by to-morrow he'll be the most weary man in Padua!''

One of the soldiers caught hold of me but another told him to let me go. ''Leave the child. She looks as though she'll be dead by evening.'' He didn't know that it was my mother's blood and not my own that soaked my shift. The priests believe there is great value in any piece of a martyr's robe that is stained with his holy blood; and I wondered if some of the love of my mother still stayed with me in this great, dark stain.

The door into the stable courtyard was wedged as we had left it. I had hoped that Celestina would have found her way home; but she wasn't there. The inn shutters had been broken open; the wine barrels were staved in and the hams had gone from the rafters. I wondered if the dead man were still lying in the store-room. I called and called for Bernard, but he didn't come.

I went into the little room where my mother and I had been together. The woolen cover was still there, and I pulled it over me and tried to go to sleep.

My hand touched something in the dark. It was the little manikin that my mother had made for me out of straw.

CHAPTER SEVEN

the farm

I cannot remember how long I stayed in the deserted inn, but it must have been more than a week. I was so very alone. I could not even meet my mother when I was asleep, nor did my Shining One come to me in a vision. The smell of death slunk into my room through the thin partition, so I knew that the dead man was still lying there. I prayed very hard that his soul was at peace, although I had not the courage to go and say an Ave over the body in which it had lived.

Somehow I felt sure that Bernard was alive, and I kept thinking that he would come and find me. But at last I realized that now I had to look after myself, had to find the food I ate and the place I slept in; and for a companion I had only my own heart. I lived on the raw turnips I found in the shed at the back of the house, and as the hens had not been stolen from the coop I had an egg nearly every day. The inn-keeper's wife had left some of her clothes behind, and rolled up with a piece of embroidery there was a needle and a hank of blue thread, which I used to shorten a woolen overdress so that I could wear it. It didn't seem like stealing, because if I had not taken it someone else would have done so.

I had propped open the small door into the yard in case Celestina found her way home, and I went to the stable many times every day to see if she had come back. But I never saw her again. I hoped that she was safely dead, because she would have forgotten what it was like to have people unkind to her, and would not be able to understand if they got angry and beat her. One of the many things that had always made me feel a stranger when I went to church, was that though the priests said God had created heaven and earth, they also said that animals had no souls. Why would they not teach what they must, surely, have known to be true; that animals are our younger brothers? If man is cruel to an animal, He that is the Father of both of them will rise up in wrath; even as an ordinary father would beat his eldest son if he stoned the youngest in the family as it slept in its cradle.

Very early one morning I went down and hid near the East Gate to see if there was any way of leaving the town without being questioned. I remembered what my mother had told me, that no one with the mark of the Griffin could hope for clemency in Padua, so I was frightened of being searched. I saw that some of the people who lived inside the walls were going out to work in the fields and that with them were many children. I slipped out of the shadow and joined the crowd, and the warden of the gate never noticed that there was a stranger amongst the others.

Everything I possessed I had tied in a bundle which I carried over my shoulder on a stick; a cloak I had made out of a woolen bed-cover, the blood-stained shift, some turnips, and five eggs. I walked, on and on, through the bleak vineyards. The vines looked cold and dead; the grapes had all been gathered but a few leaves still clung to the black stumps. That night I slept in a copse; a thin rain was falling, and I knew that soon I should have to find a roof to sleep under, for winter was coming.

The days were like a dream from which I could not wake, a dream of being tired, and cold, and hungry—at first hunger was the worst, but then it was the tiredness, because at night it was too cold to sleep.

One night I crept into a haystack for shelter. It was much warmer than a field and the mice made friendly noises as they scuttled through it. In the morning the farmer found me there. I tried to run away, and when he caught me I covered my face with my arms because I thought he was going to beat me. But he was kind, as Donnelli had been. He took me into the house, where his five children were eating at a long table, and said I might share their food. I thought it would be wonderful not to be hungry any more; but it hurt, as if I had eaten a live rat instead of a bowlful of pease porridge. Soon I was very sick, so I had to explain that it was because I had eaten nothing for three days. The farmer did not ask me where I had come from or why I was nearly starving; he seemed to know that I did not want to talk about it, and he said I must go and rest in his daughter's bed. I fell asleep at once and it was dark when I woke. A little girl brought me a cup of goat's milk and a posset of herbs, and after I had drunk them I felt much stronger and went to sleep again.

Next morning Giorgio, the farmer, told me as his wife had just died he needed some one to look after the baby and the youngest boy who was only three years old, and that if I would do it I could stay on as long as I liked.

I was very grateful to him, and in time grew to be quite happy living there. I used to milk the goats and often helped to feed the pigs and the oxen, as well as cooking for the whole family and washing all their clothes in the stream which ran through the pasture. Except during the winter, the farm produce was taken into market every week. I liked market days, for Giorgio used to take me and the children with him in the ox-cart to the nearest town. The two youngest children spent the day with their great-aunt, who lived there, but the other three had to run errands for their father. I used to take a heavy basket, filled with fruit, or eggs, or cheese, from door to door. Sometimes when I was tired of carrying it, I put it down and started singing one of the songs my mother had taught me. When people came out of their houses to drive the beggar away, I told them that I had not come to beg but to offer them a fine bargain, and quite often they were nice to me and gave me a fair price.

By the time I was thirteen my hair had grown long and I wore it in two braids. The work on the farm was hard but in the two years I was there I grew tall, and stronger than I had ever been before. One day followed another, like a pattern endlessly repeated on a roll of stamped velvet. I might have stayed there until I was grown up; perhaps married the son of a neighboring farmer, borne his children, looked after his house, and lived very close to the earth until I forgot what lay beyond it; had I not gone into the town one day to take a cheese of my own making to the wife of the inn-keeper.

I wonder what I should have done if I could have known how that day would change the color of my life. Should I have still gone out to meet experience, or chosen to stay at the farm and live as a peasant?

new lute

I was going alone into the town, so instead of taking the ox-cart I rode one of the pannier donkeys and led another. The cheese I made was sprinkled with wild thyme to give it the special flavor of the district, and I put two discs of it, packed between reed mats and then wrapped in fresh leaves to keep them cool, into one of the panniers, and, in the other, two fine capons and fifty eggs.

I followed the path through the woods instead of the high road, for it was very pleasant in the shade. It was hot, even for July. The dust was fine as flour, and the donkeys ambled through it quietly as shadows. The air danced in the heat but the watching trees were still. I had to wait at the ford while a herd of oxen were driven across, for although the water was low, except at the point where the path crossed it the river banks were steep and wooded.

The "Blue Boar" was on the outskirts of the town, on the north side of the market square. The inn-keeper's wife always asked me to stay and chat with her when I brought produce from the farm, and as usual I shared their midday meal. The rich mutton stew, hot and greasy, reeked of garlic, but though I was not hungry I ate some of it while she gossiped about her neighbors and the people who were lodging with her.

"We have some vagabond players here. I was going to let

81

them sleep on the straw in the empty stable. But, oh no! That was not good enough for them. They might have been nobles and not mummers from the airs they gave themselves. 'We must have a room with a window, and the pallet cover changed....' I should have turned them away if I had not seen the color of their money, it was gold as well as silver! I hope it was not earned by cutting throats or they may slit mine! One of them is courteous enough—a grown man though he is no taller than a child of ten. The woman is a singer—a strumpet, too, if ever I saw one!'' I was hardly listening to her. Her voice droned on like a blowfly in a butter churn. ''The big one is more trouble than the other two put together. He goes about stripped to the waist. I suppose he hopes the kitchen girls will grow hot at the sight of his muscles, and they would if I didn't keep after them, silly giggling wenches! And boast! You would think he were an emperor to hear him talk! 'I, Bernard, will do this. I, Bernard, the strong-man!''

Suddenly I realized what she had said:

''Bernard! You said his name was Bernard? Tell me quickly—is his hair curly, straw yellow? Can he bend an iron bar and lift a sling with four stone cannon balls in it with one hand?''

''That's the man. Where have you seen him, for they say they are strangers here? When I asked them if they were going on to Padua he said, 'No! It is an accursed town!' More of his silly talk—why should Padua be accursed unless all its scholars—its a great place for scholars, so I've heard—are learning sorcerer's tricks?''

''Where is Bernard? Is he still here? I must see him.''

''Asleep in the room at the top of the stairs, unless he's gone out when my back's been turned. Sleep half the day and roister at night—that's what they do, instead of taking the sun for their hourglass like good Christians.''

I ran up the stairs. I listened, but could not hear anything. The door was not bolted, and it swung open when I pulled the latch string. Bernard was fast asleep. His head was pillowed on the crook of his arm, and he looked like a statue of some colossus of the ancients, for he was naked because of the heat. I said his name very quietly. He stirred. A little louder I said, "Bernard!" His eyes opened. For a moment they blinked sleepily, then terror shone out of them. He cowered back in the corner and, crossing himself, he babbled, "You can't come back. You were buried in consecrated ground. I stayed in Padua till I was sure of that. I paid gold for masses to be said for your soul. Where is Olivia? Why is she not with you?"

"It was Olivia who died. Don't be frightened, Bernard. I'm Carola, grown a little taller but the same Carola."

"They told me you had been buried with your mother...."

"The priest may have thought I was killed after I ran away from him."

"I promised Olivia that I'd look after you, and I never found you. She must be sitting among the saints hating me for betraying her."

He began to cry noisily, like a child. He had always been like a child. My own childhood seemed such a long time ago that I had almost forgotten it, but since I had lived on the farm I had learned the ways of children. I comforted him, as I would have comforted little Giorgio if he had fallen down and hurt himself, and at last I made him believe that no one could have found me—I did not ask why he had never gone back to the inn to look for me.

We talked all the afternoon. I told Bernard about the farm, how strong I had grown since I had been there, how I always had enough to eat and although the work was hard I liked it; about the children, and all the little things I could think of that would make him feel that I was safe. It was evening before I said I must go.

Bernard was amazed when I talked of going, "How could you go now that I have found you again? You will soon re-

83

member what your mother taught you of lute playing. We need a lute player—we had one, but she was cozened by a mercenary and followed him back to France. Besides myself, there is Petruchio, the jester. He has not yet decided to join with us but he soon will, for we have journeyed together for the last month. He is a jester fit for a palace, his jests sting my eyes with laughter-tears and make my ribs ache, even when I have heard the same one fifty times. You would like him, Carola, and your mother would have liked him too. Then there is Lucia. She is a singer. Her voice has not the sweetness that your mother's had, but men always gather to listen to her. She has a good heart and a kindly tongue. I must be honest with you. I think your mother would not have liked Lucia, but then your mother was nearer to a saint than a woman. Yes, sometimes in her blue fall she looked like the Madonna herself—and that's not blasphemy now she is in heaven. Don't be too strict in your thoughts of Lucia. You never liked priests, did you, Carola? Nuns and priests have the same bones—bones are about all they do have, their flesh is so chill—and a nun values virginity above all things. But nuns are nuns and Lucia is Lucia, so don't think harshly of her because they follow different trades.''

''Bernard, I have never said I was going to stay with you. How can I? There are the children to feed and the cows to milk and cheeses to be made....''

''I shall not hurry you. Go back to your farm and I shall come to you there—or no, perhaps they do not hold with players, I shall wait here until you see me next market day. Despite what you tell me, I cannot believe that the Carola I knew, the one who was so keen on adventure and excitement, wants to spend the rest of her life quiet as a stalled ox.''

When I left Bernard I thought I should see him only once again, to say good-bye. But I suppose I had grown too used to wandering to be content to stay all my life in the same place. Bernard seemed the only link that was left between me and the life I had lived with my mother. We had gone through so many things together, and he had been very kind to me after his fashion. I had always been fond of him, even when he was being difficult; and perhaps I began to share his hopes again, and saw myself as a musician, a maker of songs that would be played by famous troubadours.

I was very sad when I had to say good-bye to Giorgio and the children. I think they believed I should soon return to them with a fortune, or else find a wandering life did not suit me any longer, so that I should come back to them and never want to go away again. Giorgio gave me my riding donkey as a parting gift, and some clothes that had been part of his wife's dowry. I thought it would hurt him to part with them, but he said she would rather I wore them than have them shut away in her dower chest. He told me that he would always think of me as a foster daughter who had gone away to visit some relations, and that I was to remember that his house would always be ready to welcome me home. I promised that somehow I would come back to stay with them, perhaps in the autumn but surely before that time next year; and the children stood with Giorgio at the gate, waving until I was out of sight.

I kept my promise to go back to the farm, in the spring of the following year. I began to call the children before I turned the last corner of the path through the woods. Somehow I expected to see them waiting for me at the gate, as though they knew I was coming back.

Where the farm had been there were only a few blackened walls. A neighbor told me the plague had passed that way at the end of the summer: and in four days Giorgio and his children were dead. The herbs which were burned to purify the house had set light to a hanging, and the fire had spread until everything was destroyed.

CHAPTER EIGHT

the Jester

When I came to the ''Blue Boar'', where Bernard waited for me to join him, I saw a young man looking down at me from an upper window. His forehead was broad and calm; and his eyes had the look of a poet or a philosopher. There was something strange and remote about his face; as if a man whose profile might have been struck on one of those ancient coins sometimes turned up by a plough had come to life again in this modern Italy. I did not see him again until evening, and then for a moment I did not recognize him in the little hunchback wearing particolored clothes: Petruchio, the jester.

Although Bernard was sure that our prosperity was due to his leadership, it was Petruchio who brought it to us. There are many strong-men, many singers and lutanists, but I think Petruchio must have been unique among jesters. The landlord of an inn where he stayed soon found the truth of the old proverb, ''Laughter is the brother of thirst, and wine the friend of both of them.'' Instead of stopping at the inn for a little while on their way home from work, people who listened to Petruchio stayed until the landlord put up the shutters—which was done only when they had spent all their money. They would gather round him, eager and intent as children, while he told them stories, in a voice so flexible that he could change it to fit the humor of each of his characters until they became as real as any company of actors could have made them. He would tell of the legendary exploits of famous crusaders until the dim room rang with the clang of sword on armor as Christian and infidel joined in battle for the Holy City. In another mood he would unravel the silken skeins that lovers weave; tales of fair women and impetuous gallants with a cuckold or a jealous woman as the butt. And of these was this story:

There was once a lady of rare beauty, and of an even more rare wit. Her family was impoverished and had no money for her dowry; and so full were they of false pride that they kept their daughter shut away in their decaying house so that no lover should expose their poverty by demanding her hand in marriage. The father was a recluse and a scholar; only on rare occasions did anyone visit him, and even then it was only another antiquary of venerable years.

The desire to collect the relics of a vanished past is usually confined to the nobility. But one day there came to the house of Rosalda's father—for Rosalda was the lady whose wit I am going to expound to you—a prosperous merchant who wished to discover whether a marble torso, which had been uncovered while the foundation of his new terrace was being dug, was as valuable as rumor said it to be. He had brought the statue with him in his traveling coach; and while it was being unwrapped from the cotton quilts in which it had been swathed to protect it against the rough journey, the merchant, whose name was Ricardo, saw the beautiful daughter of the antiquary looking down at him from a high window.

Though Ricardo was fat and coarse, and nearly sixty years of age, he fell in love with Rosalda as impetuously as though he had been a youth. Far from demanding a dowry, he offered ten thousand gold pieces, a fortune that a conte might have envied, to be paid to her father on the day she became his bride.

They were married with almost princely splendor; and it is said that in her cloth of silver bridal robes Rosalda was so beautiful that the cardinal lost his way through the marriage ceremony and several of the choristers forgot the bridal hymn and broke into a song of praise—but it may be that this has been added to the story recently.

Ricardo was rich; he had a house full of rare furniture and hangings, which poorer men of better taste than he had chosen for him; his bride was more beautiful than any woman in the duchy: but there was one thing that Ricardo did not possess, and no one except his wife knew what he lacked. He had paid over nearly half his fortune to alchemists, and had taken more than a hundred potions; some made him sick, some racked his bowls, and some had no effect at all—but still his manhood hung down from his loins, like a catkin from a hazel twig.

The patience of Rosalda, though sufficient for most women, was not inexhaustible. It may be that she had not the gift of fidelity, or perhaps the young gallant whom she met on one of her walks in the public gardens had been more than fairly endowed with the power to compel a woman's heart. Their first meeting was followed by another; and in a time so short that I will not tell you the exact number of days—lest you think Rosalda did not display sufficient of the reluctance required by modesty—she had told him how easy it was to climb in at her window.

For a few weeks the lovers were very happy, and the bed curtains might have been the cliffs that surrounded an island of bliss. But they had forgotten that the sun shining on an apricot not only warms, but ripens it; and so does a lover bring fruitfulness to a woman.

Rosalda was prepared to leave the house of her husband and cleave to her lover, until she found that he was not the son of a rich noble, as she had fondly believed, but a student whose resources barely covered the rent of an attic over the shop of a cloth-merchant. He was more than eager to share it with her, but Rosalda, upbraiding him for so deceiving her, told him that her sympathy would be only with the fish if she saw his corpse floating down the river.

Though the clothes of the period of which I am telling you were well designed for the concealment of such feminine mishaps, Rosalda knew that she must speedily find a way out of this impasse. (I have told you several times that she was a woman of wit, and when I have told you what she did, I think you will agree with me.)

The next night her husband was wakened while it was still dark, to find his wife bending over him and apparently trying to take a dagger out of his hand. He sat up and demanded what she was doing. And she said, ''May the saints be thanked that I have got you safely back to bed, my dear husband. You came into my room uttering fearful cries. This dagger was in your hand, and you seemed convinced there was an assassin lurking behind the curtains. I dared not call out to you, for I knew that if a sleep walker is wakened he will go mad. You shouted to the assassin to come out from behind the curtains, and when the folds never stirred—how could they when there was no one there?—you lunged at them, again and again. Come to my room, Ricardo, and see what you have done! My beautiful damask! It came all the way from Verona, and now it is slashed to rags!''

The old man was bewildered, but obeying his imperious wife he followed her into her room and saw what he took to be proof that he had indeed walked in his sleep.

The following night he saw yet more evidence of his somnambulant activities. This time it seemed he had wrenched open his wife's jewel casket and stamped on one of her necklaces, fortunately one of which she had never been fond. The filigree was twisted and broken, and it was still lying where he had flung it among the ashes. He was even more worried than he had been on the first night; for to replace the necklace would cost him more than twice as much as to send to Verona for new damask.

Five days went by, and each of them added to Ricardo's increasing alarm; for it seemed he could not sleep without causing damage to some valuable, even if ugly, possession. The necklace had been costly enough, but now he must commission an artist to make a faithful copy of the portrait of his elder sister, a rich woman with no direct heir, lest she saw herself grotesquely defaced. The very morning he was on the point of summoning a foreign physician, who was famous for his powers over strange manifestations, Rosalda came to his room and fondly embraced him, saying, ''I had begun to despair that my beauty was not sufficient to be worthy of your attention. But, oh, Ricardo! How have you been able to conceal your ardor from me for so long? Did you keep me starved for love to sharpen my appetite? Oh cruel husband! And yet I must forgive you, for surely no woman ever knew such bliss, such transports, as we shared last night! I thought I was a mild and temperate being, now I know myself a flame of jealousy, and if I see you cast a single glance at any other woman I think I should consume her with my wrath!''

Oh poor Ricardo! Did he never doubt that sleep brought powers to him he knew not when he woke? I cannot tell you, for this is the end of my story. But it is said that Rosalda's child grew into a fine boy, and throughout all Italy there could not be found a more doting father or husband than was Ricardo.

Laughing harlot

The first time I saw Lucia she was berating a drunken stable-boy with a flow of oaths a muleteer would have envied. The evening sun was still strong, and it showed up the circles of fard on her cheeks and the angry flesh where she had plucked out all her eyebrows in imitation of a lady of fashion. Her hair was a hard, brittle yellow, a yellow which nature had never seen and even a painter could not find on his palette. It was elaborately curled, and tied up with many little bows of dirty green and tinsel ribbon, looking as though a magpie had built its nest on her head. She must have thought me a peasant girl, sheep-stupid, who could easily be dazzled by her flamboyant charms, and I thought her worthless as a pedlar's trinket. But we had to share a room, so for the comfort of both of us we maintained the courtesies.

I wondered if she would be jealous of Bernard's fondness

90

for me, but I found that his feelings meant nothing to her. She had many lovers, and was as careless of them as is a rich woman with her dresses. For some she had a passing fondness; but usually she discarded them with no more stirring of the heart than a noble's wife feels when her mirror tells her that olive green dulls the pallor of her skin and she gives away a roll of velvet of this color to her tire-woman.

Bernard gave me a lute, not so mellow as mother's had been but sweet enough, and soon I was able to play the accompaniments to Lucia's songs. She was friendly to me, and offered to show me how to curl my hair, and told me I could help myself from her fard pots—I think it annoyed her that I never did so.

It is curious what people will do to change themselves for fashion. Every week or two the roots of Lucia's hair would begin to show that nature had intended it to be an ordinary brown and she would have to dye it again. She put on a wide, crownless hat of stiff, coarse straw, and pulling all her hair up through the crown she spread it out on the brim. Then she would ask me to pomade her head with an evil-smelling paste, which had to be moistened every time it dried, and while this was being done she had to sit for three or four hours in the full sunlight. When I asked her if she realized that what she was putting on her head was cows' urine, she said, ''Of course I do. It is the same as the wife of a noble would use, only she would buy it, for a gold piece, from an alchemist who called it an 'Elixir of the Indies', because he had dissolved a little musk in it. You put yourself very high, Carola, if your stomach is more queasy than a princess's! It not only makes my hair beautiful, but it saves my nails being worn out by scratching, for on lice it is a scourge like the plague!''

She seldom brought men into our room, and she told me that when she did I could pretend to be asleep. I think she was surprised that I always went outside and waited there until I heard her patron depart. She usually plied her trade in a dark archway or a shadowy corner of the yard, for she said,

''A hungry man can satisfy himself just as easily if he eats his food standing up as he can if he is sitting at a table. A clever harlot will make her patron so impatient that he can't wait to go up to her room but must needs take his pleasure at the first chance—once they lie down, like as not they go to sleep afterwards and snore for half the night!''

Lucia went to Mass every Sunday. She used to wash the paint off her face, cover her hair with a modest coif, and put on a plain gown of dark-colored wool or fustian—like the pious wife of a farmer or shopkeeper. If men tried to cozen her on Sunday you would think she was a prioress to see how haughty she became; though I think no prioress could have praised her indignation so strongly! Once I asked her if a priest had ever refused her absolution unless she gave an oath to refrain from the same sin in the future. She looked surprised and said, ''What sin?''

''I thought the Church held fornication to be the shortest road to hell.''

''The commandment against adultery is one that only wives need lose their sleep over, and I have no marriage bonds to break.''

''Yet you think it would be a deadly sin to fornicate on a Sunday.''

''Sin—why sin? God Himself rested on the seventh day and decreed thereafter that once a week all men should rest from their labors, and women too. On Sundays the shutters are not taken down from the booths in the market, so why should I follow my trade? You may think harlotry is less work than pleasure, but it is work—dull as a milkmaid's, though more profitable.''

''I have always been told that harlots were very lustful; that they follow their trade because their flesh is avid for such things.''

''Carola, sometimes to hear you talk one would think you had been brought up in a convent, or else been the tire-woman in a palace and helped to smuggle lovers behind the bed-curtains of a duchess! There may be women whose loins are eager as a man's, I have heard tell of it although I never met one. When Bernard lifts his weights he is pleased if the crowd cheer him; Petruchio is glad when his hearers roll on the floor doubled with laughter at his jests; and I take pride in my trade too—and a good trade it is. I give more pleasure than a barrel of wine to any man. They come to me fierce as turkey cocks and leave me mild as lambs—and glad to pay for it! Yes, and their wives get a good night's sleep, and perhaps a trinket or a ribbon that buys their husband a quiet mind. We take a pride in work well done; it's hard work, but better paid than most things women do.''

''You never wanted to get married, and have children and live an ordinary sort of life?''

''Marry! What should I get from marriage? I'd marry a noble or a man with money-bags quick enough; but that kind never ask me. What should I do as a peasant's wife? Spend half my life heavy with child to mother louts; cook and scrub and look after animals; welcome my husband when he told me to—and not get a word of thanks or a bronze piece for my trouble? There are only two kinds of women—not counting nuns, and such like, for they are not women at all: dutiful wives, who don't get thanked, and harlots, who get paid.''

In time I grew to be very fond of Lucia, and I realized that she had qualities that many respectable women might well have envied. She was honest, and kind, and I have seen her give the money she had just earned to a beggar or a crippled child. She was always gay, and she never complained when a journey was hard, or we had to go hungry and sleep in a field because a mule had gone lame and we could not reach the next village before nightfall. She never brewed trouble between men, never turned her patrons into rivals so that they fought over her; and I have heard her tell a youth how to be gentle with his bride so that she would love him, instead of hating him, when he first bedded her. I have seen her stop a tavern brawl more quickly than a score of mercenaries could have done. She would stride amongst them shouting as if she were a captain commanding his troops. They always seemed to obey her, and many a man has been saved a knife thrust, or a slit throat, through her courage.

I think St. Peter will welcome Lucia, and her kindred.

CHAPTER NINE

Companions on a Journey

I had known Petruchio quite a long time before I discovered there were many things I could talk about with him to which Bernard and Lucia would not have listened. Perhaps it was because when he stood beside me he reached only to my shoulder that I was slow in realizing how great he was; or it may have been because I lived with people who did not look for wisdom from a jester that at first I did not hear it in his voice.

When we were traveling through the marsh country I was attacked by the fever that comes from the mists of the low ground. In the south there had been a poor vintage and people had little money to give to players. We were on our way to Tuscany, where the people are not so dependent on the grape harvest. Bernard and Lucia decided to press on, but Petruchio said that he would stay with me.

For the first few days that I was alone with him I must have been very ill. There was no longer a sharp line drawn between my dream world and the world my body lived in. Even when I slept I could not escape into tranquillity, and it seemed that the demons of the shades stood beside the straw on which I lay and mocked at me. Yet through the grey twilight of disembodied shapes I would hear the voice of Petruchio, strong and gentle; and always it brought me comfort.

His hands that tended me were long and beautifully shaped; as though they would be familiar with a painter's brush; and as I grew stronger, with him I found more happiness than I had ever known. I no longer felt a desolate stranger; we were like two travelers, who, content in each other's company, can journey through a land whose language and customs are unfamiliar, and yet find there no hostility, for this very strangeness is a new interest to be shared.

I used to tell him how sometimes in my dreams I could fly, darting through the air like a bird, or resting upon it as though I floated upon still water; and to him this was no more curious than if I had told him that yesterday I had walked through the forest to gather pinekernels. Even my visions of the Shining One became more luminous now that I could talk of them to Petruchio, for he had given me a deeper understanding, both of myself and of the mysteries. It was he who showed me that what I had experienced was true, not only of myself but of all people of earth who wished to acquire it; and that sleep-memory is no more a special favor of the Gods, or the seal of a divine compassion, than is the practiced skill of a ploughman who can drive a straight furrow across a field.

When I was well again we set forth to rejoin Bernard and Lucia. In the evenings I used to play my lute, and Petruchio taught me the value of a falling harmony; how to weave a new thread into an old tune to bring it gaiety, or make a silver melody by pledging sorrow in a minor key.

I shall always remember how one day Petruchio said to me, ''Carola, I think you are impatient of this world, as once I was. You feel that it is a somber twilight and even its brightest colors are dim, like a picture that has hung too long in a smoky room. But there is happiness on earth if you can find it. There is much beauty in the world which God gave to men for their refreshment: if we do not accept His gift it is not God who has withheld this joy, but we who deny it to ourselves. We are all born into a small dominion, and it is wiser to cultivate our own field than to envy the wide lands of a neighbor. There was a time when I should have envied Bernard, because his body is strong as a tree that has age in its branches; but this was before I learned that even if one is born a dwarf one can do much to train oneself to forget this small imprisonment.''

I said, ''Perhaps we could make our lives follow a pattern of our own choosing if they were not influenced by other people's; but they are. The chain which binds us to sorrow is made of so many links. Why did my father destroy my mother's happiness? Why did the Republic elect that duke instead of another to rule Padua? Why did the pack-mule break its leg so that we stayed there when the townspeople revolted? Why did the blood make Celestina break away from me so that we followed her? Why did the rebel's knife find my mother's heart and not mine? So many links! And if any of them had not been forged, circumstance would have bound me prisoner with a different chain.''

''Though there are some things that we must undergo which are beyond the temporal power of ourselves to change, there are many that are influenced by our own approach to life. A drover may overload his mules until they die of exhaustion, but God does not give His children a burden they are not strong enough to carry. We bewilder our decisions with needless anxieties; forgetting that all difficulties have been sent to us because they are necessary for our advancement, and if we search well we shall always find within us the strength to overcome them.''

''But, Petruchio, the happy lover walks in joy and the galley slave groans at the oar—surely our approach to life cannot alter the circumstances into which we have been born?''

''If the pattern of three lives were identical, so that three men experienced the same difficulties and the same pleasures, and each man told you the story of his life, you might think one was a happy philosopher, one a fool, and the third the twin brother of melancholy.''

We had been traveling since early morning and were resting during the midday heat in a little wood on the top of a hill. The river was low between the quiet fields, and the Umbrian plain was drowsy in the sun. While we were looking out from the shade to this pleasant scene Petruchio said, ''When two men look at the same landscape they do not see the same things. What should I see if I were a noble? That little hill would be the site for a summer villa, and its slopes could be terraced into gardens leading down to the river. By the water's edge I should build a marble pavilion where a pleasure boat would always be moored. The vineyards and the rich pastures would belong to my estate, and I should ride across those water meadows when I unjessed my falcons. If I were a painter I should see none of these things. It is the high clouds, and that pilgrimage of cypresses on the distant slope, which would first hold my eyes. I should ponder on my colors, trying to judge if sienna red, or umber blended with vermilion would best match the quiet warmth of that farmhouse roof; how I should echo the shadows of that distant field, or capture the sorrow of the willows, who languish for their own beauty as did the young Narcissus. Have I proved to you, Carola, that vision comes from the soul behind the eyes?''

''All whom I have met during my life, Petruchio, have been unhappy because they long for something that is just out of their reach. None of them possesses the secret of contentment; none of them has achieved your strange tranquillity. How did you find peace, Petruchio? If you told me I might find some quietness.''

Window Without Shutters

This is what Petruchio told me, of his childhood and of how he gained his wisdom:

I can remember my mother clearly, although she died when

I was still a child. Even when I was very young her eyes told me that I was not as other children, though as yet I could not understand what kept her love away from me. It was only when I was older, after she was dead, that I knew how angry and bewildered she must have been that I was born of her; for in the community in which she lived it was believed that a deformed child was a sign of God's wrath. She and my father must have suspected each other of some hidden sin—a sin from which they had never been absolved because they had concealed it from the priest. Every time they looked at me they must have been reminded of the other's guilt. Or was it their own hearts they searched to find what had brought me into their lives? Did they give each other the love they denied me, or was I the seed from which hatred grew between them?

If my mother had borne other children she might have forgiven me the shame I had brought upon them. But I was an only child. I heard it whispered that I was not begotten by my father but by a devil who had visited my mother in the shape of her husband. Some even said that I was born with horns on my forehead, and that under my hair there were scars where my mother had burnt them off with a hot iron.

I used to go by myself into the woods beyond the village so that I should not see myself in other people's eyes. In my loneliness I grew familiar with my heart. It told me that man is solitary even though he is always in company, and that his heart is a country in which he must walk alone; but the boundaries of this country are limited only by his thoughts, and he may travel to far dominions though he never leaves the door of his house.

I felt that somewhere there was a pattern: just, and beautiful, and clear: which would show me what I longed to know. The village people used to kneel before the crucifix in the little church, to kiss the feet of the dead Christ, and sometimes I went there when the church was empty to ask the Lord of Pity to tell me why He had set me apart. It was so easy to believe that God had created all beauty, but it was hard to understand why that same God, who loved the strength of mountains and made the poplar trees soar toward heaven, should have imprisoned a soul in a body such as mine: yet I knew that I had a soul, for I felt it, urgent and alive, within me. I knew that when I looked out through my eyes, as a man may look out at a landscape through a window, it was not the dwarf who saw, but I. Not only Petruchio but the ''I that am I'' had come from God in the long past, and in the remote future would return to Him.

So long as I kept out of my father's way he let me sleep in the straw next to the cow-byre, and every evening a bowl of food was put out there for me when the animals were fed. It is difficult for a dwarf to earn his living, but I managed to get work at the inn, where I cleaned the stables and looked after the mules. The inn-keeper said that a mule would never savage me, because we were both children of the same father; and if he saw one of them trying to kick me while I was grooming it, he used to laugh and say there was a brawl in Satan's nursery.

When I was thirteen, a prosperous band of strolling players stayed there for the night on their way to the next big town. One of them saw me when I came to lead their pack-animals round to the yard. He must have found out who I was from the innkeeper, for late that evening I heard my father shouting for me. I thought he must be going to beat me again; but it was to tell me that he had at last found a use for his only son, having sold me to the strolling players for twenty silver pieces. I could not understand why they should want me, for it was not until later I learned that players are always glad to find a dwarf whose mind does not share in the deformity of his body, to train as a jester.

Until then I had done everything I could to forget I was different from other people; I even tried to walk always in the shade so that my shadow would not remind me of myself. Now, I was never allowed to forget that I was a dwarf, for it had become my profession. I had to wear clothes, half-red, half-yellow, and my hump was padded with horse-hair to make it even more monstrous. I could no longer hide away from people in case they mocked at me: I had to do everything I could to make them laugh, and until my wit was keen enough to make them laugh *with* me they must laugh *at* me.

Sometimes it was very difficult to remember God, and I began to doubt the voice of my own heart. How could I trust in a Lord of Pity when I met no followers of His teaching—in these days there are few men who have tears to weep for any grief other than their own? God is infinite compassion; but even a man of compassion needs no jester to make him smile, so why had He made me a jester? Even though some people were kind to me, no man made me his friend; for in friendship there must be equality, and none would admit equality with a dwarf.

I seldom went to Mass, but now I thought that in the confessional the priest, who would only hear my voice and not see my body was twisted, would talk to me as he talked to other men. So I went to the church hoping to find strength and comfort.

''Father, I have not come to tell you of my sin but to ask you to tell me of heavenly things so that I may learn how to avoid sin in the future; for there are questions to which I must know the answer if my faith is to be strong. We are told God's justice is without a flaw; yet we know the laws of man are corrupt, and it seems the laws of heaven follow the same course. If every soul is part of God surely all men are born with an equality of spirit and should be given an equal chance to tend the host that is within them. Why then are some born with health and some as cripples? Why do some wear furred robes in winter while others have only thin rags to hide their sores? And greater than this, why does the temper of men's hearts, which governs their way of life, show such a strange diversity? It cannot be that a man's heart is born of his parents, for that wise men have fathered tyrants and sinners begotten saints is a fact that all must recognize.''

The priest answered me, ''You must not question these things, my son. They are the will of God.''

But I went on, ''What is the plan behind this outward shadow? If God is just, where is His justice? It cannot be His will that His children suffer; so are our torments of our own creating and our joys our own reward? Is it true that man is born again into life, not in heaven but on earth? A great tree has seen dawn increase to noon and fade to evening many a thousand times before it grows into its strength: do we not need as many births and deaths before we are cleansed of the desires of the flesh and become mighty in spirit?''

I listened but there was no answer; and leaving the confessional I saw that the priest's door stood open. He had not stayed to listen. I passed him as I went out of the church; I knew it was the same priest, for he crossed himself when he saw me and his long nose twitched as though he smelled heresy.

For a time I tried to deny God and His dark brother, Satan. I saw mankind only with the eyes of this world and was blind to the realities of the spirit. I still knew that God created Earth, but I thought He had grown weary of it and turned His virtue to some other star; as a sculptor who finds a flaw in his marble turns to a stone more worthy of his skill.

When I was a child I too had known a Shining One who sometimes talked to me in sleep. For many years I had forgotten him, but now I found that when I woke in the morning, though I could not remember clearly, I knew I had been in his company. But still I could not understand why I had been born a dwarf, until I had a strange dream which taught me that there is a truth in the world of which the men of our time are not aware.

In my dream I saw myself walking along a narrow road that crossed a marsh on a high causeway; and the road turned neither to the right hand nor to the left, but led on to the horizon. On an island in the marsh there was a marble tower from whence came music tender to my ear, and beside me I saw a green path that led down from the causeway towards it. I followed the path until I came to the tower. The door was shut, but I opened it and barred it behind me. I climbed the winding stair I found within, and it was lit by narrow windows. Through the windows I could see the causeway that carried the road I had been following, and I closed the shutters so that I should not be reminded of my journey.

The time came when I no longer wished to dwell in the tower, although she who had beguiled me with her voice was very beautiful, and I tried to leave it and return to the road I had left. But the bolts had rusted into their sockets and I could not open the door. It was the same with the shutters over the windows, them also I could not move. I ran back to the room but it was empty; and I was alone and afraid.

For a long time I beat against the closed door, until my hands were scarred and bleeding. Then, at the top of the tower, I found a window which I had never seen before. It had no shutter and it was so high from the ground that I could see many travelers going along the causeway. Sometimes I saw one take the path that led to my tower; I longed for him to come and release me, but I knew that I must call out to him to return whence he had come and not to follow me into prison. It was difficult to warn them, for the tower was so high and they were far away, but one by one they heard and turned back.

Content grew in me until it filled my heart, for I was no longer a prisoner in a high tower but he that tended the beacon of a lighthouse. And one day I found that all the windows were open, and the door stood wide on its hinges: and I was free.

When I woke from my dream I knew why I had been born a dwarf. I knew it was not God who had made me a prisoner, for my body was a house I had built with my own hands. When the time came that I had learned contentment this burden would fall from my shoulders. And, upright, I should stride forth on the long journey.

Then in the bird's songs and the storm, in the breeze whispering through the standing corn and in the murmurous brooks, I heard the voice of God. When pride, and fear, and shame released their hold on me, I saw that God is life and all that lives is God. The young grass is His tenderness and the soaring poplars His aspiration; the oxen are His patience and the rivers His generosity.

I used to go into the woods and feel myself one with Him in the celestial unity. I was a tree stretching out her branches to clasp the wind; I was the bud on a hawthorn twig flinging wide her petals to the young morning; I was a mole tunneling through the warm earth to make her nest in the enfolding dark. I was impetuous as a dragonfly, and quiet as a raindrop shining on a leaf. Though I was a dwarf I was God; and when I cried out my name, the vines and the sparrows, the willow trees and the oxen, echoed ''And I!'' ''And I!''

CHAPTER TEN

love and lucia

It was nearly two years after I met Lucia that I noticed a change in her, and at first I did not realize that it was because she and Bernard had fallen in love with each other. She sang love songs when she thought no one was listening, and wore her red velvet dress, which she used to keep for fiestas, when there was only Bernard to admire her. Now if one of the men who had been listening to her singing in a tavern tried to pull her down onto his lap, she no longer threw her arms round his neck as he fumbled with her bodice, but tweaked his nose or scratched his face in a fury. If the innkeeper grew angry at seeing his patron so disgruntled, Bernard, instead of telling Lucia not to be a fool—as once he would have done, used to

103

ask him, "Do you want me to show you how a man's head can be twisted off his body like the stalk of an over-ripe pear?"

Bernard in love reminded me of a dancing bear when a wooden spoon, sticky with honey, is held just out of its reach. He was always finding some excuse to be alone with Lucia, and when we were traveling he might say, "Listening to Petruchio and Carola talking together makes me as sleepy as if I had eaten a troughful of suet pudding"; and then ask Lucia to go ahead of us and keep him company. He was very generous to her and gave her a new dress of fine cloth with a satin underbodice, but when he offered to buy her a pair of earrings from a pedlar she was scornful of them and said they were too gaudy and only fit for a strumpet, and she asked him to give her a little silver crucifix instead—like the one my mother had worn.

Lucia, who once had so despised all housewife's work, used to go into the kitchens and offer to help with the cooking, just so that she could learn to make the things that Bernard liked to eat. She always hoped he would marry her. I don't know what difference it would have made if he had been her husband, for already they worked together, traveled together, slept together on the same pallet; so she could not have seen any more of him had a cardinal united them.

She came to love him with an almost idolatrous devotion. When he smiled at her again after one of his moods of dank despondency, from which he suffered so often, her eyes lit up as if she were a peasant woman praying in front of a miraculous virgin and saw the wooden lips curve into a smile. Now that she was possessed by this strange foster-child of love she no longer saw him as he was. I once saw myself in an old mirror distorted almost beyond recognition, and it was as if Lucia's eyes had become a mirror which reflected Bernard so that all the follies that distorted him were smoothed out. His stupidities turned to wisdom; his irritation to a just wrath; he was no longer a tavern entertainer amusing himself with a reformed harlot, but some god of the ancients raising a mortal to his own stature.

Sanðra

When I was sixteen we stayed from June until after the vintage in a Tuscan village. As we were to be there such a long time, instead of lodging at the inn we lived in a little house which was owned by the landlord of the "Pig and Winepress." It was small, and had only two rooms, but it stood by itself in a vineyard that sloped down to a stream. I found it very tranquil—perhaps because I knew that for awhile I should sleep in the same place to-day, and tomorrow, and again tomorrow.

Bernard and Lucia shared the smaller room, and Petruchio slept on a straw pallet under the vine trellis that shaded the south wall. He was always happier when he could sleep under the night sky, and he used to say that when the stars twinkled it was because they shook at some Olympian jest and sometimes he could hear an echo of the gods' laughter. The larger room was furnished with a table and two benches. There I did all the cooking, and I slept in a cupboard bed which was built into the wall. I smiled when I thought how scornful Maria would be if she could see my kitchen. I had no spit, no rows of copper pans, no carp to stuff with goose livers and herbs: only an iron cooking-pot that hung from the chimney chain, two earthen bowls, a knife and some wooden spoons. There was not even a pair of bellows, and I had to blow on the reluctant flames to kindle the sticks I had collected.

We played every evening at one or other of the village wineshops. One day a traveling artist, who painted inn signs, heard me singing, and he promised that he would paint for my pleasure so long as I would sing for his. I told him that Lucia was the singer and I only the lute player, but he said,

"There may be painters in Italy who are much greater than I am, but I think my treatment of an ear, a throat, or the curve of a shoulder, unrivaled—it is unfortunate that no one shares my opinion! No doubt there are singers whom some might claim were sweeter than you—but I put no value on other people's judgment!"

He told me to call him Sandra, but I don't believe that was his real name; because, although he pretended to be a vagabond, I think that once he must have been rich, or at least had a noble patron, for his clothes, though old, were of fine quality and his voice had the ring of a great house. He loved sitting in a tavern where he could watch people without their noticing, because to him they were as exciting as an old parchment to a scholar. He showed me a portfolio filled with sheets of fair paper, and some of them were covered with many drawings; a nose, a hand, a woman in sorrow, a child in joy. He used to make quick drawings of Bernard, and they made you see the strength stored in his swelling muscles, and the skin moist with the sweat of effort.

Sandra often came to our house. He made life-size drawings of me on the wall. In one I was playing a lute, with my hair unbraided and bound with a chaplet of vine leaves; there was a Carola stirring the cooking pot, and a Carola sitting in the sun plucking a capon. So lively were the lines of his red chalk that I began to think I had three sisters.

Every morning he filled the bucket for me at the stream, and often he went with me to the fields on the other side of the river to gather mushrooms or cooking herbs.

I was very happy while he was there, and I began to hope that he was poor, as we were, so that he might decide to join us, and travel north when we moved on. I found that I could talk to him almost as easily as I could to Petruchio, for he was never afraid of heresy. He did not believe that things happened in the way I told him they did, but he was not imprisoned in the little world of things that people can see, and hear, and touch with their hands. When I told him that I could fly when I was asleep, he thought I must be dreaming into the future. He said, ''One day men will make themselves wings. I think Icarus was a man who became a legend, a man who was trying to do something that one day many people will be able to do. If a bird can fly by the power of its own wings there must be sufficient buoyancy in the air to sustain my weight, if I can but find the way in which my strength should be utilized to overcome the attraction of the earth. It may be that I myself will challenge an eagle to a race! What consternation there will be in rookeries when I descend upon them! I shall draw men as a bird must see them—not striding like giants but as puny midgets, squat and foreshortened, their upturned faces gaping in wonderment! Will they run into their churches to seek protection from this monster of the skies?''

I said to him, ''Perhaps I could teach you to fly my way before you are ready to show me yours.''

''I am too impatient to wait for sleep to show me things. It is from earth I wish to rend the secrets, not from heaven. The earth herself is full of miracles, she is only waiting for a man to persuade her to perform them for him. Visions and prayers are fit for nuns and priests, but I am too content with what my eyes can see to wish for their sight. Carola, why do you welcome me into your house and share your food with me—me, a drifting vagabond who sometimes forgets even to thank you for your charity.''

''Because I know that you are one of my kind of people. I have met so few of them—I think only my mother and Petruchio.''

''How did you know I was?''

''It was that first day in the tavern. You were sitting on the bench under the window, drawing Petruchio while he was jesting. I was watching you, and I saw that you drew only his hands, his long, beautiful hands, and his face. Any one who had ever seen Petruchio would have recognized him from your drawing; but they would never have known that he was a dwarf. They would see him, as I see him, wise and beautiful, with heaven in his eyes and kindliness in his speech.''

Sandra was pleased. ''One day I shall be a great painter. Even cardinals will forget that I am a heretic and beg me to decorate their cathedrals; princes will cry my name in greeting, hoping that I may be so gracious as to lay my colors on their palace walls. When that time comes you may see yourself as a goddess, and Petruchio as the Shepherd of God.''

''It may take you a long time to become so famous. Will you still remember a lute player, and a jester?''

''It may be that I shall have forgotten the sound of your voice, but the way the hair grows from your brow, the curve of your wrist, the arch of your foot when you walk so lightly through the meadows, are stored away in my portfolio, ready to make my eyes see you again. It may be that I shall have forgotten how I have laughed with Petruchio, how I have talked with him of strange philosophies through the long evenings of a Tuscan summer, but when I need to paint St. Michael, or perhaps the young St. John, or a hand riven to a crucifix, it will be Petruchio that I shall see. When you see my pictures, Carola, will you think of me?''

''My life is in taverns. We do not go to cities where there are great cathedrals, nor play to entertain princes and cardinals. Perhaps in the future, when both of us are dead, I may return to Italy and see them.''

''Sweet Carola, when you are dead, if any of the phantasies are true, you will be playing a lute among the clouds—and your poor Sandra will surely be in hell, painting the brides of Satan for a wage!''

''Don't you believe anything I have told you?''

''They are beautiful legends, and I believe in everything that is beautiful with that part of me which is an artist—but I am also a man, and not a visionary. It is in my drawings I shall find my immortality.''

He often came to the house very early, before I was

awake, but I would know he had been there, for when I opened the door I found my bucket had already been filled with clear river water—and there would be a flower floating in it as a greeting. One morning, instead of water there were six gold pieces in it. With them was a drawing of Sandra, dressed as a rich courtier, kneeling before a goddess with my face.

I used to watch for him to come back, but I never saw him again. Whether he became a great artist I never knew, because he did not tell me his name.

Ghost of the Griffin

The landlord of the Inn of the Three Eagles shone with importance when he told us we had been summoned to play at the palazzo outside the village. I could see that, in his eyes, instead of a beggarly troop of wanderers, we had suddenly become artists of distinction; artists unfortunately suffering poverty, too often the twin sister of genius, during those early struggles which the sleek jesters and musicians attached to a wealthy household like to recount to their less fortunate brethren.

Even Bernard's belief in a brave and splendid future had begun to dim, but now he was as full of bombast as a barrel of new wine. He told Lucia and me that by Christmas we should be wearing fur-lined gowns, and grumble at the joltings when we traveled in a coach.

He put his beard in curling rags and spent the morning practicing his feats of strength in the inn yard. He had taken to wearing his hair in short curls, after the statue of an athlete which he had seen in Florence. His skin was whiter than a fair woman's, and the hair, hard and metallic as gold wire, sprang arrogantly forth from his mighty chest; but his legs always looked too small for his huge arms and shoulders. He was shaped like the wedges that quarrymen drive into a flaw in the marble to split out the block.

Lucia's excitement was clouded because she was discontented with her best dress; but after she had held the crimson velvet over a steaming cauldron and caught up all the pulled threads, I persuaded her that by candlelight no one would see that it was a little shabby.

It was not the first palazzo we had played in, though it was by far the most splendid. We went there at six o'clock, and were told to wait in the kitchen until we were summoned to give our performance. The kitchen was smaller than the one I had known as a child, but it was still more than four times as large as the main room of the tavern. The servants seemed to think themselves superior to entertainers, and none of them spoke to us while we were waiting. Even the man who came to bring us to the banqueting room did not deign to speak, but beckoned to us as if we were a row of deaf mutes.

We followed him along winding passages, whose flagstones were greasy with food spilled over the years of hurrying table-runners. All the rooms we passed through were very magnificient in the Florentine style. The furniture and carvings glittered with gold leaf, and the floors were spread with carpets, or inlaid with different colored marble in patterns as elaborate as those of a marquetry cabinet. There was no plain surface where the eye could rest, for even the window shutters were painted with satyrs' masks or garlands of roses and laurel. One of the ceiling paintings was still unfinished: a plump goddess gazed at a lover who had not yet appeared, though where he should have been a hand and shoulder were roughed in—the hand held a trident, so perhaps she was waiting for Neptune.

About thirty men were seated at the long table in the banqueting hall. There were many courses in the kitchen still to be presented to them, but several of the guests were already far gone in wine. They took little notice of us when we entered, and even when Lucia began to sing, beyond a few careless glances, the company paid no attention to her.

There was enough of the old Lucia in her for this to make her angry. She had been standing beside the musicians' bench, but now she began to walk round the table as she sang. From ballads she changed to tavern songs, rough and bawdy, and the men's interest began to quicken.

When Bernard saw the look that Lucia was beginning to kindle in the men's eyes, he tried to distract their attention to himself. He staggered forward, carrying in each hand a sling holding three cannon balls; it was the greatest weight which Bernard, or perhaps any strong-man, had ever lifted. He waited for the applause. Only the host looked at him and said, "Prodigious!" in a bored voice.

When I first came in I had noticed that one of the men was sprawled forward across the table. His face was hidden in his arms and the breath whistled from his open mouth. Lucia seemed to have made a conquest of the man next to him. He was handsome enough, at least Lucia seemed to think so, and when he pulled her down beside him she only pretended to resist and laughed as her gown slipped from her shoulder. Perhaps she thought that a noble should be allowed his pleasures, or she may have forgotten that Bernard was in the room.

I noticed that a man sitting near the host was staring at me. I thought I must have seen him riding past in a procession, or perhaps played in a tavern where he had lodged, for his face had a vague familiarity. It was only when I heard some one call him Deccio that I remembered him. It was he whose mockery had caused my father to brand me.

I saw that he was puzzled, though he cannot have recognized me, for I had been a child then; but something in my face must have served to bridge the ten years between this banquet and Orlanzo's. A man near him was telling his neighbor how his brother's life had been attempted by an assassin. Deccio interrupted them, "I can tell a stranger tale than that of an assassin; mine is of an assassin who hid behind a tapestry. It is the tale of how I made Orlanzo of the Griffin acknowledge his bastard...."

He told it vividly, and soon all the company were listening to him. When he had finished someone asked, ''What happened to the child?''

Deccio flicked a crumb from his sleeve before continuing. ''That is the squalid ending to a romantic story. The child's mother was a kitchen wench, and when Orlanzo went to Spain she became the leman of one of the workmen he had sent to make the castle ready for his bride, and she followed the man back to his own country. I have heard that Orlanzo was in a fine wrath about it for a time. He even talked of sending horsemen after them and having the Spaniard put to death for daring to steal away his child. I think he would have done so if Isabella had not persuaded him to show clemency.... She was a pretty child with a high, proud spirit—curious, when her mother was a strumpet...''

I picked up a full goblet and flung the wine in Deccio's face, ''Rinse out your lying mouth, Deccio!''

Everyone was still with amazement, as if a half-eaten sucking-pig had got up from its gold dish and run squealing along the table. Two servants seized me, and were trying to drag me from the room when their master halted them. ''Let her stay.'' Then he turned to me. ''I am interested. Tell me, why should a lute player insult my guest? Do you wear a hair shirt under your dress, and, finding that too little penance, want to have the skin flayed from your back? Or are you tired of lute playing and wish to lose a hand? Or shall we give one of your pretty ears to Deccio as a balm for his pride? I am magnanimous, you may choose.''

''The lash. May it curl over my shoulders to flay this brand out of my flesh! And let that little popinjay carry out my punishment himself!'' I tore open my bodice, ''There, Deccio, do you recognize the Griffin's seal? Come, take a whip and cut it from my flesh. It will make a prettier ending for your story than the lies you have invented round my mother's name.''

Lucia was staring at me, her mouth half-open in horror.

112

She tried to climb off the cushioned bench and knocked against the man who was asleep. His head rolled from the shelter of his arm. There was a pool of black vomit by his mouth. At a sign from the steward two of the servants went to pick him up. When they saw his face there was a cry, ''The pox! The pox!'' The servants would have let him fall but they dared not, and they carried him from the room.

I spoke to Deccio again, ''You have two uninvited guests at your table, a ghost of the Griffin and a pestilence. I am waiting, Deccio; have you forgotten that you are to flog me?''

He cringed away from me, as if I held the flail and he were the suppliant. ''Send her away! Send them all away! The Griffin's brood are all in league with Satan. If we lift a hand against her we shall all die of the pestilence. Go! Go!'' He threw me a purse of gold. ''Call off your familiars! Don't send the pox to revenge you.''

''You need not fear me, Deccio. For though I am of the Griffin's blood my mother watches over me from heaven.''

As I walked slowly out of the room, Lucia ran back to pick up the purse which I had left where it had fallen. When we passed through the kitchen on our way out of the place we saw that the servants had already heard of the pestilence, for they shrank from us.

Late that night a messenger rode into the inn-yard. Their was a packet for me. In it there was a sheet of paper and a ring. On the ring was carved the arms of the Griffin with the bar sinister, the arms that I had seen in the picture in the long gallery, the arms of my great-great-uncle, who had also been a bastard. With the ring was a letter. ''I, the grandson of the Bastard of the Griffin, salute another of my kindred. If you take this ring to the House of the White Sisters, a league beyond the town of Perugia, they will give you sanctuary, for their benefactress is a kinswoman of our blood.''

I never knew which of the company had sent it to me. I wore the ring on a cord round my neck and never told Bernard or Lucia that I possessed it. Nor did I tell Petruchio, for I was afraid he would try to persuade me to go into the convent. I kept the ring, for the word ''sanctuary'' had a kindly sound; but I knew I should never need it while Petruchio was alive.

With some of Deccio's money I bought two riding jennets, so that we should all be mounted; and the rest of it was divided among us, five gold pieces to each. I sewed three of my coins into my dress; for I had known too often what it felt like to go hungry because we believed overmuch in the future.

The landlord was angry and suspicious when he knew we were leaving so hurriedly. He must have thought that when the news that we had played at the palazzo spread through the town people would flock to his inn to hear us. He tried to prevent us going by demanding that we stayed there till Bernard had paid all the money he owed. I have seldom seen a man look more surprised than did that innkeeper when Bernard threw him two gold pieces as carelessly as if he were a rich merchant throwing a lead token to a beggar.

We left the town long before midday. Instead of taking the high road, we crossed the open country on bypaths and for the first three days stopped at no house or inn, for I did not trust Deccio. I thought he would soon be ashamed of his fear and perhaps send his servants after us to accuse us of theft. It would be so easy for him to deny giving me the gold; and the truth of a strolling player weighs nothing against the lie of a noble.

Bernard sang as he rode. He was full of confidence; he was already famous, already cardinals and princes quarreled amongst themselves over who should have ''Bernard the Strongest Man'' in his train. He had come to believe that it was he who had earned the gold, and that it had been wrung from Deccio through admiration for his giant strength. We decided to go on until we came to a big town, for now that we could afford to lodge at a good inn it would be easier to persuade a prosperous landlord, in Bernard's words, ''to

114

let us honor him by entertaining his guests.''

We had been traveling fast for several days and meant to stay at the next village until Petruchio rejoined us. His mule had gone lame so he had stopped at a farm where he would lodge until it was sound. The sky was overcast and the wind cold, but Lucia often complained of being too hot. Her face was flushed and she kept pressing her hand to her eyes as if the light hurt them. Bernard tried to cheer her by saying that she would feel better after a hot meal with hot spiced wine to make her sleep. He said he would ride on ahead to the next inn so that there should be food ready when she arrived. She was grateful for his concern; but when he asked what dishes she would like, she said the word food made her queasy and the smell of it would bring on a retching.

We crossed the bridge into a large village just before night-fall. The inn was well-found but there was only one private room unoccupied. Lucia asked me to share it with her and told Bernard he could sleep with the other men. He pretended to be offended that she did not want him, but we both knew he was longing to find someone to gamble with and found it irksome to be with a sick woman.

It was only a short time since Lucia's child had begun to stir in her womb—she was so happy when she knew that Bernard had got her with child, and I think he had promised to marry her before it was born. Neither Lucia nor I knew anything of child-bearing, but she tried to make me, and herself, believe that this sickness, this grinding pain in her back and loins, this mounting fever, was what many woman with child suffer before their bellies swell. She said, ''It must be because I have been so well that all these ills have come on me at the same time.''

I helped her into bed and brought her a bowl of broth, but she could not drink it. She began to be sick, with a sickness that tore at her bowls and left her exhausted. The pain in her head grew worse and her eyes hurt as though hot irons had left the sockets empty. I laid cloths steeped in vinegar on her forehead, but they brought her no ease. I sat beside her in the dark, stroking her face to try to quieten her.

It must have been nearly dawn when suddenly I realized that her skin was no longer smooth. It was as though there were grains of coarse gravel under it. I touched her neck, her chest. Everywhere the rash was spreading. I lit the candle and leaned over her. She was half asleep, breathing heavily through her mouth. Her skin was a dusky red—and under it the pox had begun to grow.

I stood quite still while my thoughts ran back and forth like a hare coursed by greyhounds.... If they discover that Lucia has the pox she will be turned away from the inn. It is her only chance, to be kept warm and quiet. It would kill her to go into the cold air. Is there a physician in the village? What use if there is? He would not go near smallpox or the plague except for a fee that only the very rich could pay. Perhaps the inn-keeper loves money more than he fears the pox. Between us we have enough money to bribe him, unless he is very frightened. I will promise him that I will stay shut in with Lucia. No one need come into our room. They could leave the things I need for her outside the door, and go away before I open it....

I covered Lucia up and went down to find Bernard. He was sleeping on one of the trestle tables in the front room. Without disturbing the other sleepers, I woke him and made him come outside. I said, ''Lucia has smallpox.'' For a moment he did not realize what I had said, for he was still fuddled. I pulled his sleeve. ''Lucia is very ill. The pox.''

He snatched his arm away from me, ''I may have caught it from her! You must not touch me, Carola, you have just come from her....''

I had no time even to despise him. ''Find where the inn-keeper sleeps. Go to him at once and offer him ten gold pieces if he will promise to let her stay here until she is cured.''

''Who will take food to her? I cannot. The pox is

stronger than I. It might kill me. It *would* kill me...."

"You had better search for some of the courage you boast of, Bernard! You will have to leave the things I shall need outside our door. I promise to give you time to run away before I take them in. I shall tell you what I want through the door, so there will be little danger for you. If when you call me you hear no answer you can tell a priest to come and bury us."

I waited in the courtyard. But when the outer door creaked open I saw, not Bernard but the inn-keeper. He said that being a man of charity—which when I looked at his face I knew was only another name for avarice—he had consented to let us stay. "I cannot allow you to remain in my best room, but there is a smaller one you can have."

"She is too ill to be moved."

"If she is too ill to be moved you can take her out of the village to die. It is what any other landlord would make you do."

"I cannot carry her alone."

"I will help you. I have had the pox, and lightning seldom returns to a tree it has already struck."

I wrapped Lucia in warm covers and between us we carried her to a bare room over the stable.

From the sound of his voice I knew that Bernard was terrified every time he came to the door. I was afraid he might not come back, so I told him that if he dared to stay away I should creep down in the night and throw the stained cover off Lucia's bed over him and breathe the pestilence into his snoring mouth; and that his only hope of escaping it lay in obeying me.

Before the fever reached its height Lucia miscarried. Twice on the farm I had helped Giorgio with a cow that could not deliver her calf, but I was very ignorant. I expected the dead baby to be like a new-born child, only much smaller, like a doll. Perhaps it had not been in her womb as long as she thought. I did not know if all babies would have looked like

117

that, or if this slimy horror meant that Lucia would have mothered a monster if it had grown. I felt like an animal, dull and stupid, trying to help another. She moaned like one. Her eyes were wide and bewildered as the eyes of a dying ox. She did not realize she had lost her child, but after it had been expelled she was in less pain. I did not know how old the child must be before it should be buried in consecrated ground. It seemed blasphemy to say a prayer over the thing hidden under the filthy straw in the bucket, yet I could not bear it to be thrown with the other refuse on the midden in the courtyard. I told Bernard to take it into the woods and bury everything very deep, so that the cur dogs could not dig it up.

When the retching stopped, I fed Lucia on sips of wine and goat's milk, or broth with fresh hog's blood mixed in it, which was what Giorgio's aunt had told me to give the children when they were ill. The granules under her skin swelled until they were as large as dried peas. Then they turned into watery nodules, so close together that they ran into little putrescent pools. Her body stank as though it had been long dead in hot weather; her labored breath was like the wind from a charnel house. I kept on thinking she was about to die. Perhaps if I had known what the future held for her I should not have fought to keep her alive.

When the pus hardened into scabs she grew a little stronger. I knew that the scabs must not be touched until they fell off of their own accord. I used to kneel beside her, holding her hands and saying, over and over again, "Lucia, you must not scratch off your scabs. I know it is so much more difficult to bear than any pain, but you *must* be brave, Lucia, or you will be scarred."

She used to whimper and try to writhe away from me. "I can't bear it! I can't bear it! There are thousands of lice, fierce as hornets, feeding on me. Why don't you kill them, Carola? Let go my hands! I am going mad—*mad!* You are driving me mad, Carola. Have you no pity?"

As her strength began to come back, it was more difficult

to restrain her. Sometimes after I had struggled with her she looked as though she hated me. I had swathed her hands in thick cloth, tied on firmly round her wrists with twine, so she was as helpless as a baby in its swaddling bands. I was afraid she might tear off the bandages with her teeth, so I only dared to rest when she was asleep. I slept so lightly that I woke when I heard her move.

At last the scabs began to dry, and the edges of some of them had already curled away from the skin. I thought I had won my battle with the pestilence for Lucia's beauty. But I must have been more exhausted than I realized, for I fell into a sleep so deep that it was like death.

When I woke I saw that Lucia had managed to free her hands. Her face and breasts were pitted with raw, oozing flesh, where she had clawed off the scabs.

CHAPTER ELEVEN

the Òrab

While Lucia kept to our room she did not realize how terribly she was disfigured, for I had told her that our little mirror had been stolen while she was ill. When she was strong enough to go out I could no longer prevent her knowing how her face had changed, but she still believed that in time the pox-marks would fade, and that when they did Bernard would find he still loved her.

As the weeks passed she came to realize that she would never regain her beauty, and then it was not only her beauty she had lost, but her pride. It was as though she were a changeling; as though an evil spirit had carried away the Lucia I knew and left in her place a woman with the same body but with a different heart. She knew Bernard took other women, but now there were no turbulent scenes, no outbreaks of jealousy—and no reconciliations.

Now that she could not compel his love she tried desperately to buy his affection. When she told Bernard that she had been to the market to buy his favorite cheese, I knew that she had only gone there on her way to the village usurer, who paid her well for hiring her body to his idiot son. She gave all the money she earned to Bernard, who lost it at dice. He never asked her where the money came from and pretended to think it was part of their savings; but he must have known he had spent them long since, and guessed what she was doing.

Once the coupling of bodies had been an incident in Lucia's trade, and her heart was unawakened as a nun's. She had been like a deaf woman who has learned the postures of a dance until she can carry out the pattern faultlessly, yet who has never heard the music that creates the rhythm which she follows. Now that she could hear love's melody she was tortured by the harsh discords she played on it; and every time she prostituted her body she was dull with shame. I knew what she was suffering, for I remembered how, before she loved Bernard, she had once told me, ''Harlots should be cold as the Apennines in winter, for if the warmth of love should end this wintry solitude their tears would flow like freshets in the spring.''

She no longer went to Mass, and began to question me about my dreams. ''Carola, you used to tell me that when you were asleep you could fly, and do many strange things. I laughed at you for I thought you mad, but now I know it was I who was foolish. What potion did you take to gain these powers? Who gave it to you—or have you the secret of this magical formula?''

''I need no drugs or incantations to leave my body when it is asleep. Lucia, you believe that you have a soul, that there is something within you which is far greater than your flesh; and you believe that this soul lives on when the body dies. Is it so difficult to believe that death is not the only freedom from earth? While sleep closes our eyes to this world we can see what lies beyond the outward form. When we return, some of us may remember what we have seen, but we remember only if we have trained ourselves to do so. If you have no sleep-memory it does not mean that you have not had experiences such as I have had, it only means that you cannot recall them. In this life I have found no one, except Petruchio, who knows of the nature of sleep, for it has become a greater mystery even than death. Many men expatiate on where the soul goes when the body dies, and yet they never guess that, to all mankind, sleep is a little death, a little freedom.''

She did not recognize that what I told her was true; she thought I was trying to hide some secret knowledge from her. From a small bag, which she always wore under her clothes, she took everything of value she possessed, and tried to bribe me with her trinkets. Then she fell on her knees and besought me to help her. ''Help me to be free of my body so that I can follow Bernard. When he lies with another woman I will be between them. When he mounts her she shall be only the bed on which we lie together. Carola, you told me you heard music. For me there is no music but Bernard's voice—could I hear that? I knew a thousand ways to stir him; his body was a lute on which my fingers could play wild music and subtle harmonies. Once I had a body that a famous courtesan might envy, and Bernard desired me above all women. Then it was he who craved my favors and I who granted them to our delight. When he got me with child I was glad because I thought that it would enhance my beauty—painters delight in the curve of a fruitful belly, and though they have the eyes of poets they have the loins of men. It seemed that Bernard discovered a new kindliness for me; he was no longer impatient when I was tired; he was not rough with me even when he was stupid with wine.... I cannot forget his face when he saw me crusted with the pox. You tried to make me believe it was you who kept him from me when I was ill because the fever demon might attack him too; that he stayed away because he knew you were caring for me and he must keep strong so as to earn our lodging. I tried so hard to believe you, but I always knew it was because it would have disgusted him to see me; to see lips that he had kissed, cracked and blackened, and a body that had curved so often to his own, swollen and corrupted. I could have died then, Carola, but you made me go on living. You made me live, you must give me something to live for! I loved my body, for it brought me love. Now I hate it, for the sight of it breeds hatred, or worse—indifference. Carola, you used to tell me that when you were asleep you sometimes wore a different form. Teach me how to appear to him as I used to be, for of what use is my love, my skill, when my skin is pitted like a dusty courtyard with the first heavy drops of rain? The songs I sang still echo clearly in my ears, but now my voice is harsh. I am no longer Lucia the sweet singer; Lucia, the woman whom many mean desired and whom none dared approach for fear of the jealousy of Bernard, the strongest of all men. Now I am Lucia the drab, the harlot who is unskilful at her trade.''

I tried to make her see that Bernard was not worth loving, but I could not change her.

I was unhappy, for I loved Lucia, so I went to Petruchio to see if he could teach me how to help her. I asked him, ''What is this strange fever that fires the blood and lulls the mind to sleep? Does the sound we think nightingales come from Pan's pipes, and is the patter of his goat's feet echoed by the pulses of women? Do the snake-root and the purple nightshade distil their subtle poison on the air, so that under the spell of their miasma humans forget their godliness? Their body chokes their spirit, as ivy shrouds a tree, until their eyes become vacant as a cow's; a cow that goes lowing after a sulky bull until he, of his own desire, swells her smooth flanks and leaves her lowing again—with calving pains! Why use the name of love for such bewildered cravings of the flesh! Is it from God or devil that it comes? Or is it some rank distillation of the earth, brewed from dead bones, and sweat, and unborn seed? Tell me whence it comes, Petruchio, so that I may protect myself against this evil!''

''Once love and lust were twins and walked together in fair company. Now we seldom find love in hand with lust. The love of God, the love of friends, the love of kindliness; troubadours seldom sing of love like this—it is lovers' bodies they immortalize. Even the Church has sullied the first lovers, Adam and Eve, who came into the world to bear their children as vessels in which one day would burn the light of godhead. Lovers may seek each other, not to assuage some torment of the blood, but to escape from the long loneliness of mortals; to achieve some vision of that future in which we shall be able to share each other's memories.

I seemed to hear an echo, ''in some strange land where mermaids and dragons dwell, where gazelles talk and flowers sing madrigals''; and I said, ''Once I thought I might meet someone with whom I could share not only flesh but soul, not only soul but spirit. I believed that love could illuminate all things, and that our bodies would be like flint and steel to kindle light. Now I no longer let myself believe that this is possible, for if I did I might give my heart into a man's keeping—and feel it break.''

''The time will come—though it will not be on earth— when I shall remember how cool the moss felt under your bare feet when Carola ran through the meadows in the dawn, and you will see yourself through Petruchio's eyes. Only then will you know what his heart held for you, know his fears and all his vain ambitions. And this will show you how love could be on earth, even though it were guised in ugly flesh, imprisoned, mute. A love that cannot be told—and only shared in some far heaven.''

love potion

After we had moved on to the next town I noticed that Lucia seemed wrapped in a strange excitement; and at first I thought she had found another lover. The inn where we stayed was small and overcrowded, and Lucia and I shared a little room which overlooked the stable yard. The floor boards had shrunk, and when the mules were picketed below us the acrid smell of their urine and the fretting of their hooves on the cobbles kept me awake.

One day a mule train stopped there soon after daybreak. Lucia was still sleeping—a fly was crawling across her face but it did not disturb her. Her shift had slipped off one shoulder, for the drawstring was broken, and showed her breast with its deep, purple stains. Her hair, brittle as dry grass, was stiff with nits; once she would have plastered it with cow-dung to destroy them, but now she was indifferent. I was glad my mother had taught me to oil my hair before braiding it, or the lice might have got into mine.

When she woke I pretended to be asleep, for I was tired and did not want to talk. I heard her straw bed rustling and saw her take out a little phial that she must have hidden there. She held it between her hands, fondling it as if it were infinitely precious. I thought she was going to try to kill herself. I sprang up, crying out, ''Don't Lucia! Don't take it!''

I tried to snatch the phial, but she thrust me angrily away. ''You are a fool, Carola! It's not poison, it's a love potion.''

''Where did you get it? Who gave it to you?''

She refused to answer, and kept murmuring to herself, ''Sofia has promised, she has *promised*, to bring back Bernard's love for me. Soon he will see me as I used to be, and not as I am....''

I had to shake her before I could make her listen to me. ''Lucia, there is no magic in that potion. It is some filth, or it may be a drug that would make Bernard crave a woman even if he were impotent. If you increase his lust why should he turn to you to bring himself ease? And if he did—would you be less lonely after he had left you again? You have told me, Lucia, that before you loved Bernard you had known scores of men, yet none of them ever possessed your heart. How do you hope to hold Bernard through his body, when no one could hold you through yours? Why will you not believe that your body is only a house that you live in? Be proud of it, as a good housewife is proud, but remember it has a doorway through which you may come and go, and windows which you can see out of. If you forget this, it will no longer be a dwelling place for your soul, but a prison where you are shut away in the dark.''

''It is easy to despise something that has never been important to you! You are content to talk of heaven with a dwarf—you have never found it, as I have, in a man's arms. How can you understand my craving for Bernard when you have never had a lover? You mock at love potions! How do you know that if you took them they would not stir your quiet blood? Perhaps the saints are colder even than you, and that is why they have never listened to my prayers! In hell there must be many who would not scorn to help a woman who is going to join them when she dies. You told me you know nothing of the black arts, so how can you judge what sorcery can do? You feign to despise all incantations—perhaps it is because you know of none! Sofia's father was an alchemist and his father before him: she can bring back spirits from the dead to obey her will. Do you imagine that all sorcerers are charlatans and fools!''

''I think that if this daughter of an alchemist has the power to summon spirits to her aid, they are the spirits of the newly dead who are lonely for the brothels, the wineshops where assassins gathered, the squalor and filth with which they are familiar on earth. Think of the faces of the men we see watching us when we play: and the faces of the beggars, and the lepers, and of the pestilent princes who ride through the streets. It is their kind who are the confidants of wise-women and sorcerers. You would not have listened to the counsel of such people when they lived. Why should you listen to them because their bodies have died?''

In our struggle for the phial the pallet-cover had fallen off. Sitting huddled in the dirty straw, Lucia looked like a mad woman, as she spat out, ''Do you dare deny all powers to Lucifer?''

It seemed impossible to reason with her, but I said, ''I think it is true that before he became a Prince of Darkness, Lucifer had first to become an archangel: and he who has been an archangel must keep his power, his rare nobility, even when he leads the Horde of the Shadows. The little sorcerers who call upon Lucifer have no more the right to claim his protection than has the fat cardinal of Spezia to claim the protection of God. There was a time, Lucia, a time on this earth though perhaps not in this country, when the truths I try to tell you would have seemed no madness, no heresy, but so natural they hardly called for speech. Now men are always supplicants to some outside power, for they have forgotten their own godliness. They pray to saints, or try to invoke demons; but they do not look into their own hearts for truth. People have come to fear God—I think they fear him more than they fear the devil. They have been told for so long that they are sinners, that all earthly pleasures are sent to lure them along the path to the burning pit, that they feel a greater fellowship with the Prince of Darkness than with the Lord of Hosts. The Church has forgotten what it must once have known, for it holds that death imprisons men in purgatory until they are changed into angels, or else condemns them to the eternal fire. I feel as though I had always known that our time on earth is very long; that there is no hell, though the gates of heaven are not reached by one death, perhaps not by a thousand deaths; and men do not go into purgatory when they die but when they are born.''

126

Lonely Valleys

When I saw that nothing I could say would prevent Lucia seeking out the alchemist's daughter, I went to Petruchio, for I hoped that he might give me some power of speech by which I could prove to her that to follow the path of sorcery would be to leave the causeway and walk in the mire. I said to him:

"Petruchio, when I tell Lucia that during sleep the soul leaves the body, she looks at me as though some fever had entered into my blood. She denies the truth of her spirit, and yet believes in strange, satanic powers. It is as though she could hear bats, as though the shrill squeak of those flying shadows of the night were loud in her ears, and yet was deaf to larks when they made the air tumultuous with sound. She listens for the whispers of demons and hobgoblins, but when the angels come to cherish her she armors herself against their comfort. Whence came this knowledge that is within me— this knowledge that I cannot share with Lucia? I hear an echo of an ancient wisdom, an echo that I follow through the lonely valleys, longing to see him whose voice brought it forth from the silence. I am tormented by this longing to hear what I have once heard, to see those visions for lack of which my eyes are blind with tears. Long ago, far away, Truth lifted her veil and smiled on me. She took me for her pupil and gave me a part to speak in her great comedy—or was it tragedy even in that time? Now, though I search for words to find Lucia's heart she will not listen. What can I do, Petruchio?"

"Though I, too, have some knowledge of the past I cannot tell you what road you followed to reach our meeting-place. But this I do know, that within you there is much of heaven. I am like a man who on a dark night can see a light shining in the distance. I do not know, nor do I care, whether this light shines from scented taper or from consecrated wax, whether it is held in the hands of a bride or burns serenely beside a bier; I can only say that the darkness in which I walk

127

is lightened and that I will always follow where it leads."

"Why are people bemused with devil's breath? They see his vapors in their ills, his curse in their misfortune—even his favors in their prosperity. Why do they hold this liege to Satan?"

"When God and His celestial company have so few servants here to tend their lamps, the world is dark; and little evil ones grow bold in the darkness. The bat, the owl, the black rat and the toad, are brave as lions and eagles when the sun has hid herself away. If there were men of wisdom, clear eyes and silver tongued, to guide us, then it would be as if the gods themselves were here. Satan would fall before St. Michael's sword; goblins would flee from nymphs, witches from cherubim; roses would climb where now the ivy creeps and golden poplars crown the cypress slopes."

"What of the sorcerers and the alchemists, Petruchio, would the earth gape to plunge them into hell?"

"I think most of them would be unchanged; would still be men, without power either for good or evil, who follow their trade of mixing the noisome brews by which a foolish woman tempts her love; would still be guileful rogues, cheating the simple minds who can be bewildered by their words. But among them might be some who had received the sable accolade from Lucifer; and these would follow him into his stronghold of the underworld and there stand siege—until men let the torches gutter on the wind and he could again ride out upon the earth."

"And what of the witches—are they all kin to sorcerers?"

"Some who are called witches or heretics would once have been hailed as priests, for they try to bring a light into the world; and they cherish their small flame, although they know it may kindle the pyre on which they burn."

"Is that why Lucia is frightened when I talk to her? Is it because she fears I may be declared a heretic?"

"People are frightened of what is beyond the compass of

their understanding; and I think she is not frightened for you, but of you. And it is my fear for you, Carola, that what will bring you the most unhappiness in this life is that when you open your heart you will not see love in the eyes of those who listen to you, but fear.''

''Why should they fear me when I tell them that sleep is an awakening; when I tell them that death is not a gaunt stranger but a friend?''

''It is easier to hate than to love; it is easier to be afraid than to have courage; it is easier to disbelieve than to earn wisdom. When we are walking in the twilight our eyes become accustomed to it and we can see the road we follow; but, because we cannot see very far, if there is a chasm at the side of the road its depths do not call to us. If we try to walk in the same twilight after our eyes have been dazzled by staring at a flame, then we are bewildered by the darkness. That is why many people are afraid of the light, because they know that after they have seen it, for a little while the shadows grow more somber.''

''Once they have found it, why can they not stay always in the light?''

''For a short time we may live in the light of another, and our own darkness is made luminous. But, to all of us, the time comes when we must kindle our own flame: we must shield it between our hands though it may burn our flesh, for if the winds of faint-heartedness extinguish it, then is the rekindling a hundred times more difficult than the first lighting. The oil which feeds this flame may be our heart's blood or our tears; but we must not grudge it—for at the last it will show us the gates of paradise.''

CHAPTER TWELVE

the Alchemist's Daughter

Bernard had gone off to a town about twenty leagues distant, because he had heard that at its annual fair the champion of the wrestling bouts received five gold pieces. Lucia was determined to pour her potion into his wine as soon as he returned, and when I tried to argue with her she refused to listen. So at last I decided to seek out the alchemist's daughter, to try either to frighten her into refusing to see Lucia any more, or, if she had some measure of knowledge by which she could recognize mine, to convince her that she must abandon the practice of the black arts.

I expected Sofia to be an old hag, small and wizened under her trappings of witchcraft, with piercing eyes and dirty, claw-like hands. But she was younger than Lucia, not very tall, though plump and strongly built, her dark hair neatly smoothed, and her breasts round and matronly under the green woolen bodice. She welcomed me into her house as warmly as if I had been a farmer's wife come to discuss cheesemaking with a friendly neighbor; which surprised me very much until I found that Lucia had told her all about me. She must have thought me a wise-woman, for to me she made no mysteries; and soon I was sure that she brewed her potions with as little guile as an honest kitchen girl.

Although her father had been an alchemist, I think from what she told me that he must have been more of a scholar than a sorcerer. He had known of the virtues of herbs, and from them made healing draughts, not only for human beings but for animals. Sofia had helped him in his work, gathering plants and grinding up the spices brought by merchants from the East.

He had taught her Latin, so she could read the manuscripts, on calfskin, which she had found in an iron box after his death. She showed one of them to me, running her finger along the lines of faded brown writing as she read out: "To cure the Bloody Flux, both of the lungs and the bowels"—then there was a list of herbals, of which I only recognized cowslip root and oak bark—"these to be pounded with fish livers and hogs' blood, and of this a great spoonful at the sun's rising and setting."

"Did your father often make cures?" I asked her.

"He gave health to more people than ever did a duke's physician! He cured so many that they thought him a sorcerer, even though he denied it. Sometimes I told him he was more of a cook than an alchemist, for most of his remedies were nearer broths than potions. There is a weed which grows in the streams near here, that he stewed in a little water and then squeezed, and gave the juice to children when their gums bled or their lips were cracked—he always said it was the best cure for the scurvy. Then he gave sorrel broth for boils, and infused wild peppermint for sleeplessness. If anyone came to him with the bellyswell he told them to fast for three days except for a cupful of hot olive oil and hogs' blood, two parts to one, three times a day. He never believed in sorcerers' tricks, and told people to follow some ritual or recite an incantation only when he knew they were too credulous to obey him without it. He always said that if he knew someone would be greatly benefited by an infusion of herbs, but would drink it only if he told them the herbs had been gathered in a garden in the Indies the gate of which was guarded by a seven-headed serpent whose name they had to invoke in prayer, it made no difference if they thought it was the prayer and not the peppermint that had cured their windy colic. I have seen children who were puny weaklings grow strong and beautiful after they were brought to him. He believed that long ago men worshipped the sun instead of God. He would have been declared a heretic if the priests had known that he was a kind of sun worshipper himself. He used to tell mothers that his potions were made active by the sun—and explain how the potion could feel the sun's rays through the flesh just as a seed feels it through the ground—and they must let the sun shine on the child's body until the virtue contained in the potion came up through the skin and drove out all the evil humors. They would never have obeyed him unless they had believed him to be a magician, for lots of mothers would rather let their child whimper its way into the grave than let it lie naked on the grass.''

''If you do not believe in charms and sorcery why did you give a love potion to Lucia?''

''If she had not come to me she would have gone to some other wise-woman—and at least there are not poisonous drugs in mine.''

''It is as I thought; wise-women are only tricksters—or, at best, herbalists.''

Sofia was indignant. ''Because I do not dabble in the black arts you need not think I am ignorant of alchemy. Other wise-women have told me their secrets—powerful enough they are, too, without a demon's aid.''

She told me some of them: ''Take of hot mule-dung three parts and of snakes' fat two parts. Pound them to a paste with a blending of powdered amber and fennel seed. Enough of this to cover the left thumb nail will keep a man faithful to the woman who dissolves it in his wine, even if he has to leave her for forty days.'' Another one was, ''Take the udder of a goat, the genitals of an ape, the womb of a bitch, and seethe them well in vinegar. In the liquid that will flow from them by the ninth day, soak linen cloths and bind these on the breasts for three days before the full moon. This will make the withered paps of an old nun, or a grandmother, as taut and rounded as the breasts of a young virgin.''

She expected me to be impressed by the extent of her knowledge. I said, rather scornfully, ''Surely nuns and grandmothers have other things than their breasts to think about.''

"You would be surprised how many clients I have had for that brew."

"And when they find it does them no good?"

Sofia laughed, "They think it is their own fault; for I always tell them that before I used it on myself mine were like a pair of empty wineskins—so they think they have had proof of its powers."

"Isn't it difficult, Sofia, to make people believe you hold magical secrets?"

"It is easy to convince the fools—and their whispers soon spread through the town. If I think someone is sufficiently credulous I tell them to meet me at midnight in the deserted hut by the river—few people will go there at night, for it is supposed to be haunted by the leper who died in it. They have to wait outside until they hear the night owl hoot three times, and when they enter they are permitted to see me in the shape I assume to fly through the night on my broomstick."

She opened a cupboard. "Here are my properties, the pointed hat, the cloak painted with red and black symbols of the stars, the stuffed lizard. They make me into a terrifying witch!" She laughed. "Then there is Filippo. Filippo is my familiar; some even say it is the shape I prefer to live in, and that I only change into a woman when I hear a human being approaching.

"Who is Filippo?"

"Go outside and wait while you count a hundred. Then scratch on the door and you shall see Filippo."

I did as she told me. When I opened the door, at first I thought the room empty. Then I saw, sitting on a low stool beside the hearth, an enormous toad. It seemed to stare at me. Its mouth opened and shut as if it were talking a language I could not hear. An owl hooted—an owl hooting in the daytime is an evil omen. The toad flopped from the stool and hopped purposefully towards the half-opened cupboard. As it crossed the sill the door closed behind it.

After a moment the latch lifted again and Sofia stepped

out. I must have looked very surprised for she started to laugh. ''Come, Carola, I will show you. It must be true that I can change myself into a toad! See, the cupboard is empty, the toad has vanished.''

There was nothing in the cupboard, not even a cobweb. I tapped the walls but they appeared to be quite solid. She was delighted at my not being able to see how the trick was done, and when I admitted I could not solve the mystery she showed me how part of the back of the cupboard slid to one side. We climbed through into another room and I saw the toad sitting in a basket by the fire. Sofia went over and stroked it. ''It was my father who trained Filippo. He is always fed in the cupboard, and to call him I hoot like an owl. He loves milk and raw meat; and before he is fed he is put on the stool in the front room—it takes him a few moments to make up his mind to hop down, so I have time to get out of the room. You only saw it by daylight, but even you would have found it impressive if you had just walked along through the wood to keep a midnight appointment with a witch. When they see Filippo hopping across the room they think they have come too early and taken me unawares.''

the Dark familiar

I enjoyed being in Sofia's company and often went with her to gather plants. Whether we went into the hills beyond the village, or along the bank of the river and through the water meadows until we came to the deep woods, Sofia was always hoping to find a mandrake. Mandrakes are so rare that only the richest alchemists have mandragora to sell. When I asked her what they looked like, she did not seem to know. I said, ''How then will you recognize it?''

''I shall know it because it will begin to whimper when I approach. A magpie can speak like a man, but a mandrake can scream louder than a woman being delivered of her first

134

child. It can be pulled only on the midnight of the full moon or else whosoever gathers it will die. Some say that, even then, it is best to tie to it a black dog which pulls up the plant in trying to free itself. But I shall be safe because I have been told to plug my ears with tallow from a candle that has burnt by the bier of a virgin, so that I shall not hear the mandrake scream as it is drawn from the ground.''

When we wanted to bathe in the river we had to go a long way above the town until we found a secluded place, for Sofia said that if any of her patrons saw us swimming they would no longer believe in her, because every one knew witches feared water and would not cross it even on a broomstick.

Although the white surf of the cherry blossom had browned and vanished, the air was very thin and clear, and the water looked brittle in the sunshine. I lay as still as a water-lily leaf and let the lazy current carry me downstream. There was an aisle of poplars along the river bank. Fragments of dreams awoke to their rhythm.... Poplars turned from trees to colonnades of stone. I was on another river, under a bluer, a remote yet more familiar, sky. A little swirl of the current washed a strand of my hair across my eyes. It was strange to see it long and umber red, for it seemed that it should be black and cut to shoulder length.... Sofia called out to me that I was drifting past the place where we had left our clothes—and I woke from a fond day-dream.

As I climbed the bank I scratched my leg on a bramble, so Sofia rubbed it with wild sage to stop the bleeding. I had brought food, tied up in a red cotton handkerchief; black bread, goats' cheese and a meat pasty. I wondered if the pasty had been made from the kid that died the night before—but I was hungry and it was strong of garlic.

After we had eaten, Sofia stretched herself out in the sun and went to sleep. It was very still on the edge of the woods and I saw a squirrel chasing its mate through the branches of an oak tree. I lay face downwards, and watched a little green beetle adventuring through a forest of grass. I was warm and

135

contented, and my body was soaking up the sunshine as a sop of bread soaks up wine.

Suddenly Sofia sat bolt upright. She dug her fingers into the turf; her eyes were shut and her body twitched convulsively. She sucked in great gulps of air as if she were thirsty. Then she began to speak; a babble of words, too fast for me to understand. I was frightened—a shadow seemed to have fallen over the wood. I wanted to run away from the voice that came from Sofia's mouth. Then the voice changed. It was a voice I knew. The words came slowly, as if they were formed with cruel effort. ''Carola, Carolissima, listen to me! It is so long since I have spoken to you...''

I cried out. Sofia sighed, stretched herself, and knuckled her eyes. She seemed to remember nothing of what had happened. When I asked her if she had dreamed, she looked surprised and said, ''If I cried out in my sleep it was no dream but because the pasty lies so heavy.''

Could the voice really have been my mother's? Why did I doubt it? It was so like her voice. She alone had called me Carolissima. I knew that men could be possessed of devils; why could I not believe that they might be possessed of angels? Why was I afraid instead of eager? I wished that I could believe that Sofia had tried to trick me, that she had disguised her voice and played the mummer. I even told myself that to believe she had been possessed was to be as credulous as the village women who thought that Filippo was her familiar. It was impossible to explain how I knew that the voice which had spoken to me was not Sofia's. Surely it was right that I should listen to this voice which spoke to me through Sofia—Sofia, who was no witch, no blood sister of vampire or werewolf?

For the next few days I was kept very busy; the axle of a noble's traveling coach had broken and he and his retinue had to stay at the inn until it was repaired, so I could not visit Sofia. I was sent by the innkeeper on an errand to an outlying farm, and when I was returning through the woods at dusk I heard a voice calling me, "Carola, Carolissima, where are you?" It was far away, yet clear as the fading echo of a bronze bell. It grew clearer, stronger, and then seemed to die away. Always the same words, "Carolissima. Where are you, my Carolissima?" "Where are you, my Carolissima?" I forgot that I was grown up, forgot that my mother had been dead nearly seven years. I was a child again, a child who had been playing in the garden with her greyhound puppy until she heard her mother calling her.

I ran along the path in the direction whence the sound came, frightened, though I knew not why, yet strangely drawn to it. I met Sofia walking towards me. She looked surprised to see me, and said she had passed no one on the way.

The next time that I knew Sofia's body was being used by a familiar, we were in her cottage. She had asked me to share her supper and had been showing me how to make a special stew, of hare spiced with freshly gathered thyme. While it bubbled in the pot hanging from the chimney chain she stirred it with an iron ladle. Then she drew the logs apart and left it to simmer over the quiet heat. It was very peaceful sitting by the glowing embers which diffused the darkness. We had been talking, but now Sofia had fallen silent and I thought she was asleep.

Suddenly I realized that her breathing had altered as it had done when she had slept on the river bank. Her hands had grown rigid and her eyes were rolled back under the half-open lids. Then my mother's voice issued from her mouth, "Carola. Why do you not answer me? Have you forgotten me, as Orlanzo forgot me? It is so difficult to speak to you. I made your body, Carola—will you not let me use it now that I am a lonely ghost? You used to trust me, Carola. Perhaps you do not believe that it is I? Could Sofia know of the little chest with the fifteen drawers where the jewels were kept?... Of the scarlet collar your father gave you for Mimetta...how we listened to the tapping of Isabella's stick...of the house in

Perugia which I never found on earth and which I cannot find in heaven? Let me use your body. Unbar your will that closes it against me.... I am so lonely, so lonely without you...."

I called, "Mother! Mother!" But the room was empty except for Sofia snoring by the fire.

I had no clear memory to guide me, and yet an echo of an older knowledge warned me that the voices of angels do not come forth from the mouths of men, though devils can command the tongues of their servants on earth. It seemed that this warning was suddenly clear before me, as if long ago I had heard it spoken by one whose voice I had never forgotten. But what if my intuition were untrue; if my mother had spoken to me from the other side of death and I had closed my ears to her? Did she weep in the flowery valleys of some tranquil heaven because her daughter denied her? Had it been pain and torment to her to clothe herself in flesh so as to speak to me—and I had not listened? The voice had been her voice and not Sofia's; the words her words and not Sofia's? Why did I deny her with the innermost part of me—when my heart and my reason believed that she had returned?

I used to go into the woods hoping that in their silence my Shining One would counsel me. But I was alone, shut away in my flesh, with only the little that Carola knew to guide me. Even talking to Petruchio brought me no comfort. He warned me that possession was one of the black arts—but why should I believe him? I began to think I was keeping my mother away from me not through wisdom but through cowardice.

I lay down in a glade hidden among close-growing elder bushes. I prayed that my mother should enter my body, and that as a sign that she had used it, I should return to find my body in a different place and with no memory of how it got there.... I thought of a calm, enfolding darkness; darkness that wrapped me round; deeper and deeper; warm, soft, impenetrable; down, down; nothing...nothing...nothing....

Then a terror came upon me. Terror fiercer than vipers, more consuming than fire. I was in the ultimate darkness. Round me clustered the spiders that spin shrouds for the damned and the toads that echo the footsteps of the condemned. The wings of bats were loathsome on my flesh and I could not move. I tried to scream, but my mouth was choked with the feathers of dead carrion birds. I tried to force my heavy eyelids open with my hands....

I was no longer in the dark. I could see the sky, the sky that had forsaken me. I lived with horror till I was wide awake; then I ran to the river and tore off my clothes. I swam upstream, trying to cleanse my body from the filth that had come with the evil that had entered it. I knew how the lepers felt, unclean, unclean.

Because her familiar had tempted me into evil I never wanted to see Sofia again. I kept away from all the places where we had been together, and avoided the path to her house as if it were a lepers' walk. If I had not heard the bleating of the black kid, there is much that I might never have understood.

When I heard it I thought it must have strayed from its mother, or perhaps got caught in a thicket. I ran towards the sound, which came from a clearing among some trees. The kid lay in the middle of a five-pointed star drawn in the dust. Its legs were tied together with a crimson cord. Sofia, carrying a knife and a bowl of hammered silver, was walking round it in a circle, chanting an incantation in a language I could not undersand. I stood in the shadow, to watch a witch at her unholy rites. At last she cut the kid's throat, her voice never ceasing its monotonous rhythm, and held back its head so that the blood flowed into the bowl. She slit its belly and poured out the entrails; searching among them as if she hoped for a sign. Her arms and the front of her dress were dark with blood. After a time she buried the body in the center of the pentagon and smoothed all her symbols from the dust. She carried the bowl back to her cottage. I followed her; and watching through a chink in the shutters, I saw her smear the blood upon the door lintel and above the windows. With nettles dipped in the blood I saw her make the sign of the Cross over every opening into the house and on the hearthstone.

I thought these must be some of the blasphemous rites of the Black Mass—until I saw her face as she knelt to pray. Then I knew that this was no witch propitiating her overlord, but a girl seeking protection from the forces of which she went in terror. I forgot that I had been afraid of her and remembered only the Sofia who had been my friend. I called out a greeting to her before I opened the door. When she saw me she pretended that her preparations had been made to impress one of her patrons. I told her she need not lie to me. As she talked to me I realized that her fears had been more terrible than mine.

''I did not want to tell you, Carola. I made it happen, and I ought to be strong enough to bear it alone. I never believed in demons, or angels. I thought that death was the end of everything, and there were no angels, no familiars or demons; but only flesh rotting away in graves, or dungeons, or in gibbet chains. I never thought it was wicked to pretend to be a witch—it was like telling tales to children. I may have taken a malicious advantage of their fears, but I was not aware of evil. When the demons first entered my house I thought it was a neighbor taking her revenge. One morning I came down to find a stool overturned and a cauldron of stew tipped into the ashes. But it still happened even when I covered the latch with wax, so that I knew it had not been moved. I put river sand on the hearth, but it was never marked by any footprint. I made sure there was no other human being in the house, but when I woke I found the wineskin slit, and the threads of the cloth I was weaving torn from the loom, and the cheeses hidden under the kindlingwood. I bought a crucifix and always wore it next to my skin, but even that did not protect me. I paid gold to a pedlar for a piece of unicorn's horn, which is the most powerful of all talismans, and next morning I found my witch's cloak rent in pieces. I dared not to go to the priest, for he might betray me to the Council, who would burn me as a witch. I put St. John's wort over the lintel, and still they came. I wound a cord, plaited from the hair of a dead man's beard and a strand from the left braid of a virgin, round the hasp of the bolt. I have stolen consecrated oil and put it upon the hinges. But still the demons come to remind me that they wait for my soul to carry it to Hell."

CHAPTER THIRTEEN

the Lotus

I knew that hermits, and many of the saints, had lived as solitaries because when they were alone they were nearer to God. I had asked for counsel, and had not received it. Perhaps it had been given to me, and I had not heard because the noise of the little things of earth was too loud in my ears. The time had come when I must seek knowledge and not wait for it. At the inn there was no quietness; there, I could not achieve the stillness that was necessary to receive wisdom—and some measure of wisdom I must have, for without it I was powerless to help Sofia. I told her she must have courage, for I was going away to search for a powerful talisman—I could not tell her the name of it was Truth—with which to combat the dark forces that surrounded her.

I put only bread and two waterskins in the panniers, and rode up into the hills. On the first day I saw scattered farms, and shepherds with their flocks. I passed them, and rode on and on, until I came to a little valley among the peaks, where the mark of God's hand upon the mountains had not been blurred by man.

There was pasture among the rocks, and a pool of clear water, very deep and cold, in which I swam at dawn and at dusk. Only the eagles were nearer to the sky than I was; and the people who lived far below in the valleys seemed as alien to me as a fish does to a bird. In the silence I could hear the voice of my spirit: and my soul grew in the quietness, as do the flowers of an alpine meadow when the snows melt.

I saw a vision of the I that am I...and stood upon a great plain.

Upon my right hand and upon my left hand was a line of people stretching to the horizon. They were in single file: old women, and girls, and children; warriors, and scribes, and priests, and husbandmen. Their faces were strange to me, yet they were as familiar as my own. I knew the grain of the wood in the staff of that pilgrim; the temper of the sword in that young warrior's hand; the weight of the child in the arms of that woman; the joy of the girl dressed for a festival. Their skins were of different colors, for they had come from all over the earth; and some wore loin cloths and some were crowned. One by one they reached me, and I saw that their eyes were a mirror in which I was reflected. They were all I's who had been on earth. Upon my other hand there were still many upon the path. I could not tell their faces, nor their clothes, nor their country, nor even whether they were men or women, for I had not yet been born into them to make them live.

I knew that somewhere in this multitude was the I who knew what Carola longed to know. I saw a girl wearing a white tunic. Her hair was black and cut to shoulder length, and in her hand she carried a blue lotus, its petals open. I stretched out my hand to take this flower she held out to me. I knew that if I possessed it I should remember all this girl had known—perhaps remember all that this vast company had known. The wisdom on her forehead would be on my fore-head also; her strength would be my strength; her stillness my stillness.

Then a man, who had been nearer to me than she was in this long procession, stepped between us. He was tall, hawk-faced, wearing the head-dress of a captain in Pharaoh's army, in the time when, though the temples of Egypt were the mightiest ever built by man, the Light in them guttered on the altars and evil stood in the sanctuaries. I knew that he had been a warrior for the Light. He showed me his sword; the blade was dark, as though it had been held in the smoke of a flame; I knew that he had fought for the Light with a dark weapon. The sword was between me and the girl of the far older Egypt. I knew, though I know not how I knew, that only when the blade between us was no longer tarnished could I receive the lotus from her hand; and that when I did receive it she and I would again be one.

The girl with the lotus, and the warrior, passed on together. Beyond them was a woman who spoke to me, saying, ''You are not ready to receive the knowledge which you once possessed; nor shall you receive it until that which holds it from you has been undone. I am you, but since that time, and what I learned of you may know. When you wake, what I know will be part of Carola. You will not remember how you know it, but things that have been obscured from you will be made clear. You may not be able to explain how you know you gained this experience, but you will no longer stand at the fork of two paths wondering which one to take. You will see that the right-hand leads to the hills, and the left-hand to a swamp where the dead are rotting....''

I awoke: and the memory of my vision was strong upon me. It was as though I had been blind and now I could see; as though I had been deaf and could hear; as though I had been crippled and could race the wind. I was ready to leave the high place and bring news to the plain.

What I must tell Sofia was clear, as if I were reading it from a scroll.... ''It is not your house you must barricade against demons, but it is the bars of your will which must close the gateway of your body against them. Because at some time in the past you have allowed your body to be used by the spirit of another, now it can be possessed without your knowledge. It is written in the Laws of the Gods, 'To one spirit there shall be one flesh. He that puts on the flesh of another shall suffer Our condemnation; and with him, he that alloweth this betrayal of the tenement of the Host shall suffer also.' ' '

I knew that it was Sofia's body, but not Sofia herself, that had overturned the cauldron and broken the wooden stool; and that these things had been sent to bring fear to her so that she would be unable to armor herself against evil. I knew that the voice which had spoken to me through Sofia's mouth had come from a follower of the Shadow, who mimicked my mother so that I might be deluded into joining his followers. I knew also, that the terror which had come upon me when I tried to place the guiding rein of my body in another's hand had not come from an evil source, but had been sent to me as a warning.

I knew that the time had been when priests could cast out devils, not by ritual but by power; and they triumphed in their conflict through the keen tempering of their will. I knew not whether I had the strength to do this thing; but somewhere in the concourse of my past there lay a seed of power which by my own actions I must bring to fruit. Somehow I would teach Sofia to train her will—so that she should no longer be a servant of the evil ones, but a sword against them.

Witch-Burning

It seemed that I rode with an invisible company, of the people I had been and would become. I, who had always been so lonely, was one with a multitude; they were beyond the limitations of my earthly consciousness, yet all of them were within me. It was their experience which set my values of good and evil—values that might not be part of the ultimate truth, but were true for Carola. They spoke to me as one voice, the voice of my conscience, and though I knew the theme of their chorus, I longed to hear each speaking alone, so that I should know my past and make ready for the future.

I must have ridden further into the hills than I had realized, for it was three days before I came down among the farms and villages. I saw a man driving a stubborn ox between a row of vines, and thought how strange it was that the last time I had seen a human being I had been Carola the lute player, the girl who had strange visions but knew not why. Now my body had taken on a new impermanence, and it was no more part of me than the dress I wore; I should use it for a little while, and when the time came to put away this flesh, death would be my tirewoman and birth would fashion me a new garment.

After the track I was following joined the high road, I asked a muleteer how far I was from my own village, and he told me that it was more than five leagues distant. I hoped to reach Sofia's house before nightfall, so when I came to a town I decided that it would be quicker to go through it than to skirt the walls by the bridle path. The houses seemed to press towards each other across the narrow street. I had become so used to breathing the clean air of the hills that I had forgotten the stench of human beings who lived crowded together. In the gutter there was a dead dog—a crawling mound of flies. A woman emptied a bucket of slops from a balcony, and two children were sailing a fleet of walnut shells in a puddle of filth, but except for them the streets were deserted.

As I rode up towards the principal square, I heard the muttering of a crowd. It reminded me of the sound I had heard before the revolt in Padua, and I would have turned back by the way I had come, had not my curiosity been stronger than my apprehension. I dismounted, tied the jennet to a hitching-post, and walked towards an archway through which I could see people running about behind the crowd, trying to get a better view of what was happening. As I joined them I realized they had not gathered together from a

145

spirit of rebellion, for most of them looked pleased or excited. I heard fragments of conversation, ''The procession should be here soon.... They say she is young and pretty, and you would never know she was...Antonia said she was going to leave her children at home, but I brought mine. It's good for them to...''

I thought they must be waiting to see the bridal procession of the daughter of some rich noble. I knew Lucia would like to hear about it, so I worked my way forward through the crowd. When I knew what they had come to watch I tried to get away. But the press was so thick I could not move. A witch or a heretic was going to be burnt.

The stake had been erected in the middle of the square, on a high stone like the plinth of a statue. Faggots were piled round it except where a narrow passage way had been left for the condemned to mount the pyre. There were soldiers standing by it, wearing black tunics over their body armor and black plumes in their helmets. I knew it was the soldiers who would carry out the burning; for when the Church has chosen her victims she hands them over to the Civil Authority for her sentence to be executed. There were one or two solemn faces among the crowd that had gathered to see one of their kindred burnt alive, but most of them might have come to watch wrestlers or a bear-baiting.

The Church had grown even more savage in its war against heresy since the new religion from the north had begun to gather power. How can people believe they are followers of the Christ of Compassion when the Church that bears His name thinks heaven can be gained by ritual, and that ritual is so important that a divergence in its practices turns fellow Christians into mortal enemies? The knowledge of Truth brings courage to those who have heard her voice, but from what source do these martyrs draw their strength? How can they die for points of ritual; die for a faith that has obscured its truth; die believing in priests that are not priests? How can the people watch their faith polluted, used as a weapon against them in the hands of crafty prelates and scholarly cardinals? They seem to have forgotten the teaching of Christ, they remember only a dead man on a crucifix, a man who died by torture. Is that why they allow this needless martyrdom?...

A bell began tolling. A procession wound through an archway on the far side of the square. It was led by monks in brown habits, their cowls drawn down over their tonsures. They chanted the Office of the Dead as they shuffled slowly forward. The crowd was silent, expectant; in a moment they would see the condemned.

She was enveloped in the ceremonial Cloak of the Damned. It was of white, coarse fabric, painted with red and yellow flames. The pointed hood concealed her face. At first I thought she was screaming. Then I heard, more terrible than screams, that she was laughing; laughing as if Satan himself had told her the ultimate jest against humanity. I thought it must be some poor madwoman who had been accused of having the Evil Eye. Between the gusts of laughter she would scream blasphemies, horrid and obscene, not against the Church but against the Christ. The high, cracked voice was harsh as a carrion crow's. Then she would be silent for a moment, as if she listened for a hellish answer to her gibe, and then she would laugh—and laugh.

The shrouded figure did not try to resist as it was lifted on to the pyre by two soldiers. Her hands and feet were wrenched backwards and chained round the stake. The woman seemed indifferent to what was being done to her, and never ceased from her satanic laughter. A dignitary of the Church, in black robes, began reading to her from a parchment with seals of purple wax. ''You have been tried by the Tribunal of the Church with scrupulous justice and in accordance with the divine will of the Holy Trinity. We, the Church of God upon Earth, find you guilty of the abominable crime of witchcraft and of other divers heresies. In our infinite mercy and compassion had you confessed of your sins you would have received absolution before you died and thus saved your soul from eternal damnation. But you have chosen to go to your death unrepentant, so the flames that consume your flesh will be but a foretaste of the hell-fire which you will suffer throughout eternity.''

A soldier climbed on to the pyre and pulled off the cloak that had hidden the condemned woman. She was leaning back against the stake, her black hair falling loose to her waist. For a moment I could not believe who it was that I saw there.... It couldn't be Sofia. I had come to save Sofia.... She was in her house waiting for me. I was going to drive away the demons.... I screamed out, ''Sofia! Sofia!'' The man next to me put his hand over my mouth. ''Keep quiet, you fool! You can't save her. To admit you are the friend of a witch is the quickest way of mounting the pyre yourself.'' I struggled, but he held me back.

Everything seemed curiously still. Sofia had stopped laughing. She was staring round, dazed and frightened, as though she were waking from a nightmare and trying to reassure herself that she was safe in her own room. Then I knew that the voice that had laughed its blasphemies was the voice of the dark familiar. I knew that Sofia did not know what was happening to her—perhaps she did not even remember her trial or know that she had been proclaimed a witch. She said slowly and clearly, as though she were a child bewildered at being punished for something it has not done, ''What are you doing to me? What are you doing? I have not done anything. How did I get here?''

A soldier, carrying a torch flaming with pitch, stepped forward to kindle the brushwood piled round her feet. She said to him, ''Don't! Don't! *Please* don't!''

He hesitated, but at a word from the officer he plunged the lighted brand under the faggots. He stood watching the fire take hold. Then I saw him sway on his feet and double up as he vomited.

The flames sprang up, sharp and clear. Someone beside

me said, "The wood is too dry for the smoke to smother her before she burns."

I fought to free myself.... If only I could get to her, make her see me before she died. I must let her know that she was not alone.... But the man who held me was too strong, or too compassionate, to let me escape.

The bigger faggots caught. Sparks showered up round the stake, and through them I could see Sofia as if she were being drowned in burning rain. The bark curled away from the green stake as the clothes charred from her body. The flames roared up, louder and louder; but not so loud as Sofia's screams—"Don't! Don't! Don't!..." on and on, until they lost all humanity in an extremity of pain.

CHAPTER FOURTEEN

fugitive

I cannot remember how I got away from the place where they had killed Sofia. I only know that somehow I was free of the town, galloping through the dusk to find Petruchio. I reached the inn after the shutters had been put up; and when I clattered into the yard no light showed at any of the windows. I threw up a stone into Lucia's room to try to waken her, but the window stared blank and empty and the broken shutter banged to and fro in the forlorn wind. I saw a glimmer of light as the kitchen door opened. I saw it was Petruchio and that he was very disturbed. In a low voice he said, "Thank God that you are safe, my Carola! There was a fiesta yesterday and every one is sleeping heavily, otherwise they might have heard you. I have kept the panniers of the pack mules filled against your return. We must hurry...."

I could not understand what he was talking about, or why

he should want me to start on a journey when I was so tired. I supposed that Bernard and Lucia had set off without us and that for some reason Petruchio was impatient to join them. "I can't go on anywhere to-night, Petruchio. You must tell the others that I will follow them when I have slept. I am too tired to think, too tired to eat. I only want to sleep—if the inn is full a corner of the stable will do.

He took no notice of my protests and said, even more urgently, "I must get you away from here, there is no time for explanations. You must believe me, Carola, and do exactly as I tell you—otherwise you will endanger both of us."

He would not even let the jennet drink at the trough before he made me remount. He led us out by the little door that gave from the cow byre into the pasture, and across a field until we came to a copse. Then he tied the rein to a tree and told me to wait for him.

It seemed only a few minutes before he was with me again, riding his own mule and leading another. I was too tired to wonder where we were going, and only just managed to keep in the saddle. I could tell by the sound the hooves made that we were not following a road. I heard a cock crowing in the distance, and once a dog barked at us from a silent house. When it grew light Petruchio led the way along a stream which ran between high banks, in a miniature ravine, to a hidden grassy beach where there was enough room for us and the animals to rest. I started to question him, but I must have fallen asleep before he answered me.

When I woke it was early evening. Petruchio had made a fire between two flat stones, and the fish he had caught were roasting in the embers. I realized I was very hungry. I felt much stronger after I had eaten, and drunk some glowing cordial that Petruchio had brought with him.

Before he let me ask any questions, he made me tell everything that had happened to me since I left him. As I finished describing my vision, he interrupted me, "That vision was true; but, my Carola, it is perilous knowledge to hold in our time; a time when the Church condemns as heretics all who profess powers it cannot understand. It is so difficult to refrain from speaking of what you know to be true, but you must guard your speech, or you will be condemned out of your own mouth.''

"Petruchio, you talk as though you thought me a sorcerer...."

"I think that? No, Carola, but the Church would. It has forgotten that once all true priests could travel beyond the outward form of the world; now it only remembers that there is a stinking canal along which the followers of Satan come to bewilder mortals. All who receive news, either from the source of light or from the darkness, now suffer the same punishments from ignorant authority. The Church is right to condemn sorcerers, to condemn those who allow themselves to be possessed; for the angels do not descend upon men, though men can train themselves to soar to heavenly dominions. It is not only sorcerers whom the Church destroys, but all who would bring back the forgotten wisdom of Christ's teaching into their dead ritual.''

I realized that he was trying to warn me of the danger of consorting with people like Sofia, and yet to spare me the pain of knowing what she had suffered. I said, ''I watched Sofia burnt as a witch. The Church was only the instrument of her death; it was her dark familiar that brought her to the fire. Yet if the Church knew the true powers behind their own rituals they would have cast out the devil that possessed her, and put a seal upon her so that it could never enter her again...."

While I was describing what I had seen it was almost as though I could still hear Sofia's screams. Petruchio took my hand, and comforted me as if I were a child. Then he told me why we were fugitives from the village: ''When Lucia found that you had gone, she was very distressed. I told her that you would come back, that you had gone away for a few days

151

because solitude had become necessary to you; but she would not believe me and insisted on going to Sofia's house to see if you were there. When she came back to the inn I could see that she was terrified. She had found some of the villagers setting fire to the house, and they had told her that Sofia had been taken before the Papal Authority to be brought to trial for witchcraft. There were rumors that other women had joined with Sofia in the Black Mass, some said that one of them was a girl with red hair who had often been seen going with her into the woods. Lucia knew they meant you, Carola, and thought that they would soon recognize the lute player at the inn as being she whom they suspected of being the consort of a witch.

''Lucia was afraid that you might have told someone how she had gone to Sofia for a love potion, so she barred herself into her room and would not open to any one. I managed to persuade Bernard to take her away with him, though he is more frightened of sorcery than of the plague. He pretended to think you were never coming back, that you had received warning of Sofia's betrayal and had fled without waiting for us to go with you. Lucia did not believe him, for she left me the crucifix she wore, the one Bernard gave her, to give to you when I saw you again. She said it would protect you against demons, if you had not already sold yourself into their keeping. I knew that when you had received what you had gone up into the hills to find, you would come back. I prayed that it might be when everyone was asleep, for the inn-keeper is avaricious and the Church pays well for news of heresy....''

I think I wept. I had ridden down from the hills strong in the memory of truth; I had been so sure that somehow I should find strength to destroy the dark power that threatened Sofia—and I had stood in a crowd to watch her die alone. I had tried to help Lucia to live, I had loved her and she had been my friend for more than four years. Once she had railed at me for not believing in witchcraft, for warning her against sorcery, for scorning love potions; now she had fled from me because she feared my heresy.

Reluctant Troubadour

Petruchio and I lived much as we had done when we were with Bernard and Lucia; but we kept away from the roads we had traveled before.

It was easier to earn money by writing serenades than by lute playing, so I began to follow the traditions of a troubadour. I would be told a woman's name, the color of her hair and eyes, and in an hour be expected to have written verses that praised her doubtful charms as if she were a goddess. By making a few changes, I could use the same lines over again; and sometimes more prosperous scriveners paid me to do their work for them.

It made me impatient that men had not even the wit to beguile women into folly without another woman helping them. One day, when I was feeling more impatient than usual, I said to Petruchio, "It is a strange world that we live in. You earn your bread by making men laugh—when if they thought of themselves they would weep, and I earn mine by weaving a tapestry of lies. In the last month I have made more than fifty songs for men to sing to their mistresses; young mistresses, scornful mistresses, eager mistresses— even dead mistresses! I write songs of love that is unending, for men to sing who do not even know that life is unending. All over Italy troubadours are singing of happy lovers. Are there not a diversity of lies that they must always play upon one theme! Why do they not sing of goats that can mutter like priests, of cauldrons of water that freeze when they are hung over a fire, or trees that uproot themselves and fly into the sky?''

''Perhaps it is not love, but what men seek from it which

is at fault," he said. "If man hopes for permanence from that which is impermanent he must find sorrow. To love only the flesh, is to love a flower believing that when it withers one's heart will die."

He was holding a poplar spray in his hand. I noticed how much thinner his hands had become, as if soon they would be transparent as a skeleton leaf. He pointed at the tree from which the twig had come. "Look at the rosy bronze of that poplar. Its leaves are newly unfurled, for it is spring; but soon they will be green, and then autumn will mint them for winter to swirl like smoke upon the wind. We do not regret their seasonable change, because it is the spirit of the poplar which we love; the spirit which manifests itself in the beauty that our eyes can see. If men and women could love each other with this knowledge, they would find happiness in love, for they would glory in the spring without fearing the autumn. They would know that although this body dies, another will be born. And greater than this, Carola, for their comfort; they would know that though upon the earth they had grown old, though their skin was withered and their hair without luster, they had but to sleep to enter into youth; to see each other as they once had been, to see each other as they had longed to be—fair and radiant in the image of God."

the Conte's Jest

Sometimes, when we had made enough money at the last village, we lodged at a farmhouse instead of an inn. Early in May we came to a farm where we were made so welcome that we stayed for nearly a month. The farmer's wife told Petruchio that we could be her guests as long as it suited us, for the stories he told her more than paid for our food. She was very fat, and wore dirty cotton dresses printed in wide stripes, which, on her, looked like the staves of a wine barrel. Her nose and mouth seemed ridiculously small for her large face, almost as if she had been blown up like a pig's bladder at a fair, and her eyes were black and glossy as currants. Even when she shouted at one of her children or scolded her sour and withered little husband, there was a broad kindness behind her anger. I have seen her hit her husband over the head with an iron ladle, so hard that it cut the scalp even through his thick hair, with as little malice as when she scolded the baby for trying to crawl into the hot ashes on the hearth.

She had a herd of goats, six nannies, and a fierce old billygoat which she called Tonio because she said it reminded her of her father-in-law. She would add, with a fat chuckle, looking towards her husband to see if she had roused him, "Old Tonio and young Tonio are like enough to be twins instead of father and son." But her husband went on picking his teeth with a splinter of wood he had pulled off one of the benches, and pretended he had not heard. He hated the goat, and was always trying to persuade her to have its throat cut and let it go into a stew. But even when it ate all the young shoots off the vine arbor, or pulled down the clothesline and trampled on her best dress, which she had hung in the sun because she had overspiced it against the moth, she refused to have it beaten.

I think she looked upon her husband and the goat in the same way: she thought it a weakness in herself to be so fond of them, but knew that in spite of the annoyance they caused her, she would weep bitterly when either of them died—and whenever she remembered this she was grateful to them for being alive.

Sometimes Petruchio told me stories that he never told to any one else. I remember him saying, "The ears of a dwarf hear many strange tales that men conceal from people of their own stature. Sometimes they talk to me from their hearts, as they would talk to a favorite dog, without using words to conceal their secrets."

He went on, "Once, when I was journeying through Tuscany with a troupe of mummers, we were commanded to play at a banquet given in the honor of a prince of the Church. A conte, who was among the guests, found that I could easily provoke his laughter; and when he heard that I was making my way towards the south, he offered me a place in one of his baggage wagons, making it a condition that I must relieve his boredom during the three nights he would have to lodge in taverns before reaching home. I agreed to go with him, though I wondered why he needed a jester to protect him from his thoughts, as I had heard that his young wife was famous for her beauty. During the journey he talked of the wars, of the countries he had visited, but he never mentioned his wife save on one occasion. He had invited me to travel in his coach, and he told me that the coffer which he never allowed to be out of his sight held gifts for her, gifts he had searched far to find, for her beauty was of such rare quality that only a subtle tribute was worthy of it.

''I expected that we should part at the last halting place, and I was surprised when he insisted on my accompanying him to his palazzo. When we alighted from his coach he told me to take the coffer and follow him. I had been prepared to see a woman of uncommon quality, but his wife far exceeded the portrait that my thoughts had painted. She stood waiting for him in the great hall of his house, and he knelt to kiss her hand as if he were her page. Her eyes were water-green; her hair, netted with pearls, seemed alloyed of gold and silver, so pale and yet so brilliant was its sheen.

''He took the coffer from me, and handed it to her as if he were a vassal bringing tribute to a beloved prince. Before she opened it, he said, 'I have searched Italy and France, sent my envoys into Spain, for gifts worthy of you, gifts that will show how well I know your heart. What do you think it is I have found for you? Has the sea given up her pearls, and will they die for envy of your skin? Or are there rubies, carved in far Cathay, to match your lips?''

''I could not understand why there was fear in her eyes as she lifted the lid. In it there was a ring, set with a fair emerald; a pair of velvet gloves, embroidered with seed pearls; an enamel comfit box; and a dagger, its hilt finely wrought with precious stones.

"She stood looking, not at the gifts but at her husband, as he said to her, 'Once I would have plucked the stars to jewel your necklaces; or left the world in darkness if you had craved the moon as a mirror for your tiring-room. For then I saw only how fair you were, how wondrous your eyes, how infinite your grace; and when I led you to our marriage bed I did not know the world held so much joy. Now, these are the gifts I bring you; a ring, to remind you of those solemn vows you pledged to me before the Cardinal; these gloves, to cover the white hands I kissed; this comfit box—does it hold sugar-plums or pearls? This dagger, is it to defend you while you sleep alone when I must leave you?

"His voice changed to mockery, 'It is three years since you became my bride; three years whose days have built a tomb for love; three years in which you have revealed your heart.'

"And then to me, 'Now, laugh, Petruchio! Often you made me laugh when I would weep. Look at her eyes, and listen to *my* jest! The ring and gloves are poisoned; the comfit box holds a live scorpion—and she can sheathe the dagger in her heart!'"

CHAPTER FIFTEEN

the 'Santa Maria'

Our wanderings had taken us eastwards, and by the height of the summer, Petruchio and I came to a little village on the Adriatic coast. It was seldom that a vessel larger than a fishing boat anchored there, and when the Santa Maria was sighted coming round the headland, the whole village turned out to watch. She was foreign built, with blunt, clumsy lines; and, as I heard later, she had been captured from the Spanish by corsairs and later retaken from them and sold as a trading ship.

I was standing on the wooden jetty when the crew came ashore. The first man to land was very tall. He wore gold ear-rings, and his striped singlet was tucked into ragged breeches of grey worsted. His blue eyes looked strangely brilliant in his sun-dark face, and in spite of his clothes, there was no doubting who was the captain of that motley crew. He asked me where he could replenish his water casks, and I showed him the way to the stream.

If the breeze had held, he would have left the same evening; but by midday there was a flat calm, and he said that his men had worked hard enough warping the *Santa Maria* to this anchorage and they could rest until there came a favorable wind.

The captain had led an adventurous life, and he had a great fund of tales to tell; of skirmishes against pirates, and of the countries he had been to on his voyages. In two or three days he and Petruchio were like brothers. They used to sit outside the inn door on a bench in the sun; drinking the rough wine and talking so hard that they never noticed the time passing. Even when the days were very hot the air was fresher by the sea, and being with the Captain, as we always called him, seemed to give Petruchio new strength, as if he were being refreshed from the other's strong vitality.

For more than a year I had seen that Petruchio was growing steadily weaker. Though he refused to talk about it, I knew he was often in pain from the way he would press his hands to his side and catch his breath as if he had been stabbed by an invisible dagger. I had tried to make him go to a physician, but he had only smiled, and said, ''They could not cure me; for I think my body so hates its own ugliness that it is trying to destroy itself.''

The night I woke to hear the wind blowing strongly from the south I could have wept—for I knew it meant that the *Santa Maria* would continue on her voyage. The Captain went on board at dawn—but there was no need of farewells: he had arranged with Petruchio for us to sail with him, and they had kept it a secret to surprise me.

I had never been on the sea before, and I was very excited at my unfamiliar surroundings. I thought the *Santa Maria* was a mighty ship, for she was the largest I had ever seen, but the Captain laughed at me, and said, ''She would look like a rowing boat alongside any of the Spanish fleet, and if you saw one of those towering galleons on the horizon you might think her great spread of sails was the cliffs of an island.''

I shared the stern cabin with both of them. The beams seemed to press down on me and the Captain warned me not to bump my head. His height was very troublesome to him in the confined space below decks, and he used to say, ''God forgot He was going to make me a sailor, or else that ships are made for little men.'' Though the cabin was shabby it must once have been handsomely appointed; there were traces of gilt and vermilion on the carved mouldings, and the tattered brocade that covered the bench under the stern windows was of fine quality. It was here that the Captain kept the many strange relics he had collected in foreign lands: a piece of amber with a fly in it; carved coral; a heavy war club; a monkey's skull, said to have magical properties, from the African coast. There was also a box of curious shells; and as he showed them to me, he told me of the beaches from which they had come. The Captain, and any guests or passengers that he carried, always drank wine. I was sorry for the sailors who had to drink from the water-cask, for after about ten days there was green scum on it. One of the men told me that on a long voyage the water became so foul that they had to hold their noses against the stink before they could swallow it without retching.

We carried a mixed cargo: silk, some hogsheads of Spanish

wine, salted fish, bark used in the tanning trade, and many other things I cannot remember. Few of the small towns along the coast had a good harbor; we anchored off-shore and the traders came out to us in a fishing boat, or the Captain went ashore to look for a new cargo. Sometimes he bought merchandise to trade, and sometimes he carried goods under charter.

I was very happy during the two months we were on the ship. At times I wished that the Captain had not a wife and five children living with his parents on a farm near Naples— he had not seen them for three years so I doubt if he can have loved them very much—because then he might have asked me to remain with him. I think I should have done so if I had had the chance; but first I should have made him promise not to leave me on land to have a lot of children I didn't want. Unfortunately he seemed to look on me more as a child than a woman of eighteen; and he always treated me as if he were a kindly uncle. It was lucky that I never fell in love with him, otherwise I might have been very unhappy, instead of merely regretful that I could not follow the sea with a man of whom I was very fond.

When we came into Venetian waters we stood away from the coast. I had been hoping that at last I should see the town I had so often traveled towards and never reached. The Captain never told me the reason why he thought it unwise to attempt trading there. Perhaps they were in a state of war, or it may only have been that the dues were too heavy.

Soon afterwards we came to the great port of Trieste. The harbor was crowded with ships from many countries, men-of-war, coastal traders, merchantmen, ships from Spain so high out of the water that they seemed top-heavy. The merchants who came aboard us used to sit for hours in the stern cabin, drinking wine with the Captain while they haggled over the value of his cargo. When at last they were in agreement, bales or barrels would be taken up out of the hold and lowered into the little boat waiting alongside, while the two who had been arguing so fiercely parted from each other with many elaborate phrases of goodwill.

It was a charter that sent us to Fiume. Until then we had been fortunate in the weather, the sun shone nearly every day and the sea remained blue and mild. We left Trieste with a favorable breeze, and were out of sight of land before we saw storm clouds blowing up from the east.

Waves seemed to follow us like angry serpents, towering to strike down onto our stern; but somehow we always seemed to out-distance them. I wanted to stay on deck, but I was ordered below. There was no light or air in the cabin, for wooden covers had been put over all the portlights and the hatches were batten down. So violent was the storm that the ship drove forward under bare yards; and the shrouds twanged like the devil's lute strings as the wind tore at them.

After a time the wind lessened, but a high sea was still running and the ship wallowed in the trough of the waves like a dying porpoise. It was so dark in the cabin that until the cook came in with some food for us and lit the lantern, I did not realize that Petruchio had been injured. A heavy chair had worked free from its lashings and fallen on his knee. The bone was not broken, but it had begun to swell and it looked very painful. Though I put poultices of hot meal on it every hour, by the following night the flesh was still red and angry and he could walk only with difficulty.

Next morning the storm had abated. The sky was blue again, with high scudding clouds, and we made fine speed under a full press of canvas. The Captain said we should reach Fiume by the following evening, but it was twelve hours later than that when we tied up alongside the stone jetty. He went ashore at once; and when he came back from the town I could see he was disturbed about something. He told us he had been offered a very favorable charter to sail direct to the African coast. It would be a dangerous voyage, not only because he must reach his destination with all speed, and so would have to chance being many days out of sight of land, but also because it was rumored that three other ships which had attempted to follow the same route had been taken by corsairs on the Barbary coast. He kept on stressing the dangers of the voyage. It seemed out of character for this man who laughed at danger to talk so much of it, until I realized that he was trying to tell us he could not take us with him.

Petruchio was always quicker witted than I was. He said that his leg would heal better on land than on sea, and that as he had always wanted to go to Fiume it would suit us very well to be landed there. The Captain at first protested against our leaving him, but we knew he was relieved—a woman and a cripple make poor additions to a fighting crew. At last it was arranged we should wait there till the *Santa Maria* returned. The Captain was confident he would complete his voyage in three months, or if the wind were favorable, he might be back even sooner.

So the *Santa Maria* sailed. We watched her until she was hull down on the horizon—and then Petruchio and I were alone in Fiume.

WINTER IN FIUME

Before he left, the Captain had found two little rooms over a ship-chandler's for us. It was on the water front, and at night I used to lie listening to the water sucking at the wooden piers of the wharf. When a ship was loading, carts used to grind over the cobblestones and I could hear the rumble of the casks as they thudded down into the holds. It was easy to tell when a ship had made port after a long voyage by the vomit on the streets outside the taverns.

We knew that in Fiume it would be difficult for Petruchio to earn money as a jester, for the frequenters of the harbor taverns were mostly foreigners who could not understand Italian. But we had saved enough money to keep us through the time the Captain expected to be away, and he had promised that on his return he would give us passage to his home port of Naples.

I hid our bag of money under a loose floor-board in my room, because Petruchio thought it unsafe to carry it about with us. His leg refused to heal, and at last even he could not bear the pain of walking and he had to keep to his room. The chandler's wife let me cook at her fire, and I used to go down to the market to buy our food. Fish was plentiful and it was easy to get meat; but at this season of the year the price of fruit or butter was too high for me to afford any. I missed being able to gather my own wild pot-herbs. I had never lived out of sight of growing things before; in all the little villages and towns where I had been it had taken only a few minutes to get out of the shadows of buildings.

Petruchio often asked me if I still had the ring which that other Bastard of the Griffin had given me, and he made me promise that if he died I should go to the House of the White Sisters for sanctuary. I had a picture of it in my mind: high, white walls, which shut away the turmoil of the world; quiet cloisters with white doves strutting among the ordered plots; and muted bells to mark the gentle hours. But I put the thought of it away from me, for I knew that there I should have no Petruchio—I was so afraid of having to live without him.

I never found out who stole our money. I think it was the squinting son of the chandler, but I knew it would be useless to accuse him; he would only have denied it and his parents would have turned us out. I did not tell Petruchio it was gone, for it would have made him unhappy to know that our livelihood depended on what I could earn.

The shop next door was owned by a meat-pickler. I earned a little money there, helping to fill the casks and nail down the lids. Much of what went into the brine tubs to feed the sailors was the refuse of the meat market. In some of the casks the meat was packed in dry salt; in others gobbets lay half-obscured in the pickling, like the brew in a sorcerer's cauldron. I saw a pig's eye floating on the surface of one of them, like a monstrous frog's spawn.

I had to find other work as well as this, for what the briner gave me was not enough to pay our lodging and buy even a little food. There was a tavern along the quay which was owned by an elderly woman. She was always dressed in black, very soberly though in cloth of a rich quality. She walked with a stick but her carriage was erect and imperious. She seemed to have a flavor of Donna Isabella, so perhaps that was why I did not go to her sooner to ask for work. But at last I had to, for I could find it nowhere else.

I went to the tavern in the morning. The shutters had not yet been taken down, but when I rattled the latch it was opened to me by a loutish boy. Just inside the door was a dais; it was surrounded by a railing, and behind this the proprietress sat at an oak table tallying up the score of the week's takings. Her voice was sharp when she asked me why I had come. Then she said, ''There is no work for you here. You are too thin. Chickens and girls should both be plump.''

''But why should my being thin affect my playing?'' Long fingers are more nimble than fat ones on the strings. Won't you hear me before deciding against me?''

''A lutanist?'' She looked surprised. ''Can you sing—not sickly romances but the kind of songs that make a sailor laugh?''

I said I would try, and sitting down on the edge of a table I began one of the songs that Lucia had sung when I first knew her, and I tried to play it as she would have done. Though I knew the woman liked it, I dared not haggle over the price. I accepted the little that she offered, and it was arranged that I should play there from six in the evening until they put the shutters up. Before I went out the woman looked at me piercingly and said, ''You understand you are here as a lutanist. It is the only thing I require you for. If you try to interfere with other people's work you will be dismissed at once. Everything here is very orderly. You are here to play the lute, and play the lute you shall and nothing else—except singing, of course."

I started work that evening. The proprietress seemed to know most of her customers by name, and I was amused to see that she made them stick their daggers into a board behind her table. One man, he must have been a newcomer, protested, and she said to him, "Did you think you would need to draw a knife in my tavern? If so you had better walk along the quay till you find a cut-throats' meeting-place. Plenty of them there are, as you will soon find! I am an honest, God-fearing woman and I will permit no brawling here."

In every way she was very strict. If a drunken man tried to grab at me as I walked between the tables, she shouted at him, and he would look sheepish as a child caught stealing sugar. If a man got truculent he found himself thrown out by the huge negro servant she employed, or, if he was sober enough to pull himself out, he might be dropped into the harbor. When they were very drunk she left them to sober up on the wharfside, because, she said, "If customers get drowned people begin to talk about it and that is bad for my business."

Opposite the door to the quay there was another, which at first I thought must be a back entrance. Then I noticed that some men walked straight across the room and through the other door and knew it could not lead into the street. But it was only when the proprietress called out to a man who was trying to pull me down beside him, "Go into the back room if you want to drop anchor between a pair of thighs!" that I realized it was not a tavern she owned but a brothel.

The drabs all lived together in the back room. There were low partitions, not reaching to the roof, between each pallet, of which there were four on either side of the room; and a dirty curtain on a string gave them each an illusion of privacy. From seven in the evening until midnight their earnings belonged to the house, and during these hours they had to wait in their cubicles for customers; but what they made at other times they kept for themselves. They had a code of rules amongst themselves which they never broke; each girl was responsible for the man she brought into the room: if he was fighting drunk and created too much of a disturbance, she had to put half his fee into the common fund from which they paid the little gutter boy who cleaned the floor. This boy sat outside the doorway with a ship's mop and a wooden bucket, and ran in to clean up the vomit at the sound of a protesting stomach; but though he was very nimble, a sour smell always clung to the floor of beaten earth.

In the day-time the girls used to gather round a large table under the high window at one end of the room, to sew, or gossip, or gamble away their earnings to each other at dice. They were much lower in the scale of harlotry than Lucia had ever been, and yet some of them had achieved a magnificient detachment. Vaccia talked about her work as if her body were a mule she hired out for a day's work to a carter. She took more trouble than did the others with her appearance, and would cut, thread by thread, the frayed edge of her velvet dress, or mend with fine careful stitches a rent in her chemise or a torn ruffle. Another of them—I think if she had had one less thought she would have been an idiot—seldom talked to anyone. She was very lousy, and used to sit scratching herself, slowly and despairingly, like a dying monkey. Maria was pregnant, but her striped skirt was very full and the old woman had not yet noticed. Maria was terrified that she would be turned out. She dreaded being alone and having to wander round the alleys looking for men; for, she told me, girls who had no protection seldom got paid anything and ran the risk of having their throats cut.

I think the proprietress had a certain fondness for me, and she was not unkind to her girls. She treated them like a mule-teer who keeps his animals in good condition so that they will make him a better profit. She went to a church in another part of the town, where prosperous merchants took their wives and families. Although she believed in hell-fire, I am sure she never thought she was in any danger of it, for she had a great opinion of her own virtues. I have heard her say that if the sailors' mothers knew how well she looked after their sons they would remember her in their prayers.

The long, cold weeks went slowly by. It was a season of bitter gales: the winds screamed down from the mountains, and the skies were low and somber, leaden as coffin seals. My cloak was threadbare, and the cold gnawed at my fingers until there was blood on my lute strings.

Petruchio used to sit at the window, watching the grey horizon for the *Santa Maria*. Sometimes we thought we recognized her rig, but as the ship grew nearer it was always a stranger. I prayed so hard for her to come back, and I should have gone on board her, even when the gales were at their height, if only she would have taken us back to the Italy we knew. Whenever a new ship came into the harbor—and there were few of them at this season—I tried to get news of her from the crew. It was in January, four months after she sailed, that I heard of her. She had foundered off Sicily with all hands.

Petruchio was desperate to get me away from Fiume, I think he already knew that he was dying, but he clung to life so fiercely that he made his body obey him. It was one evening while I was lute-playing that I found a way to get back to our own country. No ships had come into the harbor for the last two weeks, and captains were delaying their sailings until more favorable weather. Several days had gone by without my seeing a new face in the tavern, when a stranger walked in. I could see by his dress that he was not a sailor, and his fur-lined cloak showed that he was a man of substance. Even the proprietress greeted him with respect, and herself led him to a seat by the fire.

My songs seemed to please him; he made me play the ones that caught his ear till long past the time I was usually allowed to go home. He was made very welcome by the company, for he threw gold on the table and said they were all to be his guests.

He looked so prosperous, yet wine brought him self-pity; he made me sit beside him, and while he stroked my hand he told me his troubles. ''Three day I have stayed in this town listening to this accursed wind. I am a merchant; until I came to Fiume I thought a wise one, for I found these foreigners profitable to trade with. Now my business is concluded and I am trapped here by the sea. I have promised the Madonna that if she gets me safely back to Italy there shall be a new statue of her in the cathedral. But the wind is so loud I doubt whether she can hear my prayers.''

''You pray to the Madonna for a quiet passage. I pray to her for any passage, however rough, however dangerous, for it would get me back to a friendly shore.''

Then he made me tell him my story from the time the *Santa Maria* had sailed. He looked at me, the solemn, stupid look of a drunken man who thinks he still possesses a keen judgment. He spaced his words carefully, as if they were a line of stepping-stones from which he was afraid of slipping; he must judge each one separately and adjust his balance before moving on to the next. ''I am a musician as well as a merchant. You may think merchants care only for trading, not for song. But you are wrong! You may think merchants think only of money and have no generosity. That's wrong too! I will prove it to you: I'll pay your passage, and you can also take the dwarf you say you travel with. That proves I'm generous! I'll make a bargain with you—I'm no fool to have money wheedled out of me even by such a pretty face as yours. You must play the lute to me and sing, the louder and bawdier the better, to keep the noise of the winds out of my ears.... Maybe it will make me forget these accursed seas. I shall shut my eyes and listen to you, and perhaps I'll believe the ship's only swaying because I've drunk too much.''

I knew that he hoped for more than lute-playing, but I was

168

too happy at his offer to worry about the difficulties of the journey.

It was hard to believe in our good fortune, and both Petruchio and I were afraid it was only a drunkard's promise. But the merchant did not forget, and by the next evening we had sailed from Fiume.

There is little to tell of our journey. There were no great storms, though the waves were high enough for our benefactor to have no stomach for lutanists—it was too busy protesting against the sea! He was a kind man, although queasy and something of a coward. He was so overjoyed to feel firm land under his feet, that when we parted from him he further increased our gratitude by a gift of money.

The Great Physician

Petruchio pretended that he had always wanted to see the castle where I was born. I knew that this was an excuse to travel towards Perugia, so that when he died it would be easy for me to reach the convent. He could no longer ride on a mule so we traveled slowly, having to wait until there was an ox-cart with a friendly driver going in our direction.

When we were still twenty leagues from Perugia, his illness was increased by a fever. I wanted to find lodging at a farm, but he would not rest. We went on, in a cart half-full of barrels, some of wine, some of oil. They were roped together but they rolled with the jolting of the cart, so we could not lean against them. Petruchio had once told me, that of all things, a hunchback most desires to be able to lie flat on the ground and look up at the sky. He could never lie flat, and now that he had grown so thin there were sores on his shoulders and elbows because it was so difficult for him to vary his position.

We tried to hide our sorrowful thoughts from each other with an imagery of earthly contentment. Of how we should write songs, he stringing the words and I the melody; songs that would echo throughout Italy until they were heard by some great lord who would find us and be our patron. He would be a man of kindliness and riches and would give us a corner of his palace to live in. I should have a lute inlaid with olive wood and painted with flowers, in colors soft as harp-strings plucked at dusk. Petruchio would no longer be a jester, and would keep the fair sheets of paper on which he would write his philosophies, in a coffer of leather curiously deviced in scarlet and gilt, such as we had once seen in the hall of a great house. Hunger would never walk through our thoughts, and the cruel, shabby terrors of the very poor would no longer follow us.

I pillowed his head on my lap, and stroked his forehead to try to bring him sleep. His head looked too big for his body, as if it were a head carried on a pike. Pain had scored deep lines into his face; but life had written courage on his fore-head, and gentleness spoke from his mouth even while he slept.

As I watched him it seemed that I saw him, in heavy armor, on a white horse, a man stronger than Bernard even in his prime. Behind him I saw banners; one emblazoned with three gold leopards, another with a white hart on an emerald field. Then I realized what I had always known though never shaped into words: Petruchio was not a dwarf like other dwarfs, but was a knight who had been grievously wounded. A knight whose now crippled hands had known the singing downsweep of a battle-axe; whose withered legs had gripped the deep sides of a mighty war-horse as it thundered on to meet the enemy.

That night the carter stopped at a farm belonging to his cousin. They gave me some milk for Petruchio, and let us sleep on a pile of sweet hay in the corner of a barn. Moonlight pierced between the broken roof tiles in silver rods; darkness and light, clearly divided the one from the other in a sharp line.

Petruchio had slept during the day, and all through the night he was wakeful. His voice was clear and strong, and it did not seem to tire him to talk. It was as though we had reached an unspoken agreement to abandon the pretence that he was going to get well again: he knew that he was going to die, and I accepted it. He talked about it calmly, almost eagerly, as though he were setting out on a voyage, and giving me careful instructions what I must do until I was able to join him.

He was so confident, so serene, that I almost forgot how soon his voice that had so often comforted me would be beyond my hearing. ''It is strange, Carola, that even if our physicians were great men, even if they were near to the Christ in their power of healing, they would despair to cure a hunchback of his deformity. There is only one physician that will cure me. Soon I shall feel his hand on mine, and he will say, 'Rise up, my friend, for you are whole again.' And I shall be young and strong; my back will be straight as a poplar wand and my neck will carry my head proudly; there will be no clumsiness in my feet, and my thighs will be long and swift. I shall be clean and beautiful, for though Jesus cleansed lepers, Death is a greater physician.

''Even now I can feel my body loosening its hold on me, and just as at other times when I have had a fever, I can see a little further beyond the curtain. I want you to go to the House of the White Sisters not only for sanctuary—though that part of me which is still blinded by my mortality fears for the things that you might suffer if you were alone without your little dwarf to serve you.''

I felt my tears sliding down my face. I dared not brush them away, for I loved Petruchio too much to dim his freedom by my selfishness. He went on.

''We both share memory of an older time when men and women trained themselves as priests, in temples, where they shut themselves away only until they were ready to speak of what they knew. When you rode up into the hills you be-

171

came wise in your own spirit; and monks and nuns must live as solitaries. You may find women there who have taken vows only from expedience; but there must be some who know of the things we know, and they will befriend you. Remember that the starving must eat slowly; that in our time it is easier to teach people the truth through their own formulas. You must go gently with them, or they will not accept the living truth but call it heresy.

"When you have listened to your own voice in the silence and are strong in certainty, you must leave the convent and share your knowledge among the people outside, even though it will expose you to the great danger of being recognized for a renegade nun. It may take you five years, or ten, shut away alone, but I shall always wait for you on the other side of sleep....

"I wonder if you will recognize Petruchio as I shall be then? I know you will. But if I thought you would deny me in a radiant guise and think me a stranger, I would still be a crippled dwarf in heaven."

By the next evening he was too weak to climb out of the cart, but the driver was kind and carried him into the inn. I asked for a room to ourselves. The inn-keeper said he had none, until I showed him that I had money to pay.

I put Petruchio to bed, and the inn-keeper's wife brought me a bowl of hot water and towels to bathe him. His lips were dry, and I kept moistening them with wine. It seemed that the flame of his fever would split the taut skin from his bones. I bathed his body until at last the sweat dewed his forehead and gathered in the hollow of his upper lip.

Then it seemed as if winter took him into her keeping. His teeth chattered with cold. I got heated stones, wrapped in a cloth, to put at his feet; but I could not warm him. I took off my clothes and lay with him in my arms, but his cheek between my breasts was cold.

His heart was still beating under my hand, very fast and sharp, as though he had been running. Twice I thought that it had stopped. I felt him stir, and my arms tightened round him. He opened his eyes.

"My Carola, are we in a dream?"

"No, my Petruchio, we are both awake. I am here. Can you not feel my arms holding you to me?"

He smiled, "So you have died too, my beloved. I have left the cold earth, and even my lonely dreams, and we are at last together—in Paradise."

And my tears fell upon his forehead; but Petruchio did not feel them, for his body held him prisoner no longer.

CHAPTER SIXTEEN

house of the White Sisters

I stood watching the mule-train, with which I had traveled for five days, straggling away from me down the dusty road. In the distance I could see Perugia; its walls strong and purposeful against the sky, the river, moon-brilliant in the sun, coiling beneath them. The track leading up to the House of the White Sisters was narrow and stony. A bell was tolling among the olive trees, pellucid, measured, bubbles of sound rising slowly through the still air.

Because it might be a long time before I saw this outside world again, the things that belonged to it were suddenly very dear to me: the little cyclamen growing in the grass, the placid furrows green-hazed with new wheat, the blue distance of the sweeping hills. I wondered if I should be allowed to keep my lute. I sat down on the warm, sweet turf and tuned its strings; the smooth wood seemed alive under my fingers, strong and comforting as the hand of a friend. Until it was nearly evening I wandered through the melodies that Petruchio had loved, as though he still listened to me.

When I climbed up the path towards the convent, I passed a little boy driving a flock of geese. I had a single coin left, and before I pulled the bell rope that hung by the door in the high wall, I threw it to him with a greeting, and saw my last link with freedom glint in the slanting rays of the sun as it spun through the air.

The bell jangled harshly, as if it were angry at being disturbed. A little panel in the door slid back, and a face peered out at me through the iron grille. If it had not been the door of a convent I should have thought it was a man's face, so strong was the beard which sprouted from the wrinkled chin. I took the ring off my thumb and asked her to take it to the Abbess. She was old and stupid, and kept on shaking her head as she told me to go away, but at last I made her understand I wanted to speak to someone in authority. She told me to pass the ring through the grille to her. It seemed a long time before I heard her returning. She opened the door and beckoned to me to follow her; then led me along a deserted cloister surrounding a shadowy garden. The flagstones were cold to my feet: I felt alien, and alone.

The Abbess was very old. There was a calm and a serenity about her such as I had never seen except in Petruchio. She told the nun to leave us. Then she smiled, and said gently, "My child, I have been waiting for you a long time. It is more than a year since I heard your story. Tell me, what has kept you away from us?"

I told her I could not leave Petruchio, and of other things. She seemed to understand and listened very patiently; and once she exclaimed, "My poor child!" As I described how I had lived as a strolling player, she said, "More than forty years ago, I played a lute." When I showed her mine, she picked it up and played a little thread of sound, "The neck is longer than mine used to be—one forgets that fashions change."

"May I keep my lute, and play it sometimes?"

"You cannot have it with you, but I will see that it is kept safely for you. If you complete your vows you may wish for it to be given away to some poor musician, or sold to buy bread for the hungry.''

''I thought no one could get out of a convent once they had got into it.''

''That is only after a nun has taken her final vows. There are a very few who go after they have made their first profession, but novices do not always stay with us. If a novice has been put in our charge by her parents, their consent must be given to her leaving; but as you come here of your own free will, if you find that God has not called you to this vocation no one will constrain you.''

She talked to me a little longer and then summoned the nun who would instruct me in their routine.

I was taken to the storeroom where I was given a white habit of coarse wool, two undershifts, very harsh to the skin, a rope girdle, and a wooden rosary. I was shown how to tie the stiff coif with which my hair had to be covered except when I was alone in my cell. The nun was silent but not unfriendly. As I was too late to join the others at the evening meal in the refectory, she stopped at the hatch leading through to the kitchen and fetched a wooden bowl of food for me; bread and beans with gravy poured over them.

The cells opened off each side of a dark passage. The doors had a heavy iron lock and a little panel which slid back from the outside. When the nun unlocked the door she gave me her candle, ''As this is your first day here I will leave the light with you until you have finished eating, but you must realize this is a special favor and will not happen again.''

She went out and I heard the key grating in the lock. The cell was very small. One side of it was taken up by a plank bed, just wide enough for me to lie on. There was a straw pillow but no pallet, and the sole covering was a square of the same fabric as my habit. The window was high in the wall and covered with a grating; under it a ledge in the plaster wall held an earthenware pitcher. There was a black wooden crucifix over the bed, and the only other furnishing was a three-legged stool.

The pitcher was empty, except for cobwebs, and I was thirsty. When the nun came back I asked her where I could fill it. She showed me the way to the well, and how to wind up the bucket. Before she locked me in for the night, she said, ''Your food bowl is kept in your cell and you take it with you to the refectory. When next you hear the bell it will be for the First Office. Prepare yourself, and wait by the door until the cells are unlocked for the novices to go to the chapel.''

The coif was tied so tightly that it cut into my chin, but I managed to undo the knot without tearing it. Then I lay down in the dark, wondering what the other girls, shut away in their little cells like grubs in a honeycomb, were like; and whether among them I should find a friend.

Cloister Garden

Before I entered the House of the White Sisters, I thought that nuns chose their vocation because some virtue within themselves inspired the life of a religious; so at first I was surprised when the other novices gave no sign of being aware of things away from earth. Then I learned some of the many reasons, other than vocation, why girls, often against their will, were put into a convent: they might be bastards, as I was, of an influential family; they might have had to accept the cloister as the only alternative to a repugnant suitor of whom their father approved; and it was the custom among the impoverished nobility so to dispose of daughters who were not expected to make a suitable marriage. A certain sum of money was given to the Order when they entered, and a further sum when they took their final vows. If a nun brought no dowry she became one of the lay sisters, who continued to do the household work even when they had passed their novitiate. I also heard that it was a not uncommon practice for parents to dedicate their next-born to the church as a thanksgiving for the granting of some special favor. This child would be brought up very strictly, often being kept away from her own brothers and sisters, and her education would be confined to religious subjects. It was seldom that such a child questioned her destiny, and it was from among these that the few nuns who had a vital fervor seemed to have been drawn.

The White Sisters were not a strictly enclosed Order, and certain of the nuns went into the towns to nurse the sick and take food to the crippled poor, although this had been permitted only since the present abbess came into power. For a time I had to spend my days learning prayers, a cycle of words whose meaning I could not understand as they were in ritual Latin. During the long hours in the chapel I used to wonder if any of the nuns really knew how to pray. I could not believe that the gods listened to their endless formula of words, the same prayer perhaps repeated a thousand times as a penance for some small disobedience; for even if the words had once held some significance it must long since have been numbered by endless repetition. As I knelt I used to watch the rosaries slipping through the bleached fingers of the old nuns, bead after bead, on and on, like a blind ass plodding round a treadmill.

When the Abbess sent for me I was glad, for though I had not spoken to her since the day I entered I felt she was not a stranger. She was sitting at a table reading a manuscript. She let me look at it, and I saw that the margins and some of the letters were illuminated in azure and vermilion. While she turned over the pages to show me the designs which pleased her most, she said, ''There is no one here now who can do such work—this was done by one of our sisterhood who died four years ago. She was the daughter of a great painter, and he taught her his skill.''

''I thought women were not allowed to learn such things.''

She smiled, "They may learn—if anyone will teach them. Women can even be scholars. I remember the time when I—but that is forgotten now. I sent for you to find out what work you are best suited for. Can you cook, or sew, or weave?'

"I can cook well enough, but I should be much happier if you would let me work in the garden. I promise to work very hard. I have always wanted to stay long enough in one place to watch things grow. Once we had a little house and I planted some seeds, but we moved on before the buds opened."

"That can be arranged. Perhaps you shall work in the herb garden; we have a rare collection of medicinal plants, sent from foreign countries as well as from our own."

I broke in eagerly, "I know something of herbs, I used to gather them for a woman who knew how to cure the scurvy and make crippled children strong...."

"It seems we share another interest—lutes, and now herbs! Tell me, who was your friend?"

I suddenly realized that the Abbess had the authority of the church that had convicted Sofia. I drew back, "She was not important—only a village girl who had a little knowledge. Her father was an herbalist, a good man who cured many people. It is two years since I saw her, I even forget the name of her village—I have traveled through so many villages."

"Do you think, my child, that you will find it hard to be shut away in our enclosure? Will you regret your freedom? It must be difficult to get the wandering out of your blood."

"You have to wander as much as I have done before you realize the freedom that comes from staying in one place. I think the only real freedom comes from inside oneself, and when one is not preoccupied with journeyings, or anxious what the next day will bring forth, it is much easier to look into one's own heart. I have found that here already. I shall soon start remembering things very clearly, for it is quiet enough to hear myself."

The Abbess leaned back in her chair and looked at me, kindly and steadily, ''What is it that you wish to remember? It is easier to live here if we forget—forget everything that happened before we came.''

''I don't want to remember what Carola knows. I want to find out what I did long ago, hundreds of years, thousands of years ago. I need to remember the things I knew then, things that all priests knew in the past.''

''Why do you say such strange things?''

''They are not strange. I was born knowing them. Perhaps everyone is born knowing them and then people make them forget.''

She seemed to disregard that I was a novice and she the Abbess. ''Why did you come here, my child? Was it to escape from your difficulties?''

''You can't escape difficulties. They are like a wall right across the road you have to travel. When you see the wall in the distance you can shut your eyes and pretend it is not there, and when you can't go any further you can sit down in the dust and turn your back on it. You may sit there for years and years, hundreds of years, waiting for time to make the wall fall down; but time doesn't, it builds course after course of stone to make it higher.''

She smiled, ''And does the traveler ever climb the wall?''

''Oh, he has to. He hears the voices of the friends he was traveling with calling to him from the other side of it, and usually he listens and starts climbing. But if he won't climb, even when they call and call to him—there aren't very many like this but there are some—he will see a pack of wolves coming down the road after him, and fear will spur him to clamber over.''

''You talk in parables. I understand you, but it is better that you do not talk of these things to others.'' She stood up, ''Come, my child, your Abbess is going to permit herself the indulgence of visiting her flowers, and you shall come with me.''

The cool arches of the cloister were framed in a delicate tracery of the buds and leaves put forth by flowering vines that twined round the pillars, and the grass paths between the garden plots were sweet with thyme and camomile. There were many plants I had never seen before; shrubs with white stars shining from glossy leaves, rich purple sprays moving with butterflies, feathery plumes the blue of cloud shadows. It seemed that spring and autumn were both here, for vigorous spears still thrust up through the earth, beside heavy calyces of contented seeds.

An old nun was kneeling beside the far border, pressing seedlings tenderly into the ground. When she heard of Abbess's voice she got to her feet, slowly and carefully as though her bones were very brittle. "Sister Ignatia, this is the new novice. It seems that she shares our love for plants, but I have told her she must work among the pot herbs, to see if she has a gardener's hands, before I ask you to take her as a pupil. How is the little shrub that came from Spain?"

"It sickens for its own country, though I have given it every indulgence. See, here it is in the sunniest corner. There are no leaves showing, but I know it is not dead, for when I hold the stem in my hand I seem to feel the sap coursing."

They moved away along the border; pausing to look at some newly unfolded bud, to discuss an ailing vine as though it were a sick child, to break off a withered leaf. I followed them, rubbing a sprig of verbena, which the Abbess had given me, between my fingers to bring out the sharp, lemon scent. With a flurry of wings a dove flew down from the roof and began to peck at a young shoot. Sister Ignatia clapped her hands at it, "You wicked bird, fly back to the cote! Do I not scatter grain there for you twice a day so as to keep you away from my garden?" She hobbled off to see what mischief the bird had done.

The Abbess had reached a door that led from the cloister. As she lifted the latch she looked back at the garden. "Before I became Abbess there were no flowers here. When I first planted them some of the nuns thought that as a cloister is used for meditation, beauty would distract the mind from holy things. But I reminded them that God was the first gardener.'' She sighed, ''He must have been so much happier with His world before he peopled it.''

The door opened into a room I had never seen before. It was full of a strong, pungent smell that came from a copper cauldron standing on a brazier. A novice was pounding dried bark in a mortar, and another one was straining what looked like curds into a row of little pots. The walls were lined with shelves, and on them, ranged with orderly precision, were pottery jars lettered in Latin, a row of pestles, little sacks of seeds, and bundles of twigs tied up with thread.

The Abbess called me over to the window, ''This is where we grow our most precious plants. Some of them hold death as well as healing, and must be treated with discretion.'' I saw a garden surrounded by a high wall. The plots were intricately shaped, and divided each from the other by miniature hedges, the color of lavender bushes but of a different leaf. ''When you are more experienced you shall help Sister Ignatia, or if you prefer it you may work here. The friend you told me of could have used her talents with us—our cordials and herbal salves bring pilgrims even from Lombardy....''

Sofia here, allowed to work in peace, honored for her skill. Sofia, who had burned for alchemy—even though, unknown to them, she was guilty of sorcery. I thought of our days together, when we had gathered common plants to make broth for sick children. Without thinking I asked, ''Have you a mandrake?''

The Abbess pretended not to hear my question. But when we had gone into the garden, she asked, ''What do you know of mandrakes?''

''I have heard they are very valuable....''

''To sorcerers—but it is not wise to talk of sorcery here.''

''I am sorry, I....''

"We will talk of other things. Would you like to be taught how to tend the sick who come to us for healing?"

I said eagerly, "I cannot heal, but I am very eager to learn. I think it would come easily to me. It seems as though I used to know of healing, long ago. I had a friend who took the pox—sometimes when I thought she was dying I felt as though I were feeding her with my own strength, as though she were grey ashes which I was breathing into warmth again."

A bell began to clang. "My child, you must hurry or you will be late in the refectory. Do not forget there are some things of which it is only to me that you may speak freely."

"But I may talk to you?"

"I will give orders that you are to come to me once every week. I shall say that I have found it necessary to give you special instruction—for you have much to tell me!"

CHAPTER SEVENTEEN

Anthony the Glass-Maker

There was a clean austerity about this cloistered life which seemed to have an echo of familiarity, yet I realized it was not even a pale reflection, for though there was an outward likeness between this life and another I had known, there was no true unity in their resemblance. I knew that here I could have dreamed strongly, but the bell tolling for the First Office at four in the morning startled me from sleep and confused my clear memory. I wondered why it was that those who should have taught us to become wise in our spirit should have forgotten the necessity for a smooth return to earth in the training of sleep-memory, but I believed that, though teaching seemed to be withheld from the novices, some degree of vision must be held by those who had taken their vows. I thought these vows were less a declaration of faith than a symbol of their attainment to the authority of personal knowledge.

Though at first I found it difficult to train myself to wake before the clanging of the early bell, I started to remember more of the time when I had been the girl with the lotus. I knew why it was familiar to have a narrow, white room, and to live for a time shut away from the world while I trained those faculties which it was necessary for me to acquire; and I wanted to find further similarities between the life I had lived then and the one I was experiencing as Carola. That other girl, who was the wiser I, had been in a temple that was not a hive of ritual but a training place of the spirit: the priests, aware of the immensities, had taught their pupils, who were chosen from the long in years, how to follow after them.

Though I had to go to chapel with the other novices to attend the four daily offices, I learned how to dissociate my thoughts from the mumbled prayers, which sounded like an innkeeper casting up the score of his day's takings. When I prayed, it was alone in my cell, and in time I knew that I could send a ray of light streaming up to the High Place. But the effort to do so was very great; my heart seemed to stop, then thudded as if I had been running up a steep hill.

The chapel was small and bare, with white-washed walls and no color in the windows, but on the altar there was a triptych which, I think, had been the gift of one of my kinsmen. On one panel there was a young saint, like Petruchio as he might be in heaven; and I came to love it, as in my dreams I had once loved the statues of the old gods—strange gods with jackal heads, of shining power. I forget the trivial fault that caused me for the first time to have to pass the night kneeling in prayer before the altar; but I shall always remember the dream I had there....

I was standing on the third step, above me was the triptych. The halo about the serene head seemed to give forth light—it filled my eyes, brighter, warmer, more luminous. It was no longer a painting, but a living being who was before me. He wrapped his cloak, azure, and deep as midnight, about me. I was with him in the sky, traveling more smoothly than a gull gliding down the wind. Below us the star-lit clouds drifted in their mutable formations, and through their shadowy rifts I glimpsed the earth, silent and far away.

He brought me to a place where men were building a great cathedral. Time ran through my fingers; the years turned back into the past as though they were patterns on a silver ribbon. I watched stone grow from the earth as though it pulsed with the vitality of its own life. There was wisdom in this stone, wisdom alive and urgent as the sap in a tree. Pillars soared upwards, the majestic trunks of a forest aisle; carvings sprang from them like budding leaves.

I stood in the great nave. It was empty, for as yet there were no altars or choir stalls, and the windows were arches open to the sky. No musicians or choristers were there, yet all about me was music; music that was never heard from plucked strings or human throat, for it streamed from the fountain of celestial sound. Sight and hearing had become one sense, each shade had voice, each harmony its hue. I could see the beatific melody flowing through the archways, in shaft of sound and color beyond the range of mortals.

There was a man standing in the nave: a young man in the habit of a monk, with strength in his hands and godliness in his eyes. I knew he had been vouchsafed the vision whose echo was being shown to me. He belonged to the time when the teaching of Jesus sprang in men's hearts as a fount of living water, in which they were truly baptized into the virtue of Christ.

I was no longer in the nave, but in a long room; a room that might have belonged to a silversmith or an alchemist. The man of my vision stood before a crucible. He was making living color, the blue of the robe of the Madonna, the glowing crimson of the Holy Blood.

With singing patterns he filled the archways of the House of God; and when light shone through his windows, it was as though the evening wind blew upon dulcet reeds, as though angelic fingers rippled silver strings, yet soared beyond the notes that even these could bring.

They that come after may stand within this Host, and if they have ears to hear and eyes to see, they too may receive an echo of the vision which came to Anthony the Glassmaker, whose heart was open to God.

heal the sick

I worked only for a short time in the refectory garden with the other novices before Sister Ignatia claimed me as her pupil. She used to say, ''You seem to have such a kinship with the plants that if you cut your hand I think it would run with sap instead of blood!'' I was happy looking after the flowers, but after a few weeks I asked the Abbess to let me learn the virtues of those plants which God had given men to succour him. I knew that it might be a long time before I was told the secret of the formulas, but soon I was allowed to help in the preparation of herbals; distilling essences, grinding twigs and aromatic bark into powder, or covering pots of salve with a film of wax to keep them fresh.

I was impatient to be allowed to use them on the sick who came for healing, though I had seen a novice, who had joined in that work for the first time, carried fainting to her cell, and knew that she had fled from her body in horror of the things she had seen. I had received no instruction for the training of my spirit but I thought that when I had shown I did not shrink from sores I should be taught how to cleanse them with more than salves.

When I was considered to be sufficiently experienced, I was given summary advice on how to apply a bandage.

Then, as were the others, I was given a flask of lotion and a jar of salve, with which I was to cleanse, or anoint, the wounds after I had washed them with water from the well in the outer courtyard. I carried a bundle of clean rags, to be used as bandages, and as I followed the nun in authority, who took with her a basket in which were knives, gouges, and a pair of pincers, I found that I was more fearful of the things I was going to see than I had ever been when Lucia had the pox. In those days cripples and disease had been familiar to me—I could even look on the face of an old leper without flinching—but since I had been hidden from the ugliness of the flesh I could not so easily armor myself against it.

One by one the pilgrims filed through the outer door: a blind man led by a lame child; a girl with a wizened baby in her arms; an idiot boy trying to break away from his mother's restraining hold; a man cradling his diseased hand with the other; a cripple dragging himself along on his elbows, the stumps of his legs making two straight ruts in the thick dust—and still they came. Then the thin tinkle of a leper's bell as he crawled through the gate to cower in the far corner, crossing himself with what once had been a hand.

The feet of the blind man were cracked with running sores. I knelt to wash them, but he said, ''It is my eyes. Please give me back my sight. It is so dark, always so dark.''

There was a film over his eyes, like the white of an egg. I whispered to the nun, ''What can we do for him?'' She answered, ''Nothing, he will always be blind.''

The man heard her, and put out his hand to feel for the child that guided him, ''Take me home. I thought God had forgiven me, but He is still angry.''

Tears gathered in his sightless eyes and drove a glistening path down his dry cheeks. I ran after him. ''You are blind only when you are awake. Sleep and you shall see, see things more beautiful than your eyes could tell you about.''

He halted, ''I can tell by your voice that you are young. Are you blind too?''

"No, not blind as you mean, though there is so much I cannot see."

"My pity for you. I lost the sight of one eye a year before the other left me. Try and remember while you can still see, so as to take something with you into the dark."

A novice brushed past me, "Be careful, the sister is watching you. We are not allowed to talk." I went to fetch more water from the well; and left the blind man listening for my voice.

A woman was sitting in the shade of the wall with a little boy across her lap; he cannot have been more than six years old though he had the face of an old man. She was no longer young, and even the weight of that wasted body must have been a difficult burden for her to carry up the steep hill. Her face was pale with the heat, and her shoulders were heavy with fatigue. Most of the other pilgrims called out for us to come to them, or tried somehow to attract our attention, but this woman seemed almost pathetic. None of the others took any notice of her, perhaps it was so long since they had been exhausted that they did not know how after endurance has made one reach a goal one often sits placidly, drained of ambition, empty of hope. I gave her a cup of water before I took the child from her. His leg was bound to a piece of wood with strips of dirty rag. There was no childishness in his face; his eyes were wide and full as a hare's, his skin clung to the bones of his skull as if it were trying to nourish itself on this meager skeleton. His mother would have followed me, but I told her to rest there until I came back. She gave me the blurred smile of extreme weariness, and her head jerked forward as she fell into sleep.

In a corner of the courtyard there was a stone bench under an old fig tree; a bough of its rough, heavy leaves hung down and shielded the rest of the sufferers from the child's sight. I had to fetch a knife to cut the rags, for the knots were hard with crusted blood and pus. I soaked the bandage with water to loosen it, and when I took it off a splinter of bone sloughed away with it. Where the knee should have been there was a pit of rotting flesh. The stench of decay rose from it, tangible as oily smoke. The child did not cry or whimper. He looked as though he had been born into pain, and long ago had found no cry was loud enough to drown the shrieking of his flesh. I cleansed his wound as best I could and then smeared it with salve. I knew that only a miracle could give him ease. I wondered if any of the nuns were near enough to the Christ they followed to have gained so great a measure of His teaching that they could heal nearly as strongly as He had healed. I plucked at the habit of a nun who was passing. ''Tell whomsoever among you can heal most powerfully that she is needed here.''

She looked at the wound, and said kindly, ''You have done well. There is nothing more you can do except put on the bandages—there is nothing more anyone can do.''

I was bewildered, then angry, ''Do you not think this child worthy of your healing? You profess to love God. How then can you deny the healing of His Son to this child?''

''What have I denied him?''

''The only power that will make his flesh whole again. You know as well as I do that salves cannot help this child. Heal him, or fetch someone who will!''

''I know what you feel, I was the same as you when I first did this work, but even if one of us were a physician, it would do no good.'' Then as though remembering her authority, ''But you must be stronger of stomach. You will soon learn to grow less queasy.''

''Do you think I asked you to send someone else because I wished to avoid putting on the salve and wrapping the bandages?''

She nodded, ''I have been too long in charge of novices to be deceived by them.''

I think it was only then that I realized it was not lack of compassion that made her withhold the power of healing, but ignorance of its existence. And I knew why, though I had been instructed in the use of salves and balms, I had been told nothing of the mysteries; it was because no one here knew that there were mysteries.

As I looked at her, saw her bland smile, saw that she thought she had outwitted me in a petty conceit, I forgot authority and said, ''You pitiable fool!''

The Olð Abbess

When I was summoned before the Abbess, she said, ''Have two days, locked in your cell without food, taught you that it is unwise to insult those who have been put in authority over you? I am sorry that you made it necessary for me to order this punishment.''

''I didn't mind it. I am used to being hungry—and they forgot to take away my water pitcher.''

I thought she would be angry, but she took no notice of my defiance. ''Why did you call her a fool—a pitiable fool? Come, my child, do not be afraid to tell me.''

I nearly lied to her. I was so afraid that she would not understand; and I knew that if I saw the same bewilderment in her eyes as I had seen in the nun's, it would always be a barrier between us. But I took courage from the compassion which surrounded her. ''It is so difficult to explain to anyone how I know things. I suddenly find that new knowledge has become a part of me, as though I had had over my eyes a veil which had been taken away, and I could see things which had been obscure to me before. When you first told me that the sick came here to be healed I thought it was only with salves and ointments. Then I realized that such things are only the outward form of a greater necessity. I saw life as a stream flowing down from the Most High, and knew that all living things are only a channel for this same life. I knew that when I sleep my body refreshes itself from these streams, and that weariness comes only when the body thirsts for them. It seemed I saw a vision of a great lake of sweet water, and to it came pilgrims who drank and were refreshed. Amongst them were those who carried a water jar on their shoulders; they filled the jar at the lake, and carried it back to others who could not reach to the source. They held the water, cupped in their hands, to the lips of those who thirsted; and with it they cleansed their wounds, and they were healed....

"Then in a dream I saw into a narrow room, where a woman lay on a bed and a man stood beside her. Beyond the bed, mourners were kneeling; for they thought she was dying. I saw the man stretch out his hand towards the woman. And down upon his head there shone a ray of light, a light of fiery particles like drops of bright water. I saw it flow down through his head; and from his hands and his forehead it flowed out upon the woman. I saw the shadow pass from her sunken lids, and warmth return to her skin. And when the mourners saw this thing they thought it a miracle, and they knelt before him and would have kissed his feet. But he raised them up, saying, 'I am not your Master, nor am I one of His pupils. I am one whom a pupil of His pupil trained to follow after Him. Remember, it is to the source of the stream that you should look in gratitude, and not to the channel that carries the water to the cistern in your garden.'"

The Abbess paused before she answered, "It is true, my child, that it is written how Jesus not only healed the sick and cleansed lepers, but taught others that they too should do these things."

"I thought that was what you were going to teach me here; that you were only waiting for me to show some special virtue before you considered me worthy."

"And we locked you up—because you had dared to tell us that we had forgotten our Master's words. I thought I had done so much, but we have forgotten how to follow our Teacher. We pray for His intercession, we wait for His miracles, but we do not remember how to perform them to His glory.''

''I am beginning to remember how to remember. Couldn't you find which of the novices and nuns dream strongly? Then we should know which of them had undergone priestly training in the past, and though they have been born into forgetfulness they could become lively with memory; the quick instead of the dead. You follow a Master whom you know as Jesus: His truth is the same truth that has illuminated Earth since its creation. Before I came here, I heard that in a country to the north there is a man who is spreading a new teaching for which he too claims Jesus as the authority. In Papal lands those who listen to him risk martyrdom for their faith: why do men destroy each other in the name of the Lord of Compassion? Why can't they realize that all who speak the truth speak in His voice? I lived long before He was born as Jesus, but in my land His teaching was alive, and His laws were the laws of the people. Then men did not fear death, for they knew it to be as familiar as sleep; then the sick were healed not only with salves but with life, and the parched were given water from the fountain of truth and went singing on their journey.''

''You seem so sure. How can you be so sure?''

''Because I can remember. How do I know that Lucia took the pox? Because I can remember it. It is the same memory, only longer.''

''But the rest of us have no memory, so of what use is the past to us?''

''If when I entered the convent I had forgotten my days as a strolling player, those days would still have played their part in shaping the real I. All of us remember yesterday when we wake in the morning, but only a few of us can remember the yesterdays when we are born again; for the way of a true priest is slow and difficult.''

''And perilous. To me you may talk, and together we may dream that our convent walls enclose a temple such

191

as you tell me of—but it must remain a dream.''

''Are you afraid of my heresy?''

''I have no knowledge of the past, and I can only believe in the future. Yet I know that though you follow a different teaching you are no heretic.... A strange dilemma, when the Abbess must confess her ignorance to a novice! You must think that I too am a pitiable fool.''

''I think you are wise, and beautiful, and good. I love you, and I honor you for your charity towards me and because there is that within you which is shining. Why am I never afraid to talk to you? Why are you so different from the others?''

''I am a very old woman, but I have never forgotten what it is to be young.''

''It is not only that. There is so much more....''

''A nun's life before she took her vows is kept secret, so I cannot tell you who I was when I lived in the world. But I will tell you something of my story....'' She signed to me to draw my stool close to her chair. ''I was thirty-five when I came here, and I came because there was nothing more I could hope for from the world. It is more than forty years since I was outside the gates, and yet I think I am still remembered. At first it was difficult to free myself from pride. The others were afraid of me when I came here, and they whispered that my dowry could have ransomed a reigning prince. They thought I had come here as a penance, and they would not believe I had come to learn how to do good instead of evil.

''The Order was much stricter then than it has been since it came under my rule. The nuns used to scourge themselves to their penances, or they fasted until they were near death. For a time I thought this was the way to attain to God. I wore a leather belt studded with spikes next to my skin; I used to stitch nettles into my shift, and sleep on a pillow filled with thistles. Whenever I remembered the indulgences I had permitted my flesh I took pleasure in tormenting it. I was proud, though I pretended to myself that this very pride was humility, to see how soon the nuns respected me for this self-hatred which they thought to be the outward manifestation of true piety. The scourge was sweet to me, and I gloried in my power to bear fleshly torments. I drove iron nails into the palms of my hands and into my feet, as though I were able to wear a crown of thorns. When the old Abbess died they appointed me her successor. Perhaps because they honored me, perhaps because our Order was poor and they knew I should be able to increase their lands.... I looked into my heart and found that I was barren of the peace I had come here to find....

"I forgot, I have not told you why I became a nun. I was born with all the worldly things that inspire envy; power, beauty, riches—I valued them, for I had no standard by which I could judge their worth. Then God took away the only thing I loved; He left me the rest, yet He left me nothing. No one, save God, knew how my heart had shriveled inside me, that I was already in Hell, though I still walked and breathed. I knew that there were only two ways open to me: I must find peace somewhere, a peace such as I had never seen in the world, or else try to forget the bitterness that was corroding me by becoming blinded with wealth, with power, with cruelty. I turned to religion, but I had always gone through the outward observances of the church for expedience, and it brought me no ease. I still believed that death, corruption, dust, was the end of all men. I was like a man starving in a forest—he sees berries growing on a tree, they may be poison, so for a time he dares not eat them; and only when he knows he may die of hunger does he pluck them in despair. I was such a one when I entered a convent. I was not radiant with faith nor confident of God's beneficence, but I had a slender thread of hope that I might learn how to reach my heart again—if it were true that my heart waited beyond death and had not been buried for ever in a tomb.

"For a time I even increased our strict observances. Then I

began to think of the things I had left undone in the world; of the sick I had not helped, and of the poor that my fore-riders had knocked aside to make way for me. If I had flung a coin to a beggar, it was only as a gesture; when I ordered a physician to be summoned for a servant's child it was not from compassion, but because it disturbed me to know that someone was dying in my palace, disturbed me as it would have done if I had known there was a dead mouse under the damask of my bed.

"These memories of what I had done, and left undone, came between me and my prayers, between me and my God. I realized that it is not enough to approach God as a suppliant or a worshipper—one must serve Him through serving His other children; I resolved that I should teach those who came under my care that there were other ways than prayers by which they must show themselves to be the servants of the Most High. Instead of causing pain to our own bodies we should heal the bodies of others, instead of striving after our own salvation we should seek to show the way of it to others. I forbade flagellation and all such practices; I said that though austerity was rightful for us it was an indulgence to destroy our usefulness by penitential fasts.

"Through the influence of my kinsmen the writings of the greatest physicians were sent to me. I enclosed more land, planted orchards, and gardens of medicinal plants. When I first ordered the gates of the outer courtyard to be opened twice every week so that the poor could come to us for succour, some of the nuns were afraid that God would send a pestilence to the convent as a punishment for our presumption. But in time they saw that it is better to bring comfort to lepers and give food to the hungry than it is to fear for one's own soul.... Are you a witch—or something of a saint, my child? How have you unlocked the secrets which have been shut away in my heart since long before you were born?"

"Because there is no need for secrets between us. We have known each other since a long time ago."

"I have given forty years of my life for the slender hope of immortality. Yet you, my little heretic, have suddenly made me sure that these forty years have not been paid in vain.... If he had not died you might have been my grand-daughter...."

I knelt beside her and took her hand. "He will be there, waiting for you. You are going to die very soon. You won't have to be old much longer. You may think I'm mad to know about these things. I don't know how I know...."

She covered my hand with her own. "You talk of my death as though you were promising me a great inheritance."

"I am. He who loves you is in heaven with Petruchio. You are fortunate to be so much older than I am, for very soon you will be with the one you love. Then, not only when you are asleep but all the time, you will be young and beautiful as you once were. One day he will say to you, 'My love, you need no longer leave me at the summons of the convent bell,'—and you will be so very happy. The nuns will gather in the chapel to wait for you, and after a time they will grow alarmed. One of them will come to this room to look for you; and she will find that only your body is here. They will light candles about your bier; and they will weep as they pray, for they think that death is a solemn thing. But I shall try to rejoice that you are free, and forget to sorrow because you are not here any more."

So when I heard the bell tolling for the dead, I knew for whom it lamented.

CHAPTER EIGHTEEN

Green Blood

The new Abbess was of the flesh of fanatics, gaunt, thin-lipped, the sharp bones of her cheek and jaw seeming to thrust forward against the sallow skin. Hatred had been sown between us at our only meeting. She had never been in charge of the novices, but once she had taken the place of our usual nun, who was ill, for three days. I had put a spray of hawthorn into my water-pitcher, because I found that to look at flowers as I was going to sleep helped me to leave my body smoothly—it seemed that I had done this in the past, when I had been the girl with the lotus. When this woman saw it, she had taken the branch between her thin, cruel hands, breaking the stem, crushing the white petals, savagely, as though she delighted in their destruction. When I had tried to stop her she had ordered me a day's fast, and had told me that if again I took flowers into my cell I should be much more severely punished.

A few days after she assumed office I went to the cloister garden with a message for Sister Ignatia. When I saw what she was doing I thought for a moment that she must be possessed. She was tearing down a vine from the cloister wall; and round her, uprooted shrubs were already wilting in the heat. Then I saw that tears were trickling down her face. There was a smear of sap on her hand; she tried to rub it off with the sleeve of her habit. There was horror in her eyes as she saw the green stain. She might have been a murderess trying to cleanse herself of reluctant blood. I ran along the path to her, ''Sister Ignatia, what are you doing?''

She stared at me, dully, uncomprehendingly. "Destroying what it has taken me twenty years to build. Their blood is on my hands—green blood."

"But why? What has happened? I don't understand...."

"The new Abbess has decreed that flowers are a vanity of the flesh—there are to be no flowers in our enclosure, no beauty, nothing any more."

"Don't listen to her. She is wicked, cruel, evil. We will all refuse to obey her. I'm not afraid of her—none of us must be afraid of her."

"We cannot rebel. It must be God's will that He has placed her in authority over us—but my obedience is difficult, for her righteousness seems blasphemy."

"It is blasphemy. It is right that we should rebel...."

"Hush, my child, you and I must obey without questioning the authority."

"We should question it. That is what authority is for. To be questioned, and questioned, and always to be able to give the true answer. If it can't, it is no longer an authority which should be obeyed."

"It is not for women to fight crusades. And yet I have fought to protect my little green children. The snails were armored warriors who rode against them; the massed heathen tribes poured from the ant hills; wire worms ran siege tunnels among their roots and the black rust tried to poison them with its counsel of despair. I fought so hard against these enemies—but I am too old to fight for them against so powerful an adversary."

She picked up a broken rose bush; she might have been a mother picking up a child that had fallen and hurt itself. "See how strong he is, like a little tree. I remember him when he was only a shoot; I was a midwife to his mother for I cut him from her side. How eagerly I awaited his first bud. He was shy to unfold it, and I tried not to be impatient. Would it be red, or white? It was white, even the doves were ivory beside it. Every year I have counted the increase of his buds. He has never been so beautiful as he would have been this year. There would have been two hundred and five roses—surely even the angels would have paused in their flight to look at them.'' She tried to smile through her tears. "Forgive me, my child, I should be stronger in my faith. Perhaps this grief has been sent to punish me for being over fond of the earth. Even in my prayers I used to remind God which of my plants was sick, which of them was so beautiful that even He must come to see it. I thought He would understand, but I have made Him angry. I thought of Him as the great gardener, who looks after us when we are little and then teaches us to grow strong. Even the tribulations He sends us seemed like the winter snows which bring a spring blossoming to the alpine meadows....''

''He *is* like that. I am sure he hates the new Abbess as much as I hate her. She is cruel, and narrow, and ungodly....''

''Quiet, quiet! Someone will hear you, and you will be whipped for blasphemy. Forgive me for disturbing you with my frailities. Now go, my child, and leave me. I must ask Him who made them, how to tell my little green children why their foster-mother has become their destroyer.''

the Apricot

The new Abbess was like a miasma, a blight, a pestilence that poisoned our days. She seemed to delight in finding new ways to make us unhappy, and she tried to make us feel ourselves the children of sin. We were no longer allowed to speak to each other except to ask for necessities. When I was first punished for breaking this rule I asked her, ''If God meant man to be dumb why did He not leave us without the art of words, as He left the animals?'' To this question my only answer was an order to spend my next three nights on my knees in the chapel, and my days locked in my cell. To her, pleasure—even the most innocent—was a sin, and in her ears laughter was a hellish carillon. We were forbidden to run, but must walk soberly with lowered eyes, and I have heard a girl punished for watching a butterfly, or pausing in her work to listen to a thrush.

Our food had always been simple but it had been plentiful; now there was never enough of it to satisy our hunger. Though the bread was still baked twice a week, it was stored away until it was stale, or moldy, before it was given to us. Even in the coldest weather the broth was never hot; it had a clammy warmth under the congealed fat that clung to the side of the bowl. It was easier for me than for most of the others, for they had never had to learn what it feels like to go hungry. The nun who shared our meals in the refectory was fat and kindly, and I knew she was often ashamed to ladle out such meager portions. But she was too used to the habit of obedience to protest.

We were told that God watched us to record our sins, and I think many of the novices thought of Him as an omniscient eye that stared unwinkingly at them to count their little transgressions of the code laid down for them. At first I tried to foster a spirit of rebellion in the others, but they were afraid to listen and I think most of them began to look on me as a temptation placed amongst them by Satan. I became very scornful of their slavish obedience, and took a mischievous pleasure in plucking at their fears.

It had been the custom when the fruit was in season for the novices to be given a share of it, but now it was all exchanged for bread to give to the poor. Even the refectory garden had been changed. The grass paths between the plots had been cut away and the ground was divided with the orderly precision of a cemetery. Even the herbs were not allowed to share their bed with each other; but bees defeated this virginal device, and took lovers' messages from hellebor to madder, centaury to balm. Many varieties of fruit trees were crucified on the high walls: at this season the apricots were ripe; so golden with their sweetness that it seemed they must keep their sunny warmth all through the night and glow in the darkness. One of the novices, I never liked her, she was fat and stupid, ate one of them. She had always been hungry, even when our meals had been good, and I think she found the fruit in her mouth before she realized what she was doing. She was seen by the nun in charge, for now we worked under constant supervision, and was kept without food for two days and then whipped for stealing.

When she came back to us she was always weeping and muttering her prayers, and at last I got her to tell me what was the matter. "I am so very wicked. I have sinned like Eve— Eve stole an apple and God was so angry that He cursed all women because she had been a thief. If He did that to Eve for an apple He's sure to do something terrible to me for stealing an apricot. The Abbess says that Eve was destroyed by the Serpent of Evil Knowledge, and the same serpent may destroy me!"

"Don't be a fool, Octavia. Don't you believe what the Abbess tells you. She's a wicked and ignorant woman."

Her mouth fell open and she crossed herself. "Carola, that's heresy, and blasphemy, and—and—" I finished the sentence for her, "Common sense."

She crossed herself again, twice so as to make sure. "You mustn't talk to me any more, Carola. It is very wicked to try to destroy people's faith."

I laughed at her. "Never mind, Octavia, even if you never speak to me again, I promise to warn you when I see the serpent coming for you. I expect they have different-sized serpents for different people. There may be a huge, silver serpent coiled up under the pumpkin leaves, waiting for you when you have to go past them; or there may be a little green one among the lettuces, waiting to snap at your fingers; or a very long, thin, brown one lying along the bough of a cherry tree, waiting to drop down your neck."

She burst into angry tears. "You're wicked and hateful, and I think you're a witch."

"If I'm a witch, when you meet the snake you had better say, 'What is your name?' If it coils up on the path and looks at you, as I'm looking at you, you'll know it's me. I often change myself into a snake when I am by myself at night so that I can wriggle out through the grating and go for walks. I shouldn't tell anybody, or they may beat you for telling lies, and think that you believe in sorcery."

"Oh! Oh! Oh!" She couldn't think of anything to say, so she gathered up her clumsy skirts and ran away from me down the path as fast as if I were an overturned bee-skep.

Beatrice

One day, when we were weeding the orchard, I found myself next to a new novice. If there had not been a stain, like the lees of wine, on her right cheek, she would have been beautiful; her brown hair was glossy, and her lips were full and red—a mouth made for love rather than austerity. She had the cell next to mine, and I knew she was unhappy, for in the night I often heard her sobbing. I had learned a way of talking as though I were mumbling in prayer, looking straight in front of me or at my work, but this was the first time I had been near enough to whisper to her. "Don't look at me, Sister Margarita is watching but she can't hear us. What's your name? Mine is Carola."

"Beatrice. Are you sure it's safe to talk?"

"Safe enough. Anyway, Margarita is deaf, at least she pretends to be—perhaps it is only because she's sorry for us."

"Do you hate being here? Are you unhappy too?"

"I hate the Abbess. It was quite different before she came. Can't you manage to get taken away?"

She tried to brush away a tear and left a smear of earth on

her cheek. "My parents will never allow it. My mother hates me, she is ashamed of this terrible birthmark on my face. I was never allowed to go out with my sisters because she said it would spoil their chance of a rich suitor. I didn't mind really, at least not very much. But then I fell in love with someone who my Father said would be an unfavorable alliance, and I said I should marry him however much they forbade it. And the next day they brought me here. Oh! I'm so miserable." She was so moved that she forgot her caution, but Margarita was nodding sleepily and did not notice us. "His name is Fernando. I met him when he came to paint a fresco for the loggia in the house we go to in the hot weather. I had been sent there with my old nurse; I suppose Father forgot Fernando would be there too. Fernando is so handsome! He has a little golden beard, and he is much taller than I am and he writes poems almost as well as he paints. He loves me so much! He did not even mind my scar. I used to try and keep that side of my face turned away from him in case it hurt him to see it; and he said, 'If one petal of a rose is crushed it only smells the sweeter,' so I wasn't ashamed of it any more. I thought I was going to marry him—I knew he was poor and not of a noble family but I thought my Mother would be glad to see me married and away from her. I don't think she would have stopped us, but my father is very proud and he said that Fernando should have been flogged for his presumption. And I was locked in my room and we were not even allowed to say good-bye. And my sisters scolded me for trying to bring disgrace on the family. I prayed to die but God wouldn't listen—He doesn't want me—no one wants me except Fernando and I'll never see him again...."

"Poor Beatrice! But don't despair. They may change their minds...."

"They will never change—they've told every one that I have always had a vocation. I shall live here all my life. If I am very unlucky I may live to a great age—and then I'll be all alone, for even the memory of Fernando will have gone."

Less than a month later, among the poor that came to have their wounds tended I saw a boy of about fourteen who, in spite of his rags in which he was dressed, looked as though he had known hunger only in the guise of a good appetite. He stared at Beatrice, and she recognized him, for she flushed and looked quickly away. I went up to the boy and asked what I could do to help him.

He began to tell me how he suffered great agony in his stomach, "as if a viper, and a mother viper with a nest of young ones at that, had taken up her lodging in my bowls." He clutched his stomach and groaned most realistically, but I felt sure that it was only a pretense to gain entry to the convent, so I whispered to him, "You are a fine actor, I hope you are as good a messenger! You have a message, haven't you, for Beatrice? You can give it to me, I am her friend." As he still seemed uncertain whether to trust me, I said, "Is it from Fernando?"

He nodded, and still miming the sufferer, said, "Fernando has at last found where they put her. He believes that she loves him and is here against her will. Is this true? Do you know her heart?" I whispered that she dearly loved Fernando. He went on, "Fernando will wait outside the wall, at any point you tell him and at any time. He has two fast horses and man's clothes for her to wear. They will ride to the next town where a priest will be ready to marry them."

I said, "Listen carefully. Tell him to wait at the southeast corner of the convent wall from dusk until midnight three days from now. If she does not come he must wait for her every night until I can arrange her escape. Go now, someone may be watching us."

I did not have a chance to talk to Beatrice until late that afternoon, while we were raking rotten leaves and carrying them in flat rush baskets to the corner of the garden where the pumpkins grew. Beatrice was eager, yet fearful. She had been brought up to be a piece of mosaic in the pattern of her family, and had never had to make an important decision for herself: I think she had made such a stark picture of a lonely future, in which she would live on her memories of Fernando, that she was startled to find that he was a reality. When I told her that he would wait for her at dusk she said, ''But Carola, we are locked in our cells. I couldn't get to him then. I shall never be able to get to him from this hateful place!''

She began to sob, and I said, ''Stop crying! You behave as though you needed a wet nurse instead of a lover! Do you think I have forgotten we are locked in at night? That's exactly why I have chosen that time. The sisters go to their cells to rest before the Night Office and none of them will be in the garden.''

''But how will that help us if we are locked in?''

''You will be in your cell, but I shall be in the chapel. I shall confess some little sin to Sister Catherina; I shall have to choose carefully and judge her humor, for it would be very annoying if I got solitary confinement when what I want is penitential prayer in the chapel! I must be careful not to tell anything that is *true* or I shall be whipped for blasphemy! Don't worry, I shall be in the chapel the night after to-morrow. I have been punished for so many words since I have been here that now my tongue can judge phrase and punishment with as great a nicety as a wine-taster can judge a vintage.''

''I am very stupid,'' said Beatrice, ''but I still can't see how it is going to help me.''

''The nun who keeps the key of the cells, Margarita, the fat one that wheezes when she walks, doesn't go to her cell before the Night Office. She sits up in a chair in the refectory—I am nearly sure she does this every night because I have had three nights' penitential prayer this month and she has always been there. She sleeps so heavily that one day when I crept in to try to find something to eat I could have tweaked the hairs out of her beard before she heard me. The keys have been on the table each time, for she unties her girdle when she wants to settle herself down and thinks no one will see her. I'll get the keys, let you out of your cell, and lock the door behind you. In the morning, when they find a locked door and an empty cell, they will probably believe a devil came to claim his own in the night. It's a pity we haven't got a little brimstone to burn there so as to lend a touch of authority to the story! Would you like to be remembered in history as the bride of Lucifer?''

The next two days seemed interminably long. I was afraid that everyone who saw Beatrice would guess her secret, for she looked as if she were a bride already—but not a bride of Christ. I found that I had not over-judged my reading of Sister Catherina, and by the time the other novices were locked into their cells I had been safely on my knees in the chapel for two hours. When all was quiet, I took off my sandals and crept along the passage to the door of the refectory, but though Margarita was nodding she was not yet proclaiming her absence. At last, when I was almost despairing I heard first the wheezes, and then the beat and rhythm of her snores.

The keys chinked on their ring as I picked them up. She stirred, but only settled deeper in her chair.

The day before, I had quietened the lock of Beatrice's cell with a feather dipped in oil, but it still creaked when I turned it. The passage was very dark, and we had to feel our way along by the wall. There was a small breeze, and the leaves rustled furtively in the shadows. Water was dripping from the lip of a cistern, the drops clicking like the beads of a rosary. When we reached the orchard we picked up the long skirts of our habits and ran as fast as we could over the rough furrows. I gave a low whistle and a rope ladder was thrown over the wall. I kissed Beatrice and told her to hurry.

The last I ever saw of her was silhouetted against the night sky, before she jumped down into the arms of her lover.

The excitement flickered out of me. I felt cold, and alone—perhaps a little frightened. I picked two of the last pears, like bronze among their lemon-colored leaves, partly because I was hungry, partly as a small defiance. It was fortunate that I did so, for Margarita woke up when I was returning the keys, and she might not have believed me when I told her that I had been robbing the orchard if I had not been able to show her the pear I had not yet eaten. She must have been very sleepy and thought that she was dreaming, for she neither punished me herself nor reported me to the Abbess. I wondered if it had been laziness or kindness that prompted her indulgence, or whether, deep down under her unnecessary flesh, she remembered what it was like to be young.

We were told that Beatrice had been taken ill in the night; and that her family had come to fetch her away. Did the nuns think she had been carried off by Satan, or by a mortal lover?

The Ant

Beatrice was the only novice with whom I had felt even a shadow of friendship. I had tried to bridge the gap between myself and the others, but they remained hostile and suspicious. As Carola, I had never met such people before; there seemed to be no reality in them, they were like marionettes putting on a semblance of life, or actors' masks miming a bloodless vitality. I have never known women who had been brought up as they had been, though I had watched them in the distance, walking on the terraces of my father's castle, or riding in their carrying-litters through the streets. I had always thought that they would have had much to talk of; for to their houses came travelers from far countries, men of affairs, musicians, poets, so they would have plenty for their minds to feed on, and shelter in which such talents as they possessed might grow. But I found them so very stupid; small, spiteful, with wit not even tinsel bright.

There was no mirror in the convent, and we were supposed to take no heed of our appearance except in the strict neatness of our habit. When Murilla broke out in boils, not bad enough for the nuns to count her ill but very disfiguring, the others teased her about them until she wept with humiliation. They had not even the honest cruelty of the gutter urchins, they would wait until she was listening and then whisper slyly, ''How beautiful is Octavia's skin, not a blemish on all its perfection. Is it not beautiful, Murilla?'' Another girl would join in, ''Oh, we must not ask Murilla's opinion—she is above the vanities of the flesh.'' Then they would giggle together like kitchen wenches. There was no robustness in them, not even in their cruelty. Their words had not the keenness of a rapier nor the coarse weight of a bludgeon, but were like red-hot bodkins that never inflicted a fatal wound, but brought little sores that festered, and spread, and poisoned.

I wondered how Lucia would have fared if she had come here with me, Lucia as she had been when I first knew her. Would she have been able to teach them her broad humanity, or would they have worn down her strength like a low fever? I think if she could have lived here for a week she would have been less intolerant of men. She used to say, ''Men are like children. Even when their beards are grey they are still urchins brawling on a dung heap. Their love of pomp, and bombast, and glittering armies, is only the love of dressing up that children have. Men seldom escape from their own childishness, and there will be no peace in the world until women rule.'' If she had been here under the old Abbess she might have thought our life the proof of her words, but under the new one she would have seen how cruel can be the rule of women.

I remembered my vision in the mountains, and knew that away from earth my long past waited for me, all the people I had been were near to me, were ready to enter into me. Yet if I had courage, there must also be the time when I was a coward, for courage is the overcoming of cowardice; if I was generous I had been miserly—or so it seemed; if I was kind I had once been cruel; if I had sympathy I had been callous.

With Petruchio and my mother, even with the old abbess, it was that part of me which would one day join in the ultimate conquering which had shown in my eyes. I had been able to withstand the hatred of Donna Isabella, terror, loneliness, the pox; for these had been open enemies whose very presence had brought forth my courage to engage them in conflict. But man does not draw his sword to slay an ant, though the ant may sting his foot and make him lame.

Since I had teased Octavia, the novices thought that I was a witch and shrank away from me. Even when I passed them in the cloister they brushed against the wall lest the hem of my habit should touch theirs. When we were weeding a strip of ground we worked in a long row, but there was always a space left on either side of me. They used to stare at me, and cross themselves as if to ward off the Evil Eye. In a hundred little ways they tormented me. I would find the plants in the plot I tended wrenched from their careful line, and pushed carelessly into the earth so they wilted; I found the water-pot I carried on my shoulder cracked so that the water trickled out and soaked my habit; they hid my hoe in the melon patch so that I should be punished for losing it.

I had been foolish enough to tell something of my story to one of them when I first came to the convent, for she had seemed eager to be friendly. Now they whispered legends about the Griffin, malicious, stupid. Sometimes at night I used to hear their words fluttering round my cell, like blind white moths. ''The Griffin is scarlet, because it is drenched with blood.... She danced naked at fairs.... They showed her in a booth with the other monstrosities.... They say that the Griffins are vampires, murderers.... She can change herself into a snake, a snake.... When they find out what she is they will burn her...burn her...burn her.'' Then Sofia's voice above the flames, ''Don't, don't, don't.'' I could feel my heart hard and tight within me, withered as a last year's walnut. My eyelids felt hot and full with tears that were unshed because Octavia had the next cell and would hear me if I cried.

A new piece of land had been enclosed, and after the wall had been built a door was cut into it from the orchard. The earth had never been tilled, and it was rank with briars and nettles. It became a favorite punishment to make novices clear so many spans with their bare hands and only a wooden hoe to break the hard ground. One day I was working there alone among the nettles. They were like a forest of spears against me, and when I grasped them firmly others brushed against me to sear my hands. Near me there was a little thorn bush, and under its shelter a patch of turf was smooth and green. I saw that a square of it had withered, where the sod had been cut out and then replaced. Where it joined the growing turf there was a cyclamen half uprooted. Its leaves turned back like the outstretched palms of a beggar in supplication. I carried it to a safe corner and fetched water to refresh its roots. I had left my hoe lying on the turned patch, and when I came back to fetch it I heard Octavia's voice say, ''We've caught her!'' She had been lurking in a shadow of a wall buttress and from behind a clump of brambles came her three friends. She turned to them triumphantly, ''I told you she killed Beatrice with her filthy sorcery. I said I could prove it to you for I knew that a witch had to return to the grave of her victim.'' She pointed at me, ''Murderess!''

I looked at her coldly, steadily, ''A pretty story, Octavia; I am surprised that you had the intelligence to think of it.'' I pointed to the withered turf, ''Is this her grave? You must have cut her up into very small pieces, for I could span it with my two hands.''

She came a step nearer to me, ''It's no good trying to lie! We've caught you!'' The others chimed in, ''Yes, we have. Octavia said it was Beatrice. Now we know it was.''

I picked up the hoe, ''I will open her grave and see what she looks like.'' One of them gave a thin scream, ''No! No!''

I said, ''Are you too squeamish? You say I killed Beatrice,

209

and that you buried her. My thanks to you; most murderers are not so fortunate in their friends as to have their crimes so ably concealed. I have no memory of this crime. Perhaps her body will serve to remind me of the circumstance.''

They stood huddled together as I turned over the turf. Under it the earth had been disturbed. There were some withered flowers, and then something wrapped in a torn shift. I pulled aside the wrappings and saw the decomposed body of a snake. I shook my head in mock pity, ''Poor Beatrice! I should never have recognized her as the girl I knew. Not only a snake, but a dead snake! How very unfortunate for her.'' Then my voice hardened, ''Now it is my turn to question. You buried Beatrice and I dig up a snake. What have you done with her? You say I killed her, you must have seen her dead. Where is she?''

The others shrank back and pushed Octavia forward as their spokesman. She was flushed with excitement as she pointed at the dead snake. ''You know that's Beatrice. We saw you whispering to her, just like you tried to whisper to me, but poor Beatrice was foolish and listened to you. You taught her how to change herself into a snake and wriggle out through the grating. Then you were frightened she was going to betray you, so you changed yourself back again and killed her as she was trying to get back into her cell. They burn witches! I shall be glad when you are burned!''

I realized what had started this fantasy, my teasing of Octavia after she had eaten the apricot. I laughed. ''Where did you find my poor friend?''

''You know where we found her, under her window. The stone was still lying on her head where you had crushed it in. That was clever of you. Even we know that a witch must take a birth-mark with her when she changes her form, and if you had not crushed her head there would have been a red stain on the snake to prove your guilt.''

Until then I had only been scornful of their stupidity, but suddenly I felt anger pouring into me. Octavia must have seen my eyes change for she shrank back.   As I started towards her the others fled down the path uttering shrill little cries, but I knew they would not dare to tell the nuns that they had left their work without permission. I caught up with Octavia and forced her to her knees. When she tried to scream I gagged her with my girdle. In the struggle her coif fell off, and grasping her by the hair, I dragged her towards the nettle bed. I flung her down among them, for she was flabby as a sack of meal. As she cringed at my feet I said, "As I am a witch you shall be my familiar, Octavia. Your first duty will be to pluck all those nettles with your bare hands."

She was too terrified to disobey me. I sat down in the shade of the wall and watched her. Long before she finished she was sobbing with pain, and her cheeks and forehead were blistered where the nettles had lashed her across the face. When the patch was cleared I made her kneel down in front of me. Before I untied her gag I turned over a stone and picked up a wood-louse. "Look carefully at this wood-louse, Octavia, for it was someone who betrayed me. I was feeling magnanimous at the time, so instead of destroying her I turned her into this crawling dweller under stones. See, she is quite powerless. I have but to close my hand and she will be only a dirty smear." I flexed my fingers and pretended to consider, before, saying, "I think I shall let her live to-day. But do not try to disobey me, Octavia—I think that within you there is the promise of an ant."

CHAPTER NINETEEN

Snow In heaven

Sister Francesca was the only nun with whom I felt an unspoken bond of friendship. There was a strange remoteness about her, as though she belonged to a company of different flesh than ordinary women. Her eyes were the clear, remote blue of the sky washed clean by a storm, and her skin seemed to share the quality of white flowers at dusk, as though in the dark it would still reflect the light.

One day I saw her coming from the bake-house carrying a heavy wooden tray, piled with loaves of black bread. The sweat stood out on her forehead as if she were in pain, but when I tried to take the tray away from her she shook her head and hurried along the cloister. I saw she was ill, so I followed her into the empty refectory. She managed to put down the tray on one of the long benches. For a minute she stood upright, then fell as a tree falls when the axe has conquered it.

I untied her girdle and loosened the heavy folds of her habit. Then through her coarse shift I saw the springing curve of her belly. I was frightened that someone might come into the room and surprise her secret, so before I went to get water to bathe her forehead I reknotted her girdle.

When I returned I chafed her delicate wrists, and tried to send my thoughts to comfort her. It seemed a long time before she stirred. When she tried to sit up, I said, ''Don't be frightened. There is no one else here. You have fainted, and must rest for a little while.'' She lay back and closed her eyes. ''I am your friend and will not betray you. I am going to help you escape from this prison of hypocrisy. You *must* believe me.'' Her eyes, the shadowed, withdrawn eyes of a nightmare-ridden child, stared up at me—I went on, ''Yes, I know your secret. I am so glad I know it, for you must need a friend—as I do. You mustn't let the nuns make you afraid. You must go back into the world where men and women are real people, not weary puppets moved by the rope that tolls the bell for office." I heard someone approaching. "Quick! You mustn't be found like this or there will be questions...."

I managed to lift her to her feet, and when Sister Margarita came into the room, she was leaning on the table, seeming to watch me putting the bread in orderly rows as though she were afraid I might try to steal some of it.

I did not have another chance to talk to Francesca alone until the following day. I had been working in the garden, trying to break the heavy earth, still chained by frost, into furrows for the early sowing. Massing clouds were hastening the dusk when I met her in the cloister. She signed to me to follow her into the deserted chapel, then whispered that I was to kneel beside her as though we were in prayer. The chapel door always creaked when it was opened so I knew we were secure from being overheard. She looked round her to make sure we were alone. Then she seemed to take courage, "Last night I dreamed that you came into my cell. There was a light about you, and at first I thought I was seeing an angelic vision and fell on my knees in piety. Then you smiled at me and said, "It is I, Carola, the novice to whom you have entrusted your secret. You are dreaming too. Come, take my hand and I will lead you back into the past where I can prove our friend-ship...." Then I knew that I was a boy and you were a young knight of the third crusade. When you rode into battle I ran at your stirrup. The ground stank of death. I was afraid. Then the scene changed. Now it was I who rode the tired horse, and you were leading it through a barren valley, a valley of parched rocks and stunted thorn-trees. You had put off your armor and your surcoat was stained with rusty blood. Thirst was our enemy, and the pitiless sun; and in the sky death wheeled on ominous wings.... Years passed. Now we were in a different country, a country of kindly earth and watermeads, and you were old. Your wife and daughter wept that you were dying. But it was to me, your friend, that you last smiled. Why did I have this dream? Tell me, for I am bewildered by my own thoughts.''

''I but came to remind you why you may trust me. Now we wear a different armor, our enemies are unseen; they cry the air like carrion birds, ignorance curves their claws and fear their beaks. We have no castle to hold a siege, no swords of Damascus steel: we have only a little knowledge to dwell in, and a little friendship to shield our loneliness. Tell me of Francesca, for yesterday she and Carola met as strangers.''

And then Francesca told me her story. ''I was an only child, and my mother died when I was very young. My father had loved her so dearly that he took no other woman into his life, and he tried to forget his sorrows by filling his thoughts with the strategies of worldly affairs. Youth was not in our house, and my nurse was strict and would not let me play with the servant's children. The youngest son of the family whose land joined ours was near my age. The falconer who rode with him was kinsman to my nurse, perhaps more than kinsman, and every day they met in the forest. Guillimo and I played together, and neither of us wished for any other companion. When I was fourteen we were betrothed, and there were no shadows over our days. We were to have been married on the day I was fifteen. But, before I became his wife, Guillimo had to ride to the wars in the train of his uncle. He was taken prisoner of Milan, and for three years I waited news of him. Whenever I heard a horseman ride into the courtyard I thought it was his messenger. I was so sure he was alive that with my women I stitched at my bridal clothes, and with his wolfhound beside me I tarried in the glades that we had known.

''Then they told me he was dead; some said by poison, some said by a dagger. There was no sun and no moon any more. I lived in twilight as though I were already a ghost. No tears came to cool my heart, though I prayed that the compassion of the Holy Mother should bring them to my ease.

My father told me that in a convent I might find assuaging peace; and so I came here, to wait for death to fulfil my betrothal vows. But prayers did not release me, and the old Abbess taught me that there is no escape from life save by living it. Soon after my novitiate was completed there was a visitation of plague in the city. On my body the blue swellings would have had the beneficence of stigmata; yet though I saw many die who longed to live, the plague watched me, mocking, aloof, and left me unclaimed.

"Gradually I learned some measure of tranquillity. One day I was sent to answer the summons to the bedside of a dying child. When I entered the town by the Old Gate the snows were falling to bless the new year. The clouds were pigeon-grey, and the flakes fell upon me in gentleness. I followed a narrow alley in the shadow of the town wall; my feet made no sound on the drifts, and the shutters were closed, for the people kept their houses against the cold. I saw a cloaked figure approaching. He stood aside to let me pass....

"I thought it strange there should be snow in heaven. When I had walked through the gates of Paradise why had I seen no angel guarding them? In Guillimo's eyes I saw the same thoughts. I was afraid to touch him, lest it might be that angels had no substance. But he was braver than I....

"I heard a street vendor crying his wares. We drew apart. The world closed in about us. As I moved I heard the clicking of my rosary....and remembered I was a prisoner of my vows; knew that the only dowry I could bring my lover was death, for the Papal Authority shows no clemency to a man that robs Christ of a bride. I entreated him to leave me, but he would not listen. He took me into the little house where lived his foster-mother. She was away and the room was empty. He threw fresh faggots on the smoldering ashes, and we sat together in the firelight as we had used to do in the hut of a friendly woodcutter in the winter forest.

"He told me what had befallen him since I had watched him ride away. He had been kept prisoner for nearly seven years, and when he had all but despaired of freedom, the old Duke died, and he was released when the son unlocked the father's dungeons. He was so sure that he would find me waiting for him. But when he rode into the courtyard he saw that the grass grew between the flagstones before a deserted house. An old servant told him that my father was dead, and death had marked me for her own before ever I went into the convent, and I must long since have gone beyond the reach of priest or lover. Then Guillimo came to Perugia to see his foster-mother, who used to live in our village, in hope of news of me.

"He pleaded with me to ride with him to France. If it had been only my own soul that I should have condemned to hell it would have been a small price for a few years of his company. But he would have followed me to the eternal torment. At last I made him believe that we could not find our heaven upon earth, and I must live out my life in the half-world to which I had vowed myself. I told him that he must remember our meeting only as a vision of the future, and think of me as having returned from beyond the grave with fond assurances that I awaited him in heaven.

"His voice was so much clearer than my vows, and I was eager for a memory to cherish me through the long, lonely years. It was dawn before we said our last farewells; and we had lain together, in simplicity."

Desperate Concealment

I think the Madonna cannot have been more joyous than was Francesca that she should bear a child. There was about her a strange tranquillity that seemed to protect her from the fear of discovery, and she discussed our plans for the birth as calmly as if she had been instructing a midwife who would deliver her in her husband's house. I was glad that I had lived among people to whom the cycle of birth was common knowledge, for if I had not been able to count the months for her she would not have known when her child would be ready for the world. Since Lucia's miscarriage I had seen another baby born, it was to the wife of an inn-keeper with whom Petruchio and I were lodging. It had been an easy birth, for it was her fifth child, but she had moaned and cried out until her frightened husband was calling on the saints for pity.

Near the nuns' burial place there was a mound which covered what must have once been part of an old crypt. Here had been built a penitential cell shaped like a coffin, so that the one who was shut into it should think of herself as already dead and so repent more intensely of her sins. It was a rare punishment for a novice to be shut in there, but I had already experienced it. Even at midday it had been like living under the sea, for only a dim green light crept though the encroaching weeds which covered the grating in the roof. I had been there when winter was pitilessly cold; the cell had been empty save for a heap of moldly straw, and the damp floor was slippery with ice.

It was a strange place to choose for a woman to be confined, but it had what to us was the greatest of all necessities, secrecy. It was not unusual for a nun to go there for retreat, sometimes for a week, sometimes for longer, as a self-inflicted penance. She would not attend the services in the chapel or have communication with the other nuns. Every second day a small loaf and a pitcher of water were set on the ledge outside the judas, and on the last day of the prescribed period the cell door was unlocked when the nuns went to rest before the midnight office so that the penitent could return to her own cell. We decided that when this day of her release came, Francesca would wake the nun who had the key of the outer gate, telling her that it was because she had been ordered to go into town. If she carried a basket it would cause no comment; but this time the cloth which covered it would conceal not bread nor healing ointment but a new-born child. Francesca seemed quite confident that she would have the strength to walk to Perugia and return before dawn, and that by the time the convent gate closed behind her again her child would be in the arms of Guillimo's foster-mother.

I should not be able to reach the door of the cell, for the passage that led to it was closed by a gate of iron bars which was always kept locked. But the grating which opened into the cell was hidden by a thicket of elder bushes; I found that the plaster which held it in place had begun to crumble, and after working at it for several days with a rusty nail I managed to loosen it sufficiently to lift it clear. It was not large enough for me to climb through, but I could lower things down into the cell; and as I still worked with those who tended the sick, it was not difficult for me to steal rags which I hid until they should be needed.

The summer was very hot but the plague did not visit Perugia, and for many weeks no summons came for a nun to go into town. When we had almost begun to despair of getting a message to Guillimo's foster-mother, a call to go to a child dying of the pox was answered by Francesca. I had been so afraid that she might find that the foster-mother had gone away and that our careful plans were defeated, but as soon as I saw her after her return I knew that all was well.

''Francesca, has she agreed to our plans?''

''Yes. She is a brave woman; I warned her it would be dangerous to harbor a nun's child even for a day. But she only smiled and said, 'He will be my foster-grandson. My arms are for his protection and my house is to shelter him.' She told me that every week a messenger came to her from Guillimo in case word for him had come from me. He has well provided her with money, and as soon as I take the child to her she will hire a litter and set forth immediately to him.''

''Can't you go with them?''

''No, Carola, I have taken vows and I must hold to them though I have found in my love for Guillimo a blossoming of the spirit such as never came to me through cloistered austerity.''

"Your place is in the world with your child and husband. How can Guillimo bear to live knowing that you are shut away by these convent walls; that your heart longs for him as his does for you?"

"He will not think of me here. His foster-mother will tell him that I died when the child was born. It is better so, for then he will think of me as being tranquil in heaven, content to wait there until he joins me, and he will be able to rejoice in his child without sorrowing for its mother."

"Some of the nuns are very old, Francesca. You may live here alone more than fifty years."

"Through my child I shall live in the world. He will be very splendid; he will be tall, and strong with a bright chivalry. He will be in the likeness of his father, for so I have fashioned him; but he will have my eyes, and through them I shall see Guillimo and in them he shall see my love. I have kept fear away from me for he must be created only of joy, and I shall give the happiness I have never known to him for a birth gift. There will be a spring of laughter in his heart to refresh him when he has to pass through weary days. He will have the mind of a poet and through him my lover's thoughts shall be burnished into words. He will have the eyes of a painter for he must see the beauty of the world twice, for himself and for me. One day he will marry and his wife will love him even as I loved his father and they will have children in joy together."

nativity

In the second week in September Francesca went into the penitential cell. My fear of her being discovered had increased during the last weeks, for I felt that several of the nuns were watching us with suspicion. Sometimes I thought she would betray herself by the intense inward joy that shone in her eyes, but if the others noticed they must have thought it a sign of some heavenly beatitude. We were careful never to speak to each other except when we were alone and I found it increasingly more difficult to escape from supervision.

Every day I managed to avoid their vigilance long enough to reach the grating into her cell and find out how she was. The first five days she said she felt no change, and we began to fear that she had gone into the cell too soon, but on the sixth day she told me that her birth pangs had begun. I lay on the ground and saw her smiling up at me through the twilight. She walked up and down, up and down. Sometimes, when the pain gripped her yet more fiercely, she leaned against the wall for support, but she did not groan, or cry out. I asked her, ''Francesca, is the pain very terrible? If I could only be there with you to help you....''

''It is a strange pain. I never knew we were all born by such pain, but it is easy to bear, for through it I shall see my child. My son, I know that he will be a son.''

''You remember all I told you? You must tie the cord with thread or he will bleed. You've got the rags? And the shift I stole from the laundry to wrap him in?''

''Yes, yes. You must not be afraid for me. Many women must have had to bear their child alone, and I have love for a midwife and she is more skilled than any wise-woman.''

''I'll come back to you to-night.''

''Be sure they do not see you or you will betray us both. Do not be afraid for me, Carola. I am strong and there is so much joy in my heart that there is no room for fear.''

I longed to stay with her, but I dared not; for I heard the bell and had to hurry away to fill my place in the long line of kneeling figures.

All the next day I could not go to her. It seemed that the nuns had deliberately made me work where they could watch me all the time. In the morning I had to polish the candle-sticks in the chapel; two other novices were working with me and a nun sat watching us, the wooden beads of her rosary slipping through her fingers as she mumbled her endless string of prayers. In the afternoon I was sent to the laundry. The irons were heated on a grid over a charcoal brazier; it was difficult to get them to the right heat and I was afraid that I should scorch something, because I had done this before and spent two days in my cell as punishment. I worked as quickly as I could, but before I had finished it was time for us to be locked in. I prayed very hard that I should be able to go to Francesca when I slept, and bring back news of her. But I was awake most of the night and remembered only shadowy fragments of dreams that had no meaning.

The following morning I was sent with the novices that were weeding between the rows of young cherry trees in the orchard. The nun who was watching us was Margarita, the one from whom I had stolen the keys to help Beatrice escape. She sat down with her back against a tree, fanning herself with a rhubarb leaf to keep off the flies. At last she went to sleep. I dared not go out by the gate, for she was near it and I was afraid that I might waken her, so I climbed over the inner wall at a place hidden from the others by an old pear tree. I was not sure whether anyone saw me, but I was too anxious to care.

I crept along in the shadow of the wall and managed to reach the grating without being seen. I listened before I lifted it up, but I could hear nothing. For a moment I thought Francesca must be dead. I called her name, very softly. Still I heard nothing. I lay on the ground staring down into the darkness, and as my eyes got accustomed to the gloom I saw that she was not dead but sleeping, with her child in her arms. It was the first time I had ever seen her without her habit; she wore only her shift and the torn coverlet had slipped aside. The baby's dark head was pillowed on the curve of her full breast, and I thought that anyone who could condemn her would have condemned Mary when she lay in the straw with the young Jesus. I whispered her name again, and she opened her eyes. When she stirred the baby began to cry, but she gave him to suck and quietened him.

She told me to let down the rope of my girdle for she had stained cloths that I must bury. I buried the bundle in the soft mold under some bushes, near where I had hidden the basket, and covered the newly turned earth deeply with rotten leaves. I dared not stay any longer in case Margarita woke up and missed me. But before I left her Francesca held the baby up in her arms, and I managed to stretch down far enough to touch its soft head with my fingers. I said, ''Francesca, don't come back here any more. Stay with your baby. Don't leave him alone. Forget your vows, they were not made to God but only to priests; and in priests such as we know there is no godliness.''

She looked down at the child, ''God has sent this soul into my keeping. Carola, do you think it is a sign that I should cherish him above all things? Perhaps the Mother of God would have compassion for me—she cannot have forgotten the little Jesus in the Christ.''

''Your child was born of love, and all love comes from God. He has sent you this child to cherish; love is greater than vows, and courage is greater than fear. Escape, Francesca. You could bring heaven to Guillimo if you came to him with your son. You could take ship for another country and live out your lives in rich contentment. If you leave your son he will cry in the arms of a foster-mother, though she were very kind and tender to him, for it is you that he wants. Perhaps in the past he gave you his protection; now you must give him yours.''

''He seems more real than all my vows. It is not my soul I fear but for theirs.''

''There is no fear in God, that is what we have forgotten. To love another is to love God, and to feel His compassion. To-night you will leave the convent with your child. Will you be strong enough to walk?''

''For him I could walk anywhere; have any strength.''

''Don't come back any more, Francesca. Stay in the world. While love protects you, you go in no fear of hell.''

When I had to leave her I was not sure whether she would have the courage to escape into the world. The days passed and I never saw her again. Though I was lonely for her I rejoiced, for I thought of her with Guillimo and her son.

CHAPTER TWENTY

the lame nun

I had been in the solitary cell for three days. At first the longing for food tormented me, but though they gave me no water I did not suffer from thirst, for there had been heavy autumn rains and the walls were slimy with moisture. Sometimes I had to lick the brickwork, but usually by evening enough water for me to drink had collected into a little pool in the corner of the floor. It was the same cell in which Francesca had had her child. I wondered if this was because they knew I had helped her escape. Perhaps the Abbess had only accused me of practicing witchcraft to try to frighten me....

Was it three days, or was it four, since I had seen the lame nun at the door of my own cell? It had been soon after midnight office. When I had tried to question her she would not answer, but in silence beckoned me to follow her. She had seemed contemptuous, yet almost in awe of me. Before leaving me here she had said, ''Your lies are spinning your own shroud, Carola. Why did you talk of witchcraft to the novices? They whisper together, and their whispers have reached the ear of the Abbess.''

''It was only a game to frighten Octavia. She is so stupid....''

''It is unfortunate for you that they are only lies; I thought you might have been prompted by Satan, as once I was. I saw celestial visions, heard music, seemed to fly; but it was

223

Satan who had entered into me. It all happened soon after the old Abbess died. I made my recantation: but my possessor was stubborn and for a time I would not deny what I thought truth. They lamed me for my lies, the lies of Satan's prompting. See, I have one foot near to a cloven hoof."

From the concealing folds of her habit she thrust out her foot, shrunken, withered up in hideous deformity. Instead of a shoe there was a wooden block, hollowed to hold the rigid ankle to which it was bound by thongs. Yet there was a horror in her lameness greater than mutilated flesh. "Pray, Carola! Pray to the Saints to make you deaf to evil whispers; or you will be proud, as I was proud, and your visions will have such a strong reality that you will think that you can die for them. But pain blinds us to visions; there is always more pain, more pain, for they are very subtle. Recant before they cripple you; for surely you will recant at last to bring yourself some ease."

She was staring at the wall, as though she saw beyond it. She seemed to be waking from a heavy sleep. Then her eyes changed, now there was not only terror but hatred in them. "You *are* a heretic! Already you have made me betray my vow of silence. It must be true that you have practiced witchcraft...."

With two outstretched fingers she made the sign of the inverted Cross against me, the sign used to avert the Evil Eye: three times muttering, "Ave! Ave! Ave!"

I heard her limping away down the passage beyond the locked door. She thought she saw evil in me because she had not had the courage to recognize that within herself she had once possessed a glimpse of the truth which gave her the power to recognize mine. Now she must deny truth to escape from the memory of her own betrayal. She would be more cruel an enemy than even the Abbess; for I had made her look into her own heart, and see herself no longer as a martyr but as a coward, no longer a brand snatched from the pyre but one who had blinded herself with hot arrows for fear of the sun.

Since she went no one had come near me either to arraign me or to bring me food. They were foolish if they thought they could starve me until I denied my visions, for their own fasts should have taught them that when the body is weak it is easier for the spirit to shine through it.... I found that I could escape from this cold confine into the sunshine of the past, into a country which, although it was unknown to Carola, I knew to have once belonged to me.... I could escape from my chilled body into the warmth of a foreign and yet not alien sun; swim in blue pools among the lotuses; hear oarsmen chanting as my gilded barge swept on upriver.

And when I returned it was as though I saw the modern rituals silhouetted against the memory of this old peace; black as the stones of a forgotten graveyard against the pageantry of sunset. And I remembered a voice that I had loved for many thousand years, ''Fear not to die for what you know to be true.'' And I had promised to have courage, yet found it difficult to conceive of a time when Truth must be defended.

two Voices

There was a green light filtering through the grating. The air seemed heavy on me, like water, as if it were trying to drown me. I thought of the Captain, sinking down through glaucous cold when the *Santa Maria* had foundered. His bones would be white among the coral: perhaps seaweed had rooted in his skull and silvery fish were flitting through the eye-sockets. The bones of his hands would have fallen from each other, lying on the deep ocean sand like the beads of a broken rosary.

I looked down at my own hands. It was long since I had played the lute, and the fingers had lost the roughness the strings had given them.... My hands are supple with youth; it will be many years before age binds their strength with corded veins, yet perhaps to-morrow they will not belong to me. Soon they will not be warm with living blood, but colder than the clay that folds my shroud. They may be ashes, or lie with bones still clenched as though they tensed to bear my body's pain. They will not know the texture of a flower, or feel the sun-warmth of an apricot; they will have forgotten all that I taught to them, of how to quicken mute strings to melody, of how to plait a wreath to bind my hair from flowers that grow in water-meads and woods.... God must have known contentment when he made a hand; if it had not been given this subtlety, man could have wrought no beauty upon the earth: there would have been no paintings, no fretted buildings or embroideries; no marquetry, wrought goldsmith work, or swords.

Then it seemed as though I heard a voice saying, ''They shall create even as I created; for it is well that all should see that which they build. Though the fruit of beauty is in Heaven, the rind of it shall be on Earth. I made the mountains, but even they shall carve them. I made the color under the earth, but man shall find it and blend it into pleasurable patterns. I threaded silver into the fissures of the rocks, but man shall mine it and temper it to music-loving strings to lift up his heart. I have made the valleys, but man of his skill shall fashion them to ploughland so that he and his children may grow strong on the bounty of the earth.

''They shall wax mighty in my image, until of their own stature they learn simplicity. Then when they approach my throne they shall find that they are seated at my right hand. For he that is their father has become brother unto them.

''It is wise, my children, to create. For just as thy Creator brought thee forth into light, breathing into thy nostrils, taking the clay sealings from thy eyelids, opening thy mouth; so shall thine own creation return into the bosom of thy Father: to become even as I.''

And when the voice ceased I was in the stillness of manifold peace. And there was no fear in me, nor any littleness.

The light faded. Shadows seemed to be folding together

like flocks at dusk; gathering intensity, taking on the embodiment of dark life.

I heard another voice; a voice smoother than honey, warm with infinite beguilement. ''I have returned to you. I whom once you knew and loved. Let my wings enfold you in their dark peace.''

I lay in the arms of a lover. His face was moonwhite, his hair dense as the cypress shadows, his eyes were dark fire, his soaring brows winged. Power was set in his forehead like a midnight jewel; and with him came all the beauty of the night, secret and rare:

''Beauty shall be a carpet for your feet: and I will take you where the jungles seethe with vigorous green; where panthers, dark as caverns, stalk their prey, and leopards drink at star-lit forest pools.

''We will find valleys set among tall hills like chalices to hold the wine of love. And scarlet lilies, glowing in the dusk, shall stand as sentinels to our bridal bed. Birds there shall be, with iridescent wings, and moths, the purple blue of ripening grapes. A waterfall shall trace its shining path languorous ferns unfurl their heavy fronds to shield your beauty from the envious moon.

''There will I feed you on sweet memory; and with my mouth pledge you a thousand loves in timeless moment of keen ecstasy. You knew a youth magnificent as fire, and he shall return to kindle your cool flesh. You knew a love relentless as the tide, and as a beach so shall you be engulfed in passion more profound than ocean depths: then will he leave you, virginal and smooth, but to return to woo you yet again.

''Through me you are born again into men's praise. You shall wear beauty like a jasmine wreath; poets shall set a new word upon their page when they phrase beauty, and it shall be your name. And you shall sing, as yet no voice has sung, with all the crystal harmonies of dreams. You shall have craftsmen's fingers; then will I give you ores and precious stones to bring alive as goldsmith's miracles. And you shall limn your colors on a wall to make a place of painters' pilgrimage, who seeing, will think not only you but they, have become visionary through your eyes.

"You have once ruled, and we who have tasted power find other food as dust upon our tongues. Come, I will crown you with my midnight plumes to sit in judgent on a basalt throne. There shall be temples honored to your name; and sacred rams, black kids and mighty bulls shall stream their blood upon your altars. You shall protect those in our fealty, and scourge their enemies with pestilence, send down our fire to cleanse the fallow fields and from their ashes then shall our corn spring.

"Listen, and I will teach you to destroy. See, I will stand beside you at this door, and when they seek to mutilate your flesh, then shall they see me, then shall I slay them down. You shall wear my black armor, stronger than fiery onslaughts of the sun. At your command my armies shall draw sword and in their van we both shall ride the wind.

"Why are you silent? You turn away your eyes, dare you not see your destiny in mine? Is there sheep's milk in your veins instead of blood? Do you still thirst for water instead of wine; and feel the cold winds of eternity through the warm darkness of my sable wings?

"On that other journey you will walk alone. Your sandaled feet tread solitary dust—to where? To gain humility, and feel your brow pierced by a crown of thorns. Shall I look down and laugh to see you there: or will you be beside me on the heights and see below us hosts of little men, as white and blind as maggots in a corpse, who had not the courage to look into my eyes?

"You are still silent. Must I command obedience with my whips? Fear, pain, distrust, despair; all shall you feel...."

Then like a tapestry of woven light I saw the vision of the other I's. In him had been embodied my past days when I had walked triumphantly in shade. It was not Lucifer whom I had seen, but I. The I that Carola must help destroy; the I of pride, the I of love for power, the I that is the forgetting of the I.

And yet more radiant, from the eternal light I heard the voice of my companions, ''Follow the Jackal trail. Though it shall lead you through the parched deserts where no water springs: though you may have to climb those barren hills where thorns assail you, and the pitiless scourge of your own weakness. Leave not the Jackal trail. Follow it to our land where you shall hear the Word.''

And Carola refused that burnished lust when flesh has been distilled to ecstasy; the rod of power wielded against the light, the blindness of false worship, the leaden crown of temporal ambition; and that most subtle incense, men's praise for skill.

My vision faded. I was alone again; a girl with muffled thoughts shut in with flesh; Carola, who was afraid of pain.

arraignment

I heard footsteps echoing along the passage. Then the door opened to disclose the Abbess. She carried a horn lantern; in its yellow glow her face seemed disembodied against the thick darkness. Behind her in the shadows stood the lame nun. The Abbess spoke to me, her voice dead and toneless, ''I have come to hear your recantation.''

I stood up, ''I have not lied, so I have nothing to recant.''

''You confessed to the powers of a witch.''

''Not witch, but priest.''

''A witch's blasphemy!''

My body was weak, and I had to steady myself against the wall, but I managed to keep my voice clear and level. ''You are powerful within the walls of this convent, just as the Pope is powerful within the boundaries of his states. But in a time when priests were really men of God, and the light of heaven shone upon those who looked upward to the source of truth, you would have been cast out of a temple: as unworthy even to work in the gardens of the men and women who were the Guardians of Truth. You may have taken vows, but I see you, stripped of your office, a barren woman, crusted with ignorance and blind to light."

To the other nun she said, "You are right. She is under satanic influence."

I laughed at her, "You seem to have forgotten that though Satan is now an angel of darkness he is still an angel. Why should he try to extinguish the light where he knows none has been kindled? To believe that he has bewitched my tongue to beguile into evil your narrow community would be as if you believed that the King of France would bring an army into Italy to kill a spider!"

"I have long known that you were unworthy to wear our habit. In you I have seen all the evil and lust for power of the line of which you are a bastard, and none of its virtues. Even allowing that all the evil of the Griffin has flowered in you, it is still impossible to believe that you, Carola, would have dared to address me as you have done had not a follower of Satan prompted you. I know it to be my duty, not only as a bride of Christ, but as a pillar of God's most holy Church, to drive out this evil which has entered you. We shall cause it to suffer through your flesh. I have known demons take flight when they have felt hunger and thirst, but yours needs stronger measures, for it is rooted in you like the poisonous weeds that grow from a heretic's grave."

She made the sign of the inverted Cross against me. Then her voice rang forth. "I warn you, spirit that possesses the body of Carola, depart to those nether hells from whence you came! Allow the spirit of this girl to speak, to swear denial of the evil knowledge with which you have endowed her. In the name of the Trinity I bid you go! And if you stay in this envelope of flesh then shall we teach you that earth can hold more pain even than hell where burns the eternal fire!"

I mocked her, "Why make speeches to the Lords of Hell

when I, Carola, am your only audience? You accuse me of being possessed of a devil; and I answer you that if I am possessed it is only by a ray of light which shines from the source of Truth. I have said that I can leave my body when it sleeps, and visit places I have never seen and bring back clear memory of them. I have said that sometimes in my dreams I talked with those who have been my friends, and that they are not demons, nor grey ghosts in purgatory, nor even angels, but they are as they were when clothed in flesh, though they are happier and clearer eyed. I have told you that there is no death, because we die each time we go to sleep. I have told you that we are born on Earth more than a thousand times.... What more shall I tell you? That your long-preserved virginity will not bring wisdom to you? That I have seen more godliness in a girl who earned her living in a brothel than you have dreamed of? That I have heard the wisdom of the gods, not from a priest, or nun, or devout follower of his Holiness, but from a jester, a dwarf who once wore knightly armor? If these things shall brand me heretic, then I am proud to die for heresy!''

I knew that I must be a shield, not a spear, against her. I must be calm, dispassionate. I must drive hatred of her from my heart, for hatred would forge a chain between us, and with her I must make no bonds. She spoke again.

''If I were sure these blasphemies were uttered of your own will, that there was no devil whispering at your ear, I should know that it was useless further to mortify your flesh in a last attempt to save your immortal soul. But through the infinite mercy of the Church it has been decreed that even those who speak in the voice of devils, as you have spoken, or have listened to the Serpent of Evil Wisdom and gained from him a subtlety in sin, should be spared nothing that may save them from an eternity of hell fire. By all the means in our power we shall seek to drive out the thing that possesses you, even though your flesh must mortify before the devil will release his tenement.''

I sent up a silent prayer to Petruchio to give me the strength to fulfil my promise to die if need be for what I knew to be true. I said, ''You say that I have blasphemed. Are you ignorant of your own thoughts? Listen to the voice of your heart, and it will tell you that why you hate me is not because your godliness recognizes evil in me but because your own faith has failed you. The god you worship is not a god of love, but cruel and arrogant, a mightier Pope. A god who delights to hear his praises sung to feed his pride; a god who denies all godliness in man; a god who has ensouled his puppet slaves so they should bow before him, heavy with the sin into which they were born of his own will; a god who is blind to justice, who made the world into this pattern and yet condemned his own creation to be damned until he came among them as the Christ.... You cross yourself! Like an ignorant peasant passing a suicide's grave at a benighted cross-road!''

There was horror in the voice of the lame nun as she exclaimed, ''It is only the infinite mercy of God that has not allowed your evil words to strike you dead!''

Their awe of death made me more certain of my own strength, ''Death is no stranger to me, and many times I have rejoiced to hear his step approaching the door of the narrow prison of this world to set me free. Have you no memory of your own to show you that the things I say are true? Are you so shrouded in your ritual that you are deaf to your own inward voice, which must surely tell you of the many times you have died only to be reborn?''

The Abbess seemed indifferent to my taunts, as if she were content to reserve revenge. She said, ''Secure in the light of perfect faith I cannot hear your blasphemies.''

''The light of faith is like guttering corpse lights blowing in the wind. Poor flickering light that can but show the shell of death and cannot make the spirit luminous! I cannot draw upon the mighty wisdom of the gods, but of my own knowledge I have certainty that there is justice. All men are fellow-travelers through the mists of time, time that is ten thousand times longer than your creed holds the creation of earth to be, until through the long cycle of their many births each shall at last achieve a brotherhood with God.''

The last things I remember seeing were the cold, glittering eyes of the Abbess; and her dry puckered lips, colorless in the faded yellow skin, that hardly moved when she spoke.

Recant!

I must have hit my head when I fell, for there was a bruise on my temple. By the fading of the dim light I could tell I had been unconscious for several hours. There was a bowl of milk and part of a loaf on the floor beside me. I knew that this had been brought to strengthen me for further penances. Francesca had told me that it was dangerous to eat much after a long fast, so piece by piece I soaked the bread, musty with blue mold, in the milk and ate it very slowly. Someone had stripped off my habit, and I shivered in my thin shift until I saw they had left another robe for me to wear: the robe of a condemned heretic.

I wondered in what manner I should find death. I had heard it whispered that sometimes the unrepentant were strangled—would this be more terrible than the slower suffocation of smoke? I prayed to my far and yet familiar gods that I should be strong enough not to deny the knowledge they had given to me. I ought to find it very easy to die, for I had not had happiness for my companion since I was born as Carola: there was no one to weep because I had left earth, and when I could lift the tapestry to walk out of the world there would be those who would welcome me in long friendship.

When I heard the key grate in the rusty lock I thought that the Abbess had come back; but it was the lame nun. I saw that she was habited in black, the cowl pulled down to hide

233

her face. Then I knew that I must meet torture, for it was in robes like this that the monks had chanted Sofia to the pyre.

She beckoned me to follow her. I wondered if they were going to burn me.... Sometimes they used green wood to suffocate the heretics. Measured in earth time Sofia had not screamed very long, but pain cannot be measured in earth time. I must die silent. I must keep safe my knowledge that we are given nothing which is beyond our strength. I seemed to hear Petruchio's voice, ''A man may overload his ass, but God does not give His children a burden they cannot carry.'' I must throw my thoughts forward, like a stone across a river, to where Petruchio will be waiting for me. He will be very splendid in heaven. I shall put off my burnt flesh as he put off the body of a dwarf. From there this ordeal will seem a little thing. I shall hear him say, ''You were brave, my Carola.'' And I shall answer, ''It is forgotten.''

The wind blew cool on my forehead. We followed a little twisting path between high elder bushes. There seemed to be a lightness upon my body. Before he died Petruchio said that he felt his body loosen its hold on him.... Perhaps it will be very easy to die, for my body is weaker than they realize. I shall step from this earthly shell like a fish slipping between the reeds: smooth, and cool, and quiet.

We came to a wicket in a wall, and passed through. I was in the nuns' burial ground. I wondered which of the nameless mounds concealed the body of the old abbess. I thought I was to be shown my open grave.... I must think of the earth as the foster-mother of trees, as a kindly darkness where the moles hold siege—not as a suffocation pressing down on me.

It was twilight, and bats were flickering between the cypresses. I saw that the stone slab which covered an ancient tomb had been pushed back to disclose a flight of steps. Again the nun beckoned to me to follow her. It was curious that I did not try to run away, but I knew that to think of flight would be to acknowledge fear and so be vanquished by it.

The steps were of narrow bricks, worn and rose-red, and

the roof was low and vaulted. At the foot of the steps we came into a dank passage and turned to the right. We seemed to go a very long way. The lantern lit up the mouths of other tunnels and I heard rats scampering away through the darkness. The floor was dry now and seemed to be sloping upwards, though there were no more steps. At the end of the passage there was a door; it was of age-blackened wood and had two heavy iron bolts that ran into sockets in the brick-work. They were drawn back, but instead of opening it the nun put out the lantern and knocked three times. I heard the grating of other rusty bolts from the far side of the door. It opened grudgingly on stiff hinges.

I saw a room like a chapel, with a barrel-vaulted ceiling. It was empty. The walls had once been frescoed; the plaster had crumbled, but there were still traces of faded paintings. There was a rack of whips against the wall, some with new thongs unfrayed, some stiff with old blood. Irons were heating on a charcoal brazier. In the middle of the room there was a coffin-stone, shaped like a bier. At its four corners there were ropes, threaded through the rings of staples driven into the floor; and round it had been placed the four great candles that are set to watch the dead.

I felt someone watching me. In the shadows of a low doorway stood the Abbess: she too was dressed in black, but her cowl was not drawn forward to hide her face. She looked like the image of death in ignorant men's imagination: the skull seemed visible through the bleached skin, and her eyes glittered from their cavernous sockets. Her voice was slow, and level; but in it there was a hideous, musky excitement, ''It seems that Satan has a reluctant bride. There is still time for you to turn penitent.''

''I will not lie to torture!''

''Then follow me—and see your marriage bed.''

My feet felt slow and heavy; as though I were clogged in a nightmare. I followed her into the room beyond. I saw six more figures, watching me through the narrow eyeslits in their cowls. Each held a long taper, and by this light I saw masons' tools beside a pile of mortar. The walls were unplastered: here and there a brick was missing, as in a dovecote. At the far end there was a narrow shelf in the wall, but half-concealed by freshly mortared bricks. The Abbess pointed to it, "Your bridal bed, and we shall draw the curtains close. See, we are kindly, for we leave a space where Satan can depart when he has tired of you."

I bit my lip, and felt the salt blood spurt into my mouth. She grew impatient that I kept my silence, "You seem reluctant—where are those proud boasts you spoke to me? You said you would be proud to die for heresy—you *shall* be proud. Perhaps you will be the first who has died in silence: no prayers, no cries, no pitious supplications. The others have lain here many centuries; but there will be one companion next to you—no, two, a boy closed in a convent wall."

I heard my voice, as though it were far away, "You mean Francesca?"

And her voice, gloating as warm oil, "Francesca and her son. You were both fools; you thought I was deceived by all your desperate measures of concealment. I laughed, and watched you. She had to bear the child before she could receive her punishment. The child was shrived to save its soul. Francesca will have barren motherhood in hell."

"You bricked her up—alive?"

"She lived three days; and when at last her voice was silent, the baby wailed all through another night to feel her empty breast cold to his mouth...."

I must have fainted; for the next thing I knew I was stretched naked on the coffin-stone. The ropes had been knotted round my ankles and wrists, and had been drawn so taut that it seemed my bones must be wrenched from their sockets. The lame nun stood beside me with a scourge.

The voice of the Abbess, "Recant!"

Then the scourge fell; the thin skin across my breasts split wide.

"Recant!" ...I must remember they can only torture Carola; I am inviolate from them. Master, shine upon me in strength! Do not let my wisdom be blinded by the cringing of my flesh. Let Carola hear me!

The cords cut into my wrists and into my feet.... The black cowled figures are afraid, they are more afraid of me than I am of pain.

Still the blows fell, and between each that voice, "Recant!"

"Recant!" ...Why cannot I leave my body and let them destroy it? They must not make me deny truth or my spirit will die.

"Blow on the brazier to heat the irons!" I heard the lame nun stumble across the room; the click of the wooden block on her withered leg sounded like nails being driven into my coffin.... Have pity, Death; release me from this pain lest I should betray your Master. Don't let them make me scream.... I thought I had learned all pain....

"Recant!" Pity is dead, and friends, and kindliness....

"Apply the brand! You will be lame, Carola. Your legs will tail behind you in the dust like lepers' flesh. Satan will grow impatient for his bride before he takes you. And when he sees what we have done to you, even his lesser demons will give you scorn. Do you smell your own flesh burn? That is a smell which will fill your nostrils to eternity."

Please let me say something—she must't make me scream. It's so difficult to think of words. Petruchio, I am so alone. Please let me faint—only for a little while. I will come back, but I am so tired. It's been going on such a long time. It's very difficult, Petruchio, when it's been going on a long time....

"Another iron is hot. Your foot will wither like a rotten leaf, curled with the heat." She leaned over me, her voice rising to a scream, "Satan! Satan!"

Thank you Petruchio, I can speak now.... ''You speak to yourself, Abbess? You honor yourself too much. Your name is not Satan—you are only a puny underling of hell.''

the Closed Door

When I returned reluctantly to my body the crypt was empty. I knew many hours had passed, for the sentinel candles were far burned. Their calm flames seemed to watch me. Pain began to wash over me like sea, ripple by ripple, dark, spreading. It came slowly, unhurried as the tide. It engulfed my feet and crept upwards towards my breast, then lapped my bitten lips. It was not a fierce enemy as the torture had been, it called forth no courage but only a kind of desperate endurance.

I was covered with a pall, woven of stinging nettles by the fingers of meek penitents. There was fire in their leaves; they seemed to cling to my flesh, to suck my blood like vampires.

I heard the bolts being drawn back, and thought the Abbess had returned. I tried to steel my thoughts to a last defiance. I must show myself omnipotent of hatred. Then I heard the dragging footsteps of the lame nun. I thought she had come to mock me, so I feigned sleep. I felt cool water on my forehead. My bonds were slackened, and she chafed my hands to bring me back. I thought she but revived me for new torture. Then I heard her sobbing, she was talking to herself, ''They left me in the dark, but she is braver than I. I denied everything. I was afraid of the pain. If I had had her courage, I should be walking in Paradise, not be a lame woman creeping through the dark of her faith.''

I turned my head, ''What are you going to do to me?''

''Help you to escape. They are coming to brick you up alive. I can't let them do it. I loved Francesca, though I was jealous of her friendship for you, and the Abbess made me mix the mortar. She made me stay where I could hear Francesca's voice comforting her child. It was a strong child. It wailed on and on after her voice had ceased to comfort it.''

''You are very brave to try to save me; but I am afraid that I am lame too. I could never run away now. You mustn't be too sorrowful when they brick me up. I'll know that it is only for a little while. I am very weak, so I think I shall soon die. It has been a long time since I had any food, and I am very thirsty. Petruchio will take me away; and leave my body hidden in the wall.''

''No, no! You mustn't talk like that. I have brought you a cordial, and salve and rags to bind your feet. There is another entrance to these passages. I think I am the only nun who knows of it. The rats are fierce, but they are frightened of a light. I have brought you my shift to wear....''

My body looked as if it were encased in rusty armor where the blood had dried. She tried to help me, ''I cannot carry you, you must crawl if you cannot walk; but hurry! Hurry!

I pulled myself along by the rough brickwork. The floor was soft with the dust of centuries. At one place the passage was nearly blocked by a heap of rubble. It was torment to climb through the narrow opening. On and on, she trying to help me, her voice urging me to hurry. The passage began to slope upwards. There was life in the air again. The roof had fallen, and through an opening I saw a single star. I tried to thank her—I heard her running back along the passage. Slowly and painfully I climbed back into the world.

It had been raining. I was in a wood, the leaves were damp and soft, kindly to crawl on. I came to a stream. I lay beside it to drink, half in the water. It laved my wounds; and as the crusts melted I felt the blood warm against my skin as it ran afresh....

I must hide before it is light. All the countryside will be against me. To be bricked up would have been easier than to be burnt. Lucia said that if I talked too much I should be burnt. Sofia, and I, both burnt for different things that no one knows the truth of any longer. Sorcerer and priest en-

throned on the same pyre.... But I want to sleep first. I must
find somewhere to hide. I must get into the town, for Guillimo's foster-mother must hear of Francesca. She will still be
waiting for the child. I know where her house is, Francesca
told me of it so often. It is on the right after you go through
the Old Gate. If I can reach Perugia I can send someone to her
with a message....

I shall be near the river. I could drown myself before they
find me. No, even that is denied to me. I must hide near the
water; they'll never think of looking for a witch near water.
Sofia said a witch cannot cross a river even on a broomstick....

It's getting very dark; I can't see the stars any more.
There's a wall. I am going to die by a wall. Someone else
died by a wall. Yes, it was my mother. Death is kind: my
feet are very far away. I think they belong to somebody I
used to be. I used to be Carola. I'll soon forget her.

There's a door in the wall, but it's closed. I thought they
opened doors when you died. Petruchio!—open the door to
me! Petruchio!—can't you hear me? I can't stand up to
reach the latch.... I want to go to sleep....

The stone is cool, and dark, and quiet....

CHAPTER TWENTY-ONE

Return from a Dark Journey

I must be dead, for pain has set me free. There is no pain in
me. My body is without feeling, as though I were a figure in
a tapestry.... I am not alone any more. They must have un-
barred the door when I was asleep. Petruchio will tell me
when I must open my eyes. Perhaps even in heaven one must
rest from the pains of death. I must sleep, for I am still
drowsy with death....

I can see a cloud, sailing the azure reaches of the sky; perhaps it is a ship bringing to harbor souls weary with earth. It is very quiet among the clouds.... I am looking through a window. Why should there be windows in heaven? Perhaps Petruchio thought that at first I should feel strange; and has made me a room, a beautiful room, so that I should not feel naked in my soul....

I thought that I was living in a dream, though on which side of death I knew not, a dream of some quiet corner of the wide heavens. Then I realized that I was lying on a bed: a great dark bed, the foot of it carved with shells, and nymphs, and tritons blowing horns. My hands were long and pale on the green coverlet, still as the marble hands of a woman on a tomb.... Why had I been afraid that my hands were going to be destroyed, that soon they would no longer obey me? I tried to move them, and as the fingers unclasped, I knew, though I know not how I knew, that I was still on earth.

I turned my head, and saw a rich cabinet, inlaid with green and gold. I felt a cool hand on my forehead, and a woman's voice told me to be at peace. Her voice was warm and friendly as baking bread, with the tang of Tuscany in her words. "My name is Anna. You have been ill a long time, and have lain here many days...."

She was dressed in grey, with a white cap framing her face like quiet wings. I moved my hand, and found that my body was bandaged with fine cambric under the bedgown. Then I remembered the convent: and with memory came pain. I was too tired to be brave any more. I felt slow, heavy tears sliding from under my closed eyelids; and the voice of Anna comforted me as if I were a child. She pillowed my head on her arm and fed me with spoonfuls of broth that steamed in a silver bowl.

I whispered to her, "You know I am an escaped heretic? It is dangerous to take me into your house. You should not try to protect me.... I thought I had already died...."

"My master found you on his doorstep. He is great-hearted, and you will be safe in his house. He carried you up here himself and helped me bind your wounds, for we dared not summon a physician lest he should be suspicious.''

''Why should your master do this thing for me?''

''He says you belong here. It is not for me to question my master's orders.'' Then her voice grew even more tender, ''Yet would I have questioned them if he had turned you away! No one can hurt you any more, my pretty, for Anna is here to look after you. Now drink this milk. Try just a spoonful: just *one* more, for Anna's sake.''

I tried to smile, ''It seems I have become two years old again.''

''Another spoonful.''

There was a strange, pungent taste in the milk. A taste of sleep, a sleep so dark that pain soon lost me in its depths.

When next I woke into this earthly harborage of contentment, I saw an old man sitting beside me. His hair was silver under his skull-cap and his beard was like a fall of white silk; his skin was vellum-smooth, and his dark eyes brilliant beneath the strong brow. I watched him through my lashes. He wore a long gown of black velvet, with a girdle of pierced gold work, elaborately wrought. The sleeves were lined with the smooth fur of some little animal, tawny in color; and his hands were finely shaped, with a great intaglio on the little finger.

It seemed familiar that he should be sitting there beside me when I returned from some dark journey. I spoke a name which was unfamiliar to my tongue; I think ''Thoth'' was the name I called him by but I am not sure, for I cannot recapture the memory of when he bore this name. He did not speak as he bent forward and took my hand in his; yet I knew it was not the first greeting of a stranger but that I had come home to the house of a long friend.

My body was very weak and soon let my spirit from this quiet room. But when I returned I found him there; and though the shadows lengthened he still clasped my hand.

I can remember little of what happened during the next three days. The taste of the sleep-bringing drug seemed always in my mouth, and as I grew stronger so did the pain strengthen.

When I first saw my face in a mirror, for a moment I thought that I was looking at the portrait of a stranger. Under the scourge I had so often bitten my lips to stop myself from crying out, that they were split and swollen, wide as the lips of a negress. Only one lash had struck me on the face, a scarlet furrow from jaw to temple.

When Anna unwrapped the bandages to bathe my wounds, I saw that my body was barred with broken welts, lined in with the pitiless precision of the shadow of bars on the floor of a condemned cell. Even thieves are beaten on the back, and I think only women could have whipped another woman on the breasts.

Sometimes it seemed that I could still hear the voice of the Abbess.... ''Recant! Confess that the devil has prompted you to attempt to seduce us to his works! Confess, or we shall know that it is not Carola that wears this body, but Satan himself; only he could conceal this pain, for it would make any mortal woman give up the ghost!''

I would forget that now I was safe, that the pain I suffered was of healing and not destruction; and I would hear my voice screaming, although it was far away as if it were the voice of a stranger. ''I have not lied! You can kill me but I will not deny truth! Master! Give me strength not to deny your name!'' And the white wall of my room became the wall of the crypt, and I could see those women with their pitiless faces; their hands hidden in their sleeves; their eyes self-righteous, yet furtive, the eyes of the eternal torturers who have destroyed all who have tried to bring them heavenly news, even as they destroyed their Christ. They wear His tortured body on a crucifix. They think He died to save them from their sins, and do not know they killed Him for His wisdom. It is His dead body they worship; the body from which the spirit of Christ has departed even as His memory has departed from their faith…. ''Master, make me strong in my knowledge, for the light of my spirit is being drowned in pain!'' And the voice of the Abbess, falling like icy water on my forehead, drop after drop, ''Recant! Recant! Recant!…''

The blisters made by the branding iron had burst, and the memory of this cruel heat was still so fierce that I wondered how my spirit had been able to conquer, even for a little while, the screams for pity sent out by my flesh. When Anna put fresh salve on my feet I was frightened to look at them, for fear that I should see one leg drawn up and withered, and know that I was going to be lame. I was afraid she would not have the courage to tell me the truth, and so I said to her, ''How high a block shall I have to wear to help my lameness?'' And when she told me that my wounds were healing and that my legs were not shrunken, I think I cried, for I was still weak and I was very glad.

I wished Petruchio could have been here with me, for he would have been so happy in this quietness. Carlos would have been our patron, and I knew that he was not a man who needed a jester to make him laugh. He would have seen the real Petruchio, not the dwarf. I am not sure whether I talked about the sort of life Petruchio and I had imagined for ourselves, but I know that when bitter memories were very near, and I heard the screams I was not strong enough to hold back, Carlos would sit and talk to me, very gently and quietly, as though he were reading a living poem out of an old book.

''Under this window is a garden which has long waited for you; but these white walls are high to shelter you, not to keep you prisoner. Now winds are sharp, and cold fields desolate; the peaches and sweet almonds sheathe their buds, and hyacinths hide like conies in the ground. Yet soon will narcissus put forth their leafy spears to joust with winter and we shall hear the spring. Then we shall walk together in the sun, where grow gardenias and calendulas, poppies and bergamont and drifts of phlox. You shall wear dresses, soft in changing silks, and bind your flowing hair with wreaths of damask roses and white violets...."

And through his words another vision grew, of a quiet garden in this alien world where I could forget unhappiness, and pain, and endless questing—and at last find peace.

hippogriff

Every day Anna used to rub my legs with warm olive oil to bring back their strength, but the burns on my feet were slow in healing, and at first the skin that grew over the raw flesh was too fragile to bear my weight, or even the touch of a slipper of the softest Venetian leather. When I was stronger she used to carry me into the next room where a bed of cushions had been made for me on the wide window-sill.

As I lay there I used to think of the time when I should be well again—the time when I should be married to Carlos. Every day he spent many hours with me, but though I often talked to him of what I had seen in dreams and visions there was never fear in his eyes. After I had been in his house nearly three months he said to me, ''Carola, it would be easy for my heart to speak to you, if my body was not mindful of its seventy years.''

I smiled, ''We have been talking of the past, talking of centuries as though they were hours; how can you build a barrier between us with fifty little years?''

Yet I saw he was still troubled. Then he said, ''You are so young, so very beautiful, could you forsake the heritage of youth—and marry me? I have so little to offer; only my name, my deep devotion, and the temporal protection these could give you....''

''Dear Carlos, why should you so greatly honor me? Have you forgotten who I am—a bastard heretic?''

''A daughter of the Griffin—could a priest's tie change the quality of your blood? A visionary—can priestly ignorance make heretic of saint? Again I ask you, very humbly, to be my wife.''

''And I, in gratitude and love, accept.''

In the spring warmth the windows were opened wide, and I could feel health growing in my body as a plant thrusts up through the dark earth. I had bedgowns with long sleeves, embroidered at the neck and wrists with flowers in formal patterns: one was of green with stitchery of rose color; another, heliotrope with sage-green sleeves; another yellow, with ivory buttons carved like the buds of an orange tree.

My mother had shown me how to do simple embroidery, but my fingers had forgotten how to place the stitches smoothly as the scales of a fish, until Carlos brought me a design for an embroidery in silk. It was of a woman sitting under a hawthorn tree. The ground beneath her feet was brilliant with knots of flowers, and to her left there was a castle, far and mysterious on a distant hill, with a narrow road leading up to it. There was a white deer with her fawn, and in the sky two singing cherubim. The picture was enclosed in an elaborate border, of flowers and fruits with ribbons interlaced.

There was a tapestry on the wall of the sollar; it was of a forest, and in the shadow of the trees were magic animals, unicorn and zebra and hippogriff. There were two of these, one with his wings folded, when forgetful of his eagle's power he cropped the rich pasture in equine content. The other, with slow beat of mighty wings, had risen from the shadow of the trees into the light: it seemed that he grew impatient of the tapestry confines, and would fly beyond them, out across the Apennines to some far ocean where he had been born.

I used to lie and watch him, and weave fancies in which we shared together perilous adventures. With folded wings he would carry me across the landscape I could see from my windows; and we would gallop swift as the wind which silvers the grass in its passing. Perhaps we should have enemies we must escape; they would be men cloudy with earth who could see only the white horse, for the hippogriff was beyond the compass of their understanding. They would give chase, thinking to entrap us, and as they gained upon us, my celestial steed would spread his wings. We would fly over the river and then circle above them, laughing to see their rage turn to the panic terror of superstition. We would soar upwards until we were above the clouds, seeing them as an ocean of snowy hilltops far beneath us. And it might be that we would see angels, flying under the floor of Heaven on their Master's business, who would shout greetings to us as they sped past; and they would know me for a companion because my hippogriff had brought me into their company.

Carola Di Ludovici

The sunset had faded from the sky when Anna came to tell me it was time to put on my bridal dress. On the bed were clothes such as I had never seen. The chemise was fine as river mist, and the petticoat of white satin was quilted in a diamond pattern; the overdress was black velvet, heavy and lustrous, its sleeves lined with young green to match the slippers which were embroidered with silver leaves and little garnet fruit.

Anna braided my hair with pearls, and from the gold caul a great emerald hung down to jewel my forehead. The look in her eyes reminded me of the day on which my mother had put on my little green dress to wait for my father's return—I wondered if she could see me now, if she and Orlanzo were united in heaven and smiled at their daughter's peace.

Carlos waited for me in the sollar. When I tried to thank him for my dress he kissed my hand saying, ''Now that I have seen you wearing it, it is I who must thank you for so rejoicing my eyes.''

He gave me a packet, tied with a violet ribbon, and as I unwrapped it, he said, ''You already have my heart, this is but a symbol of your authority over my household as well as over its master.''

His gift was a pendant, the work of a master goldsmith. It was of three keys, their hafts fashioned into fantastic animals: a hippogriff, his body a pearl, his outspread wings enamel; a white hart, in rock crystal with an emerald collar; a zebra, striped in gold and silver, with ruby eyes.

Carlos smiled at my pleasure, saying, ''When you wear this I shall see not three keys but five. For among them are two others—the key of my heart, and the key of heaven, which you have opened for me.''

I tried not to show how deeply I was moved, ''I must grow serious to carry so weighty an authority!''

As he fastened the jewelled chain round my neck he said, ''To me you are the authority for all truth that lies concealed behind this transient world of unrealities.''

The priest who performed the marriage had been brought secretly to the house, for Carlos still feared my betrayal to the Papal Authority. The priest was an old man, but without the nobility of age; and I wondered what he would think if he knew that I was a proclaimed heretic. He hurried through the ceremonial words, eager to take the gold he had been promised for his journey from Lombardy, eager to be on the road again.

The candles were resonant as music before the tall windows. It seemed that the vows which Carlos made to me were not a betrothal but a benediction. I knew that he had asked me to marry him only because he was old, and feared to leave me without the protection of his name. My life had well prepared me for this strange marriage: I had seen only the bitterness of the love that unites men and women, my mother's tears and Lucia's despair, and so I was content to receive peace at his hands; and in return I gave him the love I would have given the father I had longed for but never known.

The door closed noiselessly behind the shuffling priest. The marriage ring was heavy on my finger: I was Carola di Ludovici, mistress of a great house, with servants at my bidding and lands and gold as walls against the world. Yet it seemed that a chill draught crept through the room, bringing the memory of other bridals that had been warm and close.... There must be no regret in my heart. Carlos cannot bring me joy but there is no sorrow in his gift. Here I shall train my spirit, and in the past I may find those things for which I now am lonely. When I talk to him of the things of my heart he is not afraid of me. He is a great scholar, and has spent his life with venerable philosophies, now he finds them kindled with my memory so that their truths are no longer obscured by words, but live on the vellum as if a knowledgeable voice had spoken them....

A thread of music plucked the silence, and was joined by other echoes, weaving a shining pattern. All senses were bemused save hearing. It was far away, yet was I one with it as was that Anthony who heard those colored shafts in the cathedral where the light still burned. O rare, celestial melody! The sound of pennants streaming in clear air, and singing swords with their brave damascene: the silver call of curlews through the mist, the ripple of light on rustling summer leaves. These did I hear, most memorable sounds: the measured chords of the long autumn dusk, the small precise note of a drop of rain; the slow surge-music of a growing tree, and the harmonic of an opening bud. Then far across the chasms of the years I heard the voices of forgotten friends; music that had been plucked from strings long dust, by hands whose bones are scattered on the wind, but which still live when memory's warm blood shall into life their muted pulses stir....

The voice of Carlos brought me back into the present; seeming very loud in the silence of the vanished music. ''The banqueting room is impatient to see the new bride of the Ludovicis. To-night it shares your youth, and forgets my age which has kept it closed for more than thirty years.''

His velvet sleeve was smooth under my fingers as he led me down the great staircase. The shallow steps were wide enough for five to walk abreast, and the marble balustrade was fretted into patterns more intricate than the leading in a cathedral window. The double doors that opened into the banqueting room were richly gilded, each divided into fifteen panels carved in high relief.

I sat at the head of the table and Carlos at the foot. I was almost bewildered by the unexpected magnificence; the room was hung with Spanish leather in faded green and gilt, and the floor, a marquetry of foreign woods, shone brilliantly as steel. The forty high-backed chairs, covered in cut-velvet out of Venice, that ranged the walls, seemed like the servitors who had attended the household in the days before Anna, and Caterina the cook, and the old steward, were the only occupants of the kitchen quarters. Six candelabra, each holding four candles of fine wax which smelled of roses as they burned, lit crystal and silver dishes, bright with fruit; and down the long table was a cloth of living flowers, all damask white.

We began the meal in great formality. I sipped rare wines, and tasted every course to please Caterina, who peeped in through the door to smile at me. But when I had eaten of the carp, her favorite dish, stuffed with dried quince and costly spices, I went and sat by Carlos.

I said, ''I have been Donna di Ludovici. Did I play her role becomingly? Now let me be Carola a little while, for I am unused to so much dignity.''

In answer he raised his goblet in a toast, ''I drink to Carola, who honors Ludovici!''

''We have been over solemn, let us be children and play at fancies. We will pretend that all those empty chairs are drawn up to the table. Now how shall we people them? In that one over there is a Cardinal of Milan. He thinks himself a great dignitary, but you and I know that he is only a fat man, with an uneasy stomach from eating too greedily of Caterina's carp. See! Beside him is the wife of that conte from Lombardy; she is a most successful courtesan, if gossip is to be believed, but the Cardinal will not hear of her adventures, to his embarrassment, until tomorrow. How unctuous he becomes at her flattery!''

Carlos caught the spirit of the game. ''The old grey-beard is a famous philosopher. He expounds his views as though they were as factual as the rising sun. Poor ancient! He little knows that before the meal is over you will have confounded all his beliefs, and shown him truth to his discomfiture.''

''Who is that youth who gazes so intently at the girl across the table?''

''A poet, but he only feigns to look at the Duke's daughter to keep his eyes from being bold when they meet yours. The anguish in his face comes from the recognition that though his verses can well praise the moon, of you they are unworthy.''

I laughed, ''It seems we have a melancholy company! How do we fail in hospitality?''

''We give them jealousy as gall to every dish; for they must see their host and his young bride are so engrossed together that they seem to dine apart.''

And so in ghostly company I drank my bridal toast.

CHAPTER TWENTY-TWO

the ark

In alcoves on each side of a narrow room, whose barrel-vaulted ceiling was painted with a dice pattern in white and terra-cotta, there were twelve statues standing on plinths of black marble. While Carlos was showing them to me he said,

"In my youth I made two journeys to Greece, once called the land of a Thousand Islands, and it was from there that I brought back five of these statues. This one is Mars, their god of warriors. This is Jupiter, the wise. This the winged Mercury, who brought messages from Olympus to men whom the gods found worthy of receiving news of their august presence. The Greeks flourished even before the fore-runners of our own country, and I think that if you had lived in their time you would have found that many things which are familiar to you would not have been foreign to their understanding."

His words reminded me of a dream I had often had as a child, and I said, "I think I did live there.... I can only remember fragments of that life, but I know I was a boy, training to be an athlete.... I used to race with six other boys along a narrow strip of white sand—between a rocky hillside and the sea. We were taught how to temper our muscles as a sword-maker tempers his blades into fine steel. Sometimes we used to fling discs, of hard pottery or of metal, to a great distance...."

"You must have been training for the Olympic games. We know, through the immortality of statues, that they used to throw a discus, such as you describe—can you remember more?"

"No, I have forgotten how to remember at will; perhaps one day I shall dream true of this time and be able to tell you. Did the Greeks train their will as well as their bodies? Had they wise priests?"

"From what I know of them through their writings, it seems they had forgotten their wisdom as have the Chris-tians. It is known they silenced the voice of one of their greatest men with hemlock."

"What did he try to teach?"

"What you are teaching me. All who are truly wise must say the same thing when they speak of that which is change-less, though they use their own parables. For there are no pagans or heretics, but only wise men and fools.''

''Did the priests of our church ever possess some inward knowledge, or did they always say, 'You must have faith,' not because they thought the mysteries beyond man's comprehension, but because they dared not open the eyes of their spirit, fearing that if they did so they would know themselves blind?''

''I think that if they had the courage to search their hearts, they would find a greater fear even than that: the fear of seeing nothing, not because of their own blindness, but because the sun and the moon were the only light in the universe; the fear of finding that the darkness of their own ignorance encompassed all mankind, and that there was no wisdom and no truth.''

''When Lucia was hungry she found more satisfaction in buying a candle to set before the statue of a saint than if she bought bread and meat for herself. Yet when I tried to talk to her of her beliefs she refused to listen. What is the value of faith, when one who holds it fears that it could be destroyed by words?''

''How did you find that certainty which needs no faith?''

''I was born with some inward knowledge. I feel that it was my heritage to be wise in my spirit, and that from some old action of mine, which my tarnished memory cannot recapture, I am shut off from my own wisdom: yet the little knowledge that I now have is too strong for anything to destroy. You, my husband, are a great scholar, and can read what men have written in many tongues. You tell me there are days in the traditions of men when my own knowledge would have been accepted, not as a strange heresy but as a fact, changeless as the stars. I can remember, although my vision is troubled by my earth thoughts, like a reflection in a windy pool, a time when priests were men of wisdom. They wore white robes, and knew of many gods. They called on them by name, standing upright in truth with their hands upstretched to the source of light. They would have known me for one who tried to follow in their path, though I but glimpsed what to them was clear vision; and they would have helped me to wear my body lightly so that my spirit could shine forth to kindle a light in others....

"The nuns seemed to hate their bodies. They believe that God created earth, and yet behave as if it were the work of the devil. They have distorted their teaching into a legend kept in a casket of hatred. They have forgotten that God created man and woman to comfort each other through the loneliness of earth: decreed they should bear children, conceived of the love of their spirit and brought forth into flesh; just as He clothed the spirit of man to walk on earth and gain that experience through which alone can come the return into His perfection."

As the weeks passed, it seemed as though I had gone back to that serene interlude when my father loved us. From Carlos I received all that Orlanzo had never given me: there was peace in his house, and kindliness in his eyes. He thought in a thousand ways to bring me happiness, as a father brings toys to enchant his child. I saw stone-masons working in the corner of the courtyard, and on asking what they did, Carlos smiled, and said it was a secret. They built a dovecote; and soon the air was drowsy with slow sound. I used to scatter grain for my white doves, and soon they grew so tame they would perch on my outstretched hand and let me smooth their feathers with my cheek. One was so bold he would fly into my room and strut on the sill, nodding his head as if in agreement with his weighty thoughts.

In our garden there were rare flowering shrubs; one, a gardenia, came from beyond the eastern seas. I loved white flowers and those with heavy scent: the tuberoses and sweet hyacinths. Beyond the lawn there grew a mulberry tree; I would lie beneath it, quiet in its branches' shade, and watch its leaves make with the sky cerulean marquetry.

Sometimes I pretended that Carlos was my child, and I would feign to scold him for sitting too long over his manuscripts. I would bring two crystal goblets, set on silver stems, and a jug of wine drawn from the casks that had come here from famous vineyards; and we would drink together, and smile.

Once he said to me, "I think, my Carola, you are born out of time. I see you dancing to Arcadian pipes on pastoral hills. You are so many women, and all most dear to me. Your spirit circles from the pigeon-cote of this small earth, knowing the sky for its true element. From your far flights you come back to the ark I built for you, and in your mouth bring hope to comfort me. So many pictures are there in my heart of you. I see you as a boy, racing the singing waves on Grecian shores: it was your swiftness their sculptors tried to carve; your eyes that laughed, your voice that spoke to them of golden lands beyond their little sight. The boy, the nymph, the winged messenger—which will I most remember as my love? You came as sunlight to a darkened room, and lit the gilding on my manuscripts. I had been deaf until I heard your lute, insentient till I felt you clasp my hand, blind till I saw you. I was so old, and weary with my years. With shuttered windows I lived in a cold house, surrounded by treasures I had brought from other lands, treasures that stood to mock me now my youth had vanished. I had searched long to find philosophy that beat with living blood, but my books burned musty incense to dead gods. I was alone, and useless, and afraid. Then I, who hear nothing beyond mortal sound, was sitting musing to the flying sparks, when suddenly it seemed I heard, 'Open the door.' I knew it was the door into the street. There were you lying; and at once I knew you had come home to me. I saw you open your eyes and smile, call me a name you say had once been mine; and then I knew the poets had not lied."

"There is one Carola you have forgotten; the heretic who might have brought you death if they had found me in your house, the dying Carola. You have heard my heresy as truth; made me forget my scars; and built for me a temple, whose walls are love. How shall I tell you of my gratitude?''

''Does the cliff thank the seas that wash her feet? Does a bird thank the air that feels its wings? Does a star thank the pilot who sets his course by it?''

It seemed I heard an echo of his voice down through the years from some forgotten past. ''The Goddess of Truth in her celestial sphere walks naked in beauty...'' and I knew that the link between us was woven of the texture of words. I said, ''Once I went on a far journey and looked through the gates of heaven and into the seven hells. I knew that manifold terrors lay in wait for me wherein I must be alone.... When I returned from that dark journey there was a lamp burning, and you were beside me, scribing on a clay tablet the words I uttered.... And there was a joy in me, and a glory, and a strength, greater than any that I since have known. In the convent I underwent another ordeal; far less than the old one, for then the fears I had to combat were beyond pain. Again I came to you by a dark road, and I thought your door was the gate of heaven that was shut against me. But you opened it. And if God and you were two painters He would grow angry with you for copying His design, so near have you made on earth His paradise.''

the Jar and the Cup

Often in the winter evenings I would go with Carlos to the room where he kept his manuscripts. He sat in a chair covered with faded orange velvet, and I on a low stool by the hearth. He would read to me of the wisdom of old philosophers, changing the diversities of their tongues into the language I could understand. Often the words held little meaning for me, and I was content to listen to the sound of his voice and watch the sparks from the blazing olive logs, like molten rain returning to heaven; but one day he read from a scroll which was said to have come from a temple built in the time of the

256

grandfather of the emperor Nero. Before he began, he said, ''The faith of this temple was neither Christian nor pagan, and, if this writing is to be believed, it followed in the tradition of a far earlier temple which stood near to a city on the seaboard of Egypt, a city famous for its learning.''

Then he read, ''For man to try to contemplate his own substance only when he is awake, is as though an astronomer tried to map the stars at high noon: for just as the light of the sun blinds us to the stars, so do the limitations of the flesh obscure the spirit, even to the bearer thereof. Man while he is on earth is like him who can only see the night sky by looking at its reflection in a pool. He who would have wisdom must learn how to make of his heart a burnished mirror, so that in it he may see himself and thus learn of his own nature. Let us consider a traveler in a desert. If he could see the stars he would know which way he was journeying, but there is a heavy burden on his back which bends forward his head so that he cannot look upward; and the sands of the desert, which in the thread of my discourse are a symbol of the things of the flesh, cannot reflect the sky. Then one day he comes to a well, and in it he sees the reflection of a star. His heart is lifted up, for at last he knows, with that certainty which could come to him only through his own vision, that there are stars in the heavens if he could but see them. He knows that he would see more of the sky, though the well be narrow, if it were not for the shadow cast into it by his body. Some men pass on, content to have seen a single star, but others stay by the well; and it is one of these we will consider. With his bare hands he dug at the rocks which surrounded the source of the water, and day by day, through bitter labor, he widened the well until it became a pool, calm and brilliant as a mirror. Now his shadow no longer obscured the reflection of the sky: first he saw three stars, and then eleven, and then he saw them in their ordinances and came to understand something of the celestial design. Only then did he realize that the water on which he had labored was the compass of his understanding, and the stars that he saw reflected therein were the light he had kindled each time he had been born into death. Strong in his vision he continued on his journey; towards that last horizon beyond which there is no dawn and no sunset.''

When Carlos finished the story he would have read on, but I told him to wait; for at that moment I felt, as several times I had felt before, that I was more than Carola; and it was as though on hearing three notes of music there had awakened in my head the theme of a ballad scored for six instruments, complete and perfect to the last harmonic.

I said, ''There were times when it seemed I knew the true meaning behind the curtain of ritual with which in the convent they obscured the light. I knew that once I had upheld those very truths they tried to make me deny; and the truth came from an old strength, though how I gained it I know not; an old wisdom, though the fullness of it I know not. Yet this I do know: there is that in each of us, a thousand times more beautiful, more wise, more strong, than we can be on earth; a part of ourselves which is beyond the limitations of flesh and so cannot be encompassed by it, which one day, when we are at last free of this little world, we shall know to be our true selves.''

The fire was hot, and the flames dazzled my eyes; it seemed they lit pictures in my forehead so that my very thoughts became luminous. I covered my eyes with my hand, yet there came not darkness but a greater brilliance.

I said, ''Listen, and Carola will speak of what the real I knows.... Long ago, men thought of that part of themselves which though born of time is one with eternity, as a great jar. Each time they were born into flesh they could take from the jar only as much water as they could carry with them in a small earthen cup. With it they must refresh themselves during their day's journey; and though they drink from the cup, the water in it is not diminished; but if they do not carry the cup carefully between their hands, the water spills from it and, soaking into the earth, is lost. At the end of their day's journey they pour what remains back into the jar; and from a full cup will come two cupfuls, and from a cup that is half empty will come but a few drops. Every traveler leaves the jar of his memory with the same small cup: but there are some who on earth become potters, and for themselves, on the wheel of life, fashion a large vessel; and behold, it is full of water even to the brim. One who does this partakes of genius, for in him there is more of his true self than is in other men. There are potters who mold a cup with two handles, so that from it other wayfarers may drink also. These may go into a place where a drought has fallen upon the land, where even the rocks are parched and there is no grass, and they will refresh those whom they find there with the water they carry, and lead them from the torrid heat. The bearer of this cup is a true priest. Of both of them other men may say, 'He does not thirst as we thirst, for he was born with a gift from God,' forgetting that each man must be his own potter, and he who has the larger cup has himself shaped the clay. Faster and faster whirls the potter's wheel: and the jar of the Father sees the cup of the Son growing nearer to Him in His own stature; and when a man can say, 'The cup and the jar are two jars that are one,' he may say also, 'I am the Son of God; and I and my Father are One.' "

I heard the voice of Carlos, "Is the name of your cup Conscience; and of the water, Experience; and of the jar, Spirit?"

"The water in the cup is conscience, experience which cannot remember the source from which it came; the water in the jar is wisdom, understanding which gushed from the rock of experience; and the jar is immortality."

"How should this parable help us in our living?"

"On earth we can suffer no thirst that the jar does not hold the water to quench. From prayer can grow a hollow reed to carry the water from the jar into the cup. It is well that man should remember his gods, at dawn, at noonday, and at sunset; for in the memory of his gods he will remember himself. Only in the overcoming of self is the freedom from self gained; only in the mirror of one's own heart can God be seen, and only in the voice of experience can His answer to all questions be heard....

"In the old years, men did not pray to God to turn them into puppets moved by His threads; they did not cry, 'House me against the wind!' but said, 'Teach me to stretch the threads on my own loom, so that I can weave a cloak in which I may walk through the great tempest and not perish.' I remember a prayer that I was taught in the long past: 'Master, help me to find that within me of which I may drink and so be refreshed to do thy work. Teach me to see thee with my eyes; to hear thee with my ears; to speak of thee with my mouth: until my sight is thy sight, my ears thy ears, my mouth thy mouth; and I am no longer alone.' If the true teaching of Jesus were remembered, in His churches would be heard, 'Lead me into temptation, so that I may find the strength to overcome it.' And His people would know that He would not send them forth into the cold until they were ready to weave a cloak; for He tempers the wind to the shorn lamb."

Then Carlos said, "It seems that you recognize your truth even behind the Christian terms which your days in the convent might have caused you to abhor."

"There is only one truth, and all who speak of it must say the same thing."

Then he asked me, "Is there more light in our modern teaching than I have seen, though long I searched for it in vain?"

And so I came to tell Carlos of the Exiles from Eden.

Exiles from Eden

In the story of Adam and Eve there is a truth which has been forgotten, a truth taught in parables since earth was young. The Church maintains that the Serpent of Evil Knowledge tempted man and woman to lust after each other, and because they listened they were cast out of Eden. Yet in the days when the meaning of this legend was understood, the serpent symbolized not evil knowledge, but wisdom. It was taken as the symbol of wisdom because it can make itself into a circle, that circle to which we attain when the past and the future are joined.

When Adam and Eve were born of God they knew no evil, and knowing no evil they knew no good, for good is the overthrowing of evil. For a time they were content, but as they grew older they began to be aware of the loneliness which had come with their separation from the Father. They asked the Serpent, who was coiled under the Tree of Life, how they could return to the land whence they had been born. And the Serpent answered, ''If you would see Him again you must go forth into earth, and eat of the fruit of destruction until you learn to create.'' So Adam and Eve set out on their long journey.

At first they were unarmed, for they had not yet wrested the sword of courage from the hand of fear. When they saw danger they fled into the shadows; but pain followed them into their hiding place, and bound them prisoner. They cried out in torment, but no one answered them until endurance came to give them their first weapon. It was a dagger, and though it was still blunt, written on the blade they saw, 'The Trained Will, which one day shall cut all fetters.''

Time passed, and Adam and Eve became leaders of men. Pride was appointed their seneschal, and he beguiled them with false counsel, for they had yet to learn that though he is a good servant he must never be allowed to take command. So they listened to him, until their leadership was taken from them lest they should betray their followers. They walked through barren valleys, and at last came to the house of humility, where the wounds of their feet were healed and the dust laved from their eyes. Then Humility summoned them to audience, and they saw her enthroned with Pride at her right hand. And Pride said to them, "Now that you have come to the house of my sister, you need fear me no longer; for you will never see me except at her side, and together we have become your friend."

Then were Adam and Eve given great riches, and they used them to surround their house with a wall of gold as a protection from the world. But a plague fell upon their estate, and when they tried to flee the pestilence they found their gateway had vanished and an unbroken wall imprisoned them. They were alone, save for a leper who shuffled after them down echoing corridors. They dared not sleep, for always they must be ready to run from the sound of his bell. They grew weary, and he came so near they could hear the breath whistling from the gaping holes that had been his nose, could smell the rotting bones in his white flesh. At last he touched them; and they found they were even as he. At the summons of their lepers' bells the walls cracked open; and they passed through into the road again.

The day came when they saw a fig tree growing by the wayside. They longed to refresh themselves from its fruit, but they stood aside to allow other pilgrims to eat. Then they saw a stranger coming towards them; and they rang their bells to warn him they were unclean. He took no heed, and led them to a spring of living water, saying, "Put off your lepers' robes and bathe." And they obeyed him, and they found their flesh was whole again. The stranger asked them, "Do you want your lepers' robes, and staves, and begging bowls, or shall I cast them away?" And they answered, "Let us be naked, for though we have nothing we are clean." Then the stranger gave each a new garment and a new staff, and showed them the path to the hills. And he said to them in parting, ''Remember, all possessions which you do not share, become a leper's possessions which no one will share.''

So Adam and Eve continue on their journey, until they shall see the green meadows of heaven, which they once knew as Eden.

CHAPTER TWENTY-THREE

Blind Alley

On the morning when I woke knowing everything that had happened to Lucia since the day I had left her to ride up into the hills, I went to Carlos to tell him of what I had seen. While I was telling him of Lucia I forgot I was Carola the wife of Carlos, and was again a strolling player. I knew he tried to comfort me, but I was so caught up in the reality of what I was describing that I remember nothing but my own words:

''When Petruchio told me that Lucia had died, it was only a few months after we parted from her that he heard of it, he let me think it was of the plague. Now I know she killed herself because she could not escape from the shackles which held her to Bernard.

''While we were both on earth I had tried to bring back her pride, told her that no human being must depend on another to this extremity—but it wasn't any use. Whatever Bernard did to her she never complained. She used to follow him about humbly as a cur; she didn't even cry out when he hit her, and she never tried to make him jealous or angry, but just wept, and obeyed, and adored him. It was not even as if she lusted after him, because after she had the pox I don't think she was ever really well enough to be eager-loined—at least she said she wasn't. I wonder if in the past it had been he who had been importunate and she who scorned; or what was the purpose that made her stay with him, even though he had turned her from a laughing harlot into a pitiful drab, from a proud courtesan into a cringing suppliant for his favors. The old Lucia would have let no man ill-treat her; but she who had once seen men grovel on the floor because she spurned them, now was without artifice, for her obsession for Bernard had taken away all her weapons.

"I think that gradually he had come to hate her; it is often that men and women hate the one to whom they bring sorrow, for in their hearts they know that to give sorrow is to receive it. In her eyes he must have seen himself as cruel and pitiless, perhaps he even began to find it difficult to believe in his own boasts. If it is true that women learn only through sorrow, I don't think Lucia can have learned anything until she loved Bernard. She knew what it was to be cold and hungry or frightened, for these are all very familiar to strolling players if they are women, but I don't think she had ever been really unhappy. Bernard taught her unhappiness, but she could not learn what unhappiness would have taught her— and so she killed herself.

"He finally deserted her at an inn where some mummers she had once known were staying. He may have thought she would be safe with them, or it may have been that he was too weary of her importunities to care what happened to her. He left her a gold piece; knowing him, I think that it was his last, for he was always generous with money if he had any.

"When she knew she would never see him again she went into a little church outside the village, to pray before the satue of St. Cecilia for courage. But the Latin words beat a rhythm in her head, 'Bernard!' 'Bernard!'; and she knew that he was the only god she believed in any more. Lucia no longer hoped for love potions, yet once more she went to an alchemist. She told him she wanted poison to kill a dog that raided her hen-roost, but he must have seen how desperate she was, for he made her pay the gold for it.

"She hid the phial in her bodice, and felt it cold as death between her tired breasts as she walked slowly back to the inn. She swept out her little room, and covered the bed-straw with her cloak. Then she lit a candle at the head and foot of the pallet, as if she were trying to make a bier for one she loved—to her it was a bier for love itself. She made a crucifix, of two sticks tied together with a strand of her hair. And kneeling before it she drank the poison.

"When the pain began, she lay down with her hands crossed on her breast, waiting for death to bring her peace. But even the alchemist had cheated her: she took a long time to die. The pain grew stronger. She tried to stop herself being sick, because she knew she had no money to buy more poison. Then the pain grew so terrible that she did not mind what happened, even if it meant she had to go on living, if only the pain would stop....

"The candles she had set were overturned; she writhed and struggled as though something was trying to tear out her bowels with iron claws. She forgot she was a woman; she was an animal, fighting against pain and then being devoured by it—until it seemed that there was no pain in the universe that was not in her own body.

"Then pain was no longer savage, but laid its heavy paws across her body to wait for her to die. She kept crying for water but no one heard her; and she was too weak to crawl to the door. She forgot she had given me her crucifix, and her hand kept fumbling at the pallid flesh of her neck to feel for its comfort. She died calling on Bernard's name, as if he were St. Anthony or the Holy Virgin.... I shall never be able to forget the sound of her voice, Bernard! Bernard! Bernard!....

"Her body was thrown into a plague pit, for the innkeeper was afraid that if it were known she had killed herself his patrons might think that her ghost walked.... He could not know that Lucia still lodged at his inn. She was no longer in pain, but she was in the dark; crying for Bernard and hearing only silence. She did not know she had done it over and over again, she thought it was happening for the first time.

"I know I have tried to go to her, but always someone held me back and told me that her time for release had not yet come. Yet she is free now, for last night I saw her; in her peace. She was dressed like the wife of a Doge, in silver brocade and a cloak of crimson velvet, sitting by a window which opened to a fair landscape. A little negro page stood by her chair, holding an open comfit box, and on a table ready to her hand there was a gold wine flagon—and a single goblet. I asked her if she remembered Bernard, but her eyes never changed and she went on smiling. And I knew she had forgotten him."

When I finished, Carlos sat very still, staring out of the window as if he were trying to read a secret written in the clouds. Then he spoke: "Sometimes I feel that in your philosophy there are terrors which only those who are born of courage dare to contemplate. The Church offers us heaven and hell; telling us little of purgatory save that it is the shadowy ante-room to paradise; yet their vision of hell has no reality for me, and I see their demons feeding the eternal fires only as monstrous puppets set to frighten children. But when you speak of what the soul must undergo, there is a quality in your words which makes them live in my mind. You have told me of the immutable justice by which you are ruled; you know of it as part of that same law which orders the waxing of the moon and summons the sun to each day's journey. Yet you have told me a story wherein I can see no justice, the story of a women driven by circumstance, driven beyond her strength to a pitiful death. You speak of death as if he were your friend, I have heard you call him the Great Inn-Keeper, the Great Physician, yet the death who came to Lucia was without pity, a dark destroyer who imprisoned her. Where is your justice that you talk of as the great law if this should be done? You have told me that there is no punishment for sin, but only a reaping: why did she gather such a bitter harvest?"

"Only Death may open the door of his Inn, and he who tries to enter as a felon shall be imprisoned. I have told you, as Petruchio first told me, that God does not give his Children a burden they cannot carry if they will but use their strength. His heart sorrows while their shoulders are bowed and they cannot look up to His face and smile, but it is a strange burden, for even He cannot take it from them; they must carry it until it has vanished. Each time that we are born there is a road which we must travel; in it there are valleys and mountains; wineshops and prisons. The road is not of our choosing, though it was made by us long since, but the manner of our journey lies in our own hands. The time we must spend on the road is allotted by God, and it has been decreed by Him that we must wait for death to summon us home. If this were not so, all of us who can see a little beyond the limitations of the flesh would put off our bodies, like a leper's cloak: for beyond death there is all that we long to find on earth, in its perfection."

He broke in, "But Lucia had no knowledge. How can she be condemned?"

"It must be that in the past she had sought the same way of escape, had been told that it was not well but did not listen, though her ears were open for the gods do not speak to the deaf. It was by her own action that she took poison."

"Her death, her pain even, I can understand. But why was she left crying alone for Bernard? Did she know she cried for him for—how long? Five years?"

"For her, time would not be measured as we know it. I heard her voice, 'Bernard! Bernard!' the words following each other in the sweeping rhythm of a scythe, for I was outside her hell. I knew that time passed, but for her it stood still. She could not see the hand that turned the hour-glass, she could see only the sand, the sand of the present."

"But why? Why?"

"She was bound into the present, cut off not only from time but from her own spirit, so that when the water from her journey as Lucia returns into the jar of her experience, with it will go a memory so strong that she will never seek the same way of escape: the escape that is no escape.''

"How do you know? How *can* you know?''

"Because once I too received a warning to which I would not listen. Then I was made to hear that voice which to some of us is louder than the voice of any other teacher, the voice of my own experience. I remember a knife that searched for my heart. My own hand held that knife. Hoping for death, hoping for oblivion, I tried to drive it further and further up under my ribs. Each time I thought, "This is the last pain...." I do not know how long I was there.... A day, a year, a century? But I will never again attempt that same futility.''

"You think that all who die by their own hand are cowards or fools?''

"Only those who try to escape from life; for there is no escape from thought or feeling in the little incident of the body's death. Yet I have known of men who have died by their own hand in glory, for they were not trying to escape. I will tell you a story—I was shown it away from earth, I cannot remember by whom or in what millennium it happened: Once there was a man whose people were besieged in a city, built on the edge of a cliff above a river. It was in a country where there are strange trees and birds of vivid plumage such as I have never seen on earth. There was a secret way out of the city, and by it the man tried to pass the enemy encampment with a message for succour to a friendly tribe. But he was taken prisoner. His captors tortured him; they knew he could show them the way the city could be taken if they could make him betray his people—I will not tell you what they did to him, except that with pain they were very subtle. Then they shut him in a dark hut; for they were afraid that if, for a few hours, he was not left unmolested he would die under their hands, as he prayed to do—in silence. He knew that his last endurance had been reached, that he could bear no more pain and to-morrow would betray even his gods if that were demanded of him. He knew there was only one way to assure that the secret way would never be revealed by him. His hands were bound behind him with a raw-hide thong, but he was able to chafe his wrist against a sharp stone until he opened a vein; not through fear of torture but to protect his people from the peril of his tongue. He thought he died as a coward, wept for the weakness of his flesh which he dared not trust to defend his spirit; and as he felt the blood trickling over his crippled hands it seemed as though all honor and courage seeped away with it. Then he heard a great shout ring through the silence, the shout of warriors welcoming a hero to their ranks. And he found that on his head was the horned helmet of the great hunters, and round him were the Wearers of the Scarlet to whom he had become brother in splendor.''

''And what of those who kill themselves when they have gone mad?''

''What is madness? Sometimes it is only that one is born wiser than the people one must live among: a seer or a visionary might seem a lunatic to merchants, and a cardinal thought a cretin in a country of the wise!''

''Carola, I once had a friend who was seized by a melancholy as other men are seized by a pox; it was as though he lived in a shroud of grief. He had great possessions, but he shut himself away from them; he had a beloved wife, but he refused to see her. His family were afraid he would destroy himself, so he was always watched from behind the arras—but at last he escaped them and strangled himself with the sleeve of his bedgown. What of him?''

''I can only guess, for of him I do not know. It may be that in the past he had brought affliction to others: perhaps by the misuse of his intellect he had brought humiliation upon them, perhaps his pride had been a scourge upon the weak, or his mockery a prelude to their despair. My grandmother so tormented her household with her tongue, and there are many such as she. The sorrows they have caused to others will come upon them at one time; all the petty deceits that others have been put to for fear of them, all the small joys they destroyed, all the needless apprehensions they fostered; small things in themselves but a mighty enemy together. They will descend like a cloud of stinging flies to make a black pall over him who gave them birth; it may be the hand of a madman which drives the dagger into such a heart; but he made the dagger when he was sane—and he will not forge another of the same metal.''

''You told me of Sofia. What if she had killed herself when she had been possessed?''

''Then it would not have been Sofia but her possessor who killed her.''

''But why was she possessed?''

''She would not have been if once she had not allowed the bodies of others to suffer that defilement. To me, Carlos, it seems the greatest of all sins to make of one's body a house for devils. Remember, there can be terrible crimes brought to a man's door of which he is innocent; a hundred eyes may have seen him drive a knife into the heart of the one he loves, and they will all bear witness to his guilt, yet it is not he, but the tenant whom he has permitted to lodge within himself who directed his hand. On earth he will suffer man's penalty for murder, away from earth he will know that in his flesh he suffers his betrayal of it; and thus he will learn that the ways of sorcery are never trodden by the feet of the wise.''

''Then there is no escape?''

''None by death from life. When I came to your house there was pain in my body, and it did not diminish when Anna changed my saffron bedgown to one of green, for it was not the silk that felt the pain but I. How then should I escape from pain by changing one body for another? For it is not the flesh of Carola that feels the pain, but I. My body is only a channel through which I must receive experience, and I shall experience only that which is necessary for the strengthening of my spirit.''

flail of the angels

After I had told Carlos of Lucia, it seemed she had come like an unquiet ghost to rob him of the measure of serenity I had given him. We still talked together of dead philosophers whose dusty manuscripts slept in his library, but even their words brought him no comfort. To him her tragedy remained a tragedy, and he could not see that it was only a fragment of mosaic in the pattern of her experience. I searched my dream-memory for what might bring back knowledge of the great justice to his heart, yet it was in the childhood of Carola I found the key to unlock the prison of his intellect.

I was gathering flowers in the cool of a summer evening, to set in the marble urns that flanked the chimney in my favorite room, when I said to Carlos, ''When I was a child I went to a fair where there was a troupe of monstrosities. Among them were twin brothers who within the womb had grown into one flesh. They were joined at the waist, turned half away from each other, and one always had to walk sideways, like a crab. They did a shambling dance, or sang in high, cracked voices; and each knew that in his brother's eyes, eyes he had never seen, shone an old, smoldering hatred of his fellow prisoner. They knew that when either died he would be the other's murderer, for from his mortifying flesh slow death would creep, to grasp the still-beating heart that so long had kept the rhythm of his own. It seems that Lucia was bound to Bernard as were those twins, by a bond of flesh, so strong that when he severed it she died, as surely as if he himself had poisoned her. For a time I thought their bond must have been forged by Satan, but now I know that this was not so. I was told, and it was far from earth I heard it, that such a love is sometimes sent to spur on those who tarry too long beside the path: I call it the Flail of the Angels.''

He sighed, ''Even your angels carry flails to drive on their unwilling penitents! Carola, it is strange, and terrible, that

271

you who are gentle should hold so dear your cruel philosophy.''

''Only injustice is cruel—and if we look beyond the outward form of temporal existence we see there is no injustice.''

His voice was weary as he said, ''The punishment of Lucia was not on earth.''

I put down my basket, and made him sit by me on a bench under the mulberry tree, before I answered. ''See, there is blood on my finger where I pricked it on a thorn. Shall I blame the rose for punishing me—or admit that it was I who grasped it carelessly?''

''Are you not juggling with words?''

''No, for it is the same with all wounds, of heart or flesh: it is we who cause them to our own sorrow. Yet this very sorrow is the seed of the corn of experience from which the living bread is milled. Lucia would not have had that tie with Bernard bound upon her unless it was necessary for her to learn what it alone could teach her. In the past she refused to listen, many times, to what was said to her in a gentle voice; and even when she had to hear a harsh command, if she had used her own powers she would have been able to obey, without suffering the pains which come to all who try to escape the destiny they themselves have made. Once she ruled others by their lust, to their destruction. Lucia was not young in spirit; she would never have allowed a man to break her pride if she had not been assailed by this strange blindness; which made her see Bernard, whom she used to laugh at for a boaster and a fool, in a form very near to her god. Through this breaking of her pride she has gained the strength that before was never hers, a strength with which she will be able to teach others how to be wise in the age of their own loins. She will show them how best the iron links, forged on the anvil of desire, can be transmuted into the gold threads of the love that receives all because it demands nothing.''

Carlos had taken a rose out of my basket, and was turning

it between his fingers as he said, ''It is curious that our language should give us ten words with which to describe the scent of a rose, and only one for the manifold variations of love.''

''Perhaps it is because even the makers of words find it easier not to look beyond the little world of the senses. If they could see more clearly, they would know that love needs a true priest, or at least a philosopher, to mark even its broad divisions. In every experience there must be some aspect of love, the love that is within us which will one day fuse with the god from whom it sprang. I see love as a ladder reaching to eternity: he who climbs it must know of every rung, for unless he has known and conquered lust, he cannot transcend the limits of the flesh, to burnish the soul and so perfect the spirit.''

''And lust is evil?''

''Only when it blinds the long in years to their own wisdom: and if they had not scorned that early rung, by which they should have grown strong in their youth, they would not be thus blinded in their age. Each rung of the ladder, rising from earth to heaven, must in its turn be climbed. Near its foot is a wolf, scenting its mate through the darkness; at its head a man about to enter paradise: yet while they climb they are part of the same whole, and when the climb is past they will still be one, with God.''

And when Carlos and I returned to the house I was his sole companion; for the memory of Lucia no longer walked with him.

CHAPTER TWENTY-FOUR

lalage

In the summer of the following year there were rumors of plague in Perugia, so Carlos took me to his house which lay three days' journey in the hills to the north-east. Although it was still early in July, I found it very hot inside the traveling coach. The two windows were covered by leather curtains to keep out the dust, and the upholstery had the stale smell of musty cloth. The long sleeves of my purple dress were tight, and the silver threads of the embroidery on my shoes had rubbed through the lining and chafed my toes. As we lurched over the deep ruts I tried not to think that an ox-cart, where one could lie down in the straw and sleep, was more comfortable than riding in a coach; nor to remember the freedom of coarse shifts and bare feet.

It was the first time I had stayed at an inn since Petruchio died. Everything was ready to welcome us: the inn-keeper bowing, and his wife, in a newly-starched cap, curtseying in the background; for Carlos had sent a servant to prepare for our arrival. There were fresh rushes strewn on the floor of our room. For dinner we had their best wine, with roasted capons followed by a syllabub, warm and very sweet.

The inn-keeper's wife was anxious about my comfort, for she believed me to be a great lady. I thought how horrified she would be if I told her I was used to sleeping in the lofts over inn stables. As I had no maidservant with me, Anna having gone ahead to make ready the house, the woman asked that she might attend me when I prepared for bed. I tried not to hurt her by my refusal, but I saw she was surprised: I could not tell her that none save Anna might see me naked, for my scars had not yet faded and anyone who saw them would realize that such a precision of lashing could have been given only to a heretic. They might even have recalled the "red-haired bride of Satan" for whom the witch-hunters had searched Perugia since the previous spring.

It was evening when we arrived at the House of the High Air. The track to it was very rough, winding up through a growth of stunted pines. The house was of one story, set on a natural terrace in the hillside. It was plastered white, frescoed with a design of formal vines, and the roof-tiles were the color of red earth. It was very different from the Perugian house: instead of hangings of tapestry or gilded leather there were plain walls, and the blue curtains were bordered with a flower pattern in faded wools, poppies and ears of wheat and marguerites. The tiled floors were bare; the chests and tables, and the long benches, were like those I had seen in the house of a prosperous farmer when Petruchio and I had played there for a wedding.

After I had rested, I went out to join Carlos on the paved terrace in front of the house. On three sides of it there was a vine pergola, in the form of a cloister. Below us the ground sloped steeply; some white goats were feeding on the crisp pasture, and their bells echoed up to us as they moved. It was here that Carlos told me the story of his first wife, Lalage....

In the days when my parents were still alive, their household was maintained in the state usual to noble families of the time. My mother, as I have already told you, was Spanish; and she possessed, as do many of her countrymen, a taste for plotting. I think that without her encouragement my father would have been content in his riches, but she turned him from a kindly man into a disappointed aspirant for power. The house was dark with intrigue, and the people who were welcome to it were not chosen for their qualities of friendship but for the weight of their influence.

I would have found my companions in painters and musicians, but such a choice was considered unworthy of a Ludovici. My mother thought that for a young man of my position to wish to be a poet was as though I shamed her by blackening my face, and carried round a comfit box like her negro page.

To escape from this stifling environment I traveled widely, but while at home I tried to adjust myself to their standards of behavior. I became famous for the elegance of my dress, and no fashion was introduced from abroad that I was not among the first to wear. I was seldom defeated in the tilt-yard, yet none guessed that my manner was heavier to wear than any armor I put on to joust. It was remarked that I was indifferent to women; but that was ascribed to my fastidiousness—or to a liking for less creditable adventures.

My companions would have been bewildered if they had known that when I went hawking it was not the power of the falcon I shared, but the pigeon's death; if they had known that when I rode against Milan, beyond the trumpets of the charge I heard the cries of the dying echo the chink of mercenaries' gold.

My mother endeavored to extend her influence even to choosing a wife for me; trying to tempt my senses with the daughter of a house with whom she hoped to make a suitable alliance. I could not forestall her disappointment by telling her that I saw only their blackened teeth and the pock marks under their fard! When I was twenty-five I had an inheritance from a great-uncle, and with it I built this house, where at times I could escape to live as a man and not a puppet. I let it be known that I was building it, but gave no clue to its position. Even my mother made no protest, for it was soon rumored that I lodged my mistress here, and this did much to calm her doubts of me.

I kept three servants, and this house became a place where poets, or artists who had no patron, could work undisturbed by the anxieties of bread or lodging. It soon became known among their fraternity that even when I was not in residence they would be welcomed, so I often played host to men I had never seen.

I was thirty-four when I returned to find a painter living here. With him was his model, a girl of eighteen whom he had got with child; less, so he told me, from a desire to take her, than because he wished to see her with a more fruitful curve to her belly as inspiration for a masterpiece of the goddess of summer. She was an incident in his craft, no more important than the selection of a panel or the blending of pigments.

When the picture was finished he went away, but she stayed on. The servants accepted her as one of themselves, as I did, and when I heard that her child was born I sent word that he was to be my godson, choosing for him the name Alcestes. Until two years later I never saw him, for I was out of Italy, and when I returned I had almost forgotten they might still be here.

As I rode up the hill I saw a woman carrying a laughing child on her shoulder. I drew rein to watch them. They were both garlanded with marguerites, and they looked strong and beautiful, rich as the earth. I felt my slow pulses stir. In her I saw embodied so many things I had once hoped for: to sit by a hearth where wood I had chopped was burning, to drink wine from grapes which I myself had planted; and at my side a woman from whom I need not hide my heart.

There was a strength about Lalage I had never seen in other women. Her hair was wheat gold, fragrant as warm hay. Her skin was unblemished, and her eyes were calm as water. Her thoughts flowed placidly as a summer river, and there was a stillness about her like the sound of corn growing. I loved her as I had once dreamed of love, for she was gentle as milk and honest as bread when you are hungry.

Soon we were married, and at my parents' death I took her to Perugia. For a time we lived there, finding contentment even among the uneasy memories of my youth. Now friends sat at my table, dining with laughter in good company, in that great room where once intrigues were brewed.

But the gods must have been jealous of such happiness; for when my son was born, Lalage died with him.

Thereafter I lived alone with the boy Alcestes. He was not like his mother, who had loved the earth. It was as if he had been born in fealty to the sea. He was always talking of ships, and would evade his tutors to pore over an old folio of charts. I longed to keep him with me, but I had learned that each man must be free to set his course by his own star. So after Alcestes became skilled in seamanship, I gave him a vessel built to his own design. He called her the *Crimson Rose*.

Sometimes a year, two years, go by before I see him. I was in sorrow for him on the night you found my door, for it was only three days since he had set out on a perilous voyage, to where men say the sea falls into space beyond the New Land.

Statue of Apollo

Even though our life at the House of the High Air had none of the formality of Perugia, I sometimes found the role of Donna Carola a little irksome. When this happened I used to go out alone, often from dawn until after nightfall, wearing a dress of grey fustian which Anna had copied for me from one of her own. At first Carlos protested at my going unattended, but he soon accepted it as one of my unpredictable fancies.

One day I wandered farther than usual and came to a narrow valley hidden in a fold of the hills. There, set in a grove of ancient ilex, I found the forgotten ruins of a house. It must have been long deserted, for turf had covered the broken walls and only the ordered ranks of the dark trees showed they had been planted by man. A spring bubbled from the mouth of what once must have been a satyr's mask, and the water flowed down into a long basin cut from the rock. The noon sun was hot, so I took off my clothes and lay there in the shade of the heavy ferns, my body cool and fish-smooth under the water.

Often I returned, for the place held a drowsy peace for me,

as though it dreamed of a secret world beyond the sight of mortals. I used to wonder who had built these walls and planted the shrubs whose children still made flowery thickets down the slope; but it was not until I had been there many times that I knew their origin.

In the heat of the day I used to sleep in the shade of a syringa, my head resting against what I thought to be a fallen column; and while there I had waking dreams of the time when the house lived. It was after one such dream that I felt the roughness of worked stone under the moss, and un-covered part of a vine-leaf chaplet. I freed the statue from its green shroud, and found it to be of a beautiful youth, either of the God of Love or of some mortal who in a nymph's arms had warmed to immortality. He seemed to smile at me, and, stranger still, in the living stone from which he had been carved, the story of the two who set him here had been pre-served, as once I had seen a fly preserved in amber. When I touched the statue it was as though I became one with him. I could see through his stone eyelids, hear with his carven ears, savor the votive incense burnt to his name, Apollo. Scene by scene, the lives of the two lovers who had been dead for many centuries, unfolded before me.

The woman wore robes such as I had seen on Roman amphorae. She had been a temple virgin, consecrate to some ritual of an ever-burning fire. The man had been a senator: I know not what rank he held, but I saw him among other men on tiered seats of marble below a dais. They wore togas of white or saffron color, and some were wreathed with bays.

For her to leave her dedicated life was to be put to death. For him to gain her was to lose all else; honor, and name, and power. So was their early love constrained to sorrow. Then to Apollo they addressed their prayers, and they were shown the worldly artifice by which their love defeated circum-stance.

Many leagues from their city he built this house for her. For labor he used slaves bought from the oars, and when the work was done he sent them as freed men to a province across the sea. When all was ready he went to his summer villa on the coast; and when he knew that a storm was coming up, he set forth with two trusted servants on what feigned to be but a short sail. They battled down the coast through monstrous waves, until a shelter cove was gained where none could see their landing. From there he reached the temple, where, by a subtle ruse, the woman joined him. They traveled swiftly, always at night and listening for pursuit, until at last they reached this sanctuary.

The world believed them dead. The priestesses feared to betray that they had lost a vestal from the temple precincts; the women of his household put ashes on their heads and wailed in the streets; the townspeople mourned their senator who they thought had been snatched from them by Neptune.

In the hot weather, awnings were stretched above the courtyard to which their rooms opened. Lucretia would lie there on a narrow couch carved in the form of a swan, while two women slaves attended her elaborate toilet. They were foreigners who spoke only a few words of her language: one of them had the proud carriage of those accustomed to being obeyed; perhaps she had belonged to a ruling family in the country from which a Roman galley had taken her. Yet she smiled as she knelt beside the couch, holding an ointment jar, or pouring from a painted flask aromatic oil with which to anoint the smooth body of her mistress. Lucretia's teeth were polished with a black powder, perhaps it was charcoal, and then she would tint the lobes of her ears and her palms with carmine. Her hair was dressed in falling curls, bound with bright ribbons or threaded with silver pins. Her tunics were of finely pleated linen, moulding the lines of her body and the springing curve of her breasts.

She and Nigellus would walk down the path between the cypresses in seeming formality, but sometimes they forgot their Roman dignity and shed it with their clothes in some secluded glade.

There were forests on the hills in those days; there Nigellus used to hunt the wild boar, his hounds startling the silence with their baying. He cannot have found it easy to abandon his senatorial life; I have heard him address the cypresses as though they were a critical audience to be won over by his wit. He began to write a political history of the years when he held office, and she to play on a stringed instrument. It had thin, clear notes, less mellow than a lute and of smaller compass.

I think they found the house cold in the depths of winter, as though they had been used to a more genial warmth than comes from open fires. Yet even when the snow had drifted against the walls, enveloped in heavy-folded cloaks of yellow wool, they left the house to make a votive offering to Apollo.

The years passed, yet nothing came to disturb their serenity. They had a child, perhaps two children: I am not sure if the baby in her arms was the same child that I saw running beside his father. She cannot have lived to be an old woman—or perhaps love gave her the semblance of immortality, for it was only in her youth that I saw her.

Together they found a joy that is rare among mortals; and still their laughter stirs that quiet air, and their love remains to bless the paths they made. There did I share an echo of their happiness; and with the statue of Apollo found companionship, for we both dreamed of that far time when men had loved us for our gods.

Carola Saw Love

For the winter we returned to Perugia, where only in sleep could I go to the house in the ilex grove. It seemed that through the eyes of the statue I saw more of my heart than I had recognized before it was stirred by the memory of the Roman lovers; as though I was no longer a watcher but waited for a lover with whom I could share their pleasures. I forgot that I once prayed to be protected against what I thought to be the miasma of desire; and remembered only that I had lived as Carola less than a quarter century. The weals had nearly faded from my skin, and my long-hidden breasts were smooth and young.

I found that in sleep I could dream within a dream....

In the drowsy heat the syringa bushes were heavy with scent, and the glade they encompassed was still green, as I had kept it with water carried from the spring. It seemed I had slipped into an ancient past when Cupid's arrows were shafted with fine gold and feathered with peace. O happy past! whose gates have long been locked against me. This is a dream, but let it bear me onward in its tide....

I sensed that some one was approaching me. I feigned to sleep, and listened for a voice I longed to hear. He spoke, ''It seems I have become a visionary; for the man who came across these hills was a clod, prosaic as a muleteer. I saw this hidden vale, cool and mysterious. I passed through the somber shadows of a grove, a grove where still the Delphic oracles might utter their sonorous prophecies. And then I reached a house as I have seen on classic urns. Yet were its pillars freshly garlanded, and shining floor mosaics caught the sun. I knew a woman waited here for me, my woman, who held all beauty in her hands. You know me, for your lips warm to mine.''

And smiling down at her, Carola saw love....

But I woke in Perugia, with Anna smiling down at me. Even before she spoke I knew she had great news. ''A messenger reached us soon after dawn. To-morrow our Alcestes will be here! He is come safe into Naples, but they had a desperate voyage and he must leave his ship there to be careened. Even now he will be galloping toward us. He is always impatient is Alcestes; he always was, even as a baby. My mother helped at his birth. He was always for adventure; before he was big enough to walk he used to crawl along the terrace to see what lay beyond it.''

She was talking more to herself than to me, while folding into a dower chest the clothes I had worn the evening before. But I knew she watched to see if I ate the curds she brought me every morning, and drank the special potion of goats' milk flavored with sweet wine which she made for me in wintry weather.

She went out to fetch a pan of glowing charcoal to fire the logs, and not until they had warmed the room did she let me get out of bed. I was so impatient to go to Carlos that I would not wait for her to dress me, but told her to fetch a fur-lined robe I had worn when I could walk no farther than the sollar, and to put on ordinary clothes would have fatigued me.

I found the steward being given orders for preparing the house in welcome to Alcestes. Carlos was saying, "...and tell Caterina there must be sucking pig, and hill mutton larded with green bacon and sprigs of rosemary. We will broach the cask of Spanish wine, for now it must be mellowed to perfection. Tell the cloth merchant to attend the house the day after to-morrow; my son will need new doublets after such a voyage."

Then Carlos saw me. "Carola, has Anna told you? Alcestes returns to-morrow!"

"She has no need to tell me, for I saw the joy in her eyes before she spoke, as I see it in yours. What can I do to add to his welcome? Shall I wear the garnet velvet or the russet? I must look very dignified, or he may disapprove your choice of his stepmother!"

"Disapprove?" he laughed. "You think my godson a fool, and blind?"

"I hope he will love me a little for your sake."

"How could he help it? But it will be for your own sake, not mine." He hesitated, "You must not be impatient with Alcestes, he has not your vision, nor my joy in it, but he will have much to tell us. Once I might have thought his wonders sailors' tales, but now I am used to wonders. And if he tells me he has seen a dragon—a hundred dragons dark against the sky, I could believe him: for through you I know of angels. Has not one put off her wings to rest a little under my roof?''

Perhaps I was almost jealous to see Carlos so eager, nearer to happiness than I had ever brought him. To greet Alcestes I dressed with care, and wore the carved emerald on my forehead. As I bound my hair under the gold caul I might have been putting on my helm to enter the tilt-yard. I knew that now I must raise the portcullis which I dropped against invasion from the world since I had come to Carlos. With Alcestes other strangers would enter the house, people who might awaken the Carola who had traveled many roads. They would remind me of the girl who had loved Sandra for a little while—only the ghost of love, but warm and near. Carlos would be content to listen to Alcestes, but his sailor's talk might take me back to the *Santa Maria;* to Fiume where I had walked hungry down the quays, searching the grey horizon for a lost sail. I would think of the Captain sinking down through the green depths; green as the light in the penitential cell where I had waited summons to the torture.

I heard a horseman clatter down the street; the voice of Carlos raised in joyful greeting.... I will not hurry, it is fit that my stepson should wait to greet me.

I stood at the head of the great staircase. A shaft of light shone down through the high window, making a vivid pool on the grey stone of the hall below. It lit a man who stood there, looking up at me.

He smiled, but I knew that he did not remember that last night we were together in Apollo's grove.

CHAPTER TWENTY-FIVE

Godson of Carlos

On the night of Alcestes' return we dined in the banqueting hall for the first time since my marriage day: Carlos sitting at the head of the table between his wife and his godson.

Only the callouses on the hands of Alcestes showed that he was more than the young man of fashion that the richness of his clothes would have had one believe: the fabric was stiff with gold threads, and the velvet of his shoulder cloak was even more lustrous than that of Genoa. After Carlos had remarked their foreign cut, Alcestes said, ''They come from Spain, where I made my first landfall after ninety days. I had nothing fit for a scullion to wear or I should not sit here aping a Spanish dandy.''

Then he began to talk of his voyage, choosing his words with such vividness that it seemed the somber tapestries melted into the shadows to give place to other scenes.... Steep alleys led down to a crowded harbor, where negresses with heavy baskets on their heads passed with processional dignity along the waterfront. Two children, their dark skins glistening in the heat, quarreled over a slice of melon. A sailor lurched out of a tavern doorway, blood streaming from his side where a knifethrust had ended a brawl.... A cloudless sky, pale with the heat, showed the becalmed horizon day after torrid day. Flying fish skimmed the sea: sometimes one fell on the deck, to be carried in triumph to the galley by the man who snatched it up.... A white beach of coral sand, the *Crimson Rose* lying helpless on her side to be careened....

Alcestes' voice, ''I made the men wrap their feet in canvas while they scraped off the weed that fouled her, for I found that the cuts made by barnacles festered in that climate and would not heal. I sent men into the woods to hunt for fresh meat, but they brought back only birds stoned from the trees.

From the brilliance of the plumage I thought the flesh would shame a peacock's, but it was flavorless and tough. That island was uninhabited, so after a few days I did not order a night watch to be kept. At the next island we reached, the natives came out to us in canoes as soon as we dropped anchor. We stood to arms, but they brought presents of flowers and fruits in tribute to friendship. At first they were afraid of our white skins, but gradually we overcame their timidity with gifts—a piece of bright cloth or a broken knife. Those shy, brown people had great dignity and were unashamed in their nakedness. The women seemed as free and happy as the men; I used to watch them swimming down through the clear water among the coral, to come up laughing, holding a shell or a streamer of colored weed gathered from the sea-bed. I told the crew that the first man to violate a woman should have his hand cut off; they grumbled among themselves but they obeyed me.

''After a time the chief accepted me as a friend; I could communicate with him by signs and even learned a few words of his language. I wanted to know if mine was the first ship from the Old Land to anchor there, so I showed him a crucifix. He took it from me and fingered it curiously; but he showed no fear, so I knew the Spaniards had not forestalled us. I stayed there nearly two moons, yet I never saw a man angry or a woman crying—it is difficult to believe that because they are heathens they must all go to hell.''

Carlos smiled at me, ''It seems that you must take Alcestes as another pupil. It shames me to think that once I too had thoughts as foolish as the one he has just expressed.''

Alcestes misunderstood him. ''You never believed all that I told you, did you, Carlos? But wait until you see the treasure I have brought home! Then you will believe that for the last two years I have seen places beyond the limits of familiar seas. I made drawings of some of the things I saw; they are crude sketches, for I never learned more than I needed to trace a chart, but will serve to show an artist what I wish to depict.'' He went on eagerly. ''There are many more islands where no white man has yet landed. The Spaniards and Portuguese are greedy of conquest, but there is still scope for a private venture. I have seen ignorant savages wearing gold ornaments, armlets and heathen amulets. They do not know the value of gold, so I think they would trade peaceably. There is great treasure there to be had by anyone with a knowledge of seamanship and a little courage.''

Carlos interrupted him, ''You used to be impatient of riches, Alcestes, when I told you there was nothing you need lack if you stayed at home. The vaults of Ludovici are still well stocked. Must you sail in search of gold when it lies ready to your hand?''

''I want *my* gold, gold that I have won for myself out of the West. I want to find my own heritage in a land to which my sails have brought me.''

''Would it be *your* gold?'' I asked him.

He looked surprised, ''Whose but mine, when I am the Captain of the ship that takes it?''

I smiled a little scornfully, ''It might be considered to belong to the people who have taken it out of the ground, for God put it there and they found it. Why should you trick it from them with your bolts of cloth and promises of friendship?''

''There will be no deceit: they don't know the value of it. To them it is only a metal like other metals.''

Carlos raised his goblet, ''A toast to the only people who know the value of gold; know it for a metal easily worked by craftsmen, yet from it have made no fetters.''

Islanð ın the West

With the mask of Donna Carola I tried to defend myself against the memory of a dream. At first I contrived never to be alone with Alcestes; but I saw that by doing so I hurt

Carlos, who imagined that I found no pleasure in the company of his godson. He gave little sign that he was more than a young man of culture who had followed the sea; yet I found that when he was with me my fingers plucked love-songs from the lute strings instead of seeking for a thread of celestial melody. I did not admit even to myself why I was eager for new clothes and wore wreaths of flowers instead of hiding my hair under a caul. So in the bastions of formality we waited, to watch whether love would raise her siege.

As Carlos had told me that Alcestes took little interest in philosophy, I usually talked the pretty nonsense expected of young women. But one day, when he had been telling me of the islands which know an eternal summer, I asked him, "Do you really believe what you said to Carlos, that those happy people are condemned to hell because they are born, and live, and die, without the offices of the Christian church?"

He seemed surprised at my question; answered it like a boy repeating a lesson. "They must; for only those who live in Christ can be redeemed."

I was sitting at an embroidery frame, and he lay at my feet before the fire. I said, "I should not like to meet your god...a cruel old man, blind to his own justice. He made this earth and peopled it. Then for many centuries, even if we accept the short span of time the Church allows since the creation, he left it to destruction. It seems that even your god knew remorse, for he came down among his forsaken people so that the few who chanced to hear his teaching might be saved by grace. He found it convenient to forget those other peoples he had caused to lived beyond the reach of messengers across oceans the ships of that time could not navigate."

Alcestes looked, almost fearfully, at the door to make sure it was shut, before saying urgently, "You must not speak like that; it is blasphemy, and worse, heresy!"

I mocked him gently, "Is it better to denounce God than His Church? As *you* judge them it would be right! for your

288

god is blind, and may be deaf as well; and we know the pyres are always eager for heretics!''

''Has Carlos heard you speak like this?''

I smiled, ''With him it is seldom necessary. He is not so foolish as his godson.''

''To speak as though you were ignorant of the power of the Church is more foolish than I could ever be!''

I knew that he was near to anger, so I asked him to find me a strand of crimson from the tangle of silks on the floor by my chair. As I threaded the needle, I said, ''If the Church were not in ignorance of her own wisdom there would be no heretics.''

''It is dangerous to speak of heretics.''

''When you know me better, Alcestes, you will find that I value my speech more than my safety. You should have sympathy with me, or why do you voyage with danger when you could have security at home?''

''The countries that still boast of chivalry are rotten with intrigue. I want to build on ground that has never been betrayed. I want to make my own laws, mint a new coinage....'' He was staring into the fire, as though the land he dreamed of took shape within the flames. ''I shall take children there, boys about twelve years old, girls a little younger. I shall choose them from the poor who slink, furtive as animals, through fetid passages of harbor towns. They are only vicious because they are oppressed. Hunger has made them thieves, fear driven them to murder. I shall take them across the seas and free them from the bondage of squalor. They shall have clean fields where the earth is rich for sowing. They will learn to laugh, and never again shall they have to watch their children die from the slow agony of starvation, or feel the pains of winter by an empty hearth.''

He looked very young; his voice sounded eager as does a boy's before his belief in the future has been tarnished. It was then I knew what I loved in him.

I said, ''You do not speak as the same man who wanted

to take gold from those brown people.''

''I must have gold, more gold than my ship could carry in one voyage! I need it to build more ships, to buy arms, ploughs, grain—a thousand things. I need it to hire physicians, botanists; to enroll masons, and carpenters, and men skilled in farming.'' He paused a moment, ''And I must find young priests who are willing to come with me.''

''Before you search for gold, search for true priests; and if you find them, be sure you do not fear to listen because they seem to speak as heretics. You may not find what you seek in the shadow of the Church, yet I think that in monasteries there are some who see beyond their ritual. Take with you priests who remember the teaching of Christ and observe not only the outward forms of their religion.''

''You never go to Mass; why then do you think my people need religion?''

''Because there is a hunger which can be satisfied only by the bread of wisdom. You might give them food, and see them starve; shelter, and see them perish; work, and see them rot in idleness; free from their oppressors, and still they would be chained like galley-slaves.''

''I do not understand you.''

''Freedom is born of the heart, and riches come from the seeing of values that cannot be weighed on a merchant's scales. Possessions cannot bring happiness until he who holds them knows how they must be used. You must teach your people how to think before you can show them how to live.''

''It is easy for you, who have everything to scorn possessions!''

''I do not scorn them; for what I have I hold in gratitude to Carlos.''

''My people will not need the balm of philosophy.''

''Truth is not a balm; it is the elixir of life. Without it your people will never grow strong, though the grain ripens and the fishermen haul in their loaded nets, for a man who forgets his gods is only half alive.''

''God will be with us; and a priest to whom we shall confess our sins and so be shrived.''

''Not even God can shrive a man of his sins, Alcestes; God can only show him how to adjust the scales. Once men went to confession seeking, not forgiveness, but to be shown how to see their own hearts. It is well that a man should tell his sorrows to a friend, for it reminds him of the kinship of all men with the Father.''

''You speak as though you held authority....''

It was I, not Carola, who answered Alcestes, ''Thousands of years ago I ruled over a country whose people lived as you wish yours to live. They were content, for their priests were men of wisdom who told them whence they had come and where their journey led them.''

Alcestes looked at me, as though in sudden recognition of reality which until then had been beyond his range of vision. He said slowly, ''Why do I believe you—even against my reason?''

''Because I have made you listen to the truth within you; and you have heard your own voice above the clamor of a world that has made you deaf.''

The evening sky dulled to twilight, to darkness; the logs glowed among the ashes; yet still we talked of his island in the west where the old wisdom should rule again.

It was then Alcestes said to me, ''Though all the men who dwelt there thought it Paradise, still would I be a prisoner if you were not beside me.''

I forgot the ties that held me to Perugia, ''When you sail I shall go with you, and together we will found a city where our dreams are born.''

It seemed I could already hear the waves of a far ocean sighing against the prow of the *Crimson Rose*. I saw those children who would have been old in sorrow led from their hovels to board the ships that followed in our wake. I saw new houses built, smelt bread baking in the ovens; heard children laugh as they played in the warm shallows. I saw myself, sitting under a tree at evening while the people gathered round me to hear stories of other times when men had not hidden their faces from the gods. I saw a funeral pyre; yet the mourners were wreathed with flowers, for they rejoiced with him who had preceded them beyond earth. I saw Alcestes and Carola, as a new Adam and a new Eve, who created an Eden they could share with others....

I heard the creak of the opening door. The light from the sconce in the passage threw the shadow of my husband across the floor. It fell between me and Alcestes; and I knew I could not sail with him, for we loved Carlos.

lament for a lute

Instead of returning to my body reluctantly, I woke to a new joy. Even Anna noticed the change in me; yet if she guessed it came from my love for Alcestes, she had no misgivings. For the first time since I had been a child I was eager for life, and I made myself believe that Alcestes would leave the sea and be content to stay with me. We shared the unspoken thought that Carlos was old, and that it would be easy to wait until time had set me free to sail to the island where we need no longer deny our love. He might have been a knight in one of the stories I had woven from the tapestries in my father's castle, and I his princess. I lived in the sweet airs of the present, trying to hold each hour of this vivid warmth to clothe them safe in memory; and keep them like the sand in an hour-glass so that through the future I could live in love.

I was content that we should not be lovers, until one day I said to Alcestes, ''If you had not taken me into your heart you might have found another woman who would have given you so much more than I.''

"What more could a man want than to love a goddess, even from afar?''

"A goddess? No, only a woman kept from your arms by barren vows.''

It was only then that Alcestes knew I was wife to Carlos only in name. I tried to make him understand that Carlos had not cheated me of my youth, but he said, "One day I will make you break your marriage vows. I think I could make you break them even if your virginity was sworn to Christ.''

Then he released me, "Is that why you seem so cold? Do you strive for the austerity of a nun?''

I thought with bitterness of cloistered days. "I find no special virtue in virginity. All women are born with it, and they may lose it for many reasons; but I have never believed it to hold magical properties.''

"No man should pretend to own what he cannot possess. Carlos will never know that to-morrow for the first time you will wake as a bride.''

It was only when I realized the horror my faint scars held for Alcestes that I knew Carlos had never told him what my life as Carola had been. I began to tell him some of the things I had seen as a strolling player, but I saw that it offended him to know that the woman who sang to him had learned her lutany from a jester and played to a harlot's singing. He knew that I was a bastard of the Griffin and had been in a convent; and he must have pictured me growing up in the cloistered seclusion usual to girls who belong to noble families by blood but not by name. Again I tried to tell him of the woman he claimed to love, but he silenced me with endearments, using his body as a shield against my mind.

I tried so hard to stay warmly in love, but as the days passed they seemed to draw me farther away from him; until even in the midst of an embrace I seemed as remote from those figures in each other's arms as had been the statue of

Apollo from the Roman lovers. Yet for a time I acquiesced, hoping in his ardor to forget the lover I had hoped to find.

I began to despise him for his reluctance to hear my history, and one night when he came through the darkness to my room, he found me waiting for him in the sollar. He was surprised to see me still wearing the dress in which I had dined with him and Carlos.

He asked, ''Am I to be your tire-woman tonight?''

''To-night, Alcestes, I am in a mood for conversation, and there is much you must hear before we quench the candles.''

He protested, but I made him listen. I told him of the time when I had played in taverns because I was hungry; of the brothel in Fiume; and of the torture. I remember myself saying, ''The scourge seemed to fall so slowly, I could watch each lash uncurling in the air. Even before they fell I felt the knotted cords tear wide my flesh; and always that pitiless voice, ''Recant! Recant!''

Alcestes pulled my hands down from my eyes, ''Have you no pity? Why must you torture me with this horror?''

His face was working as if he were a child about to cry. For a moment my only thought was to comfort him, to let him find peace in my arms. Then I grew cold with the knowledge that he was not distraught for my sake, but because I had brought torture so close to him that it seemed part of his own experience. I knew then why sometimes when we lay together I was more lonely than I had ever been since I was Carola. Suddenly I wanted to hurt him, hurt him until he had to recognize that the tears he thought to be flowing from compassion were only a sign of weakness.

I said, ''I have known only one other captain, and his following of the sea left him squeamish. I have seen him save a man's life by pouring hot pitch over the stump of a severed hand. Your crew must know how to attend their own wounds; for it seems their captain is too delicate to stomach even the hearing of pain.''

I saw the vein in his temple swell with his mounting anger,

but I went on mercilessly, ''May the *Crimson Rose* encounter only smooth waters; for a storm brings everyone close to reality, when the most sensitive must suffer with his companions!''

I think that if his nature had been a little more violent Alcestes would have killed me. His hands were at my throat. Perhaps he saw himself in my eyes, for he stumbled out of the room. I heard his footsteps echo down the passage.

I blew out the candles and drew the curtains close. The bed was cold. I was alone, in the dark.

the Crippled Sailor

At dawn I heard a horseman ride out of the courtyard; though I was too proud to run to the window I knew it was Alcestes. As I lay listening to the fading hoof-beats I knew I had demanded from him too great an understanding: it was my own fault that the memory I had hoped to keep as a talisman against the future was flawed by this bitter quarrel. I thought I might never see him again, and when Carlos told me that he had only gone to watch the refit of the *Crimson Rose*, it was as though I were a prisoner who received a stay of execution.

Alcestes was away twenty-seven days. I dreamed of him once, but the memory I brought back was so fleeting that I was not sure whether he loved or hated me on earth. When he returned, I recognized that there was to be an unspoken agreement between us to ignore the quarrel. Yet, though he behaved as though his love had suffered no change, I knew he was afraid of me. So I pretended to be remorseful that I had broken my marriage vows, saying that never again must we betray Carlos by being lovers. At last Alcestes agreed to an austere relationship, but in our hearts we both knew that the very unity of our bodies would have shown our secret thoughts, cold as a blade of steel between us.

Alcestes now spent much of his time with Pietro, a sailor he had brought back with him from the port. This man had lost his right leg below the knee, and the half-healed stump was only partly concealed by his tattered breeches. He swung along on his crutches faster than an ordinary man could walk, thrusting himself forward by the power of his huge shoulders. They had met in a tavern, and as they exchanged stories of their voyages, Pietro said he had newly come from Spain, where a rumor was taking hold that the earth was round. At first Alcestes had laughed at what he thought was a proof of the gullibility of Spaniards, but Pietro said much that gave the story credence.

Pietro's brother had been one of the crew of an ill-fated expedition whose ships had sailed from Spain in an attempt to prove this belief. It was difficult to piece the story together from the fragments that Pietro remembered. It seemed the crews had wintered on an ice-bound shore, short of provisions, mutiny threatening to divide the weary men. Time after time they thought they had found the channel that would lead beyond the barrier of New Land into a further ocean, but always it proved to be only the wide mouth of another river. They demanded to turn back, but their leader heartened them with his courage, drove them with his scorn. Still farther south: another channel—surely this is only another river? Two ships deserted, and drove before the relentless western wind on a homeward course. Between the dark shores of a desolate coast, three ships battled on, repulsed again and again by screaming winds. At last even the winds grew weary. The ships crept forward, their crews listening in apprehension for the leadsman's call. The shores fell back only to narrow again; those desolate, demon-haunted shores. Then they came to another ocean, and knew victory. They thought that a few days' voyage would bring them to the Indies; but farther and farther the horizon beckoned. One ship was lost in a storm. They came to islands. Here their leader was killed by savages. They dared not return on their outward course; even the fear of reaching the edge of the world was less than the terrors of the haunted channel. So in the faith of a dead man's vision, a solitary ship still sailed on into the west. Crippled, her timbers strained, weighed down by the water gaining in her hold, she brought her crew back to the Spanish coast, only to founder at her anchorage.

If their leader had lived to return in triumph from the east, his word would have been unchallenged. But the witness of illiterate sailors is not readily accepted by authority. Even the scholar who had made the voyage found mockers, for he seemed so much excited at the failure of the log-book to tally with the calendar. His hearers laughed, and said that any prisoner would tell him it was impossible to keep a faithful tally of days—they scratch the first month on the wall beside them, then they forget a day, or score it twice: some are even released thinking it must be spring, to find it the autumn of the previous year. ''Why should this man, shut in his little ship—a landsman, too, think it important his tally shows a different date to ours? Why is he so insistent? His mind must be turned by his privations. Why should we believe him?''

But is he right? Is the world round or flat?

These questions fired Alcestes as even his vision of the island had not done. When he was with Pietro I knew he had forgotten me: I was only a woman, who could play no part in the plans of sea-adventurers. I never told him that why I thought the world was round was because of a vision, seen after a fresco had frightened me when a child.... There is sky on the other side of the earth as well as on this side.

I tried by every means in my power to bring Alcestes back to the ambitions he had held before Pietro came; but I failed. No longer would the *Crimson Rose* sail on a quest for freedom; her course would be set on the words of a crippled sailor.

Pietro lodged at a wine-shop near the house. Almost

every day I would hear him come slowly up the steep street; a dragging footstep, then the chink of iron against a cobblestone, for now that the stump was hard enough to bear his weight he had a wooden leg.

I tried to argue that my distrust of him was caused by jealousy, but at last I was sure that he was evil. In spite of his protestations to Alcestes I knew he did not want to sail in search of honor, or to chart new seas; he was driven only by his greed for wealth. He would have liked to show his hostility towards me, but fear of Alcestes kept his enmity concealed.

Sometimes I would be in the room when they discussed preparations for the voyage. "Everything must be sacrificed to increase the distance we can sail without a landing.... If we are long becalmed what do you think is the lowest ration on which the crew can work the ship?... We might take wine for the crew to use when the water has grown too foul...."

Alcestes entrusted Pietro with money for the victualing. He ordered that only meat of good quality should go into the brine tubs, I having warned him of the filth I had seen put into them in Fiume. He would not believe me when I told him that his crew would suffer because Pietro cheated him.

I said, "You seem to think only of the voyage, Alcestes. Have you forgotten what you mean to do when it is over?"

"It is not enough that I shall have made history for Italy?"

"History belongs to the men of the future, and will they value it? You may help to prove the world is round, but will that make the people who dwell on it any happier? A shorter road to the Indies will make the merchants richer; they will have more of the precious seeds of the pepper tree to weigh against their gold. Spices will not stave off hunger from the poor—but perhaps you have forgotten them?"

"Of course I have not forgotten, but a man cannot live on dreams. It is easy to talk of an island where the people are ruled to their contentment; it is easy to talk of Paradise, but one still has to wake to commonplace reality."

"When we talked of that island together it seemed more than a dream."

"Once I thought you more than mortal; but you are only a woman, though gracious and of a brilliant wit. You told me we shared those dreams, and I began to believe you. I thought it was I who had faith in priests that ruled with visionary power, for it seemed you told me of things I had once known, and that love could turn a seaman into a poet who was content to dream."

"So you have awakened, Alcestes! Do you find your world grey, or splendid?"

"I find it a man's world; a world where men rule, seek for new lands, new thoughts. A world in which women should be content to play their part; to be loved, to be ready to welcome their heroes home, to bear sons—and daughters to please the sons of other women. Why will you not be content to be a woman, Carola?"

"Was I such a very disappointing mistress?"

"I think that you have been too much—and too little. You never let me think that I was the sun in your universe, though that is a compliment which all women should pay to the men they love; in that you were too little. In your eyes I did not see myself as a hero, as a man has a right to see himself in a woman's eyes; my love for you showed me my weakness instead of my power."

"Then why do you say I gave you too much?"

Suddenly I saw a flash of that which shone behind the dreamer, the lover, the sea-captain. He said, "You asked me what was too much? Only that you have shown me something in yourself which will make all other women, however virtuous, however beautiful, seem tavern drabs beside the thought of you."

We kissed each other, as we had used to do; and there was no longer a barrier between us.

CHAPTER TWENTY-SIX

the 'Crimson Rose'

I think Carlos knew that everything in the Perugian house served to remind me of Alcestes, for the day after he had ridden away to join his ship Carlos took me to the House of the High Air. If he guessed that I and his godson had been lovers, he gave no sign. He was gentle with me as he had always been; perhaps if there was any change in his manner it was that he treated me with an added tenderness, as though I were recovering from an illness.

I put away the bright dresses I had worn for Alcestes; now I chose the somber colors of a matron and wore a coif over my hair. I no longer wished to go out alone, but tried to fill my days with the cares of a housewife. I started to embroider new curtains for the principal room, using sad blues and cypress green to suit my mood. I even spent long hours in the kitchen with Caterina, learning how to make quince preserve or to dry mushrooms for winter use.

Carlos seemed absorbed in translating Greek parchments into Latin. He had a table carried out to the vine arbor by the terrace, where he would sit, poring over the text, and then adding to the meticulous brown letters that barred the page, line after line. Sometimes he would have his food taken out there instead of coming in to join me, and even when he thanked me for sharpening a fresh quill for him his thoughts seemed far away. Though I seldom saw Alcestes in my dreams, there were times when I knew I had seen him yet could not remember where. Had he reached those islands of eternal summer where we had once thought to be together? Had he proved the Spanish sailors right, and so would return to Italy out of the East? I would wake warm from his arms, open my eyes thinking to find my head pillowed on his shoulder, and weep for loneliness of him. Sometimes I knew that he was in danger, and for many nights I could get no news of his safety in spite of my fervent prayers.

We had little contact with the outside world, but after we had been there a few weeks I knew that Carlos was seriously disturbed. I questioned him, but he only told me that in Perugia there was trouble which might delay our return to the city. I thought there must have been a riot among the towns-people and that Carlos tried to conceal it from me because he feared it would remind me of the sorrow of Padua. Only when he had to explain why we must pass the winter in the hills did I learn that a kinsman of the Griffin had slain an envoy of His Holiness, and in revenge the Papal States had sent their mercenaries against the town, and with it fell the power of the House which had ruled Perugia for so long, the House whose tributary blood ran in my veins.

Days followed days in endless pattern, storing the somber months into a year. Twice Carlos received news of Alcestes, and I learned that he still listened to Pietro's counsel, and that none of my prayers that he should see the evil in the crippled sailor had been answered.

Then in a dream again I saw Alcestes. I was with him on the *Crimson Rose*. Many of the crew were ill, and there were few to man the yards. Although there was still a sufficiency of hard bread, some of the sailors were near starvation, for the teeth had fallen from their oozing gums and they could not chew it. They scraped the biscuit with their knives until it made a little pile of powder in the palm of the hand, then they tried to lick it up with their swollen tongues. Some of them soaked the biscuit in their water ration, but they soon found this increased their thirst unbearably, for each man had only a quarter pannikin, served out night and morning from the stinking residue in the last half-empty cask.

The waves had risen after weeks of oily calm; a sail was stretched on the poop to catch the rain, but only a little fresh water had been collected before the first seas broke over the deck. The wind seemed to leap at the ship like a flight of demons. It tore the heavy canvas from the numbed fingers of the men on the main yard; one of them hurtled down, to lie sprawled on the deck like a rag doll discarded by an angry child. The waves could not wash him overboard, for his leg was jambed against a hatch, but they sluiced the blood which trickled from the corner of his mouth, until it ran no longer.

The ship was driving forward under bare spars, tatters of canvas cracking in the wind. They had lashed the rudder from the lower deck, for two helmsmen had been carried away by the seas. The port-lights of the stern cabin had been stove in; the sky globe and a little cask of spirits were rolling to and fro in the dirty water.

I heard a crash above the noise of the storm and knew a mast had fallen. I saw Alcestes hacking with an axe at the shrouds which held it to the bulwarks. I thought the ship must turn over and drown everyone aboard her, but as she was freed of the mast she slowly righted herself.

The moon shone for a moment through the hurrying clouds—it seemed as if the peak of the storm had passed, but it only waited to gather to itself a greater fury.

I saw the spar fall on Alcestes. I heard him scream. I tried to reach him....

I woke knowing he was dead, longing for the power to return to him so that our bodies could drift on the same current into the peace below the storm. Then I realized that it was only in my spirit that I had seen his body die, and that, enclosed in Carola, I might live to be very old.

I knew that if Carlos saw me I should betray my bitter knowledge, and I wished to protect him from this grief as long as it were possible. I feigned illness, so that I could keep to my room and close fast the shutters against the unheeding sun that shone serenely though my earth was dark.

The illness I feigned became a reality. I fell into a low fever; at night I was plagued with an icy sweating and I coughed until my handkerchief was stained with blood. Through Anna I persuaded Carlos not to come near me, fearing that if he did so the same fever would attack him.

When next I saw him it was difficult to believe that he too had not been very ill. His face looked as though it were molded in wax and the skin showed no vitality of blood. Carlos who for so long withstood the siege of age, had become its prisoner.

Storm Wrack

In the autumn of 1536 we returned to Perugia. Even though our house was some distance from the town gate I could see, above the city wall, that many of the buildings still showed the blackening of fire. Our sevants had traveled with us, and when we came to the house we found the dust of more than two years lying undisturbed. I went to my room; the hinges of the shutters were stiff with rust and they opened grudgingly. The bed carvings were clouded with cobwebs, and as I drew back a hanging, moths fluttered out blindly from the musty velvet. In the little casket where once I had kept my fard pots I found the scarf I had waved from the window when Alcestes rode away; out of its folds fell the sprig of verbena he had picked for me.

The snows came early that year, and only the pattern of birds' feet marked the white lawn under my window. Carlos seldom left his room, for he found the stairs arduous to climb. The flames were greedy for the logs on the wide hearth, but even they seemed powerless to warm his chill transparency. I knew that he was drawing near to the close of his years, and I prayed that the news of Alcestes' death should not come to disturb him.

It was early in the new year when I was awakened by a knocking on the outer door. It seemed a summons that I had long awaited in fear. I snatched up a tiring robe and ran down the passage to where a little window overlooked the street. The door was hidden from me by a deep embrasure, but in the freshly fallen snow I saw the track I dreaded, the line of single footprints beside the marks, regular as the knots on a scourge, where Pietro's wooden leg had pierced the frozen crust.

I listened, but no sound came from the servants' quarters.... I must open the door before anyone hears him knocking. I ran down the stairs and drew back the heavy bolts. I beckoned Pietro to follow me, and took him into a little ante-room which opened off the hall. He told me he had come to tell Carlos that Alcestes was dead, watching me narrowly to see how I took the news. He must have thought me callous, for he would not believe me when I told him I knew of it already.

He demanded to see Carlos. I told him that my husband was ill, dying, that he could see no one. But Pietro would not believe me. I tried to bribe him to go away, but he had always hated me since I tried to warn Alcestes against him. I pulled off my rings, and said I should give him a bag of gold as well, if only he would go in peace. I should not have let him see how desperately I wanted to keep him away from Carlos. At last he found a way to make me fear him, and I had no power once he knew I was afraid. I ordered him to go: he laughed at me. I tried by every means to thwart him, even going on my knees to plead; for peace to Carlos was worth more than my pride, even if it must be humbled to Pietro.

He stood there in front of me, swaying backwards and forward, his wooden leg braced against a dower chest. I noticed that now he only wore a ring in his right ear, the left ear had rotted away. A half-healed scar seared his face like a brand; his lips were red and moist in the coarse beard. He mocked me, ''Perhaps I will take the gold and leave the old man to drool out his last days in complacency—yet he would reward me well for news of his son's death. I could tell him how I saw Alcestes die, no longer the gallant captain but just an ordinary man like any of us. His legs were pinned under a fallen spar; the flesh was so pulped they were nearly severed. After the first screams he was brave enough, I'll say that for him. Some of the other men were for putting him out of his pain. They said they would not let even a cur-dog die like that: two or three of them were blubbering like children, but I told them to leave him be. They had to take their orders from me now, for Alcestes had always made it plain that I was to be captain when he died. You tried to warn him against Pietro, didn't you, my pretty? You despised Pietro, the lout, the brutish sailor; but I had a cleverer tongue than you had with your lover, for all your fine ways. You thought I didn't know what a fine pair of cuckold's horns you had grown on your husband. You think you're cleverer than Pietro. You think I don't know why you're afraid of my seeing Carlos. It isn't Alcestes' death you are afraid of him knowing, but what Alcestes did when he was living. Your fine lover is dead now; he will never come home to you any more. Even the sea-witches didn't want him, or they would have pulled him overboard instead of letting him die with the waves washing over him. He always said he'd die on the deck of his ship; the spar must have heard him and pinned him down to it!''

I ran to the door and stretched my arms across it, barring the way to the tower room. I thought Pietro would never dare to injure me, for he must have known that to do so would be to risk death by the felons' iron. He lurched forward and tore me away from the door. I fell. He poised his wooded leg like a pike against my breast. He taunted me, ''Shall I skewer you to your fine floor, my pretty?''

I thought he was going to kill me. I lay there, waiting to feel the iron-shod leg drive down through my flesh. Then I saw him pick up something from the settle behind him: and felt a blow on my head that sent me spinning into the darkness.

I heard Anna's voice, as though it came from far away, ''Her poor hands are grave-cold; she must have been lying here a long time. She must have stumbled in the dark and hit her head on the corner of that chest.''

I tried to speak, ''Pietro, where is he? Has he gone?''

"Gone these two years. You are safe with Anna. You have had a little fall and hurt your head."

"Carlos.... I must go to Carlos. Pietro the sailor is with him."

"There is no one here. You are caught up in a night-mare."

"No, no! he was real, I saw him! I will show you his tracks in the snow.

I struggled to the door and flung it open; Anna, bewildered yet obedient, supporting me. The footprints I had seen in the dawn were still there, and beside them the fresher marks of Pietro in haste for his life. I would have sent after him, for then I should have delighted to see him torn by the felons' irons, the punishment for common people who assault one of a noble family. But I was too weary even for revenge. Of what use to kill a viper when its fangs have already driven home their venom? Let him go free from the penalty of men, for demons watch to claim him for their own; and hell can stretch pain farther than the rack.

I said to Anna, "I must go to Carlos."

My weary thoughts ran ahead of me along the passage.... Please let Carlos understand why I did not tell him of Alcestes. I thought he would die before this sorrow came upon him. I thought they would soon be young together beyond death. Now he will die in fear because I have lied to him. He used to say he would not be a stranger in heaven because I had shown it to him. Now he will think I lied in all things. I must cover the bruise on my forehead or he will question me about it.

I stood at the top of the narrow stairs that led to his room. What shall I see when I open the door? Will he order me from his sight? Will he send me away, and die here alone and afraid?

Carlos was lying on the bed; his face against the pillows white as stone. I knelt beside him. He was so still I thought him already dead. I held his hand against my cheek, calling his name very softly.

He tried to stroke my hair. ''Alcestes is dead, Carola, I am so old, yet it was he who was first to die. You know when it happened, didn't you? I saw by your eyes that you knew, but I had not the courage to ask you to put it into words. You were brave to try not to share your sorrow with me. We loved Alcestes. We should have shared the sorrow of his death together, not alone. I shall be with him very soon. I wonder if he is still steering a fair ship? Shall I, who hate ships, find a heaven on the sea...my heaven must be with Alcestes till he makes landfall.''

He seemed to sleep for a little while. Then he spoke to me again, and his voice was stronger than I had heard it for many days.

''I have not your vision, Carola. I can only see my heaven as it might be on earth. I have lit my age with dreams of a future when I shall see you again. You will still look as you do now, but there will be no shadow of old sorrows in your eyes. I shall be a poet by whom beauty is born in words; for only a poet could tell you of his love. I shall have seen you in the sky and in the winter trees, heard your voice down the wind and in the long waves that follow a storm.

''You will be gathering wild flowers in a summer meadow, your hair live to the wind that bows the grass in homage to you. I shall have crossed the hills before dawn; I shall come to your meadow when the sun is rising, and when I see you I shall know that it has risen. When you see me you will pause, as though startled to see a stranger: I shall come towards you, and you will hold out your hands to meet mine, for you will know me. Then together we shall go to the house I have built for love; and you will find your name upon the lintel, and upon the hearth, and above the windows....''

His eyes were wide open, as though he saw far beyond the walls that hid away the sky. Only once more did he speak as Carlos; a whisper like the breeze through standing corn.

"When I am dead do not pray for my soul. Pray that when we are born again it is in my youth that I shall see you."

two effigies

While still a young man Carlos had brought home from Greece the stone for his sarcophagus. It had been carved when Michele, still a young sculptor that fame had not yet taken into her train, had captured the quick ambitions of his youth in this ageless marble. He was dressed as a young gallant, smiling as though he dreamed of Lalage, whom he had not yet seen on earth.

Now, as he had wished, he lay in state; not on a bier before the high altar, but in the side chapel where the Ludovicis were buried. He had left a manuscript of instructions for his funeral, "Before the lid is set on my sarcophagus I will lie for a day and a night; wearing not grave-clothes but my scholar's robe. Let my death bring no sorrow to those I love, for they must rejoice now that I am free of my age."

As I had read these words I wondered if while he wrote them Carlos thought of the Two Lands, where the people knew death as a friend, built their tombs while they were still young and went there with flowers on days of festival.

Anna wanted to stay with me while I kept watch through the night, but I told her that I wished to be alone. The coffin-lid, on which lay the effigy, was on the floor of the chapel, ready to be lifted into place. The face of Carlos was quiet as ivory. They seemed to share the same carven austerity: it was difficult to believe that one had housed his spirit, and the other only the memory of his youth. What form did the spirit of Carlos now wear? Was he a young man, in the foreign ruff he had affected, with the hilt of his small-sword jeweled with emeralds? Did he feel his pulses hurry with youth as when he had loved the beautiful Lalage? Or did he find the tranquillity of age a more serene habiliment?

It was the first time I had been in a church since I had escaped from the convent, yet here I did not feel a heretic. The flames of the tall candles flickered in the draught.... I seemed to see the marble figure of the young Carlos stir into life. He rose from off the tomb and came towards me. Now he wore a violet doublet and crimson trunk hose. His pointed beard was black, perfumed with ambergris; the single ruby in his right ear glistened as it caught the light. As I went towards him I found I was wearing a blue dress, the first of the many dresses he had given me when he was an old man.

His hand was warm on mine. We stood there together; and faintly, as though through a mist, I saw the corpse of an old man on a bier, and kneeling beside it a woman whose face was hidden by a mourning veil. I wondered how she had come in without my hearing her; and then I knew that she was Carola—asleep.

Hand in hand the young Carlos and I went from the church. We walked along the town walls, and saw the river glinting far below us in the first rays of the rising sun. We came to the wall of our garden and climbed over it. I could feel the cracks in the plaster, rough under my fingers.

No longer did snowdrifts cover the bare earth; for it was a garden where spring and autumn joined with summer. The mulberry tree was in fruit above the hyacinths; there was blossom on the same bough as ripening plums.

At first I was a little shy of the young Carlos. We talked together of the old man he had been; and he spoke of him with the fond indulgence that youth has for age. "You were very patient with me, Carola. It was you who first showed me this garden as we see it now. Sometimes even in sleep I was an old man, and you took me here and said that for me to pace these paths in my black robe was as if I brought winter to the flowers. You showed me how to meet Lalage again. It would have distressed her if she had seen me old and sorrowful.''

I asked him, ''Can you remember what you knew when you were the old Carlos?''

''Yes, I can remember. But much of that time is grey, and difficult to see from here. I am still too near to death, as though I had drunk deeply of wine and were bemused. I used to tell you that you had made me believe in miracles, yet I did not know that death could work so great a miracle as to give an old man back his youth.''

''Carlos, did you know that I and Alcestes had been lovers?''

He smiled, ''Even the old Carlos knew that, but he loved you both for your courtesy and silence. He was so contemptuous of his own weakness that would not let him pretend an anger that he could not feel, an anger that would have left you free to go with his godson to your happiness. Will you forgive that old man, Carola?''

''Do the stars ask forgiveness for setting the pilot on his course?''

We were looking up at the house when the window of my room opened. A woman leaned out of it, a woman whose brow was calm as a summer river. Carlos turned to me, ''There is Lalage.'' He paused, as if a little bewildered, ''I had a dream, a dream that she and the child were dead. But I am here waiting for her. She will soon bring my son down to join me.''

The woman came across the lawn towards us. Carlos took her in his arms. Over his shoulder she smiled at me; and I knew that it was she who had caused the garden to flower for him.

I awakened. It was early morning and the sun flowed down through the high windows. I put up my hand and felt the heavy mourning veil.

I knew Carlos had found his heaven, and yet I wept. I knelt beside two statues, of my father and a young lover, and on earth they could not speak to me.

CHAPTER TWENTY-SEVEN

torch light

Anna hoped that with the coming of the warm weather my cough would pass; but it never released its hold on me. Yet I found peace, for I was weary of being Carola. When autumn came it seemed as though my spirit consumed my flesh, as if it were wax that burnt to light my dusk. I knew my Shining One was often near; knew that from death's face would shine his eyes, and I should feel his hand on mine again, strength in his fingers, wisdom on his palm.

If I had been in truth a troubadour, I could have set my thoughts upon a page to leave a record; so that some other one who hears what I hear, sees what I would see, could look down through the years and know a friend. What should I set there if I knew the words? What have I learned as my philosophy through this short life of twenty-seven years?

I have seen time as a slow river, fed by myriad streams, whose source came down from Heaven in life's rain. It soaked into the earth; then trickled forth over the pebbles of a narrow rill, and as it threaded in between the rocks it learned of their immutability.

Then it knew moss grew on this barren stone; and as the channel deepened, it heard the whisper of the water plants, and felt their long leaves flowing in its course, tug at their roots. It passed between the shafts of growing reeds, and heard them stirring in the morning wind, with a murmur of bird cries and the coming storm.

Soon there were dragon-flies, which lighted for a moment and skimmed on, but left a bright gleam from their fugitive wings. Contemplative frogs croaked from the bank; and fish flashed through the shadows and were gone. Then the stream widened, into shining pools where animals came down at night to drink. The water curved the footprints they had made; the narrow prints of oryxes and deer; the claws of leopards, the cruel pads of wolves. Yet wider pools, where unicorns came down at evening; the hippogriff folded his wings to slake his thirst, and the great paws of lions set in the earth their seal of majesty.

Still it flows on: then feeds a ripple, a ripple echoing from a laughing child; and in the shallows this same child shall bathe, and beat the quiet water with its hands into bright drops. The child has grown, now he sits on the bank and carves a boat; gives it a twig for mast, a leaf for sail and launches it into the stream of time. Onward this boat is borne, till hollowed logs are poled by men who sing of trackless hills where trees strive to the light.

Then are there torches mirrored in its flood, war torches with destruction in their flames; and in the rapids long canoes are wrecked where blood weaves through the pools like scarlet weeds. Here the stream narrows. Now is the water dark, for towering cliffs obscure the sun away; as deeper, ever deeper, drives the cleft into the mountains. Its course must change, a rock wall bars the path. But where the stream has seemingly to end, a man stands poised above it; naked, alone, holding a fish spear in his upraised hand, searching the flood with no fear in his eyes, searching to see that which he longs to find—the fish, the scarlet fish, which knows the sea.

Now ever faster is the water's plunge; down rapids and by perilous ravines, weary with foam, yet urgent to press on. It joins a marsh, silent and choked with reeds, whose placid shallows drowse in noon-day heat. But on it travels over flats of mud, through lazy meads and over languorous falls. Now it is wider, now it can hear the chant of fishermen that cast their glittering nets. Then quietly, with no tumult, it flows on to join the river of eternity.

Now is it one in slow processional with all the myriads of its brother streams. Now are there boats in splendid pageantry: the silver barges of proud memory; the spreading purple sails of rulership; the patient rhythm of the rowers' arms and the clear vision of the steering-oar. Caught in the shallows there are other boats; where mourners weep the melancholy tide, where sable veils obscure the figure-head and the black masts curve no sail to the wind. These mourners do not see the lovers pass; lovers whose boats move without sound of oars, with masts that have put forth their leaves again; whose decks are violets and whose prows are doves.

The river widens: far away, yet clear at evening, it can hear the rising music of the sea; that sea whose other shores no man can know, until the stream of time has carried him from mountain into plant, from beast to steersman.

Then man may set his course under the sky, for he can see the star that pilots him to harbor in the Islands of the Blessed.

I have seen the wisdom of the gods as fire; from that dim past when all-embracing power men know as God created earth; and sent the children from another moon to teach those others, newly born as man. These little people came down from the woods, the caves, the shelters hollowed from the cliffs, to where a moon-born sat by a friendly fire that warmed their chill mortality. Yet they had made no torch to kindle there, and were content to come forth from the dark to receive comfort from a counsellor.

A thousand years, a thousand thousand years, have aged the earth. Now are the ones who called the moon their home returned to join the dwellers on the heights. Now little men must kindle their own fire. No longer through the shadows of the plain do great fires blaze; but little points of light, from twigs, from burning leaves, gleam through the night. Their light is pale as star-reflecting pools, yet does it thread the valleys, and its sparks are carried on the questing breeze of dawn. Some sparks fall into marshes and are quenched; but others blaze a path through tinder grass of gained experience. Some flee from their stifling huts before the roar of memory's bright flame. They are afraid that it may sear their flesh, and comes to blind their leaden-lidded eyes. They build new huts on deserts of grey ash where no wood grows to feed another flame. But there are others who plunge in the fire, and from cold ashes like a phoenix rise, seeing the distant earth, shadowed and cold; while the long feathers of their soaring wings strong on the air circle towards the sun.

Then came the land where lived the long in years. There temple-beaconed hills flowed to the sea; makers of moon paths built serene causeways, worn by multitudinous way-farers.

Then wisdom's wreath lost sovereignty: on basalt thrones sat men in empty robes; they ruled by power and scorned humility. Now priests were bowed with mitres: no buds un-folded on the lotuses, and looking-pools reflected nothing-ness. Yet power stalked through the land, that tarnished power when men assail the gods. No longer did the shadows flee the light, for men rode out to battle in their hate; priests wielded magic only to show their strength, and sorrow settled heavy on the land. Yet in the hills a pale light still endured; and from it came a cry, ''Master, hast thou forgotten us?''

Then came the Voice to man. ''Since you have brought desecration on my land, and made my noonday into night: now is the time come when that which I created shall be destroyed. You who hear my voice within your heart shall follow the path of the moon across the sea to far countries where the soil is yet untilled. There must you learn again to plant your corn, and when its virtue has entered into you, then shall you find a tree. From it you will cut a living branch; and you must learn patience until the sap and the leaves upon it have returned into its strength. Then from it you shall carve a torch, and in the fullness of my time there shall come amongst you one who holds fire in his hand: and you will be no longer in darkness. Those of you who do not hear my voice shall stay, and I will speak to you on the evening of the seventh moon. There is no place in my land where you can hide from the echoes of my voice: even the deaf shall hear it, and the ears of the dead shall be open; for I shall speak above the thunder. Yea, beside my voice the thunder shall be as the whisper of wind in the grass. The clouds shall be as mountains before you, and their color shall be of the darkness of your own hearts. Then there shall fall a stillness; and you shall see death, in the likeness of death. In the stillness shall come a small sound, and in the dust, you shall see the circle you have forgotten; the circle, in the heavy drops of rain. And the drops shall build themselves to rods, and the rods even into pillars of water. The water shall rise over the valleys, and drive you, even as you drove your torch-bearers, into the hills. And the water shall be as the floor of a temple, whose pillars are water and whose roof is cloud. And one by one the hills shall vanish, and you shall crowd together in your fear; on the islands that were mountains. But on the fortieth day there shall be no land: and the water will have buried the dead.''

When the Great Rain had cleansed the earth so that again it could become a place of fire, the flames burned in their serenity. The river of the Two Lands reflected the beacons which marked its course; and a light was set in the masts of the boats, and it was in their prows also: even the oars were luminous.

Then once again did man forget his gods. The mightiest temples shadowed men dressed as priests and incense swirled through barren sanctuaries.

The sacrificial fires had burnt to ash; cold were the altars set to absent gods.

Then in the gathering darkness of the west a star fell from the heavens, a child was born. A child with wisdom living on his tongue, a child with eyes that had seen many moons yet knew horizon for eternity. And men brought torches to him in their hands for kindling, that in His flame grew bright. He spoke; the leaves hushed and the birds were still, to listen. Even the hurrying clouds stayed in their course, bound were the waves, silent the running brooks, in honor of celestial majesty. The rising sun lit battlemented hills. Then from their caves swarmed leather-pinioned bats, and stealthy panthers left their jungle lairs; imperial eagles, dead yet purple-jessed, swooped down upon the Galilean shore; destruction in their claws, death in their hearts.

The Morning Star returned into the sky.

Still did the light He kindled blaze on earth. From hand to hand the line of torches passed, unquenched, undying: and with each torch together went the word, ''Is your torch seasoned for this kindling?''

Then men forgot the Word: and brought green wood, wood without age, with sap not turned to strength, wood that can smolder but gives forth no light. No more were torches lifted to the wind, the wind that streamed their far flames on the air, but in great buildings flickered and grew dim; buildings where stood tall candles of cold wax, and golden lamps were empty of live oil. And these green torches sent forth perilous smoke: it suffocated throats that would have prayed, and blinded with tears the eyes that would have seen. There was no sound but the hissing of wet wood.

A pall of smoke has drifted over earth; the smoke of pyres has joined it, and the sack of cities. It drifts across the chaos of men's wars and hides the sun.

Then speaks the Voice to man: ''Did I not course the heavens with my stars: send memory to guide you through the dark; and set my sun to watch you through the day? Till you were ready to kindle your own brand I sent my children to build my fires for you. I send the flames, but you must carry them. If you set torches guttering on the wind, then is the darkness born of your own grief. You give green torches into puppet hands, think triple crowns can give a man my sight. Amongst you there are men with radiant eyes whom you could follow: yet you deny their name, and with it, mine. Honor the holder of the living flame above your kings! Honor no priest that does not hear my voice! Honor no light that does not show my face, and with my face, your own!''

the Carola I Wore

It seemed that I was already separate from my body. It was not Carola whose hair Anna braided, nor Carola who drank the cordials to please her Anna. It was as though I watched her try to mend my dress, and wondered why she wept to see the velvet threadbare when I knew I had to wear it so short a while.

Even when rain darkened the sky I would not allow the shutters to be closed. I lived with the sky; to wake, to sleep, to dream. To see the dawn; Aurora's dawn, rosy with cherubim, or that grey stealth when night with quiet hands draws back the shade that guards the dark from heavy-lidded day. The scudding clouds of autumn called down the wind with greetings to me; and the calm evening brought contentment; closed away my fears, hushed vain regrets for living in the world.

I knew that death brought no imperious summons, but waited, calm and patient, by that stream which carried me towards him: so quiet a stream, silver between the banks where grew strange flowers that with their fleeting scent bemused my thoughts....

No longer was the music of the spheres remote from me. Sometimes I would try to find a thread of it upon my lute, a thread of sound in that great harmony. And then it seemed that I could hear myself as one small note in a titanic surge; one note, yet must the string be sweetly tuned and forged of silver. So Carola waited, ready to join the slow procession of the other I's, for the circle of her life was nearly joined.

Those hands on the green coverlet are not mine, but Carola's: hands that have played a lute, and clenched with pain; such quiet, thin hands, no longer trying to keep their hold on life. It could not be Carola who thought of what I knew, for Carola had been a heretic. She was so proud of heresy: saw priest and abbess as dark enemies. It was as though she hated a blind man for his sightless eyes, or mocked the deaf. I should have been compassionate to those nuns who seemed to live while coffined in their creed; and with compassion I might have found their hearts, and shown them the living Christ on the crucifix.

She had fought for her half-remembered truths against their creed; not wise enough to know that in His light shone the same truth that has lit this dark earth since it was born of time. Every clear flame is like, each unto each; some may be tapers that only light a room; some blaze as beacons on a mountain crest; yet are they one. The light of the Two Lands was the light of Christ; the light that burned before the flood was sent, the light that has shone for long millennia since those first fires were kindled from the moon. All heavenly truths are spoken in one voice, spoken in multiplicity of tongues, by priest, by husbandman, by child, by sage. The stars sing the same song that the grass hears as the wind passes; and within each of us is that clear spark which the cold wind of circumstance shall blow into a flame. Then, torches in our hand, no longer flaring but still upon the air, we shall be one with heaven's radiance.

Down through the years has my far memory come, to Italy, where Carola lived a day and now stops at the Inn of Death to rest, before she takes another path—to where? What will my name be? How will my flesh be carved? Shall I be born again to wear a crown; or must I be poor, and hungry, and alone; hungry for more than bread, thirsty for water that I cannot find, the water only the wise can pour for me? Perhaps I may look back to this kindly room, and with a brighter memory see myself who once was Carola. Then will my hands be strong: a warrior's hands, a priest's, a poet's? Shall I be wise in words, so Carola's thoughts may find expression in another age when men are not afraid of heresy? How many lives, how many, many lives, must pass before my torch shall blaze the dark? How long before my clear voice shall be heard above the crowds that mutter in their fear? I found the strength to die for heresy; give me that greater strength, to live for truth.

Death, give me courage to die as Carola.... There are people in the room, people who are strange to me, people I have not summoned. There is a murmer I used to be afraid of.... Water is dripping from the lip of a cistern.... The air is heavy with incense; it has made it more difficult to breathe. They have shut the windows against me. Why have they sent for a nun and a priest to watch me? Anna must have been afraid for my soul.

Backwards and forwards the censer swings.... They have put bread without virtue on my tongue. I feel them make the sign of the cross upon my forehead.

The sand is whispering through the hour-glass. How many times must it be turned again till I am free?

Anna is weeping, but I am not strong enough to bring her comfort. I am alone with these three strangers. I never thought that death would be another loneliness. I thought Petruchio and my Shining One would come for me....

It is only Carola who is alone: I am in company.

The stars are singing, and I can hear them, yet they are far away. The silver string is clearly tuned, the string that is Carola. It will be true when the silver cord is broken, the silver cord that binds me to this earth. Now I can hear that melody Carola longed for yet never heard: that strange tune from the other side of sound.

I have become a lute where music lives. I hear, I hear—all other sound is mute, in harmonies that bear me as a stream down to the tide where dreams are born into reality....

Yet I must look once more through Carola's eyes; those eyes through which I saw this little world while I was blind to vision. The music has grown so loud that they must hear it.... I see them cross themselves, and I know they have heard an echo from the stars.

I see their eyes.... Even in death they are afraid of me, of Carola.

Then on a bier, with quiet, folded hands, lay that cold

lamp where once my spirit burned. No word they spoke of
the music they had heard. They knew not whence it came,
but asked themselves, ''Was it the song of angels, or satanic
heralds? Have we seen saint or devil?''

They would not bury me in holy ground: and so that
shroud which had been Carola, in secrecy was laid into the
earth.

There does she lie, the Carola I wore. And her white
doves walk softly on her grave.